A LITTLE GENTLE PERSUASION

Kathy Keller

Leesburg, Virginia

Kathy Keller
Leesburg, VA 20176
www.kathykeller.com

Publisher's Note: This is a work of fiction. Names, characters, places, and incidents are a product of the author's imagination. Locales and public names are sometimes used for atmospheric purposes. Any resemblance to actual people, living or dead, or to businesses, companies, events, institutions, or locales is completely coincidental.

A Little Gentle Persuasion/ Kathy Keller. -- 1st ed.
ISBN 978-1-7370503-6-0

"Oh, East is East, and West is West, and never the twain shall meet, Till Earth and Sky stand presently at God's great Judgment Seat; But there is neither East nor West, Border, nor Breed, nor Birth, When two strong [people] stand face to face, though they come from the ends of the earth!"

----Rudyard Kipling 1889

Table of Contents

CHAPTER ONE

An Avenue of Escape

Boston –September 1874

"Miss Devon! Miss Devon! I got it!"

The maid burst into her mistress's bedroom suite, excitedly waving the latest edition of Beadle's dime novel of the Wild West.

"It just come in. I got the first copy."

Devon Wainwright quickly set aside her needlepoint. "Perhaps this day will not end as bleak as it began. Did Mrs. Thomas see you?"

The young maid shook her head. "No, miss, I was most careful."

"Well done, Bridget. Close the door and come sit beside me. We shall read a few pages."

Bridget closed the door and joined her mistress on the settee, equals for a moment in their thirst for adventure.

Devon read aloud their cowboy hero's latest escapade—surpassing more than the intended "few pages." They were so engrossed in the story they jumped when there came a loud knock on the door.

"Mrs. Wainwright," called the housekeeper.

"It's Mrs. Thomas," whispered Devon. She shoved the dime novel into Bridget's hands. "Quick. Hide it."

Bridget jumped up and ran to throw the novel under the bed.

"Mrs. Wainwright," the housekeeper called out again.

"One minute, Mrs. Thomas."

At a nod from Bridget, Devon opened the door.

"What is it, Mrs. Thomas?" she asked with a touch of annoyance. "You know I don't like to be disturbed while I am doing my needlepoint."

"Your pardon, Mrs. Wainwright. I heard talking."

"I was dictating instructions to Bridget to take to the dressmaker," said Devon.

"I thought you were doing needlepoint."

"Can I not do both, Mrs. Thomas?"

The housekeeper looked past her into the room. Bridget stood with lowered eyes, one might think in subservience. But Mrs. Thomas could sense a conspiracy a mile away, and her nose was twitching now.

"Is there something else, Mrs. Thomas?" asked Devon.

"There is a gentleman to see you, madam."

"Who is it?"

"He said his name is Mr. Grafton. He gave me this card."

Devon took the card and read it: *William Grafton, Investigator, Pinkerton Detective Agency.*

"What does he want?" she asked in alarm. "Is it about the debts? Has he come to collect?"

"He wouldn't say, madam. He said he has instructions to speak only with you," said the housekeeper. "Shall I tell him that you are not available to see him?"

Devon sighed resignedly. "No, he will keep coming back. I shall have to face the creditors sooner or later. Tell him I will join him shortly.

"Yes, madam."

The housekeeper left.

"Oh, madam, will we be turned out? Will I have to leave your employ?" cried Bridget.

"It will not come to that, Bridget. If I must, I shall marry Mr. Birdwell," replied Devon dismally.

Devon entered the parlor to find a middle-aged, nondescript man of medium height and stocky build dressed in a plain brown suit. Her stomach dropped. His stern bearing left her with little doubt that he, indeed, was there to demand payment.

"My housekeeper informed me that you wish to speak with me," she said, striving to keep her voice steady. She had decided that she was going to maintain her dignity at all costs, but she hadn't ruled out playing on his sympathy if need be.

"You are Mrs. Devon Toller Wainwright?" he asked.

Devon braced herself. "I am."

"I am William Grafton with the Pinkerton Detective Agency."

"Yes, I know. My housekeeper gave me your card. What…what business have you with me, sir?"

"Do you have an aunt by the name of Clarissa Cain, Mrs. Wainwright?"

Devon wrinkled her brow, nonplussed. "Yes, I have an aunt by that name."

"I regret to inform you that Miss Cain passed away six months ago."

Devon looked at him blankly for a moment before it registered that he wasn't there to collect on her debts, and she let out a little laugh of relief. She noticed, then, the odd look the detective gave her.

"Your pardon, Mr. Grafton, I had thought you to be here for a more unpleasant purpose."

"I would think the death of a family member to be unpleasant enough, madam."

Devon gave him a rueful smile. "Yes, of course, it is. The passing of my aunt is unfortunate news. But you must understand that I scarcely knew her."

"Be that as it may, Mrs. Wainwright, she was sufficiently acquainted with you to have left you a sizable estate consisting of a house, land, and a generous purse."

Devon regarded the detective with surprise. "There must be some mistake, sir."

"There is no mistake. The will is very clear," said the detective. "There is, however, a time constraint, and you must claim your inheritance in person."

"Where might that be?"

"A town called Blue Springs in the Colorado Territory."

"The Colorado Territory…" Devon slowly sat down on a chair overwhelmed by the news. "That is quite a distance away. What is the time constraint, Mr. Grafton?"

"Three weeks, madam."

"Three weeks! Why was I not notified upon my aunt's death?"

"You were…several times, in fact," replied the detective. "But your aunt's attorney never received a reply. In a last attempt to fulfill his obligation, Mr. Stilwell contacted my office in Boston and asked that the news be delivered to you in person. If you desire to lay claim to your inheritance, I am charged with making the travel arrangements for you. All expenses will be reimbursed by the estate."

Devon was silent as thoughts raced willy-nilly through her mind.

"Mrs. Wainwright?" prodded the detective.

Devon looked at him. "I hardly know what to say, Mr. Grafton. I have never made a decision of this enormity before." Come to think of it, she had never made any decision of significance on her own.

"Would you like some time to consider the matter, Mrs. Wainwright? You have a few days to think on it and still make the deadline if you choose to go forward."

Devon jumped up from the chair. "No…no, Mr. Grafton, I do not need more time. Please make the arrangements for two. A companion shall accompany me."

"Very good, madam. How soon do you wish to leave?"

"Tomorrow, if possible."

"I shall check the train schedules and reserve the tickets. But the train can take you only as far as Colorado Springs," he advised. "From there, you shall have to make your own arrangements at the depot for a stagecoach to carry you the rest of the way to Blue Springs."

Devon nodded. "I understand. Thank you, Mr. Grafton."

She saw the detective to the door.

"Is all well, Mrs. Wainwright?" inquired the housekeeper.

Devon whirled about, startled. The woman always seemed to quietly materialize out of nowhere.

"Yes, everything is fine, Mrs. Thomas," she replied shortly. "Mr. Grafton was understanding of my predicament."

"Very good, madam."

When the housekeeper left, Devon hurried up the stairs calling for Bridget.

The maid came running. "What's amiss, madam?" she cried in alarm.

"Start packing our clothes," said Devon in a whispered tone.

"Oh, miss, have we been turned out?"

"No, Bridget, we are traveling to Blue Springs in the Colorado Territory."

"Colorado!"

"Hush, keep your voice down."

Bridget stared agog at her mistress. "Miss Devon, are ye feelin' well? Shall I fetch the doctor?"

"No, I'm fine. Now start packing before my mother hears of it. Mrs. Thomas has a direct line to her."

"But I do na understand," fretted Bridget.

Devon quickly explained the nature of the detective's visit.

"An inheritance…oh, Miss Devon, 'tis the luck of the Irish," breathed the maid, her eyes wide with amazement.

"No, Bridget, 'tis Providence."

"But what about Mr. Birdwell, miss? All is bein' arranged for ye to marry him."

Devon gave a derisive snort. "My mother can marry him. They are of the same age. Now hurry. Tell Jonas to bring the trunks in from the stable and to be circumspect about it. I don't want Mrs. Thomas to alert my mother."

Bridget's eyes shone with excitement. "Yes, ma'am." She started for the door, then stopped and ran back to retrieve the dime novel from under the bed. "'Twill be a long trip," she said with an impish smile. "We shall have need of a distraction."

"Good idea," said Devon. "Gather the other ones as well."

The girls rose early the next morning. Neither had been able to sleep a wink in their excitement.

The last of the trunks were being loaded in a wagon, when a carriage came racing down the quiet, tree-lined street and lurched to a stop behind a hansom cab. A stately, older woman, cane in hand, alighted from the carriage and marched imperiously up the walk to the house.

Devon and Bridget were coming down the stairs, when they encountered Devon's mother standing squarely in the foyer.

"Mother, what a surprise," remarked Devon dully.

"What is this I hear about you running off to some godforsaken place on the other side of the country?" quizzed Agatha Cain Toller.

Devon didn't flinch at the domineering tone. For the first time, she felt a measure of control.

"You're late, Mother. I had expected you last evening. Mrs. Thomas must be slipping."

"Don't be flippant, Devon. It doesn't become you." Mrs. Toller tapped her cane on the floor. "Bridget, tell Jonas to bring those trunks back in here."

"Bridget doesn't work for you, Mother. Bridget, wait outside in the cab," countermanded Devon.

"Yes, ma'am." The servant girl edged past Mrs. Toller and hurried out the door.

"Mother, did you know that Aunt Clarissa had died?" asked Devon.

"I had word of it," replied Mrs. Toller.

"She was your sister, and this is all the more you can mourn her?"

Mrs. Toller gave a scornful sniff. "You did not know your aunt. Clarissa was headstrong, disrespectful of the rules and convention. Had not my father disavowed her, she would have brought shame to our name. Now, take those bags upstairs and forget this nonsense. If Mr. Birdwell gets wind of your willfulness, he may have a change of heart about marrying you."

"I hope so, Mother. I do not wish to marry him."

"You have no choice, daughter. You must remarry."

"Why? You did not remarry after Father died."

"Your father left me in comfortable circumstances. Alas, Mr. Wainwright has left you penniless with his foolish investments. You are lucky I was able to make the match with Mr. Birdwell. You should be grateful to me."

"Yes, your first choice worked out so well for me."

Agatha ignored her daughter's sarcasm. "You are 30 years old, and while you have retained your figure and remain comely enough, your prospects are limited, particularly with so many of the suitable young men having been lost to that dreadful war. You should consider yourself lucky that someone like Mr. Birdwell has taken an interest in you, and that he seems not to care that you apparently lack the constitution to bear children. He has wealth and pedigree, and he has agreed to quietly clear your debts to spare your name. Now that shall be the end of it."

Devon squared her shoulders. "No, Mother, it shall not be the end of it. I have given Robert's solicitor power of attorney to sell the house and auction the furnishings to settle the accounts."

"That is an act of desperation and humiliation—Devon, this is not like you. Have you taken leave of your senses?"

"No, Mother, I have just found them."

"Be sensible, daughter. You have no money to speak of. Whatever are you going to do without funds? You'll not see a penny from me."

"I do not need money from you. Aunt Clarissa has left me a sizable inheritance, and the expense of the trip is being reimbursed by the estate." Devon paused, struck with sudden insight. "Having one's own money is so liberating for a woman," she said in wonderment.

"You still have need of money in your purse," her mother curtly reminded her.

"I have sold my jewelry."

Agatha was aghast. "You sold your jewelry! Robert must be turning over in his grave."

"Robert had already sold many of the pieces to cover his debts, Mother. And, I will have quite enough money once I claim the inheritance."

Mrs. Toller scoffed. "How much wealth could Clarissa have possessed running a boarding house? She would lure you out there even from the grave to spite me."

Another thought occurred to Devon, and she regarded her mother closely. "The detective told me that Aunt Clarissa's attorney contacted me several times over the months regarding my inheritance. Mrs. Thomas intercepted the notices for you, didn't she?"

When Agatha looked away, Devon knew that she was right.

"How could you, Mother?"

"I was looking after your interests," retorted Mrs. Toller.

"Well, now, I shall be doing that myself."

Mrs. Toller tapped her cane. "I forbid you to leave here, miss. If I must, I shall have you locked in your room until you come to your senses."

"Contrary to what you and my staff may think, they do not work for you, and I am no longer a child," said Devon, moving past her mother. "All my life, I have had decisions made for me by Father, then Robert, and now by you. From hereon, I will be making my own decisions."

Agatha Toller followed her daughter out the door. "You are being headstrong just like Clarissa. Nothing good will come of this. Mark my words."

As Devon continued down the walk, Mrs. Toller furiously tapped her cane. "There is nothing but Indians, outlaws, and uncivilized ruffians out there—Devon, come back here this minute!" she shouted.

Devon got into the cab.

"Goodbye, Mother."

CHAPTER TWO

East Meets West

The train pulled into the station at Colorado Springs. The day was sunny and bright and the temperature milder than Devon would have anticipated for this time of the year.

She stepped down from the passenger train car and looked around her, feeling much more heartened. The area looked to be civilized and prosperous. After viewing the crude towns along the way and the dotting of sod homes across the prairie landscape, she had begun to have some misgivings about making the trip.

She turned to her companion. "Bridget, please see to the trunks and bags while I secure passage for us on the stage," she instructed. "That must be the coach there. Hopefully, there will not be a long wait."

"Yes, ma'am."

Devon walked inside the train depot and went up to the window marked McCLELLAND AND SPOTSWOOD STAGE LINE.

"I require passage for two on the stagecoach to Blue Springs," she said to the clerk.

The clerk looked up from his ledger. "The passenger stage left yesterday, ma'am. You will have to wait a couple of days for the next one. There's a nice hotel in town where you can stay."

Devon smiled. "I am sure the hotel is very nice, but I have an urgent need to get to Blue Springs."

It was a bit of a fib. She still had some time left until her deadline, but she was tired of traveling and ready for the journey to end. Aside from that, her funds were dwindling.

The clerk was not moved.

"I'm sorry, ma'am. You will have to wait until the next stage. The new track is finished. You can take the train by way of Pueblo to Canon City now and take the stagecoach from there," he suggested.

"When is the train to arrive here?" she asked.

"Tomorrow."

"And when will the stagecoach leave Canon City?"

"About three days."

Devon gave a sigh of irritation. "What about that coach outside? Where is that going?"

The clerk hesitated. "To Blue Springs—but it is not taking passengers."

"Why not? It is a passenger coach, is it not?"

"Yes, but—"

"Is the coach broken down?"

"No."

"Then kindly sell me two tickets on it," insisted Devon.

The clerk peered over his spectacles at her. She was prettier than most of the women who passed through here looking for husbands. Her dress, speech, and manner marked her as a member of the Eastern elite, who, along with English gentry, often visited Colorado Springs, and he wondered why she wasn't casting her net for a husband here. Blue Springs hardly seemed the logical choice for a woman like her. But then she did have red hair. Perhaps she was one of *those* women.

Devon cleared her throat. "Are you going to sell me passage on this stagecoach or not?"

Noting the set look on her face, he could see that the woman was not going to be swayed, and he was tired of taking abuse all morning from other angry passengers seeking passage to Blue Springs. Charlie can sort this one out, he decided.

"That'll be \$12," he said.

Devon emerged from the depot and walked over to the stagecoach.

"Bridget, why are the trunks and bags not aboard?"

"The driver told the porter that he wasn't takin' any passengers, miss."

"Well, we shall see about that," said Devon. "Driver," she called, striding over to him.

A stocky, middle-aged man of average height with a bewhiskered, craggy face turned and touched the brim of his slouch hat. "Ma'am?"

"I require that the trunks and bags of my companion and myself be secured on this conveyance," she said.

"Sorry ma'am. It's like I told the little lady over there, this stage ain't takin' no passengers today."

"I am bound that you are, sir. I have two tickets to say that you will," replied Devon staunchly.

"Did Samuel give ya them tickets?" he asked in surprise.

"He did."

The driver regarded her for a long moment seeing the same intractability in her that the depot clerk had seen.

"Suit yerself, ma'am, but Cort ain't gonna like it."

Devon didn't know who Cort was, but she didn't much care.

She and Bridget had just settled themselves inside the stagecoach, when a man approached and came to a halt when he saw them.

He swung his gaze to the driver. "I said no passengers, Charlie. No passengers means no passengers."

The driver shrugged. "I told 'em, but Samuel sold 'em tickets, and the redhead ain't takin' 'no' fer an answer. I figured you could deal with it. I jest get paid to drive," he said, climbing up to his seat.

"What the hell was Samuel thinking?" grumbled the man. He pulled open the door. "Sorry, ladies, but this coach is full. You will have to take the next stage."

Devon lifted her chin a notch and turned her head to coolly regard him. She found his large size and the shotgun that he held at his side intimidating but tried not to show it. According to the dime novels, it wasn't wise to display fear.

"I see no other passengers," she responded. "And, as I have purchased passage for my companion and myself to Blue Springs, I fail to see the problem, Mr.—"

"Templeton. And you are—"

"Mrs. Wainwright. This is my companion, Miss Ryan."

Bridget stared wide-eyed at the man. He looked like the quintessential hero straight out of the dime novels from his boots and fringed buckskin jacket to the Boss of the Plains Stetson hat. Devon was not so enthralled. To her, with his authoritative manner, he represented everyone who had, heretofore, tried to control her life.

Templeton returned Devon's gaze just as coolly. "The problem is, Mrs. Wainwright, I have reserved this coach, and I have no wish to share it with any other passengers. Is that clear enough for you?"

Devon stiffened. "What is clear, Mr. Templeton, is that you have no manners. And the fact is that I hold tickets for travel on this stagecoach. Unless the company wishes for me to file a charge of fraud against it, my companion and I are taking this coach to Blue Springs. Do I make *myself* clear?"

Templeton eyes narrowed, and he studied her for a long moment. He was used to encountering strong women in this wild land and often admired their moxie, but he had little tolerance for willfulness. He could force her and her companion from the coach, but he couldn't risk making a scene now. Everything had to appear normal. He looked up at the driver.

A grin split Charlie's weathered features. "Told ya."

Templeton snorted and handed up the cash box to Charlie, then climbed into the coach and sat down beside Devon. She shot him a look of disapproval. The butt of the shotgun that he laid across his lap touched her thigh, and the width of his shoulders took up half the space when he settled back against the seat. If he noticed her displeasure, he didn't show it. Instead, he propped his long legs on the middle jump seat and pulled his hat down over his eyes.

"Enjoy the ride, ladies. Don't say I didn't warn you," he said.

Devon raised a brow, and she and Bridget glanced uncertainly at each other wondering what he meant by that.

At the other end of the depot, an interested party watched closely. A rider approached from the direction of Colorado City, dismounted, and walked up to him.

The onlooker glanced at the rider perturbed. "Where the hell ya been, Pete? The stage is readying to leave."

"Ain't yer no never mind, Rix."

Rix snorted. "If you mess this up because of a woman, Billy will have yer hide."

"Ain't no call to worry none 'bout me. What's the word? Is there a cash box or not?"

Rix nodded. "And Templeton is on board with two women."

Pete looked at him in surprise. "Templeton! Since when is he a messenger shotgun?"

"Since there's $25,000 in currency in the cash box," responded Rix. "He's sittin' inside the stagecoach. I think he wants it to appear there ain't no box on board."

"Twenty-five thousand!" exclaimed Pete. "Are ya sure? That's more'n we thought."

"I heard the agent say."

"Shit. Templeton ain't gonna give that up without a fight." Pete spit out his chaw and frowned. "It don't seem right that Billy always gets half the stakes when we're takin' all the risk. He don't even ride in on most jobs."

"He'll ride in on this one when he hears that Templeton is on the stage," said Rix.

"What's Billy's beef with Templeton?"

Rix shrugged. "Billy don't always need a reason. Templeton has been a thorn in his side since his days with the Colorado Rangers. Even worse, he's a Yankee."

The men fell silent as they continued to observe the stagecoach.

"What's Billy doin' with all that loot he's collectin'?" Pete suddenly asked.

Rix shrugged again. "Don't know an' I ain't askin'. Billy shot the last man who wondered on it. You ain't happy with your cut, then leave. But Billy's been hintin' at a job so big after this one you can live out the rest of your life in Mexico off your take."

Pete snorted. "It better be damn big."

"You best get goin'," said Rix. "The stage is leavin'."

As the stagecoach pulled out, Pete mounted his horse and galloped off.

The conveyance was open on both sides, and Devon and Bridget soon began to cough and sneeze as the horses kicked up clouds of dirt. Grimacing, Devon took out a handkerchief to fan away the dust but with little effect. She had never been on a stagecoach before. Clearly, she had not foreseen this discomfort.

Hearing her grumblings of discontent, Templeton remarked: "You'll get used to it."

Devon glared at him but held her tongue.

The road was bumpy. At one point, the coach hit a rut, and she was thrown against him. She quickly regained her seat, but apparently it wasn't quick enough. Templeton raised his hat and looked at her, then wordlessly pointed to the leather straps that hung down from the roof.

A sharp remark was on the tip of her tongue, but he dropped the hat over his eyes again, effectively cutting her off.

Devon fumed. She had never encountered such rudeness.

An hour and a half into the trip, the stagecoach pulled off the road and came to a stop before a small cabin with a barn and corral.

"Have we arrived?" Devon wondered aloud with mixed feelings.

Templeton roused and glanced at her in surprise. "Not hardly. We're changing horses. There will be three more stops today. You can stretch your legs then."

A man hurried out from the barn leading a team of fresh horses and quickly switched out the other team with them. In less than 10 minutes, the stagecoach was back on the road.

At the next stop, the ladies were allowed 10 minutes to attend to their needs and to quench their thirst. It was a new experience for Devon to drink water from a ladle—a community ladle at that! Templeton shook his head as he watched her trying not to touch her lips to the rim as she drank.

"Bridget and I have not eaten since leaving the train this morning," complained Devon at the third stop. "Is there no food at these places?"

"Not at swing stations," said Templeton.

"Are we expected to starve then?" she asked irritably, gazing about the dull, barren landscape.

"The next stop is a home station. You can get food and lodging for the night there."

Devon swung her attention back to him. "Lodging? How far is Blue Springs?"

"Another day from the home station."

"Another day! I cannot abide this travel another day, Mr. Templeton."

"I reckon you'll have to, ma'am."

"Get on board," yelled the driver.

Templeton opened the door, and Bridget readily took her seat. Devon didn't move.

"Ma'am? Unless you wish to walk…"

Devon glared at him and climbed back into the stagecoach.

As the journey continued, she didn't think it was possible to be any more miserable. Her arm ached and her legs were cramped as she kept a tight grasp on the hanger and her feet braced against the jump seat, determined not to fall into Mr. Templeton's lap again. Bridget, however, seemed to take the trip in stride, Devon noted with a measure of irritation. To the young maid, everything was an adventure.

They traveled to the other side of Pikes Peak. When they rode through the pass, Devon's and Bridgett's jaws dropped as huge walls of pink granite, brown sandstone, and shale suddenly rose up to surround them.

"Oh, miss, I ain't never seen anything like this before," breathed Bridget awestruck.

"Nor I," said Devon.

Templeton watched them, inwardly amused, as the women swiveled their heads from one side to the other so as not to miss any of the spectacle.

Outside of Canon City, the mountains gave way to a plateau, and the stagecoach pulled off the road again to stop at a much larger complex than the swing stations. The stone and timber dwelling was three times bigger and, in addition to the stables, the station also had a blacksmith, a repair shop, and a telegraph.

At the blare of the bugle, a tall, thin man and a short, round woman, both older, came hurrying out of the building. Templeton got out of the coach and went to greet them.

"Cort Templeton, I ain't seen ya in a coon's age," said the woman. "Look how thin ya are. You need a woman to take care of you."

"If I could find one like you, I might think on it," returned Templeton with a wink.

The woman broke into a jovial laugh. "You ain't changed a bit."

Templeton waved and shouted greetings to the smithy and the wheelwright.

"Since when do you ride as messenger, Cort?" questioned the station manager.

"Never mind that now, Silas," interrupted his wife. "Cort and Charlie most likely can do with some water and food. Time for talk later."

"I have two passengers with me," said Templeton.

The older woman beamed with delight when Devon and Bridget walked up with Charlie.

"This is Mrs. Wainwright and her companion Miss Ryan," said Cort. "Ladies, this is Silas Webster and his wife Maisy."

Maisy quickly ushered the girls inside. "Come in, come in and sit yourselves down, ladies, whilst I get you some water to drink. It's been a spell since I've had the company of females."

Silas Webster laughed to Cort and Charlie as they followed the women inside. "See how soon she forgets our comfort when ladies are around. No matter. I got somethin' better'n water to wet our whistles."

"You stayin' the night, Cort?" asked Maisy hopefully.

Templeton nodded. "Are you expecting any more stages?"

"Not 'til tomorrow afternoon," replied Silas.

Templeton looked at Devon and Bridget. "You're in luck. Maisy is the best cook in the Colorado Territory."

The older woman chuckled. "He's partial to any cooking that ain't his own."

"Silas, I need you to send a wire to Blue Springs," said Templeton.

"Sure thing."

The men walked over to a corner of the room where there was a desk with a telegraph key.

Devon looked around her as she took off her cape and removed her hat. The room was large and held several dining tables and chairs. There was a cook stove at the far end and a huge stone fireplace in the middle of one wall. Next to the stove was a door that led into the Websters' private rooms.

Dusk was falling and the air was turning cooler. Charlie laid a fire. When Silas and Templeton finished with the telegraph, the three men sat down at a table with a bottle of whiskey. A short while later, the blacksmith and the wheelwright joined them.

The Websters were warm and welcoming. The room felt cozy and Devon, at last, felt some measure of comfort. The ladies shared one table, while the men sat at another discussing politics. After serving up plates of fried chicken, beans, and biscuits, Maisy sat down to eat with Devon and Bridget. When the older woman learned that they were from Boston, she peppered them with questions about the big city.

"You had wash basins and a bathing tub with running water? Imagine that," she remarked in wonder.

"Yes, and three water closets," added Bridget.

Maisy wrinkled her brow in confusion. "What might a water closet be?"

When Devon explained about the flush toilet, the older woman was amazed.

"My, my, but we must seem a backward land to you. How come ya to travel here?" asked Maisy.

"I am traveling to Blue Springs to settle my late aunt's affairs," replied Devon.

Bridget and Devon helped Maisy gather and clean the dishes—another new experience for Devon—while the men sat in front of the fire smoking and enjoying a last drink. Presently, the blacksmith and the wheelwright retired to their rooms behind their shops.

"Mother, we best be preparin' to turn in now," said Silas. "Cort and Charlie are wantin' to get an early start."

Devon was wondering where she and Bridget were going to sleep, when Maisy instructed her husband to take out the beds.

Silas went to a long, wooden bench underneath the front window, opened the lid, and took out blankets and rolled-up pallets stuffed with straw.

"Best make your beds by the fire," he said, handing a pallet and a blanket to each of the surprised ladies. "The nights is turnin' colder."

"And ya best make use of the necessary now," advised Maisy. "The animals like to come out after dark. Take the lantern hangin' by the door."

Devon and Bridget looked at each other, then dropped their beds and rushed to the door.

Devon had never imagined having to use outdoor privies on this trip, and Bridget had had to explain to her that the corn cobs hanging outside of them were intended to be used as toilet paper. Devon was still aghast at the idea, and Templeton had to chuckle at the look of disgust on her face every time she had to make use of a necessary.

The girls soon returned with Devon grumbling as usual. "Honestly, Bridget, I don't know how people put up with such crudity. I nearly faint from the odor." She stopped and looked around.

"The Websters retired," said Cort. Anticipating her next question, he pointed to the sink. "There's a bucket of water to prime the pump in the morning. You can make use of it to wash your hands. Soap is somewhere around there."

"Thank you, Mr. Templeton," replied Devon primly. "At least it isn't a horse's water trough."

The ladies washed their hands and prepared their bedding, placing the pallets near the fireplace. Templeton continued to sit at the table finishing his glass of whiskey.

Bridget settled down quickly, but Devon had a difficult time of it. Despite the straw mattress, the floor was hard. The stagecoach driver snored loudly, and her bustle and steel boned corset denied her any comfort. Templeton watched her with amusement as she tossed and turned. At one point, she sat up with a huff of exasperation and yanked the pins from her hair, releasing wavy, auburn tresses to tumble down her back.

She was a head turner he had to admit. Her face was fairly symmetrical, her nose straight and well proportioned. Nicely arched dark brows and long black lashes provided a startling contrast to her bright blue eyes. Few men noticed such details about a woman. They tended to register only whether she was attractive or not. But Templeton was a student of structure and gave study to it.

He returned his attention to the fire. He had to keep his thoughts focused on the plan, particularly now that two women had unwittingly involved themselves in it.

Devon glanced over at him. A lock of light brown hair fell casually across his forehead. It seemed incongruous with his stern, angular features that betrayed little emotion—except for expressions of forbearance and annoyance, which he seemed to favor most with her.

She wondered if he had been in the war. He would be of the age, and it might account for his taciturn manner. It was clear that the man not only didn't suffer fools—he didn't suffer anyone, she thought as she finally settled into a comfortable spot.

The next morning, Devon and Bridget were awakened by the sounds and smells of cooking and the early morning light streaming into the room. As uncomfortable as she had been, Devon was surprised that she had slept at all.

"There's a pail of water on the table if ya be wantin' to refresh yourselves," said Maisy.

The girls stiffly got to their feet and stretched. Devon looked around her. Except for Mrs. Webster, they were alone.

"Where are Mr. Templeton and the driver?" she asked in alarm.

Before Mrs. Webster could answer, Devon ran to the door and threw it open only to run squarely into Cort.

"I-I thought you had left," she stammered, quickly stepping back from him.

He gave her his usual look of forbearance. "Go have your breakfast, Mrs. Wainwright. It is the last food you will see before getting to Blue Springs."

He walked past her into the room, followed by the driver.

Devon continued to regard Templeton with suspicion. Throughout the meal, she kept her eye on him and the driver. Her fears were not unfounded. Cort had entertained the thought of leaving the women behind. But he knew the scene Devon would make, and, again, he couldn't trust that he wasn't being surveilled.

When Devon saw the driver get up and leave the dwelling, she quickly redressed her hair, such as she was able, set her hat, and thanked Mrs. Webster for her hospitality, then hustled Bridget outside to the stagecoach. When Templeton arrived, he found the ladies firmly ensconced in their seats. With a beleaguered sigh, he climbed in and sat down.

While eager to resume the journey, Devon was not so eager to resume it inside a stagecoach. She soon forgot her discomfort, however, as she and Bridget became caught up in the spectacular scenery, once again, as the road twisted through mountain passes and followed along the Arkansas River.

At the second swing station stop, Cort called out to the manager: "Hector, is Sanger here yet?"

"Yeah. I'll get him."

Hector disappeared inside the cabin. Seconds later, a young man moseyed out armed with a shotgun and munching on an apple. He yanked open the door on Devon and Bridget's side and froze, startled by the presence of the two women.

"Uh, Cort, I thought you said no passengers," he said.

"Change of plans," replied Templeton. "Get in."

Bridget slid over, and the young man got in and sat down next to her, still bewildered. Eyeing Bridget more closely, he chucked the half-eaten apple out the window and snatched the bowler hat off his head.

"Brett Sanger, ma'am," he said, a warm grin crinkling his brown eyes.

Bridget smiled shyly. "I'm Bridget Ryan. This is Mrs. Wainwright, my employer."

He looked at Devon. "A pleasure, ma'am."

Devon raised a brow and nodded stiffly. "Mr. Sanger."

He was a pleasant looking young man, in need of a haircut and a shave, but he raised no red flags to Devon—except that he carried a shotgun, too. Her eyes shifted from Sanger to Templeton. Something was in the wind. All manner of thoughts ran through her mind none of which were comforting.

They had gone a few more miles when the driver shouted out: "We're in Long Horn Sheep Canyon, Cort. The curve is comin' up. Best make ready."

To the surprise of the ladies, Templeton and Sanger immediately dropped the leather curtains on the sides and secured them, then pulled up the pocket windows on the doors.

"What's amiss?" asked Devon, becoming alarmed.

"A robbery," replied Templeton.

Devon looked at him. His manner was so casual she couldn't believe she had heard him correctly. Before she could open her mouth, there came a thump on the roof from the driver, and both men assumed a more serious air as the stagecoach maneuvered the hairpin curve.

"Ladies, move to the jump seat and sit in the center," ordered Templeton.

"Mr. Templeton—"

"Do as I say, Mrs. Wainwright."

Devon and Bridget quickly scrambled to the jump seat.

Brett moved to where Devon had been sitting and peeked out the side of the curtain. "They're comin', Cort. Looks like eight of 'em. Hagen is with 'em."

Templeton took out a revolver from his shoulder holster. "Do you know how to use a gun, Mrs. Wainwright?"

Devon looked at him, appalled. "Of course not. I'm from Boston."

Sanger snickered. "Doesn't anyone have a gun in Boston?"

"Not civilized people," retorted Devon. "Mr. Templeton, I demand to know what this is all about."

"Be quiet," he answered.

There was the warning sound of gunshot. Templeton holstered the revolver, and he and Sanger readied their shotguns as Charlie brought the stagecoach to a halt. Devon could hear a voice shouting for the driver to throw down the cash box. Bridget gasped and both women tensed when two men peered through the door windows, one on each side of the stagecoach.

"Looks like just the two women," one of them yelled out.

"Where's Templeton?" a voice shouted back.

"Can't see. The windows is dusty."

"Well, open the doors, you idiots!"

At the sound of the handles being unlatched, Templeton and Sanger kicked open the doors with all of their force, catching the unsuspecting robbers hard in the chest and sending them sprawling on the ground, the wind knocked out of them. With the attention of the other outlaws momentarily diverted by the action, Charlie whipped out his rifle and began shooting.

"Get on the floor and keep your heads down!" Templeton yelled to the women. He and Brett cocked their firearms and jumped out of the coach.

Their eyes wide with fear, Devon and Bridget immediately dropped to the floor. Everything had happened so fast.

"Oh, Miss Devon, we should have stayed in Boston. We're gonna die for sure," wailed Bridget as a shot whizzed through the coach just over their heads.

With the sound of more gunshots, the horses whinnied and pranced. Devon banged her head against the seat when the coach suddenly lurched forward, and her heart leaped to her throat as she imagined a runaway coach plunging them over a cliff. Bridget's cries became louder, unnerving Devon more.

"Hold the horses, Charlie," yelled Templeton.

"I'm tryin'," the driver shouted back.

Another volley of shots was exchanged before what was left of the battered gang galloped off. Charlie struggled with the horses a little longer before bringing them under control.

"You okay, Charlie?" asked Templeton.

"Yeah." The driver picked up his hat from the floor of the driver's seat. "Hells bells and damnation!" he exclaimed, sticking his finger through a bullet hole in the crown. "The bastards got my lucky hat."

Two robbers lay moaning on the ground, still trying to catch their breath from having the stagecoach doors crashed into their ribs. Templeton and Sanger yanked them roughly to their feet.

"You have room on top for these two?" asked Templeton.

Charlie nodded. "You bet."

"Brett, ride shotgun to keep an eye on them," directed Cort.

"I think you broke my ribs," complained one of the robbers as Templeton propelled him forward.

"He'll break your head if you don't get a move on," said Sanger, pushing the other prisoner ahead.

While Sanger securely tied the two robbers to the roof of the coach, Templeton corralled one of the outlaws' horses, tied it to the back of the stagecoach, and hefted the body of a dead outlaw over it.

"Too bad he ain't Hagen," remarked the driver.

When Templeton pulled open the door, he was surprised to find the women still huddled on the floor.

"You can get up now," he said.

Devon and Bridget cautiously raised their heads.

"Are they gone?" asked Devon.

Templeton nodded.

"What if they come back?" whimpered Bridget.

"They won't," he said.

Devon and Bridget sat up and shakily took their seats. Templeton swung himself inside beside Devon, and the coach took off once again.

"Who were those men?" asked Devon, breathing heavily as her heart continued to pound hard against her chest.

"The Hagen gang," replied Cort.

"Are they murderers?"

"Most likely."

The women gasped.

"Dear God, we might have been killed," said Devon.

"Welcome to the Wild West, Mrs. Wainwright."

"But in the dime novels, bandits were gentlemen…like Black Bart," said Bridget.

"Dime novels tend to exaggerate, Miss Ryan."

"Have you ever been shot?" she asked.

"Hush, Bridget. You mustn't bother Mr. Templeton with such questions," chided Devon.

They rode in silence, then, as Cort tried to figure Hagen's next move, and the ladies struggled to come to terms with their mortality. Periodically, Devon glanced sideways at him. She had no idea what to make of this man. He could have been just as easily killed today, and yet he appeared unfazed.

"How did you know the stagecoach would be attacked?" she questioned at length.

"They thought we were carrying a cash box," replied Templeton, detecting a note of suspicion in her tone. "It stood to reason."

"How did you know it would be at that spot?"

"The curve, Mrs. Wainwright."

"What does a curve matter?"

"The stagecoach has to slow down. And we are a few miles from the next swing station. The horses are beginning to play out and not likely able to outrun the bandits," explained Templeton. "It is all very logical, Mrs. Wainwright."

Devon bristled at his patronizing manner. "Why didn't you warn us that you were at risk of being robbed?" she demanded to know.

"Would you have believed me and reconsidered your plans?"

"No. I would have thought it a ploy given your manner at the time," responded Devon crisply.

"Then I am absolved in the matter."

"No, Mr. Templeton, you are not! Had your approach been more honest, I would have reconsidered taking the next stage."

Sanger suddenly banged on the side of the coach. "Cort, look what's on the ridge."

"I saw them," Templeton shouted back.

Devon was not about to be blindsided again and leaned past Templeton to look out the window. She drew back with a gasp.

"What is it?" asked Bridget.

"Indians," replied Devon.

Terror flashed across the girls' faces as they mentally recalled accounts in the newspapers of Indian atrocities against white settlers.

"Oh, madam, the stories said Indians are partial to women with red and yellow hair," squeaked Bridget, still unnerved by the robbery attempt.

"What do you think they want?" cried out Sanger. "The prisoners are gettin' nervous."

"They're probably riled up about the Brunot Treaty," responded Templeton.

"What should we do?"

"Nothing. Ignore them."

Devon looked at Templeton as though he had lost his mind. "Ignore them! How can you be so cavalier about Indians? I demand that you make ready your firearms."

"Oh yes, please, Mr. Templeton," pleaded Bridget.

"Your scalps are safe, ladies. They will not attack," he said.

"How can you be so sure?" quizzed Devon.

"It's a Ute hunting party. The latest treaty gives them hunting rights as long as they remain peaceful. They will not risk losing that."

"Logic again, Mr. Templeton?" questioned Devon with heavy sarcasm. "Indians have committed terrible acts against white people. One can ill afford to let down his guard for even a moment."

"The white man and his government have committed just as many atrocities and indignities against them, if not more."

"How so?" challenged Devon.

"Settlers have descended upon their lands like locusts, killing off their buffalo, destroying their food supply. They've brought disease and have disrespected Indian customs and sacred grounds," replied Templeton. "Every time ore is discovered on Native land, the government rewrites the treaty and moves the people to land less hospitable than the last."

"That is no reason for them to kill indiscriminately like—"

"Savages?"

"Well, yes."

"Did you ever hear of the Sand Creek Massacre in 1864 or the Marias River Massacre in 1870, Mrs. Wainwright?"

"No."

"Suffice it to know, there is savagery on both sides."

He settled back then, pulled his hat over his eyes, and folded his arms across his chest, ending the conversation.

Devon inwardly fumed at his careless disregard for their safety, and she and Bridget kept a tense, vigilant eye in his stead as the Indians continued to follow along for a few more miles before disappearing from sight. Even then, Devon couldn't relax. Outlaws…Indians—what kind of place was this that death was viewed so casually?

When the stagecoach rolled into Blue Springs a few hours later without further incident, Devon breathed a sigh of relief. She couldn't take any more surprises this day.

The town was on the southwest side of the Arkansas River. The driver crossed the bridge and drove up Front Street past the livery stables, the stage line office, a barber shop, gun shop, butcher shop, post office, and telegraph office, then turned onto a street lined with various other shops and businesses, the anchor buildings being the dancehall and saloon and hotel.

When the driver brought the horses to a stop in front of the hotel, Templeton shoved back his hat, opened the door, and stepped out of the stagecoach. To Devon's surprise, he waited to hand down her and Bridget.

Devon looked around her at the town. She wasn't sure what she had expected, but it wasn't dusty, muddy streets and a colorless landscape.

She suddenly clutched her chest when she saw the robber draped lifelessly over a horse tied behind the stagecoach. "Is that man dead?"

"Deader than a doornail," said Sanger.

"We've been trailing a dead man all day?" shrieked Devon. She gagged and clamped a hand over her mouth.

An older man of slight stature wearing a deputy's badge hurried over to the stage. He stopped in surprise when he saw the ladies. "I thought there weren't supposed to be no passengers, Cort."

"Never mind, Jasper. Did the stage get through yesterday with the cash box?"

"Yeah. The decoy worked great. I see ya got some prisoners and a stiff one." Jasper spit a stream of tobacco juice in the dirt, and Devon fixed him with such a withering glare he nearly swallowed his plug of chaw. "Ah, sorry, ma'am…. I'll jest take this here body to the undertaker," he quickly volunteered.

"Good idea," replied Templeton, holding back a snicker.

When Jasper went to untie the horse from the stagecoach, Devon angrily rounded on Templeton. "You planned for that robbery to happen? How dare you not tell us! Bridget and I were frightened half out of our wits, not to mention the fact that we could have been killed! Furthermore…"

Templeton calmly regarded her, amusement twitching at the corners of his mouth as the feather in her hat limply wagged in time to her tirade. Her hair had lost some pins, and she impatiently brushed tendrils away from her face. Her suit was rumpled with smudges of dirt, her bustle was slightly askew—definitely not the lady who had boarded the stagecoach two days ago.

"If you remember, Mrs. Wainwright, you admitted that you wouldn't have believed me if I had told you the plan," said Templeton when she had finished.

Devon bristled. "Well, perhaps if you had told me that you had deliberately set yourself up to be robbed, I would have."

"I doubt it. You were dead set on taking this stage, and I couldn't risk tipping my hand with a scene. Most likely, we were being watched. Everything had to appear normal."

Devon was searching for a stinging retort, when Bridget tactfully suggested: "Madam, the day is coming to an end. Perhaps you should see to your matters before Mr. Stilwell leaves his office."

Devon took a deep breath and gathered herself. "Yes, Bridget, you are quite right. This is not getting us anywhere when *some* people cannot admit to a mistake and proffer a proper apology."

"I quite agree, madam," replied Templeton, giving her a pointed look.

Devon bristled again. "Will someone please direct me to Mr. Stilwell's place of business?"

"Across the street next to the bank," said Cort. "What do you want with Frank Stilwell?"

"Not that it is any of your business, he was my aunt's attorney," replied Devon. "When she passed, he notified me that I had inherited her property here."

Templeton's eyes narrowed as he studied her closer. "Who was your aunt?" he questioned, though he already had a pretty good idea. He could see the resemblance now. The red hair and stubborn character were clear giveaways.

"My aunt's name was Clarissa Cain," replied Devon.

A look of bewilderment crossed Templeton's face. "You don't mean Sadie Smith?"

"No, I mean Clarissa Cain. She runs—ran— a boarding house in town."

"Was your aunt a striking woman with red hair like yours?"

"I never met her, but it sounds like a description I've heard of her," responded Devon impatiently. "I assume you work for the stagecoach company, Mr. Templeton. Please see that the bags and trunks are sent to my aunt's boarding house. Do you know where that is?"

"I believe so. I was acquainted with your aunt, Mrs. Wainwright."

"I suppose everyone is acquainted in a town this size. Come along, Bridget."

Bridget discreetly straightened her mistress' bustle, and they crossed the street.

The driver came to stand beside Templeton. "She's Sadie's kin? Why didn't you tell her, Cort?"

"If you knew anything about women, Charlie, you would know that she isn't the type you tell anything to. She has to find out for herself."

"Guess that's why I ain't married," said the driver. 'How long do you think she'll stay?"

"Not long."

The driver sighed wistfully. "Too bad. Don't get many women around here, especially ones that look like her."

"Consider yourself lucky," returned Templeton. "A woman like her complicates a man's life. Besides, she's married."

"Married...what kind of husband would let her cross the country by herself?"

"She probably didn't bother to consult him," replied Templeton dryly.

"She is a mite willful." The driver stroked his beard thoughtfully. "Her companion is right pretty. Is she married?"

Templeton laughed. "C'mon, Charlie, she's young enough to be your daughter."

"I ain't that old," retorted Charlie. "I still got plenty of kick in my pants."

"Be that as it may, I'd be willing to bet that Sanger is planning to woo her himself. He couldn't take his eyes off Miss Ryan from the moment he saw her."

Charlie snorted. "Brett is just a kid—betwixt hay and grass."

"So is Miss Ryan. Leave them alone. Come on, I'll buy you a drink at the saloon after we check in at the stage line office."

"Oh, all right," grumbled the driver. "But I ain't that old. Hey, you gonna deliver the ladies' belongin's—bein' that you work for the stagecoach line?" he asked with a snicker.

Templeton cracked a smile. "Mrs. Wainwright seems to make a lot of assumptions, doesn't she?"

Devon and Bridget walked down the wide boardwalk. Blue Springs was not the bustling community that Colorado Springs was, but it wasn't as bad as she had thought upon first sight. It had a certain charm to it.

The wood buildings were neatly painted and well-kept, and though the architecture was unsophisticated, there was an attempt to copy Victorian design with the use of decorative fretting, turned posts, and overhangs. When they came to the general store, she and Bridget peeked through the window. It appeared to be well stocked.

They continued on. The boardwalk stepped down to street level at this point and Devon and Bridget crossed an alley, then stepped back onto a lower boardwalk and passed by the jail and marshal's office.

They crossed another alley and stepped up to a higher walkway again before coming to the bank. As directed, the attorney's office was next to it. A plaque bearing Frank Stilwell's name was affixed to the front of the building next to the door.

The ladies entered and encountered a bespectacled clerk who gave them an odd look. When Devon announced herself, the clerk scurried into a back room. Minutes later, a lean, attractive man with greying hair and neatly trimmed mustache emerged. Devon was gratified to see that he was a gentleman of some elegance and manners and wondered what he was doing out here in a place like this.

"Mrs. Wainwright," he greeted warmly, regarding her with some surprise. "I was pleased to receive notice from the detective that I could expect your arrival. When I had no reply from my previous notices, I feared you to be declining your inheritance. Your aunt was most desirous that you should be a beneficiary of her estate. I would have been quite dismayed had I failed in my duty."

"Thank you, Mr. Stilwell. This is my companion, Miss Ryan."

The attorney gave a slight bow. "A pleasure, Miss Ryan."

"Mr. Stilwell, I must confess to some confusion on the matter," said Devon. "I was not acquainted with my aunt. I wonder that my mother, her sister, was not named the beneficiary of the estate instead."

The attorney hesitated. "I'm afraid I cannot answer that, Mrs. Wainwright. But I can tell you that your aunt was very fond of you."

Devon looked at the attorney in surprise. "I cannot think why. We had no contact that I can recall."

"She still kept track of her family. If I may say so, Mrs. Wainwright, you bear a strong resemblance to your aunt."

"Indeed. I would not know I am sorry to say. Mr. Stilwell, I understand there is a house."

"Yes. I have been seeing to its upkeep."

"Good. I am anxious to settle in as soon as possible. My companion and I have had a long journey and a rather trying day."

"Of course, madam. Stagecoach travel can be rather tedious," commented the attorney, again taking note of Devon's disheveled appearance.

"Tedious, sir, would have been far more preferable to what Miss Ryan and I experienced," responded Devon stoutly.

"How so, madam?"

"Robbers attacked our coach, and a band of Indians followed for miles in plain sight."

Stilwell looked at her, alarmed. "Good heavens, dear lady. I hope that you and your companion were not harmed."

"No, Mr. Stilwell, just shaken. I am not sure that we will remain here beyond the time necessary to claim my inheritance."

"I can assure you, Mrs. Wainwright, our town is quite safe. The marshal and his deputies keep matters well-in-hand."

"We shall see, sir. May we proceed, Mr. Stilwell? Miss Ryan and I are very tired."

"Certainly, madam. There are just a few papers for you to sign." He turned to his clerk. "Tobias, please see to Miss Ryan's comfort while Mrs. Wainwright and I take care of the details in my office."

"Yes, sir."

"Mr. Stilwell, are there still boarders in the house?" asked Devon, as she followed the attorney into his private office.

"No, they all departed after your aunt's funeral. Please sit down, Mrs. Wainwright."

As Devon sat down in the leather chair, he took his seat behind the desk. After some rifling in his desk drawer, the attorney produced some documents.

"I need your signature on these three pages, Mrs. Wainwright."

Devon started to read through the papers and stopped. "The name on these papers is Sadie Smith nee Clarissa Cain."

"Your aunt changed her name many years ago," said the attorney.

"Then Mr. Templeton was right," she murmured to herself. "Mr. Stilwell, why did she change her name?"

"It is not uncommon for a young woman to do so upon leaving home, especially under the circumstances of your aunt," explained Stilwell. "I understand there was a bitter estrangement."

"I don't know the details, but I was told that my grandfather disavowed her," said Devon.

"Suffice it to know, Mrs. Wainwright, Sadie was a very proud and independent woman."

Devon suddenly felt a deep sense of gratitude to her aunt, for it was only because of her aunt's legacy that Devon had had the wherewithal to defy her mother and declare her own independence.

"It must have taken great strength and courage for Aunt Clarissa to strike out on her own and succeed in a world so hostile to women," remarked Devon as she signed the papers. "Did you know her well, Mr. Stilwell?"

The attorney smiled wistfully. "Yes, I am proud to say…for many years. I admired her very much."

"Did she have a good life…a happy life?" asked Devon.

"As all of us do, she had regrets," admitted Stilwell. "But they were few."

"I am happy to hear that, sir. The detective mentioned that there was a purse and additional land."

"Yes. The bank is holding an account for you in the amount of $53,000. The remainder of Sadie's money went into a trust for the continued benefit of Blue Springs."

The attorney took out three more documents.

"These are the deeds to the house and to two parcels of land," he said. "Sadie had started to make plans for a ranch on the parcel of land outside of town. This other parcel is in the Cripple Creek area. Can't for the life of me figure how she came by that one. Most likely from a miner down on his luck. Sadie was a soft touch for a sad story."

Devon was astonished. "I had no idea the estate was so sizable."

"Your aunt knew how to run a business. Her house is across the street at the end of the block."

Stilwell took a key from a side drawer and handed it to her. "This belongs to you now, Mrs. Wainwright. If I may, I would like to suggest that you keep the land deeds in a safe place. One never knows when or where gold or silver might be discovered around here, in which case certain people would find the land worth appropriating by hook or by crook."

Devon nodded. "Thank you, sir, for your services and your counsel.… Mr. Stilwell, how did my aunt die?" she asked in afterthought.

The attorney hesitated. "Regrettably, she fell down the stairs."

"How sad. Where is she buried? I should like to pay my respects."

"Of course. Sadie is buried in the church cemetery outside of town. Is there anything more that you require of me at the moment, Mrs. Wainwright?"

"Oh, there is the matter of the reimbursement for my travel expenses," Devon suddenly remembered.

"Say no more, madam." The attorney took out a notebook and tore out a bank note. "Give this to Henry Parker at the bank and have him send an accounting to me."

Devon looked at the bank note. "It is blank. You are this trusting?"

Stilwell smiled. "It is your money, Mrs. Wainwright."

Hit once again with a new sense of liberation, she gave a little laugh. "Yes…yes, it is, isn't it?" Devon frowned then with another thought. "Will Mr. Parker allow me a conference, sir?"

"Why ever not, madam?"

"In Boston, a woman can do business in a bank only through her husband or, if a widow, through her solicitor."

Stilwell smiled again. "That is in the East. You will find life here quite different, madam."

Their business concluded, the attorney ushered her out to the reception room.

When Devon and Bridget departed, Stilwell stood at the window and watched as they walked across the street, his mood contemplative.

"Tobias, tell Marshal Templeton I would like a word with him."

"Yes, sir."

CHAPTER THREE

The Inheritance

Devon left the attorney's office buoyed by her prospects. It had rained the night before, and she and Bridget had to pick their way across the muddy street.

There was no boardwalk at this end of town. A building was under construction. A sign indicated that it was to be the new town hall and courthouse.

Next to it was a town square of sorts with a gazebo, though there was no grass or plantings of flowers as there would have been in Boston—just dirt and more mud. Come to think of it, there wasn't a blade of grass or a shade tree to be seen anywhere, she suddenly realized. It was no wonder the place had such a stark look to it.

On the other side of the gazebo at the very end of the block, the girls came to a house on a large plot of land surrounded by an iron fence. Standing outside of the gate, they stared in wonder at the elegant Victorian mansion. The roof was red, the exterior dark blue with cream colored trim and fretwork, and a large porch curved around to a turret on one side.

"Oh, madam, it looks to be quite fine," said Bridget.

Devon nodded and opened the gate. It looked to be quite fine, indeed, even by Boston standards. She hadn't expected to find anything so nice in a town of dirt streets and wooden buildings with flat roofs and false fronts.

"Are you sure this is the right house?" asked Bridget as they walked up the steps to the front porch.

Devon took out the key from her reticule and inserted it in the lock of the door. "I dare say that it is," she replied as she turned the knob and opened the door.

They stepped inside to a generous foyer with a large chandelier, dark stained moldings, and walls covered in cream-colored wallpaper with gold flocking. A wine-colored carpet ran up the middle of the steps of a wide, sweeping staircase with a three-quarter turn.

Mesmerized, the girls continued into a large parlor off the foyer. It was dark. When Devon drew open the heavy drapes, she and Bridget looked around the room, again pleasantly surprised by the tasteful furnishings.

The curtains were dark red against olive green walls and white trim. The sofa and straight chairs were upholstered in a continuous tapestry scene, and a rug with a floral design covered the wood floor.

In the alcove of the turret was a large card table. A fireplace framed with an intricately carved wood surround was against an interior wall. And in the corner near a window was an item dear to Devon's heart.

"Oh look, miss, there's a piano," said Bridget. "You will be able to play again."

Devon walked over to it and smiled as she ran her fingers up and down the keyboard of the rosewood square grand piano. It was still in tune.

"And I shall play it when we are settled," she said. "Come, let us see the rest of the house, Bridget."

They walked across the foyer into another large room, which Devon assumed was the dining room. Here, the walls were mauve in color and the drapes green, and a fine carpet of oriental design covered the floor. But in place of a formal dining table and chairs, Devon was surprised to find the room set up with tea tables, lounges and upholstered chairs like another parlor.

A door opened into a butler's pantry, and Devon and Bridget passed through it into the kitchen. It too, was of a generous size well supplied with a step-up cook stove, a sink with cold running water, pots and pans, and a variety of modern cooking utensils.

There was a large worktable in the center of the room and, next to it, a smaller table with four chairs. Devon was particularly perplexed to find a pantry filled with bottles of liquor and cupboards full of fine china and crystal when there was no formal dining room.

She walked over to a door and opened it and let out a cry of joy. "Look, Bridget, there is a bathing room with a sink and a tub."

As in Boston, the tin tub was in the shape of a shoe, but plumbing pipes were exposed instead of hidden away in a fine wooden box. The tap produced only cold water when Devon tried it, but there was a small furnace-like oddity affixed at one end of a side arm.

"I think this must heat the bath water," she surmised. "And look, Bridget, there is a drain in the tub. You won't have to bucket out the water. Such a marvel in a place like this."

Much heartened, the ladies walked through another doorway that opened directly into a hallway taking them back to the foyer. Devon led the way up the stairs to the second floor.

Here, they found four bedrooms on one side of the hall that were roughly the same size and just as tastefully styled as the downstairs rooms. Each was comfortably furnished with a rug, lace curtains, a wood bed frame, washstand, dresser, globe table lamp, and straight chairs with the backs and seats covered in petit point.

On the other side of the hall were two more bedrooms. One was much like the others, but the last room was a large, elegant suite decorated with gold damask drapes and green-striped and floral wallpaper.

Devon was agog as she walked into the cozy sitting room. A Victorian wine-colored sofa and upholstered chair were arranged in front of a fireplace. Next to the sofa was a round table flanked by two straight chairs with tapestry seats. On the other side of the room in front of a window was a French desk. And two large rugs of geometric design in green and gold carpeted the floor.

Drapes separated the sleeping area that could be closed off by pocket doors for complete privacy. Here, against the east wall, was a beautiful, ornately carved bed with a small table on one side and a high-backed dresser angled in the corner on the other side. Next to the dresser stood a large armoire. A washstand and mirrored vanity made of the same solid and burled walnut as the bed, dresser, and armoire stood against the west wall.

"Oh, madam, 'tis the most beautiful room I've ever seen," said Bridget in awe.

"Yes, it is," replied Devon, much impressed herself. "It would seem that my aunt had very good taste."

There were French doors on the west side of the suite, and Devon walked across the room to open them. When she stepped onto the balcony, her breath caught at the panoramic view of the snow-capped mountains caught in the light of the setting sun.

"Bridget, come see this," she cried.

Bridget hurried to the balcony and was awed by the spectacular scene as well. And the two of them watched spellbound for several minutes before returning inside.

"This must have been my aunt's bedroom," said Devon. "I shall make this suite mine, Bridget. You may take the room next to it as it is larger than the others."

"Yes, madam."

Devon glanced around her. "It is getting dark. We should light some lamps."

She found some matches and lit the lamp in the sitting room and one on the table by the bed. When she turned, she caught a glimpse of herself in the full-length floor mirror and gasped.

"Oh, dear heaven!" she exclaimed. "My suit...my hair!"

She mournfully lifted the ostrich plume on her hat; it drooped again. "Oh, Bridget," she cried, "this has been a dreadful two days. My nerves are fraught."

"Perhaps you'll feel better after havin' some supper," suggested Bridget. "That nice Mr. Sanger told me of a restaurant at the hotel."

Devon took off her hat and unbuttoned her jacket. "I think I shall enjoy a bath more first."

Bridget had just finished helping her strip down to her chemise, corset, and drawers, when they heard a noise downstairs.

"Did you hear that?" asked Devon.

Bridget nodded, her eyes round with fear.

"Did you lock the door?"

"No, I thought you locked it," replied Bridget.

Devon looked around her. She pulled open the armoire. It still held her aunt's clothes, and she took out a silk robe, put it on, and grabbed a parasol. Cautiously, she went to the door and looked out into the hall. They heard another thump.

"Get a lamp and stay behind me, Bridget."

Bridget grabbed the smaller lamp from the bed table. They walked down the hall and cautiously crept down the stairs to the foyer shrouded in shadow.

"I think someone is in the kitchen," whispered Devon.

Bridget set the lamp on a table. "We should go for the marshal."

As a dark hulking figure came around the corner, the women screamed, and Devon began beating him with the parasol.

Bridget stared wide-eyed, immobilized.

The intruder wrestled the umbrella from Devon's hands, and she pelted him with her fists. He spun her around and wrapped his arms around her to subdue her.

"Run, Bridget! Run for the marshal!" she shouted.

Bridget snapped out of her stupor and started for the door.

"Stop!" yelled the intruder. "That won't be necessary."

Bridget turned back and held up the lamp. "Mr. Templeton?"

Cort dropped his arms from around Devon, and she whirled about. "You! What are you doing here?!" she sputtered furiously. "I thought you were—never mind what I thought. You scared us half out of our wits! My heart is practically pounding out of my chest."

"Calm down. I was delivering your trunks and bags," he replied. "I knocked, but no one answered. I figured you were out."

"So you just walked in and made yourself at home?"

"The door was unlocked, and we tend to be more casual here, Mrs. Wainwright. The hotel restaurant sent some food over for you. I put it in the kitchen."

Devon blushed as his eye was drawn to her cleavage that swelled provocatively above the chemise and corset, and she quickly drew the robe closed.

"I don't care how casual matters are here," she snapped. "In the future, I insist that—" She broke off when the door suddenly swung open, and two men noisily entered.

"Hey, Miss Sadie, we got them baths like ya want, an' we got gold in our pockets. We's good'n ready. Been up in them mountains since—" They stopped in their tracks at the sight of Devon.

"Well, hey honey, you must be new," said one. "Will, Sadie has a redhead."

Devon and Bridget stared at the men incredulously.

"Who are you?" Devon questioned sharply.

The men snatched the bowlers from their heads. "I'm Delbert Hainey, ma'am. And this here's my brother Will."

"I like her," said Will, smiling at Bridget.

Bridget gasped and moved closer to Templeton.

Devon had had enough intrusions for the night. "Is there an Open House sign in front of this property, Mr. Hainey?" she inquired brusquely.

"I ain't seen one, ma'am."

"Then why are you walking into this house at will?"

The brothers looked at each other in confusion.

"Everyone walks into Miss Sadie's house," said Delbert. He looked around him. "Where is Miss Sadie? She'll tell ya."

Templeton stepped forward. "Miss Sadie passed away six months ago, boys."

The men looked genuinely shocked and aggrieved.

"Aw, not Miss Sadie," said Will. "Ain't never met a finer woman with a heart as big as hers."

"Yes, we will all miss her," agreed Templeton. "This is Mrs. Wainwright, Sadie's niece."

Will turned to Devon. "We're real sorry, ma'am, ain't we, Delbert?"

Delbert nodded. "When will ya be open fer business again?"

Devon looked at the men in dismay. "You were boarders here?"

The Hainey brothers laughed.

"Boarders—that's a good one, ain't it, Will?"

"What are you doing here then?" she demanded to know.

"Miss Sadie had the best pleasure house this side of Denver," replied Delbert.

"Now, Delbert, Miss Sadie said we wasn't to call it that. She said we was to call it a...a salon," Will proudly recalled.

Devon's jaw dropped. "No, you must be mistaken. My aunt ran a boarding house...a respectable boarding house."

The Hainey brothers laughed again.

"We ain't mistaken, ma'am," said Will. "Delbert and me been comin' here fer as long as we been prospectin'."

Devon looked at Templeton, horrified. "Is this true? Was my aunt a...a purveyor of flesh?"

"She was in the business of entertainment," he replied. "The house was as much a place for socialization as it was for...for female companionship."

Devon nearly swooned and grabbed hold of the banister for support. "Dear God, this house was a brothel."

"A salon," Will corrected her.

Devon glared at the miner, causing him to take a step back. She turned an accusatory eye on Templeton then. "You knew that Sadie Smith was my Aunt Clarissa, didn't you?"

"I suspected," admitted Templeton. "I thought there to be a resemblance."

"Yet, you said nothing of this?"

"I figured Stilwell would explain things to you." Cort turned to the brothers. "Delbert, you boys will have to take your business to the Golden Nugget Saloon."

"Aw, the girls ain't as pretty there," he complained. "An' there ain't no redheads at the saloon."

"They ain't as nice neither," interjected Will. "They cheat ya and pick yer pockets. Can't trust 'em, Marshal."

"Marshal…" Devon rounded on Templeton in astonishment. "You are the marshal?"

Templeton moved his jacket aside to display a gold star with the word marshal emblazoned on it pinned to his vest.

"And Mr. Sanger?"

"My deputy."

Devon's chest heaved with mounting anger. "It would seem that you are not inclined to be forthcoming, Mr. Templeton."

"Only when there is no point to it, Mrs. Wainwright."

Devon looked at him in disbelief. "You saw no point in disclosing the fact that you and Mr. Sanger were lawmen in the midst of a robbery?!"

"Can't see as how it would have changed anything," he replied.

"It would have given Bridget and me considerable peace of mind!" she exploded.

"Do you think you'll reopen Miss Sadie's salon, ma'am?" interrupted Delbert on a hopeful note.

Devon turned snapping blue eyes on him. "No! Now leave—the both of you! Get out!" she shouted shrilly, pointing to the door.

The miners recoiled and ran into each other in their haste to run out of the house.

Devon put a hand to her forehead as she felt a dull ache coming on. "Dear God, my mother was right," she moaned. "She said no good would come of this venture. I will never hear the end of it. 'Tis little wonder Clarissa changed her name," she rambled on.

"I think you are being a little hard on your aunt, Mrs. Wainwright. It takes a strong woman to command her own life and a smart one to be successful at it—particularly out here," said Templeton. "You might give Sadie some credit."

Devon looked at him. "I should applaud her for being the madam of a brothel instead of a respectable schoolteacher or the proprietor of a respectable boarding house? Of course, you would think so. You are a man," she shot back scathingly.

"Perhaps Sadie found more freedom in this choice," he responded.

"No amount of freedom is worth the price of one's dignity, Mr. Templeton."

"Apparently, you measure dignity by a different yardstick," said Cort, pointedly eyeing her state of undress.

Devon reddened and pulled the robe closer around her. "I did not invite those men—or you, for that matter—to violate my privacy. This was a wholly unexpected event beyond my control."

"Life is a series of unexpected events beyond one's control, Mrs. Wainwright. Shouldn't your aunt be given the same benefit of the doubt as you expect others to give to you this night?"

"It is not the same thing. My aunt chose a course, Mr. Templeton. How proud of it could she be if she changed her name and led her family to believe she was running a boarding house?"

"She *was* running a boarding house in a manner of speaking," said Cort. "Her girls were her boarders."

Devon glared at him. "I do not make that distinction."

"The Cherokee Indians have a saying, Mrs. Wainwright: 'Do not judge a man until you have walked a mile in his shoes'…. Do you want your trunks taken to your rooms before I leave?"

"No," she replied shortly. "Bridget and I will take care of them ourselves. Please leave."

He picked up his hat from the foyer table and opened the door. "I would advise you to set your lock tonight, Mrs. Wainwright. The miners are leaving their claims for the winter and are starting to come into town now. Miss Sadie's house was always the first place they came after cleaning up."

Bridget let out a cry of alarm. "Oh, madam."

"Bridget, we will handle it," said Devon, her tone firm. "And never call me 'madam' again."

Templeton snickered. "Goodnight, ladies. Best eat that food before it gets cold."

Devon hurried to lock the door after him.

The reminder of the food made her realize that she was hungry now, and she turned to Bridget. "We will eat first, then I *will* enjoy a bath," she declared resolutely.

They walked into the kitchen. Devon took out plates and silverware while Bridget set out the food. Even in view of the the fact that the house had been a bordello, Devon was still amazed by the fine place settings when the only place to eat appeared to be in the kitchen and the majority of the clientele were miners, who couldn't possibly have had an appreciation for the finer things in life.

The dinner was a simple fare of chicken fricassee, potatoes and onions, and biscuits with honey, but it proved to be much tastier than Devon had expected, and she and Bridget greedily consumed every last morsel. By the end, Devon was feeling less distressed.

"Shall I prepare your bath now, Miss Devon?" asked Bridget.

"After we see to the trunks and bags," she replied.

Devon carried the lamp into the foyer and set it on the table.

"You lift this side of the trunk, and I'll lift the other," she instructed.

She discarded her robe for more mobility, and they took up their positions. Grunting, they struggled to move the trunk.

"We ain't never gonna get it up them stairs," puffed Bridget, setting down her end in defeat.

"That is what the grasshopper said to the ant," lectured Devon.

Suddenly, there came a rattling of the door.

"Hey, Sadie," a man called out. "Unlock the door."

"Yeah, we ain't seen girls in a long time."

Devon and Bridget froze.

"Miners," whispered Bridget, fearfully. "What should we do?"

"Nothing. They will go away soon," said Devon.

But they didn't go away, instead becoming more boisterous and demanding as they shook the door.

"We're closed. Go away!" shouted Devon.

The door suddenly burst open and in strode four men.

"There they are, boys," said one.

"Sadie's got some new girls. There's a redhead and another one with yeller hair!" exclaimed another.

"Where're the other girls?" asked a third miner.

Devon grabbed the parasol from the hall table. "Go away! This establishment is closed."

The miners laughed. "Miss Sadie always was a joker."

One of the men grabbed for Devon, and she promptly hit him with the parasol.

"Say, ya got an arm on ya, lady," he remarked, massaging the top of his head.

"I'll take her," said another man, reaching for Bridget.

Bridget backed away and picked up a candle holder, jabbing it at him to hold him at bay.

The miner grinned. "Hey, Zeke, this one wants to play."

When he lunged for Bridget, she swung the candle holder. He feigned to the right and grabbed her around the waist, lifting her off her feet.

Devon was momentarily distracted by Bridget's cries, and Zeke took advantage of the opportunity to knock the parasol out of her hands and laughingly hoist her over his shoulder.

"These girls got spunk," he said as Devon pounded him on the back and loudly protested. "How much is Miss Sadie chargin' for ya, honey?"

"Whatever it is, we'll pay it," shouted the other two miners enthusiastically.

Templeton was making his nightly rounds of the town, when he heard the commotion coming from Sadie's house. He had a good idea what the problem was and hurried over to it, but the scene into which he walked was chaos on a scale he was not expecting.

"Hold it!" he shouted. "Stop!"

His deep voice carried authoritatively over the noise. Everyone went still and all eyes turned to him.

"Zeke...Josiah, put the ladies down," he ordered. "They are not Miss Sadie's girls."

The miners regarded each other in confusion, and Zeke and Josiah slowly set Devon and Bridget on their feet.

"She's dressed like one," said Zeke looking at Devon.

Templeton's eye took in Devon's scantily clad figure. "Uh, well that may be, Zeke, but she is not a lady of the line."

Devon blushed profusely and crossed her arms over her chest to shield herself. "Bridget, the robe," she whispered.

Bridget quickly retrieved the garment and handed it to her mistress.

"What's goin' on, Cort?" asked Josiah. "Where's Miss Sadie?"

Templeton explained for the second time that Miss Sadie had died, that the establishment was closed, and that Devon was Miss Sadie's niece who had come to settle her aunt's affairs.

The miners' reactions were much the same as those of the Hainey brothers.

"You mean we took a bath an' bought these here suits fer nothin'?" complained Zeke.

"I'm sure the girls at the saloon will appreciate your efforts," replied Templeton.

"Them girls ain't as pretty," grumbled another.

Josiah shook his head. "Things sure ain't gonna be the same without Miss Sadie," he said with a mournful sigh. He looked at Devon and Bridget. "Sorry, ladies, if we frightened ya. Come along, boys."

At the door, Zeke turned to Devon: "Do ya think ya will—"

"NO!" she shouted.

The disappointed miners filed out, throwing last yearnful glances at Devon and Bridget.

Templeton went to examine the door. "The lock is broken. I'll see about getting it fixed tomorrow. In the meantime, Deputy Hale will keep watch on the house tonight."

"I doubt I shall sleep a wink," said Devon, still shaken. She was suddenly struck with a horrifying thought. "Mr. Templeton, what are the chances of keeping everything that happened here tonight quiet?"

"None, Mrs. Wainwright," he replied succinctly. "Miners are notoriously loose-lipped."

Devon was mortified. Only one day in Blue Springs and she was already the subject of scandal.

CHAPTER FOUR

No Way Out

The next morning, Templeton sat eating breakfast with Deputy Sanger at the hotel restaurant.

Sanger laughed heartily as Cort recounted the night's events. "Zeke actually threw Mrs. Wainwright over his shoulder? Bet she wasn't happy 'bout that," he chortled.

"There was a lot of yelling," admitted Templeton with a hint of humor in his eye.

"Was the package as good unwrapped?" quizzed Brett.

"Let's just say that I can understand the miners' keen disappointment that she wasn't one of Miss Sadie's girls," the marshal replied.

Sanger took a sip of coffee. "What about Miss Ryan?"

"She was holding her own," Templeton assured him.

"Maybe we should continue to keep watch over the ladies with the miners in town, Cort—just until the word gets around."

"Maybe."

"I'll tell Jasper that I can take the watch tonight."

"I'm sure Jasper will appreciate that," said Templeton, suppressing his amusement at the deputy's quick offer.

Sanger glanced out the window. "Speak of the devil…look there. Mrs. Wainwright is crossin' the street. Where do you suppose she's headin' in such a hurry? She sure don't look happy."

"Looks like she's aiming to see Stilwell," observed Templeton.

Sanger shook his head. "Sure wouldn't want to be him. No sir, I surely wouldn't."

Devon marched into the attorney's office.

"Is Mr. Stilwell here?" she asked the clerk in a clipped tone.

"Yes, ma'am. I'll tell him that you wish to see him."

"No, I shall tell him myself." She strode past the astonished clerk into the private office. "Mr. Stilwell!"

Startled, the attorney jumped up from his chair. "Mrs. Wainwright, what a pleasant surprise. Did you find everything to your satisfaction?"

"No, Mr. Stilwell, I did not, and this is not a social call," she bit off.

"Oh, dear. Is something wrong?" he asked anxiously.

"Yes, Mr. Stilwell, something most certainly is wrong. You seem to have omitted the fact that my aunt was the proprietor of a house of ill repute. My family and I were under the impression that she ran a respectable boarding house, not a boarding house for prostitutes!"

The attorney swallowed hard. "Oh. I was hoping to give you a few days to settle in before telling you."

"When were you going to tell me that my companion and I could expect to be besieged by miners seeking certain comforts? Those miners thought we were ladies of the line, Mr. Stilwell!" she exclaimed shrilly. "I am still mortified by the very idea of it. God only knows what might have occurred had not the marshal intervened when he did."

The attorney paled. "Good heavens. Weather must have forced them from their claims early. I am very sorry, Mrs. Wainwright. Please accept my humblest apologies."

"It was shocking enough to have to learn from my aunt's 'clients' the true nature of her business, but your failure to give full disclosure also resulted in a misunderstanding that has now placed me at the center of a scandal I shall never live down. I am afraid this changes everything, sir."

"How so?"

"I cannot accept this legacy, Mr. Stilwell, and I cannot possibly stay here with this stain upon my brow. My companion and I are returning to Boston. We shall leave on the first stage for Colorado Springs."

"But you cannot leave, Mrs. Wainwright."

"I dare say that I can, Mr. Stilwell. I am not a prisoner."

"Apologies, madam. What I meant to convey is that your aunt wanted you to have this inheritance. Won't you take a few days to reconsider? All totaled, we are talking about a very sizable estate."

"I have made up my mind, Mr. Stilwell. Give everything to the town," said Devon. "I will not be the stuff of gossip." On that note, she turned and swept out of the office.

The clerk looked up in surprise as Devon stormed past him and departed the building. Minutes later, his employer came rushing out of the back room.

"Tobias, take this note to the marshal. He's usually at the restaurant this hour of the morning. Quickly, man, quickly!"

As Devon marched down the boardwalk past the bank and the marshal's office, she heard a piano playing the lively folk song "Goodbye, Liza Jane" and stopped. It was coming from the Golden Nugget Saloon across the street.

Music to Devon was like catnip to a cat. Unable to help herself, she crossed the street and peered over the swing doors into the saloon. When her gaze took in the scantily clad women draped provocatively across men gambling and drinking, Devon drew back in shock.

"May I help you?" inquired a male voice.

Devon jumped and turned to see that a distinguished-looking gentleman had come up behind her. She blushed, dismayed to be caught outside such a place. "I-I was just walking past," she stammered. "I heard the music."

He smiled and tipped his hat, his teeth white against his dark hair and features. "My name is Matthew Chandler, proprietor of this fine establishment," he said in a smooth, Southern drawl. "And you must be Mrs. Wainwright. Checking out the competition, are you?"

He was suave, handsome, and well-mannered, obviously of a class akin to her own, and Devon was surprised to find that he was the owner of such a place. She couldn't help wondering how he had fallen into such a degradable occupation.

"News travels fast, Mr. Chandler, but apparently not in the interest of accuracy," she said, recovering her composure.

"I beg your pardon, Mrs. Wainwright?"

"I do not intend to resume my aunt's business, Mr. Chandler. You may have it all to yourself."

"You are not returning to Boston I hope."

"Yes, as a matter of fact, I am."

"What a pity."

She looked at him curiously. "You seem to know a great deal about me."

"There isn't much I don't hear owning a saloon, Mrs. Wainwright." He chuckled. "You are the talk of the town."

Devon became flushed, and she took a deep breath. "What…what is being said?" she asked haltingly.

"They call you the red-haired siren. I've had to break up a couple of fights between those claiming bragging rights and those defending your virtue. Is it true that Zeke had you over his shoulder?"

"Oh, good Lord! I shall surely have to leave town now!" exclaimed Devon.

Chandler burst into laughter.

"Well, I'm glad you think it's funny," she remarked crisply. "My reputation is at stake."

"Not to worry, Mrs. Wainwright. It will blow over soon and the miners will be on to something else. If you like, I do have some leverage. I own the only saloon in town for the time being."

"Thank you, Mr. Chandler. I will be grateful for anything you can do to put an end to the matter."

"Consider it done, madam. Might I assume that you are a widow or divorcee?"

"Why might you assume that, sir?"

"No man worth his salt would allow his wife to travel across the country alone."

"I am not alone, Mr. Chandler. I am accompanied by my companion."

The charismatic gambler smiled. "I stand by my observation, Mrs. Wainwright."

"I am a widow," said Devon.

"My condolences, madam. Perhaps you would allow me to take you to dinner at the hotel tonight to welcome you to Blue Springs."

"I'm sorry, Mr. Chandler. I have much to attend to at the moment."

"Perhaps later, then, before you leave town."

"Thank you, but I intend to leave on next stage. I am on my way to the stage line office now to make arrangements."

"A pity indeed and Blue Spring's loss." He paused. "Mrs. Wainwright, if you intend to sell the house, I will make you a generous offer for it."

"Thank you, Mr. Chandler, but you shall have to take up the matter with Mr. Stilwell. The house is not mine to sell."

Chandler raised a brow in surprise. "How so? You are the benefactor, are you not?"

"I am not accepting the inheritance. Good day, Mr. Chandler," she replied, impatient to be on her way.

Chandler had more questions but didn't try to detain her. He lit a cheroot, watching the sway of her hips as Devon crossed the street.

"Haven't you learned that high and mighty ladies like her are trouble, Matt?"

Chandler turned his head to the sultry, dark-haired woman standing in the doorway of the saloon. "Haven't you learned that trouble is the spice of life, Belle?"

Belle pushed open the swing doors and strolled over to him when his eye turned back to watch Devon. "Don't tell me you believe that stuff about girls with red hair." She raised a hand to caress the back of his neck. "You know I can show you a better time," she cooed in his ear.

"Maybe later," he said.

Belle gave a huff of annoyance. "She said she is leaving, Matt."

"I would lay odds against it," he replied.

"Why?"

"She has too much of Sadie in her."

As Devon turned the corner and continued down the boardwalk, she wasn't sure what to make of Matthew Chandler. He was attractive, charming, and well-mannered but too cultured for the unruliness of the West and too well styled for the nature of his business. But then, so had been her aunt.

What was it about this place that drew such people to disrespect their families and reject their social positions? Whatever it was, thought Devon, she would have none of it, forgetting that just a day ago she had admired and praised her aunt's courage for doing just that.

With a determined gait, Devon walked into the office of the stagecoach line. She was brought up short when she saw the marshal conversing with the clerk. They ceased their conversation and looked at her.

"Mr. Templeton," she acknowledged stiffly.

"Mrs. Wainwright."

"Can I do something for you, ma'am?" asked the clerk.

She hesitated and glanced at the marshal, hoping that he would take the hint to leave, but he showed no such inclination.

"I wish to purchase two tickets to Colorado Springs on the next stage," she said. "Is there one leaving tomorrow?"

"No, ma'am. The stage to Colorado Springs ain't comin' back through for three more days," replied the clerk.

"Well then, I wish to purchase two tickets on it," replied Devon.

"Yes, ma'am. I can sell you tickets for the roof."

"The roof!"

"Yes, ma'am. The coach is full up inside."

"I am not sitting on the roof," she declared, indignant. "I cannot even imagine how one manages such a thing."

"Oh, it isn't so bad," said Templeton. "I've heard of only a few passengers falling off. But I would advise you to dress warm and take a slicker with you. On the bright side, the tickets are cheaper."

Devon glared at him. "I don't care if the tickets are free. I will not entertain the thought. Apart from the indignity of it, passengers on the roof are the first to be shot in the event of a robbery."

Templeton shrugged. "Just make sure the coach isn't carrying a cash box."

Devon looked at the clerk. "Is it?"

"I cannot say, ma'am."

"Perhaps you can get a passenger to exchange seats with you for a price," suggested Cort.

Devon dismissed the idea. She couldn't offer much reward, and who in his right mind would make such an exchange?

"When is the stage after that one due?" she asked.

"Six days, ma'am. With the miners coming in for the winter, the coaches have been mostly full up. You'll have to check back to see if there are any seats open."

Devon let out a deep sigh of annoyance. "Rest assured, sir, I will."

"So soon to leave Blue Springs, Mrs. Wainwright?" asked Templeton.

"It would seem that it is not to be soon enough," she retorted. "Good day."

When she walked briskly out the door, the clerk looked at Cort. "Whew. She ain't happy. Are you sure about this?"

"We'll have to see, Jeremiah. Just make sure there are only roof seats open on the next couple of stages."

The clerk nodded.

Devon returned home not in a good mood.

"Bridget!" she shouted.

Bridget quickly appeared from the parlor. "Yes, madam—I mean miss?" she amended at Devon's glare.

"We are leaving on the stage in nine days if there is space."

Bridget looked at her mistress in surprise. "But I just unpacked the trunks."

"Then, you shall have to repack them."

"But why, Miss Devon? We just got here."

"Because, Bridget, I refuse to accept an inheritance as this," replied Devon, removing her hat and setting it on the foyer table. "And I will not be the subject of gossip. Talk is all over town about our mishap with the miners last night."

"But where would we go, miss? We can't go back to Boston. You will have to admit to your mother that she was right, and you will have to marry Mr. Birdwell."

Devon sighed heavily. Bridget was right. If she returned to Boston, her mother would be insufferable. Heaven forbid that Agatha Toller should ever learn of her sister's vocation. Devon would never hear the end of that either. And without an income, she would have no choice but to marry Mr. Birdwell. The very thought of it made her cringe.

Devon massaged her temples, a dull ache behind her eyes. What could she do? There was no such thing as bending one's principles a little. They were either co-opted or not. To accept just the legacy's purse was still accepting the inheritance in her mind. She would have to reject all of it or none of it. She moaned. Independence was not as freeing as she had thought. It carried with it problems requiring decisions that she was unaccustomed to deliberating.

"Are you all right, miss?" asked Bridget, concerned.

Devon looked at her. "No, Bridget, I am not, but I suppose I shall have to be. We will stay," she announced. "But only until another option presents itself. In the meantime, I shall not take a penny of that money from the estate—except to reimburse our travel—and we will not remain in this house."

"Where will we stay, miss? The hotel will be too costly."

Devon frowned. Even with the travel reimbursement she felt entitled to take, she had only enough money to see them through for a few months, but not if she had to pay $24 a month for them to stay in the hotel and take meals there.

"I am still much perturbed with Mr. Stilwell, but perhaps he can suggest a more modest alternative," she said. "I shall consult with him."

CHAPTER FIVE

Lopsided Logic

Mr. Stilwell was delighted to be given the opportunity to redeem himself with Mrs. Wainwright. But, as it turned out, he could be of no help in her quest. Devon was shocked to find that her only modest lodging alternatives were tents and hastily constructed shacks, which she was quick to veto.

After her disappointing meeting with the attorney, Devon sought refuge in bathing room. She moaned with contentment as she leaned back against the tub and closed her eyes, reveling in her first real bath since leaving Boston.

The encounter with the miners had been so unsettling she had been too fearful of being left vulnerable in the event of another intrusion, but now two days had passed without incident, and she felt comfortable enough to take the risk.

Devon sighed. There was no way she could give up this luxury for a community tub and a shack or a tent. But how could she continue to stay in the house without accepting the inheritance—not to mention live in what had been a bordello?

She was at her wit's end, when a solution suddenly dawned on her. It was so simple. How could she not have thought of it before? Hearing movement in the kitchen, Devon quickly got out of the tub and slipped on her robe, eager to share her plan.

"Bridget," she called, pulling open the door, "I know how we can—" She stopped short when she came face to face with the marshal.

The corner of his mouth twitched. "Having trouble finding your clothes, Mrs. Wainwright?"

Devon blushed and pulled the robe tighter around her. "Am I never to know privacy in this place?!" she exclaimed in exasperation.

"I came to fix the lock on your door," said Templeton, unfazed by her temper. "Sadie stored some tools under the sink. Miss Ryan gave me leave to enter." He bent down to search for a screwdriver.

"Didn't Bridget tell you that I was engaged in a bath?"

The marshal stood up with the tool in his hand. "She neglected to mention it. Miss Ryan is a bit distracted at the moment."

"Distracted…by what?" asked Devon, putting some space between them.

"You would do better to ask by whom," he replied.

Devon heaved a sigh of annoyance. She, too, had noticed Bridget's interest in the deputy.

"I did not bring Bridget with me from Boston to have her head turned by some young man she has known for two days. I feel a responsibility toward her as a—"

"Mother. I understand," said Cort.

Devon glared at him. "I was going to say as a sister."

"Your pardon. But you needn't concern yourself, Mrs. Wainwright. Brett is a man of his word."

"Be that as it may, I have much to accomplish and shall require Bridget's full attention to her duties, Mr. Templeton. I would appreciate it if Deputy Sanger would refrain from being a distraction."

"I will relay that to him," replied Cort. "Stilwell tells me that you are renouncing your legacy. Is that why you are leaving town?"

"News travels fast here, doesn't it?"

"It's a small town and strangers invite curiosity."

"I see. Well, as it so happens, I have changed my mind about leaving—for the time being—until I see my way clear," she was quick to quantify. "Thank you for coming to fix the lock."

"Keeping townspeople safe is part of my job, Mrs. Wainwright."

Devon started to leave the kitchen when a thought came to her, and she turned back to him. "Marshal, what is this fascination miners seem to hold for women with red hair?"

The corners of Templeton's mouth twitched again with an imperceptible smile. "They are of the belief that such women possess, shall we say, a more passionate nature, Mrs. Wainwright."

Devon became flushed as the look he gave her seemed to beg the question that she most certainly was not going to dignify with an answer.

"Well, ain't you a chip off the old block, red hair and all," declared a small, wiry woman bustling into the kitchen. "Hey there, Marshal."

"Hello, Nettie."

"Who are you?" Devon demanded to know.

"This is Nettie Thornbush," said Templeton. "Sadie ran the business, and Nettie ran the house."

"When I heard Sadie's kin was here, I come straight up from Saguache," said Nettie. "Don't you worry none, missy—"

"Mrs. Wainwright," corrected Devon.

"Right. Don't ya worry none. We'll get this place set up and ready for business in no time. But I don't do no cookin' after 10 o'clock," she warned.

Devon let out a shriek and fled the kitchen.

Nettie looked at Templeton stupefied. "What set her off?"

"It's a long story," he replied.

Later that day, Templeton sat at a table in the Golden Nugget Saloon finishing a glass of whiskey.

"Hello, Cort. Heard you had some trouble on the route," said Matthew Chandler.

"Some," responded Templeton.

"The currency for the town got through. You caught two of Hagen's men and shot up his gang pretty good. It was a clever play. What are you going to do next time?"

"Capture Hagen."

"Good luck."

Chandler sat down. He pulled out a tin of cheroots and held it out to Templeton. Templeton ignored the offer. Chandler gave a slight smile. The snub wasn't unexpected. He took out a cheroot and slipped the tin into his vest pocket.

Cort glanced at him. "Something on your mind, Matt?"

"I saw Mrs. Wainwright this morning," the saloon proprietor commented, casually lighting the thin cigar. "She's a lot like Sadie."

"I wouldn't let her hear you say that," said Templeton. "She's pretty miffed to find that her aunt was a madam and her inheritance a parlor house."

Chandler chuckled. "She did seem to be in a tizzy about something. She said she's leaving on the next stage."

"She has changed her mind."

"Is that so?"

Templeton looked at Chandler, curious. "Why so interested, Matt?"

Chandler shrugged. "I offered to buy the house, but she said she wasn't accepting the legacy and the house wasn't hers to sell. Has that changed as well?"

"You'll have to ask her."

Chandler took another drag on the cigar and blew a puff of smoke in the air. "Care to make a wager, Cort?"

"Depends on what I'm wagering."

"How long Mrs. Wainwright stays in Blue Springs."

Templeton snorted. "That's a fool's bet."

"Why is that?"

"She's a woman and unpredictable by nature."

Chandler smiled. "That's what makes it interesting."

"Okay, my bet is that she leaves before the first snowfall," said Templeton.

"Possibly. I'm betting her stay is longer."

"Why?"

Chandler smiled again. "Intuition." He rose from the chair. "The drink is on the house."

"I prefer to pay," responded Templeton.

"You haven't changed, Cort."

"Neither have you, Matt. Stay away from Mrs. Wainwright."

"We aren't kids anymore, Cort. Even you have to admit she's a very comely woman…. I think the lady can take care of herself."

Templeton's eyes narrowed as he watched Chandler cross the floor and climb the stairs to his suite.

Deputy Sanger strode in and sat down in the chair vacated by Chandler and signaled to the bartender for a drink. "He's buying," he said, pointing to Templeton.

Templeton raised a brow. "Why am I doing that?"

"To thank me."

"For what?"

"For information you'll be interested in."

"Have you figured out who is tipping off Hagen about the payrolls?" asked Templeton.

"No. Better than that. Bridget—I mean Miss Ryan—told me that Mrs. Wainwright is a widow. Her husband passed away a year ago."

"Why would that interest me?" questioned Cort.

Sanger grinned. "Oh, I don't know. Maybe because she's pretty. Maybe because you were there to take care of the miners last night. and went to fix her lock instead of sending Jasper."

"It's part of the job, Brett."

Sanger shot the marshal a smug smile. "If you say so."

"I say so." Templeton stood up and threw a couple of coins on the table. "For the record, I know about Mrs. Wainwright being a widow."

Sanger looked at him in surprise. "When did she tell you?"

"She didn't."

"How do you know then?"

"I'm the marshal. I know about everybody in my town."

"I'll bet you didn't know she was fixin' to leave but had a change of plans."

"Know that, too."

"Damn. Where ya goin'?"

"To do my job," said Templeton, giving his deputy a pointed look. "By the way, Mrs. Wainwright thinks you're too much of a distraction for Miss Ryan."

"What's that to mean?" asked Brett with some hesitation.

"Pick your time better." Templeton paused with another thought. "Keep an eye on Chandler. He's up to something."

* * * * *

Devon was supervising two men on the installation of a large sign in the front yard when Cort walked up.

"Still having trouble with the miners, Mrs. Wainwright?"

Devon turned to him. "Good morning, Marshal. Not for a few days. I think you can return your deputies to their other duties now. This sign should settle the matter."

Cort read the sign: CLOSED FOR BUSINESS. "It might settle things if the miner can read," he said.

"They can't read?"

"Most can, a few can't. I'll have a deputy keep watch for a few more nights just in case," replied Cort.

Devon massaged her forehead, the dull ache once again building to a pounding force.

"Headache?" inquired Templeton.

Devon nodded.

"Do you tire easier…have trouble sleeping?"

"Yes. Bridget is feeling under the weather, too. How did you know?" she asked.

"It's called mountain sickness."

Devon's eyes widened, and she clasped a hand to her chest in alarm. "Dear God. Is it fatal?"

"Not unless you have a problem with your heart," replied Templeton. "The elevation here is higher than in Boston…the air is thinner. Take it easy for a few weeks. You'll get used to it. Stilwell said you wanted to visit your aunt's gravesite. I'm going out that way if you want to ride along."

Devon shook her head. "No. I've changed my mind. I have no respect to pay my aunt."

At that moment, Bridget and a loudly grumbling Nettie came out of the house carrying armloads of linen. Sanger followed with a mattress and threw it on a pile of other mattresses. When he saw Templeton, he walked over with a sheepish smile.

"The ladies needed some help," he said.

"I see that," replied Cort. "When you can tear yourself away, there are some matters at the office that need tended. I'm going out to the Proctor place to see how Thaddeus is getting on after the accident."

"Yes, sir."

Cort turned to his attention back to Devon. "If you need help, you might consider hiring some of the miners."

Devon shuddered. "After past occurrences, I think not, Marshal."

"The boys didn't mean any disrespect, Mrs. Wainwright. They're always a bit rambunctious when they first come off the mountain, but they're not a bad lot. Give them a few days to settle down. Nettie knows which ones will do right by you."

"Even if I took your advice, I can't spare any money to pay them," said Devon.

"It is my understanding that Sadie left you plenty of money."

Devon lifted her chin a notch. "I told you. I am not accepting the inheritance. It is ill-gotten gains as far as I am concerned."

"I thought you might have changed your mind since you are living in the house and appear to be making changes," said Templeton. "Is that not a violation of your values?"

"Oh, I have not accepted the house, Marshal. After Mr. Stilwell showed me other housing options, he and I came to an agreement that I would rent this house for one dollar a month and could make certain changes, which I am doing with my own money," she explained.

Templeton stared at her. He had never heard such lopsided logic. "It must have been quite a dilemma for you," he remarked dryly.

"Yes, until I came up with this plan, it was quite a conundrum," she admitted in all seriousness. "And as my funds are limited, Mr. Chandler has agreed to buy all of the furnishings I wish to sell. Some of the parlor furniture I suppose I shall have to keep and have reupholstered."

"Why go to the bother and expense if you're not planning to stay in Blue Springs?" questioned Templeton, still trying to follow the maze of her mind.

Devon looked at him, appalled. "Surely, you don't expect me to reside in a bordello in the meantime, Marshal."

"Apologies, Mrs. Wainwright. What do you plan to do when your money runs out? How will you support yourself? How will you leave here?"

Devon hesitated. "I'll think of something," she said with more confidence than she felt.

Templeton studied her for a moment. "Mrs. Wainwright, the way I see it, Sadie left you a house, money, and land. She did not leave you the business. Just because you disagree with the way your aunt made her money does not make your inheritance ill-gotten. Sadie came by her wealth honestly. It is not illegal to operate a parlor house or a brothel in Blue Springs."

"Thank you for your opinion, Marshal," Devon replied stiffly. "Now, if you'll excuse me, I have much work to do."

* * * * *

As Devon and Bridget continued to be plagued by mountain sickness, Devon began to give some thought to the marshal's remark about the legitimacy of her aunt's legacy and to his suggestion that she hire some miners to do the work.

After much wrestling with her conscience, she decided it would be acceptable for her to use some of her aunt's money as long as it was used for the maintenance of the house and not for herself, concluding that there was no connection between the two concepts. And the next morning, Devon took herself off to the bank to make the arrangements for periodic withdrawals.

Again, taking Templeton's advice, she approached Nettie about helping her gather a work force. Once the word got out that she was hiring, there was a stampede of applicants to the door, and Devon suspected that word of her unfortunate 'incident' with the miners had something to do with it.

Nettie steered her to the more reliable workers, which luckily were not the miners of her acquaintance, and Devon hired a half-dozen men. As the men worked, however, they waxed nostalgic—at times a little too graphically for Devon's comfort—as they lamented the systematic purging of their favorite haunt. When they looked at her, Devon was certain they were trying to imagine her in her state of undress on that hapless night, and she soon turned over management of the workers to Nettie.

The feisty housekeeper proved to be adept at keeping the men in line and sober. In a few weeks' time, all vestiges of sin had been scrubbed, scraped, and painted away to Devon's satisfaction. Anything that could not be cleaned or covered over to suit her was replaced.

True to his word, Matthew Chandler bought the furnishings she wanted to sell. The reclining lounges and chairs in the dining room turned second parlor were the first to go. The sofa and chairs in the

main parlor Devon felt she could live with if she had them reupholstered. As for the bedrooms, once she got rid of all the bedding, she
decided the basic furnishings were tasteful enough to stay.

CHAPTER SIX

Ladies of the Line

It was a week before Devon found the time to go through her aunt's clothes in the armoire. She found that Clarissa's—Sadie's—taste for elegance had carried over to her taste in clothes as well. At least something of her aunt's upper-class instruction had remained with her, thought Devon.

There was nothing vulgar or cheap about the style or material of her aunt's wardrobe. In fact, the gowns were oddly glamorous in a distinctly unglamorous place.

As Devon examined a dozen gowns of varying degrees of formality, she was struck by the thought that her aunt seemed to have had two sides to her. She was obviously a woman of great style and taste, educated, intelligent with a head for business. How did she end up in such a disreputable occupation? It was a question that continued to plague Devon. The pride and gratitude that she had felt towards her aunt upon her arrival had dissolved into anger and disgust at the discovery of the shameful truth.

Devon transferred her clothes to the armoire after carefully packing away her aunt's dresses, shoes, and toiletries in the trunks. As she rummaged in a drawer, she came upon two photographs. In one, she saw a stately woman—tall and striking—standing in front of a stately home. She looked to Devon to be in her thirties, and she wondered if this was her aunt.

The woman seemed vaguely familiar to her. She thought about it for a minute before remembering that the woman had come to the house once when Devon was about four years old. Her mother had been very displeased to find the pretty lady talking to her daughter, and she had sent Devon from the room. Devon recalled hearing the two women argue bitterly before the lady left the house. Afterward, her mother had told her to never speak to this woman and to tell her if she ever saw the lady again. Devon never did.

The other picture was of a group of girls—likewise beautiful, well-dressed and well-groomed—standing in front of the same house. Devon guessed them to be Miss Sadie's girls, though one might take them to be leading members of society.

Devon continued to study the pictures, fascinated by these "ladies of the line." They appeared to be happy and prosperous, which she found both mystifying and disturbing. How could a woman who sold her body be happy? How could a woman find the "act" tolerable enough to embrace it as an occupation and still smile in a picture? She, Devon, had been respectably married and had found the act to be not in the least enjoyable or memorable but a dreaded, repugnant chore. If she had to make a living at it, Devon was quite certain she would starve to death.

She laid the pictures on the bed and continued to go through her aunt's drawers. They contained handkerchiefs and various articles of undergarments made of fine lawn and cambric materials.

Devon frowned. There were signs that the items had been rifled. She noticed dirty smudges on some of the garments. Bridget wouldn't have gone into the drawers without being told to do so. Even so, she wouldn't have left dirt on items or the clothes in disarray. It was as though somebody had been looking for something, thought Devon.

Nettie entered the room. "The workers want to know what they should do with them drapes in the parlor and dining room."

"Tell them to leave the drapes for now," said Devon.

"Miss Sadie paid a fortune for 'em…the rugs, too. She brought everything with her from Baltimore."

Devon turned around and looked at her. "Baltimore?"

"Yeah, she had a parlor house there," said Nettie. "Miss Sadie called it a salon after the ones in Paris—like this one. Before the war ruined everything, it was visited by every man of account."

Devon snorted. "I cannot imagine why my aunt would come here when all she would find would be illiterate miners. How high end could her 'salon' be then?"

"Some of them miners was teachers and doctors…educated people from the East lookin' fer a new start after the war," said Nettie. "But ya don't have to be educated to discover a big find on yer claim. And the bigger mines hereabouts is owned by businessmen from Chicago and New York. They all came here to Miss Sadie's. The bigwigs from the railroad and the stagecoach lines, too."

"Indeed," said Devon, not in the least bit interested. Whether one called it a parlor house or a salon, to her mind, a bordello was a bordello. "Nettie, did you go through these drawers at any time between my aunt's death and my arrival?"

"I ain't touched nothin' since Miss Sadie passed."

Devon picked up one of the photos from the bed. "Is this a picture of my aunt?"

Nettie looked at it and smiled wistfully. "Yeah, that be Miss Sadie. This picture was taken in Baltimore just before the war. Oh, she was a beauty. So many men wanted to marry her—rich, important men. But she always said 'no.' Her heart was buried with another—a sailor on a whaling ship that was lost at sea. She never liked to talk about it."

Nettie picked up the other photograph. "These were Sadie's girls." She pointed to an engaging young woman with a saucy smile and pose. "That one is Pearl. She was my favorite. She's a lot like Sadie— smart, tough. Miss Sadie sure loved them girls, an' they loved her. She was like a mother to 'em. She took care of 'em."

"She exploited them," retorted Devon.

Nettie looked at her. "No, missy, she saved 'em."

Devon snorted. "These girls were forced to offer themselves to men, Nettie. How was that saving them?"

"They was already in the business. Girls like them come from poor families," explained Nettie. "Ain't nowhere else for 'em to go but to the streets. Many are sold by their fathers, guardians, widowed mothers, and even husbands. Others are lured by sex slavers promisin' a better life. These poor souls find themselves workin' in cribs."

"What are cribs?" asked Devon.

Nettie's face clouded over. "They're horrible places, missy. The girls are forced to service 40 to 50 men a day. They get diseased and addicted to drink and drugs. If they ain't beaten to death, they kill themselves when they can't take it no more. Most of 'em don't last a year there."

Devon was horrified. She couldn't begin to imagine such an existence. "There must be other choices."

Nettie shook her head. "Ain't no other choices when ye're poor. Most can barely read or write if at all."

"Still, they can work as servants," insisted Devon.

"Some try but end up on the streets anyway."

"How is that?"

"They're raped or seduced by the master or son of the house and turned out when the mistress learns of it. Without a letter of reference, ain't nowhere for 'em to go." Nettie made a face of disgust. "The mistresses always blame the girls, never their menfolk."

Devon suddenly remembered whispered incidents where servant maids were let go under mysterious circumstances by elite families in Boston.

"Sadie took girls off the streets before the slavers got hold of 'em," continued Nettie. "She educated 'em, gave 'em a good place to live and work, gave 'em nice clothes to wear, made sure they had a doctor when they was sick, and she kept 'em free from childbearin' and disease. Yessir, Miss Sadie had strict rules. She protected her girls. Men treated them with respect or they was turned out."

Devon was fair to exploding. "You cannot tell me that these women enjoyed what they were doing."

"Sometimes Sadie took in girls that weren't suited to the business," admitted Nettie. "But she found other jobs for 'em to do in the house or paid to send 'em home. I can't say the others minded what they was doin'."

Devon scoffed. "How could they not?"

"Miss Sadie turned back to the girls half the coin they earned and taught them how to handle their money. They was free to leave at any time," said Nettie. "Some married their gents. Others opened their own houses…like Pearl. Ain't nowhere else a woman is gonna make all that money an' get a good shaggin' besides when she has an urge for it."

Devon blinked at the woman's unvarnished frankness. "I beg your pardon."

Nettie looked at Devon. "You know how it is. A woman has needs, too. Ain't no difference if she's married or not."

"Married or not, a lady does not have 'urges,'" replied Devon stiffly.

"Well, maybe a lady don't, but a woman does," returned Nettie. "'Tis human nature. Ain't normal not to."

Devon saw it was useless to argue with the woman and tried to drop the subject, but Nettie wasn't finished with her defense of her girls.

"People call them soiled doves and fallen angels," she went on, "but these girls *were* angels. During the cholera epidemic, Miss Sadie and the girls nursed the sick. After that, Miss Sadie sent for some kind of expert she read about to put in this new kind of sanitation system in town, so's the privies wouldn't pollute the wells and the river no more. An' she hired Tom Wick—he used to be a drunk—to keep the streets clean. Ain't had no cholera since, and Tom ain't a drunk no more."

Nettie set the photographs on the bed. "Yessir, they was good girls. An' Miss Sadie was a saint. She was always doin' somethin' to make things better for folks. It ain't right what they think."

"About what?" questioned Devon, half listening as she went back to searching through another drawer.

"Miss Sadie's death."

"Mr. Stilwell said she fell down the stairs."

"That's what they say."

Devon stopped and turned to Nettie. "What do you mean?"

"Nothin'. Jest an old woman yammering. I best be gettin' back to the workers, missy."

"It's Mrs. Wainwright," Devon shouted after her as Nettie left the suite.

Devon shook her head in annoyance at the woman's refusal to address her correctly. Her eye went to the photographs, and she picked up the one of Sadie's "angels" again, searching for some sign of despair on the women's faces but found none. Prostitution was a complete violation of the principles of a woman of good moral upbringing and an insult to her dignity. It was one thing to be forced to a life of degradation, but to actually choose it.... Devon simply couldn't comprehend it no matter how good the "benefits" might be.

She put the pictures away and went back to searching through the rest of the drawers. She puckered her brow in perplexity. They were in a similar state of disarray as though someone had been looking for something.

Devon went to the keepsake box on top of the bureau. It was made of rosewood and the ivory inlay on top was crudely engraved with a whaling scene. Coming from Boston, she knew it to be scrimshaw, an art form usually practiced by sailors to pass the time on a voyage. She wondered if Clarissa's—Sadie's—lost love had made the box for her aunt.

Devon lifted the lid and was surprised to find that it contained only a few cheap trinkets. Bewilderment rippled across her features. If the clothes and furnishings of the house were any indication of her aunt's taste and wealth, she found it odd that there were no expensive pieces of jewelry—unless they had been taken by whoever had rifled through the drawers.

She left the suite and went to the top of the stairs and called out for Bridget.

The girl quickly appeared from the kitchen. "Yes, Miss Devon?"

"Bridget, fetch Marshal Templeton here. I would like a word with him straightaway."

"Yes, miss."

Devon had finished with her task upstairs and was in the parlor when Bridget returned from her errand, flushed and not with the speed Devon thought possible. She made a mental note to talk the marshal again about his deputy.

"Marshal Templeton says he's busy," reported Bridget. "He says if it isn't a matter of life and death, he'll be at the hotel for supper at six o'clock tonight, and you can talk with him there."

Devon bristled. "Is that what he said?"

"Yes, miss. They was his exact words."

"Well, that's rude," huffed Devon. "Is that supposed to be an invitation to dine?"

"I think so, miss," replied Bridget.

"How silly of me to think that one might know proper etiquette in this place. I tell you, Bridget, that war between the states did more than eliminate slavery. It seems to have done away with civility as well."

"Yes, miss. Shall I take word to the marshal that you will dine with him?"

Devon hesitated. "Very well…but tell him that I am occupied until *fifteen* past the hour."

"Shall I come with you tonight?" ask Bridget on a hopeful note.

Devon arched a brow. "Well, I suppose so. We can't have Deputy Sanger eating alone now, can we? Tell Nettie not to cook supper for us."

Bridget's face lit up, and she scampered off to deliver the messages.

Another Side of the Story

At a quarter past six o'clock, Devon and Bridget walked into the hotel restaurant. Brett immediately went over to greet them.

"Good evening, Mrs. Wainwright…Miss Ryan. The marshal will be here soon. He said to tell you that he is occupied until half past the hour."

Devon bristled, and Brett became uncomfortable with the look on her face.

"He-uh-said to seat you at his table…over here," the deputy continued haltingly.

Devon didn't move as she debated her next course of action. If she stayed, she would be ceding the upper hand to the marshal. If she left, what message did that send? That her matter wasn't important enough? And how else was she to talk to him unless she went directly to his office at the jail?

Long, tense moments of uncertainty passed between Brett and Bridget before Devon made up her mind.

"Very well, Mr. Sanger, I shall wait for the marshal, but not one second longer than half past," she declared.

Brett slowly let out his breath. "Yes, madam."

Devon stiffened, and Bridget whispered to him, "Don't call her madam."

"I mean yes, ma'am," he immediately amended.

Devon and Bridget followed him over to a table by the window in the corner of the room.

"I have taken another table for Miss Ryan and me—if that's all right," added Brett, "so's you and the marshal can talk private."

Devon raised a brow. "How considerate of you, Mr. Sanger."

At a subtle nudge from Bridget, he pulled out a chair for Devon to sit down.

"Bridget—I mean Miss Ryan—and me will be over there." He pointed to a table across the room.

Devon nodded. "Is there something else, Mr. Sanger?" she asked when Brett continued to hover.

The young deputy took a deep breath. "Uh, Mrs. Wainwright, might I have your permission to walk Miss Ryan home after dinner?"

Devon looked at her companion. "How do you feel about that, Bridget?" she asked, knowing full well the answer.

"I would be ever so fine with it," replied Bridget with a shy smile.

"Indeed. All right, Mr. Sanger, you have my permission, but do not betray my trust," warned Devon.

"No, ma'am."

As Brett escorted Bridget across the room to their table, he wiped the sweat from his brow. He felt as though he had been through a trial by fire.

While Devon waited for the marshal to make his appearance, she watched the young couple interact, shyly getting to know each other, their attraction obvious and mutual. She at once envied Bridget's ignorance and pitied her naivety in matters of the heart and resolved to monitor the situation closely.

"Mrs. Wainwright, it must be my lucky night," said Matthew Chandler.

Devon looked up at the dapper gambler. "Good evening, Mr. Chandler. How so?"

"You can join me for supper."

"Well, I am—"

"I will not take 'no' for an answer again, Mrs. Wainwright."

"You will have to, Chandler. Mrs. Wainwright is dining with me tonight," broke in Templeton.

Chandler turned to see the marshal and forced a smile. "Good evening, Cort. Didn't anybody ever tell you that it is bad manners to keep a lady waiting?"

"At least I show up and make good on my promises," returned Templeton evenly.

They regarded each other for a tense moment before Chandler turned to Devon. "Another time, Mrs. Wainwright. But I must warn you that I do not give up easily," he said in his soft, Southern drawl. He gave her a warm smile and took her hand, lightly brushing his lips across it in a courtly manner.

As he moved on to another table, Devon stared after him, mesmerized. "Such a charming gentleman," she remarked.

Templeton snorted and pulled out a chair to sit down across from her. "Better check to make sure you still have all your rings."

Devon regarded the marshal with curiosity. "It would seem that you and Mr. Chandler do not hold each other in very high regard. Is it because of the war?"

"I believe you are here on another matter," Templeton replied.

Devon blinked in surprise. His tone wasn't sharp or rude, just matter of fact, but she got the message. This wasn't something he was going to discuss.

"What did you want to talk to be about?" he asked.

"I have some concerns," she said.

"About what?"

"Has anyone been in the house since my aunt died?"

"I or one of my deputies made frequent checks of it, and Frank Stilwell looked in on it," he replied. "Nothing ever appeared out of the ordinary. The doors and windows were always locked. Why?"

"Someone went through Clarissa's—Sadie's—drawers looking for something," said Devon.

"Are you sure?"

"Quite. Was my aunt known to have expensive jewelry?"

"Nettie could tell you better. Did you ask her?"

"No," said Devon.

"Nettie was devoted to Sadie. She wouldn't steal from your aunt, Mrs. Wainwright. You can trust her to tell you the truth. Why do you suspect jewelry is missing?"

"The pieces in my aunt's trinket box are not equal to her taste."

"I thought you didn't really know her. How would you know her taste?" questioned Cort.

"The pieces are cheap. All my aunt's possessions are of high quality and expense—her clothes, her toiletries, her house. With all the ore mined around here, I find it hard to believe she would own any of the jewelry in that box."

"Maybe the pieces have sentimental value to her."

"Maybe, but I think it more likely that someone stole the good jewelry and replaced it with cheap pieces hoping no one would notice the robbery."

"I'll check around."

Just then a woman approached them. "Hey, Cort, did you come in for the chicken and biscuits tonight?"

"Wouldn't miss it," he replied.

The woman looked at Devon. "You must be Mrs. Wainwright, Sadie's niece."

Devon nodded. "Does the whole town know?"

"Afraid so. No one keeps a secret for long in Blue Springs, but, even so, the red hair is a dead giveaway. I'm Rosie, the owner of this restaurant."

The woman was older than Devon, tall and thin with graying brown hair pulled back in a bun at the nape of her neck, but Devon thought her warm and friendly manner and the sparkle in her brown eyes transcended her plain physical appearance.

"It's a pleasure to meet any kin of Miss Sadie," Rosie continued. "She helped me to set up the restaurant after she built this hotel."

Devon looked at her in surprise. "My aunt built this hotel?"

"Oh, yes. The church and the school, too. In fact, she pretty much built this whole town as it is now. She was the heart and soul of Blue Springs. We all miss her. Supper is on the house tonight, Cort—for Sadie."

Templeton nodded. "Thanks, Rosie."

Rosie moved on to greet people at another table. She was obviously a sensible woman of good moral conduct, and Devon was astounded by her praise and admiration for the madam of the town brothel. Even more now, Devon felt conflicted about her aunt. How could she be the town pariah and savior at the same time?

Devon looked at Templeton. "You planned this," she said in an accusatory tone. "That is why you insisted that I talk with you here."

"No, Mrs. Wainwright, I did not plan it. But it doesn't hurt to have a different perspective. You have to forgive your aunt sometime."

"No, Marshal, I do not! She compromised her values."

"No, she compromised your Boston values," corrected Cort. "Out here, folks have a different outlook on things."

Devon stiffened. "Obviously." She rose from her seat. "You will have to excuse me. I have lost my appetite. Don't get up. I prefer to see myself home." With that, she stormed out of the restaurant.

Cort sighed and stood up to follow after her anyway to make sure that she got home without incident.

"Keep my plate warm, Rosie," he said on his way out the door.

From across the room, Matthew Chandler viewed the scene with great interest and a pleased smile. Bridget and Brett viewed it with dashed hopes that a spark might ignite between their employers or, at the least, a friendship that might make their own courtship easier to pursue.

CHAPTER EIGHT

Snake or Charmer?

Devon walked around the general store to see what goods it had to offer. She didn't expect much beyond the rudimentary and was surprised to see how well the store was supplied.

One side was stocked with foodstuffs, the other with a variety of household and personal items. She picked up some soaps to see that they were from New York. On a table were bolts of cloth and magazines from which one could order furniture and clothing. And a nearby shelf held ribbons, threads, and other sewing needs.

"May I help you?"

Devon turned around to see a pleasantly plump woman dressed in a plain brown dress and gingham apron, her gray hair braided and coiled on top of her head.

"Oh, good day," said Devon. "My companion and I are new to Blue Springs, and I have come to acquaint myself with your store."

The woman readjusted her wire-rim glasses for a closer look. "My stars in heaven—you are Miss Sadie's niece. Hiram, come meet Miss Sadie's kin," she called out excitedly to her husband.

A tall, skinny man hurried over and looked at Devon. "Well, bless my soul. It is a pleasure to meet kin of Miss Sadie," he said, enthusiastically shaking her hand. "I'm Hiram Walker and this here is my wife, Ruthie."

As with the woman at the restaurant, Devon was taken aback by their warm welcome. She had expected to be called to account for her aunt's shame and shunned by respectable people. This acceptance was totally unexpected.

"It is my pleasure to make your acquaintance as well," she said, returning a smile. "My name is Devon Wainwright."

"Yes, we know, dear. We know all about you comin' all the way from Boston," said Mrs. Walker. "You are just as pretty as everyone says, ain't she, Hiram?"

"Prettier, I would say," the proprietor replied with a wink.

A bright pink suffused Devon's face. "Thank you. You are too kind. I take it that you knew my aunt."

"Of course," replied Mrs. Walker. "Everyone knew Miss Sadie and her girls."

"If it weren't for Miss Sadie, Ruthie and me wouldna have this store," interjected her husband. "She helped us to get started. Staked us for a year…. It was a real shame 'bout Miss Sadie dyin' that way."

"Hush, Hiram. Are you planning to stay?" asked Mrs. Walker. "We like having new people move into the area."

"I cannot say," replied Devon.

"I hope them miners bustin' in on you the way they did won't scare you away. It's a good thing the marshal was there to take them in hand."

Devon forced a smile. "Yes, it was most fortunate." She hesitated, reluctant to ask. "Mrs. Walker, what did you and Mr. Walker hear about the-uh-incident?"

"Oh, just miners' talk," replied Mrs. Walker. "No one pays them any attention. Everyone knows how miners exaggerate."

Devon left the store breathing a lot easier, though she was once again assailed by uncertainty and confusion regarding her aunt. Apparently, no one seemed to mind that Sadie had been the town madam and probably a prostitute in her younger years.

"Mrs. Wainwright, hold up," called Matthew Chandler.

Devon stopped and waited for him.

"Mr. Chandler, I am surprised to see you about this early in the day," she commented when he came alongside of her.

He flashed his most charming smile. "I was hoping the morning would hold promise for me, and indeed it has."

"How so?" inquired Devon.

"I encountered you, fair maiden."

Devon blushed, finding his manner a little more forward than she was used to encountering in gentlemen. "You are too kind, sir."

"I assure you, madam, kindness has nothing to do with it. How goes the refurbishing of your house?" asked Chandler.

"Quite well," replied Devon. "I am nearly finished."

"Good. Then you have no reason to refuse my dinner invitation this evening."

"I'm sorry, Mr. Chandler. I cannot accept."

"Contrary to what the marshal might have told you, Mrs. Wainwright, I am harmless."

"Well, it is true that he doesn't hold you in very high esteem," she admitted, "but that is not why I must refuse your invitation."

"Then what is your reason, madam?"

"Please do not call me madam, Mr. Chandler. That is a title reserved for my aunt."

"My apologies, Mrs. Wainwright. But I ask again, why can you not accept my invite?"

"I do not approve of your profession, sir."

"I am an honest businessman, Mrs. Wainwright. I provide a service."

"You provide a vice," she corrected him.

"One man's virtue is another man's vice," he countered. "I run a clean game and pour a full measure of whiskey."

"The miners said your girls cheat and mistreat them."

"They are not my girls, Mrs. Wainwright. They are my business associate's enterprise. I just rent her rooms, and she splits the money on the drinks her girls sell."

"That still makes you indirectly responsible, Mr. Chandler."

Chandler smiled. "You drive a hard bargain, Mrs. Wainwright. How about this? I will speak to Miss Waters about her business practices, if you will have dinner with me."

When Devon remained uncommitted, he reminded her: "I did help you by buying your furnishings."

She hesitated. "Well, I suppose that deserves some consideration. Supper at the restaurant can't hurt."

"Actually, I was thinking of dining in my private quarters, Mrs. Wainwright."

Devon balked. "I don't think so, Mr. Chandler."

"I promise you, there will be nothing untoward. I have a very good cook and an excellent wine selection."

Devon shook her head. "No, I'm sorry. I cannot walk into a saloon."

"You won't have to. There are outside stairs to my living quarters."

"In Boston, it would not be proper for a lady to be with a gentleman in his rooms unchaperoned."

"Help is but a shout away, and you are not in Boston, Mrs. Wainwright."

"Yes, the marshal repeatedly reminds me of that," she remarked dryly.

"Shall I arrive at seven o'clock to escort you then?"

"Make that five o'clock, Mr. Chandler."

Chandler smiled. "I don't turn into a monster at dark you know."

"Five o'clock, Mr. Chandler," she restated firmly.

He took her hand and brought it to his lips. "I shall count the hours."

When Devon returned to the house and announced her plans for the evening, Bridget and Nettie were less than thrilled.

"That man can charm the skin right off a snake. Don't be losin' yer heart to that one," warned Nettie with the wag of her finger.

"Don't be silly," said Devon. "It is just a dinner engagement."

"In his rooms," Nettie stoutly pointed out. "Ain't nothin' just anythin' with Matthew Chandler, missy."

"Mrs. Wainwright," Devon corrected her for the umpteenth time. "Please refer to me as Mrs. Wainwright."

"Maybe Nettie is right," interjected Bridget. "Mr. Chandler does run a saloon and dance hall."

"Yes, that is regrettable," agreed Devon. "But he is a gentleman, which I dare say is a refreshing departure from someone else I can name."

Nettie snorted. "Just because he knows fancy words and highfalutin ways don't make Chandler a gentleman. If I was you, I'd keep my distance, missy."

"Mrs. Wain—oh, never mind," huffed Devon, conceding defeat.

"Miss Devon, think of your reputation," pleaded Bridget.

"People here didn't seem to have a problem with my aunt's profession. I doubt they will raise eyebrows if I have dinner with Mr. Chandler."

"In his rooms," Nettie pointed out again.

"I will be fine," responded Devon sternly. "And we will not discuss the matter any further."

If Matthew Chandler was nothing else, he was punctual. At his knock that evening, Nettie opened the door.

"Hello, Nettie, is Mrs. Wainwright ready?" he asked, ignoring her frosty glare.

"No!" she responded and was about to close the door on him, when Devon appeared.

"Good evening, Mr. Chandler. As it so happens, I *am* ready," she said, throwing Nettie a look of reproach.

He smiled and took her hand. "You look lovely as always, Mrs. Wainwright."

"Humph," snorted Nettie.

When Devon took his arm, Nettie slammed the door behind them.

Devon sighed. "I'm sorry, Mr. Chandler. I don't know what gets into that woman sometimes."

"Is she a member of your staff now?" he asked.

Devon gave him a rueful smile. "I'm not sure what she is. She just showed up and seems to think she runs the house now. As Bridget and I need a cook, I haven't asked her to leave."

Chandler chuckled. "Nettie is a rare bird."

He ushered Devon down the street, his manner light and jocular. By the time they reached the stairs that went up to his quarters above the dance hall and saloon, Devon was feeling more at ease.

She wasn't expecting much. When he opened the door to his apartment, she was surprised to walk into a tasteful, well-appointed parlor.

Chandler was amused by her reaction.

"You don't think that the owner of a saloon can have an appreciation for the finer things, Mrs. Wainwright?"

Devon smiled, apologetic. "I'm sorry. I hadn't expected to encounter *anything* of style in Blue Springs. If it makes you feel better, I was similarly surprised by the elegance of my aunt's house."

Chandler laughed. "It may not seem to be the case sometimes, but we are civilized out here."

"Still, it is a different land to be sure," said Devon.

"I will grant you that."

He removed the wool cape from around her shoulders and escorted her to a table that had been set with fine linen, china, and silverware. The fire in the fireplace and the light from the oil lamps and candles wrapped the room in a soft glow.

He held out a chair for her, then seated himself across the table and poured ruby red wine into crystal goblets. As Devon tasted the fine wine, she almost felt transported back to Boston. The only thing that betrayed the fact that she was sitting above a dance hall and saloon was the muted sound of the piano music.

Presently, a Chinese manservant appeared to serve up dishes of fish chowder, potatoes, squash, and trout from a sideboard before discreetly disappearing.

"What do you think?" asked Chandler when Devon had tasted enough of the dishes.

"It is delicious," she replied. "I haven't tasted chowder and trout since leaving Boston. I think you have much practice at pleasing ladies, Mr. Chandler," she teased.

Chandler chuckled. "You must have been talking with Nettie."

"She did warn me about you."

"Might I prevail upon you not to believe everything that you hear?"

Devon smiled. "What *is* true, Mr. Chandler? You know all about me. It is only fair that I know about you."

"What is it that you wish to know?"

"For one thing, how do you find yourself here and in this profession when you obviously come from a higher class?" she asked.

Chandler laughed lightly and toyed with his wine glass. "You think me the black sheep of the family?"

"The thought crossed my mind. You and my aunt seem to be two birds of a feather."

"Actually, Mrs. Wainwright, I find myself here by a twist of fate, or perhaps it is by a cruel joke of fate."

"How so, Mr. Chandler?"

He paused for a moment. "After the war, I returned home to find my life gone. The family plantation was destroyed, my older brother had been killed at Gettysburg, and my parents died just before the war's end…casualties of too much heartbreak I guess."

"I'm sorry," said Devon.

He shook off the memory and gave a resigned smile. "My story is just one among many of the same. When I heard that gold was discovered, I joined all the others trying to forget the war and came West. I drifted around and eventually found my way here."

He took a sip of wine.

"This had been a booming mining town called Last Chance—on par with Denver. I thought the name rather appropriate. But, alas, I was late to the dance. The ore played out. The town had become pretty much a ghost town."

Devon frowned. "I cannot imagine my aunt living in such a place, let alone choosing to stay."

"Well, she must have seen something about it that she thought worth saving," replied Chandler. "She had renamed the town Blue Springs and was rebuilding it with a mind to attracting families when I arrived."

Devon sighed. "I fear my aunt will forever remain a mystery to me. I cannot understand any of her actions." She regarded Chandler with more interest. "You do not strike me as being a family man. Why have you stayed?"

Chandler shrugged. "I was tired of prospecting…had nowhere else to go. I thought this place might have promise, so I bought the saloon from a fellow who wanted to return East."

He poured more wine for them.

"As it turns out my bet is paying off," he continued. "The town was slow to start, but it is steadily growing. And now that new deposits of gold and silver have been discovered in surrounding areas, Blue Springs is becoming a major supply center."

"Until that ore plays out as well," remarked Devon.

"Actually, Sadie had a plan for that," said Chandler. "Just before her death, she secured an agreement from the railroad company to build a switch line here."

"What does that signify?" asked Devon.

"It means that when all the planned railroad lines are built from Denver to Durango to Santa Fe, all business will pass through Blue Springs. Your aunt was an enterprising woman."

"Yes, so people keep telling me," Devon responded brusquely. "Marshal Templeton was in the war as well," she said, diverting the subject. "Is that why you don't get along?"

Chandler hesitated. "It goes deeper than that. Cort and I were at West Point together." He gave a slight laugh. "Would you believe we were close friends then? We knew your aunt from…from her days in Baltimore. Your pardon, madam."

"No need to be delicate, Mr. Chandler. I know she operated a brothel there, too," said Devon, disdain in her tone. "Please go on."

"There was a young girl named Jenny who helped Nettie with the house and the girls with their clothes," said Chandler, resuming the narrative. "Sadie had taken her under her wing. She was pretty and sweet. Cort and I both wooed her. To make a long story short, she chose me. We were going to be married, but war was declared and I went South to join the Confederacy. I later learned that Jenny had died."

"I'm sorry," said Devon.

"Sadie, Nettie, and Cort blamed me. I didn't see any of them again until I came here. It was quite a shock for all of us the day I rode into Blue Springs."

"Opportunity aside, I cannot fathom why you remain, Mr. Chandler. It cannot be comfortable."

"Cort and I traded fisticuffs and a few bloody noses," admitted Chandler. "But we all came to an understanding. I pay a tax on the drinks sold and run a clean establishment. At the risk of sounding smug, my business brings a lot of money into the town's coffers. And, in the end, your aunt was a businesswoman."

"Why were you blamed for Jenny's death, if I may ask?"

"She died in childbirth."

Devon blushed, immediately catching the drift. "Apologies, sir. I should not have pried."

"It was a long time ago," said Chandler. "What about your husband?"

Devon was silent for a moment. "Suffice it to say, he left it to other people to clean up his messes."

"How did he die?"

"He drank heavily and was a morphine addict."

"Regrettably, many veterans have turned to drink and drugs to dull the memory of war and the pain of their injuries," noted Chandler. "He was not alone."

"My husband was not a veteran, Mr. Chandler. I am ashamed to say he paid the $300 fee for another man to take his place in the draft. Robert had no injuries, just a weakness of character."

"I see. Well then, let us forget the pain of the past and look only to the future, Mrs. Wainwright. To start, please call me Matt. And may I call you Devon?"

Devon smiled. "You may," she replied.

CHAPTER NINE

The Barn Raising

"Hurry, Miss Devon. The wagons are gathering."

"I don't know if we should go, Bridget. We don't know the Johnsons. We have no food basket prepared."

"But we must go, Miss Devon. The whole town is turning out for the barn raising."

Devon eyed her companion with suspicion. "Deputy Sanger doesn't happen to be going, does he?"

Bridget blushed. "He said as how he might be there. Please, miss. It will be such fun. We ain't seen much of that since we come."

Nettie came bustling out of the kitchen with a large basket filled with foodstuff. "Get your bustles movin'. We're all goin'," she declared definitively.

Devon threw up her hands. "Well, I guess we are going then," she said, annoyed at the usurpation of her authority.

She and Bridget barely had time to collect their wraps before Nettie shooed them out the door.

Chandler stood on the balcony above his establishment and watched as the townspeople gathered and filled the wagons waiting to carry them to the Johnson farm. His eye found Devon as she was handed into one.

Belle came to stand beside him. "You have been seeing a lot of Mrs. Wainwright," she remarked in an accusatory tone.

"That's my business," said Chandler.

"Before she came to town, *I* was your business, Matt."

Chandler turned to coolly regard the exotic woman of Indian, French and Hispanic descent. "You were my entertainment, Belle."

"You bastard!" She raised a hand to slap his face, but he caught her wrist in a strong grip. "Templeton will kill you if you do to her what you did to that girl Jenny," she spat.

Chandler threw her off. "I'm 34 years-old, Belle. Maybe I'm ready to settle down now."

"Ha! That will be the day. You would be back in my bed in a week. Maybe your only interest in the widow is because you think the marshal has an eye for her," she suggested snidely.

"Get back to your girls, Belle…. Tell them to be nicer to the miners and to stop cheating them on the drinks."

"Or what?" she challenged.

"You can find another place to ply your trade."

Belle bristled. "You make a lot of money off those drinks and the rent I pay you. Don't tell me you are growing a conscience, Matt."

"Just do it," said Chandler.

It was nearly noon when the wagons pulled into a large field beneath a sunny but crisp autumn morning. The townspeople climbed out and joined the crowd already gathered from neighboring homesteads.

The framework of the barn was in place and several men were hammering boards to the sides. Others had started work on the roof. Children ran about laughing and shouting as they played tag. Women busily laid out food on long tables.

Devon was wondering what she should do, when Mrs. Walker thrust a bucket of water at her. "You can take this to the workers, Mrs. Wainwright. They most likely have a powerful thirst by now."

The bucket was heavy. Devon lugged it to the barn and called out that she had water. Several workers stopped and helped themselves to a ladleful. When Templeton walked up, she became flustered. She hadn't expected to see him here.

"How is the mountain sickness, Mrs. Wainwright?" he asked as he lifted the ladle of water to his lips.

"It is tolerable," she replied, avoiding his eye. "Bridget wanted to come today. I assume Deputy Sanger is here as well."

"On the roof."

"Marshal, I really would appreciate it if—"

"I'll keep Brett in line," he said, anticipating her complaint.

"Thank you. Please understand that Bridget is young," continued Devon. "She has never had a beau before. I don't want her to…to find herself in unfortunate circumstances."

"That won't happen," Templeton assured her. "Perhaps you should be more concerned about yourself, Mrs. Wainwright."

"What do you mean?"

He took another swallow of water. "It is none of my business, but a word of caution: watch your step with Chandler. He's not to be trusted."

Devon bristled. "You're right, Marshal, it isn't any of your business. But you should know that he told me about Jenny and the hard feelings it has caused between the two of you."

"He didn't tell you the whole story, Mrs. Wainwright."

"How do you know?"

"I know Matt Chandler better than you."

"People can change."

"A snake may shed its skin, but it's still a snake."

"That's unfair, Marshal, don't you think? You accuse me of being inflexible and of standing too high on my values when you stand pretty high on yours."

"I stand on principles, Mrs. Wainwright."

"What's the difference?"

"Principles are a man's word. Values, as you see them, are tenets as determined by the privileged."

Devon pursed her lips. "You, sir, are a smug, overbearing jackass," she blurted out, borrowing one of Nettie's more colorful words.

Cort raised a brow. "And you, Mrs. Wainwright, are a sanctimonious, narrow-minded prude."

"O-o-o-h! You are impossible!" she exploded.

He calmly looked at her. "You need more water."

"What?"

Templeton pointed to the bucket. "It needs refilled."

Devon yanked the ladle out of his hand, picked up the bucket and stormed off. She was glaring over her shoulder at him, when she collided with a stout, middle-aged man.

"Whoa there, young lady. Where are you going in such a hurry on this fine day?"

"Oh, apologies, sir," said Devon. "I was on my way to the well. I-I fear I was distracted."

He looked at her closer. "Ah, you are Miss Sadie's niece, I do believe. I have been most anxious to meet you. I am Pastor Clemmons."

"I am pleased to make your acquaintance, sir. I am Devon Wainwright. But I'm sure you know that, too."

"Hmm, I sense that all is not well with you, Mrs. Wainwright," he observed, hearing the edge in her tone.

"Please call me Devon, and no, all is not well with me, Pastor."

"What troubles you? It is too beautiful a day to be so bothered."

"I had words with your marshal," she replied crisply. "He was most rude."

The preacher chuckled. "Cort is not one to mince words, but I have always found him to be a fair and temperate man. Perhaps you misunderstood him."

"I assure you that I did not. He called me a sanctimonious, narrow-minded prude because I cannot condone my aunt's choice of 'occupation.' And if I meet one more person who tells me how wonderful she was, I shall surely scream," declared Devon angrily.

"I see," said the pastor. "Well, your aunt did help many people, my dear."

"She bought their goodwill."

"No, she received their gratitude. Sadie never asked for anyone's acceptance."

"Yet she appears to have gotten it. They think her a saint. How is that, Pastor?" Devon demanded to know. "I wasn't acquainted with my aunt. But I know that no woman who operates a bordello can be classified as anything other than a sinner whatever her good works. I don't care if this is the Wild West!"

Pastor Clemmons smiled. "I believe you have what we in the ministry call a crisis of conscience or moral uncertainty."

"No, I am quite certain that operating a bordello is a sin, Pastor."

"But you cannot understand why people choose only to see your aunt's good works. And the fact that they do makes you angry."

"Yes!" exclaimed Devon. "At last, someone understands."

"Why do you suppose this makes you so angry?" asked the minister.

"Well, because all my life I have done everything I was told and expected to do. I've abided by all the rules, have led a virtuous life, yet I've received no notice or reward for it. Instead, I suffered 10 years of marriage to a selfish, controlling man who treated me little better than a servant and—" Devon stopped, shocked by her outburst. "I'm sorry, Pastor Clemmons. I should not have spoken in such a manner."

The minister smiled again. "Do not be sorry for saying your piece. It is better to speak one's mind than to hold it inside. It cleanses the soul. But take heart, Miss Devon, the best rewards are the ones you least expect. Perhaps you are experiencing one right now and do not realize it."

Devon gave him a skeptical look. "How is that, Pastor?"

"You are here instead of in Boston marrying yet another man you do not love."

"How do you know that?" she asked in surprise.

Pastor Clemmons smiled and gave her a wink. "God works in mysterious ways. Have a better day, Miss Devon."

Devon stared after him in bemusement as he strolled off.

After filling a couple of water buckets, Devon was given the task of helping to serve up dishes to the men as they filed by. She wasn't used to doing anything with food except eating it. She certainly was not accustomed to serving it, and she was a bit awkward at it.

Templeton observed her efforts with a faint smile of amusement. He could readily see that she felt out of her element. When she glanced up to see him watching her, she stiffened and quickly looked away.

When the men had taken their fill and returned to work, the women filled their own plates and sat down on blankets spread out on the ground to exchange news and advice.

"Do they have barn raisings like this in Boston?" asked a young woman sitting beside Devon.

Obviously, the woman had no concept of Boston and Devon smiled. "Not that I have seen," she replied. "I'm Devon Wainwright."

"Yes, I know. I'm Penny Johnson."

"Oh, this is your barn," said Devon.

The woman smiled proudly. "Yes, this is my homestead." She turned to the apple-cheeked toddler seated next to her. "This is Emma, my youngest, and those two there," she said pointing to two little boys playing tag, "are my boys. My husband Emmett is talking with the marshal."

Devon looked over to see a tall, thin young man in earnest conversation with Marshal Templeton.

"Your aunt helped us to buy this land and set up this homestead," said Penny. "We owe so much to her."

"I am sure you earned it," responded Devon. "If you don't mind, I prefer not to talk about my aunt."

Penny cocked her head. "Cort said as how you are a mite touchy about Miss Sadie."

"Mr. Templeton should mind his own business. He should not be bothering you with mine," said Devon.

Penny regarded Devon with a keen eye. "It's a hard life out here, Mrs. Wainwright. But it was harder still where Emmett and me come from. It's pretty much the same story for most people here. The war changed a lot of things," she said on a somber note.

"Ain't none of us free from sin," she continued. "We all done things we ain't proud of to get by, but if there is goodness in the heart, we don't judge here. It was one of Miss Sadie's rules. This town she has built is all about second chances....Your aunt was a good person, Mrs. Wainwright. She gave everyone deservin' of it another chance at life. That is what you need to remember about her."

The young woman began to talk about her life struggles then and about the painful loss of a child a week after birth.

Devon felt chastened. In comparison, her complaints seemed small and petty. And she was struck by the fact that while Penny had never experienced the wealth and privileges of Devon's life, she was happy.

The young woman found humor in life instead of just hardship and heartache, and Devon found herself laughing at her stories and wry observations. Every time Penny talked about her husband and her children her face lit up, and Devon realized with sudden insight that the young woman's family and friends were her riches.

Penny wasn't learned, but she was forthright, witty, and smart, and she had a way of bringing things into a perspective Devon had never considered before. She found she liked the plain-spoken young woman. In fact, she liked everyone she had met in Blue Springs.

An hour before sunset, the barn was largely finished, and everyone piled wearily into the wagons to return to town or to their homesteads. Devon was silent throughout the trip, still conflicted and annoyed that so many people defended her aunt to her. If she was possessed of a more suspicious mind, she might think there was a large-scale conspiracy afoot.

By the time the wagons pulled into the center of town, darkness was falling. Devon was handed down from the back of a wagon and looked around for Bridget. That girl had an uncanny knack for disappearing into thin air these days, she noted irritably.

"I see before me a lady in need. Perhaps I can be of assistance," said a voice behind her.

Devon turned and smiled. "Mr. Chandler."

"Matt," he corrected her.

She laughed. "Matt. I was looking for my companion."

Chandler pointed across the street. "I believe she is busy."

By the light of the streetlamp, Devon could see that Bridget was indeed busy wrapped in the embrace of Deputy Sanger, and she gave a sigh of frustration.

"It is difficult to break the bond of young love," remarked Chandler with a chuckle. "But don't worry, the bloom will be off the rose soon enough."

"That is cynical," Devon lightly chided him.

"Perhaps but most often true," he responded. "At that age, how can one know what one's heart really desires?"

"I fear I share your sentiment," she said. "I suppose that makes me cynical as well."

"No, dear lady, I would submit it makes you wise."

He extended his arm. "May I escort you home?"

Devon laced her arm through his. "You may."

As they strolled down the street, she couldn't help comparing this charming gambler to the marshal. Matthew Chandler was endowed with dark good looks, a polished manner, and wit that made conversation with him as pleasant and easy as strolling through a meadow of wildflowers. And his soft, Southern drawl put her in mind of a gently flowing brook.

Cort Templeton, on the other hand—handsome in a rugged sense, taciturn, rigid in one regard, surprisingly progressive in another—brought to mind a swift-moving river with rapids. While he appeared laid back and deliberative on the surface, Devon came to know that inside of him was a core of principles that when run afoul of—which she seemed to do with some regularity—brought forth the full force of a character that could be exasperating and intimidating. Conversation with him was like walking through a mine field.

Was it any wonder that she found Matt Chandler's company to be the more welcome? she thought, as she relaxed on his arm.

When they arrived at the house, Chandler forestalled her as she was about to walk through the gate. She looked up at him questioningly, and he put a hand beneath her chin and lightly brushed his lips across hers in a gentle caress.

"Until next time," he said, his voice low and seductive.

Devon nodded dumbly.

The next morning, she awoke in high spirits and remained so throughout the day as she mentally revisited, again and again, Chandler's kiss.

It had been so unexpected. It was a breach of protocol in their world. A gentleman should ask a lady's permission before making such a gesture. But Chandler seemed to walk up to that line of what was allowable in polite society and charmingly step on it—and she had to admit that she was finding that exciting.

Nettie, on the other hand, was finding it alarming and decided it was time to take things into her own hands.

An Errand to Run

"Mrs. Wainwright!" shouted Nettie urgently.

Devon rushed into the kitchen. "What is it? What's wrong?" she cried in alarm.

"I ran out of flour. You need to go to the general store."

Devon stared at the older woman in disbelief. "You ran out of flour?! Good gracious, I thought there was an emergency. Can you not go to the store yourself?"

"I'm in the midst of bakin'."

"Where is Bridget?"

"She's hangin' out the wash."

Devon's chest heaved with irritation. "Oh, very well."

Now, she was running errands for a—she wasn't sure what Nettie was. She couldn't classify her as a servant. She hadn't hired her; she wasn't paying her; she couldn't fire her. The woman was just there by her own invitation running the house as well as the lives of her and Bridget.

She really must exert more control, fumed Devon, as she tied on a bonnet and pulled on her coat. She could order Nettie to leave, but the woman would probably ignore her, and Devon had to admit that, for one of such small stature, Nettie could be daunting.

As Devon walked down the boardwalk, she became aware that the men were most solicitous toward her—tipping their hats, wishing her a good day, offering their escort. This wasn't the first time. Every time she ventured out, she seemed to draw such attention. At first, she had thought it to be her imagination, but now it was occurring too frequently to dismiss. She was not unaccustomed to men noticing her, but this seemed different.

When she arrived at the general store, she saw a man hurrying toward her, no doubt to offer his assistance in opening the door for her as many of them did, and she quickly performed the task ahead of him and stepped inside.

He stopped, disappointed. When he walked on, Devon breathed a sigh of relief.

"Mrs. Wainwright, is something amiss?"

Devon turned to the storekeeper. "No, everything is fine, Mrs. Walker. I need a bag of flour."

"Certainly dear. Now where did I put them sacks?" murmured the older woman. "Sugar did ya say?"

"No, flour," repeated Devon. "Is something amiss, Mrs. Walker? You seem frazzled."

Mrs. Walker sighed. "Hiram is feeling poorly and has to stay abed today, and there is a shipment of goods to be put away and bookkeeping to do."

"I'm sorry. I hope Mr. Walker is not suffering a serious illness," said Devon.

"No, no. 'Tis his arthritis giving him a fit. That means cold weather is on the way. I told him to keep a raw potato in his pocket." The shopkeeper paused with a thought. "Mrs. Wainwright, I wonder if I might ask a favor of you."

"Of course. How can I help you, Mrs. Walker?"

"Well, a delivery needs to be made and with Hiram abed, I cannot leave the store unattended."

"I will be happy to make the delivery for you," replied Devon.

Mrs. Walker clasped her hands together. "Bless you, child."

She gathered together two packages wrapped in plain brown paper—one was the outline of a medium-size box, the other had a strange, elongated shape.

"Marshal Templeton is most anxious to get these nails and this saw," she said.

Devon's face fell. "These are for the marshal? Can't he walk across the street and pick them up himself?"

"Well, he could if he was here," replied Mrs. Walker. "He is at his homestead. You'll need to take the supplies to him there. You can use my buggy at the livery. Tell Teddy to hook up Betsy for you."

"But Mrs. Walker, I don't know where the marshal's homestead is, and I have to get this flour to Nettie."

"It's easy to find, dear. 'Tis only a few miles outside of town. Just take the road downstream along the river. When you come to a stand of trees, turn down the lane. You can see the house from the road. I'll see to it that Nettie gets her flour."

"What about Deputy Sanger or Deputy Hale?" asked Devon, desperation creeping into her voice. "One of them must be able to make the delivery."

"They're waitin' for a federal marshal to come for them prisoners. Here you go," said Mrs. Walker, plopping the packages in Devon's arms. "Oh, wait." She picked up a magazine from the counter and placed it on top. "This just come in for the marshal."

Devon looked at the magazine. *"Van Nostrand's Engineering Journal*—he reads this?"

"Oh, yes. He looks for it every month so have a care with it, or he'll have your head. Off you go now," said the shopkeeper, guiding her to the door and opening it for her.

Devon walked out of the store wondering how she had come to be in this position. Cort Templeton was the last person she wanted to see after their argument at the barn raising. And she was quite certain that he had no desire to see her. She was trying to think of a way to avoid having to make the errand, when she spied two miners who had tried to be so helpful to her earlier. Devon quickly ducked around the corner before they saw her and walked down the boardwalk to the livery stable.

Teddy the liveryman wasn't busy, and, in a short time, he had Betsy hooked up to the buggy. As Devon drove out of town, she grumbled aloud. How was it that she found herself running errands for everybody today? And what the devil kind of directions were these— follow the river downstream and turn onto the lane at the stand of trees? Didn't Blue Springs ever hear of street signs?

After about a mile, her annoyance began to abate as she succumbed to Betsy's easy gait and the tranquil flow of the river. Presently, she came to a group of scrub oak trees and saw the worn path—she certainly wouldn't call it a lane—and she hesitated for a few minutes before turning onto it. In the distance, she saw a large farmhouse and a half-finished barn nestled against other groupings of scrub oaks. As she drove closer, she could hear the sound of hammering.

Devon pulled back on the reins and brought the horse to a stop. She needed a minute to collect herself and to figure out the best way to approach the marshal. She could drop the packages on the porch for him to find later and say that she hadn't wanted to disturb him. But that might imply that she didn't have the nerve to face him. As nothing else came to mind that didn't show her to be something of a coward, she decided the best course of action would be to pretend indifference.

Cort had just finished hammering a board into place and was about to pick up another, when he sensed someone in the room and quickly turned. His features seldom betrayed much emotion, but it was clear that he was surprised to see Devon standing there.

"Mr. Walker is suffering an attack of arthritis, so Mrs. Walker asked me to deliver these packages to you," she hurriedly explained. "No one else seemed to be available."

Cort walked over to her and took the packages out of her arms. "Much obliged," he said. "I'm hoping to get the house closed up before the first snow."

Devon watched him as he laid the packages on a rough-hewn table. His hair was ruffled, a lock of light brown hair fell across his forehead, and he hadn't shaved in a few days. The two things combined gave him a curious boyish-masculine appeal that, for the moment, made him seem more approachable.

"Oh, and here is your magazine—safe and sound," she said, suddenly remembering the journal in her hand. "Mrs. Walker warned me that it had better arrive in good condition."

Amusement played at the corners of his mouth as Templeton took it from her.

Devon noticed the cot in the corner and the provisions on the makeshift table. "Do you stay here?" she asked.

"When the town is quiet and I know that Brett and Jasper can handle things," he replied.

She looked around her. "It looks to be a fine house. Did you build this yourself?"

"The neighbors helped with the framing and the roof. It has become something of a hobby."

"How long have you been building it?"

"Two years. I might actually finish it by the summer." He hesitated. "I'll show you around if you have the time."

"Yes, I would like that," she heard herself say.

As he led her around, she was amazed by his level of enterprise. The first-floor rooms could be closed off with pocket doors in the winter to maintain heat or opened to one very large room to allow cool air to circulate throughout the house in the summer months. Though a stone fireplace dominated the outside wall of the great room, there were two warm air furnaces, yet to be installed, to provide additional heat for the room as well as for the dining area and a smaller room that he had designated as an office.

As he described how he was going run pipes to heat bedrooms on the second floor, Devon saw a spark in his eyes and heard the pride in his voice.

They climbed makeshift stairs to the second floor, and Cort led her to a door. "I think you will appreciate this," he said.

He opened the door to reveal a large room with a flush toilet and a hand wash basin.

"A water closet!" she exclaimed. "How wonderful."

"I just need to make a few more adjustments to the bend and ratio of the pipe sizes," he explained.

"What about a bathing tub?"

He chuckled. "I'm working on it."

"This is quite progressive, Mr. Templeton," said Devon much impressed. "Where did you come by your interest and expertise?"

"Most likely my uncle," he replied. "My parents died from diphtheria when I was 10, and I was sent off to live with him. Uncle Tim was a tinkerer, always inventing things. He was awarded two patents but didn't have the wherewithal to develop them."

Cort smiled at the memory. "I learned a lot from him. He was a great believer in education. It was because of him that I went to West Point. After graduation, I was placed with the Army Corps of Engineers."

"So that is why your interest in this journal," said Devon.

"I like to keep abreast of the latest advances."

They returned to the main floor.

"With all of your education and skills, how is it that you find yourself a marshal out here instead of an engineer in a big city?" she questioned, curious.

Templeton was silent for a moment. "It is not easy to leave a war behind and return to ordinary life," he said. "I resigned from the Army, came West, and joined the Colorado Rangers. When your aunt heard I was in the area, she strong-armed the mayor into offering me the job of marshal. I turned it down, but Sadie could be very persuasive."

"What happened to the other marshal?"

"He was a drunk…picked a gun fight one day and lost."

"Are there that many bad men in Blue Springs?" asked Devon with some concern.

"By and large it's quiet now," said Cort. "But there are a few who walk too close to the line and bear watching."

Devon knew he was referring to Matthew Chandler but refrained from commenting. When there was no point of controversy between them, she was surprised by how easily they were able to converse.

"If the town is quiet, what is there for you to do?" she continued to question.

"The miners can sometimes get out of hand after a few too many drinks," he replied. "I also keep a check on the homesteads outside of town and help out the county sheriff when he raises a posse."

"How many people live in Blue Springs?"

"When the miners are in town and with the outlying homesteads, it is near to a thousand."

The light shining through the window reflected the gold in his hazel green eyes and gave them a translucent quality she had never noticed before, captivating her. Suddenly feeling self-conscious, she took a step back and tripped over a board on the floor.

He reached out a hand to grab hold of her arm and steady her. "Careful now."

"Thank you. I'm fine." Devon pulled away from him, annoyed with herself for being clumsy. "I—I must be going now. Bridget and Nettie will wonder where I am."

Cort walked her out to the buggy.

She climbed in and picked up the reins. "Good day, Mr. Templeton."

"Good day, Mrs. Wainwright."

As she turned the horse and buggy around and started down the lane to the road, she was left with much to consider on the return journey. The marshal, it would seem, was full of surprises when he was inclined to talk, which to her information and experience was rare.

When Devon returned home. Nettie and Bridget met her at the door.

"Ruth said you took a delivery to the marshal at his homestead. What happened?" questioned Nettie.

Devon looked at her in bewilderment. "What do you mean?"

"You were gone for so long," said Bridget. "We got worried."

"I was perfectly safe. I've been told that the level of crime here is—"

"That ain't what we mean," said Nettie brusquely. "What happened at the homestead?"

"The marshal showed me through the house he is building."

Nettie's eyes widened in surprise. "He showed ya his house?"

"Yes, and we conversed for a bit."

"You didn't bite off his head, did ya?"

Devon bristled. "Of course not."

Bridget and Nettie breathed a sigh of relief.

"Well, that's a start," said Nettie, ambling off to the kitchen.

Devon looked at Bridget. "Whatever has gotten into that woman?"

Bridget shrugged and hurried off, leaving Devon to ponder on the strange behavior of both women this day.

C H A P T E R   E L E V E N

Staking a Claim

Templeton walked into the marshal's office and shoved Sanger's feet off his desk. The dozing deputy opened his eyes in confusion. When they focused on his boss, he immediately jumped to attention.

"Cort, heh, didn't expect you back for another day."

"Why are the prisoners still here?" questioned Cort. "A federal marshal was supposed to pick them up three days ago."

"A wire come from Pueblo sayin' he was comin' at the end of the week. Had another prisoner to pick up," replied Sanger. He eyed Cort curiously. "Why are ya back early?"

"I finished what I needed to do."

Templeton took off his hat and coat and hung them on the peg, then went to his desk. He picked up the latest Wanted posters and began shuffling through them.

"I-uh-heard ya had a visitor at the house," Sanger broached slyly.

Templeton looked at him. "I can see that I'm going to have to do something about that grapevine between you and Miss Ryan."

"How did it go?"

"What?"

Sanger gave a sigh of exasperation. "The visit with Mrs. Wainwright. What'd ya think?"

"It wasn't a visit. She came to drop off my order from the general store and left. That's all there was to it," said Cort, returning his attention to the posters.

Brett grinned. "Now that ain't exactly what I heard."

"What did you hear?"

"Bridget said ya showed her through the house and that you and Mrs. Wainwright talked."

"People do talk, Brett."

"Not you and Mrs. Wainwright."

Templeton turned a level eye on the young man. "Find something to do, Deputy."

"Yes, sir," replied Sanger with a snicker.

Templeton glanced over at the prison cell. The feeling that niggled at the back of his neck when something didn't seem right niggled at it now. It was a sixth sense he had learned to heed during the war.

"Anything strange or different happen with the prisoners while I was gone?" he asked.

"Not as I noticed," replied Brett.

"Did Jasper mention anything?"

Sanger thought for a moment. "He said a man came to visit one of the prisoners—the tall one Jacks. He was a cousin or somethin'. Why?"

"Do the prisoners seem different to you?"

"Well, they ain't complainin' like they was. I figured they just got tired of it."

Templeton walked across the room to the jail cell and studied the prisoners more closely. They stared back at him, their manner insolent and much too smug for him.

"I hear you had a visitor, Jacks…a cousin," he said.

Jacks snorted. "So. What's it to ya?"

"Brett, did Jasper get a name?" asked Cort.

Sanger reached for the register on the desk and scanned the page for that date. "Yeah, here it is…Harry Hogg." Sanger wrinkled his brow. "Strange name, ain't it?"

Templeton turned back to the prisoner. "What's his real name?"

The prisoner snickered. "Just what the deputy said."

Templeton returned to his desk and took out a revolver. "Brett, bring the key and the manacles," he ordered.

As Sanger took the key ring and manacles off the hooks on the wall, the prisoners looked at each other uncertainly.

"What're ya aimin' to do?" asked the shorter one.

Templeton ignored him and trained his gun on them. "Unlock the door, Brett. Then shackle the prisoners to the other cell."

Casting curious glances at his mentor, Sanger unlocked the door.

Cort motioned to Jacks with his revolver. "You first…out."

As Jacks moved out of the cell, Sanger grabbed him and cuffed him to the bars of the next cell. He followed suit with the other prisoner. When the men were secured, Cort holstered his gun and walked into the vacated cell and began pulling apart the bedding.

"What're ya expectin' to find?" asked Brett.

"Just making sure Mr. Hogg didn't pass a weapon to his 'cousin."

The search yielded no results.

Jacks snickered. "Gettin' paranoid, ain't ya, Marshal?"

Templeton left the cell.

"Search them, Brett."

Sanger patted his hands over the men but found nothing. The prisoners smiled smugly.

"Pull off their boots," instructed Templeton.

"Hey, we got rights," protested the shorter man.

"Shut your trap," said Sanger.

He pulled off the prisoner's boots. A knife fell out on the floor from one of them. He made the same discovery in one of Jacks' boots.

Brett looked at the marshal in amazement. "The visitor must have passed the knives to them when Jasper wasn't lookin'. How'd ya know?"

"A gut feeling," said Cort. "Lock these guys in the other cell in case I overlooked something."

Templeton went back to his desk while the deputy secured the prisoners in the next cell.

"Looks like they're plannin' a jail break," said Brett, returning the key ring and manacles to the hooks on the wall.

Cort nodded. "In the next three days, I'd guess…before the federal marshal arrives. Get a description of this so-called 'cousin' from Jasper and tell him no more visitors."

"Yes, sir."

"Until then, I want an around-the-clock watch on these guys," continued Cort.

Sanger scratched his head in bewilderment. "Why wouldn't Hagen wait until the marshal takes custody of the prisoners and ambush him on the way to Pueblo?"

"He might, but I don't think he wants to risk killing a federal agent," replied Templeton. "He'll have the Army down on him then."

"I don't get why Hagen cares about them two."

"They must have some other value to him," surmised Cort.

Sanger glanced over at the prisoners. "What value could these two have? Neither of 'em looks too smart."

"Good question, Deputy. Send out some wires and see what you can find out about them. And tell Jasper to stay alert, especially at night. If I were Hagen, that's when I would make my move."

"Yes, sir."

Cort reached for his hat and coat. "I'll be at the restaurant if you need me."

As Templeton walked across the street, he saw Devon coming out of the millinery shop. Instantly, she was besieged by two gentlemen who sought to help her with her packages and walk her home. The startled look on her face changed to desperation when they began to argue with each other.

"I saw her first," shouted one.

"So what if you did? I got here first," the other man shouted back, raising his fists.

As the men squared off, Templeton stepped in. "Hold on there," he commanded. "What is Mrs. Wainwright to think of your manners?"

The men immediately lowered their fists and gave Devon a rueful smile. "Apologies, ma'am. We don't mean no disrespect," said one.

The other man nodded. "We'll both carry yer packages and see ya home. Then ya can choose between us."

A look of panic crossed Devon's features, and she looked helplessly at Templeton.

"Sorry, gentlemen, Mrs. Wainwright promised to have coffee with me," said Cort.

The two men looked at him in dismay.

"Are ya stakin' a claim, too, Marshal?" asked one.

"Mrs. Wainwright and I have some business to discuss is all."

The men breathed an audible sigh of relief.

"Glad to hear that, Marshal, ain't we, Milton?"

The other miner nodded. "Sure am."

Cort tossed each of them a coin. "Why don't you boys have a drink on me?"

The men's faces lit up.

"Thanks, Marshal. That's right decent of ya," said Milton.

They tipped their hats to Devon and hurried off to the saloon.

Devon stared after them in disbelief. "What is wrong with the men in this town? They all seem to have taken leave of their senses. Honestly, I can't walk down the street without being accosted—what do they mean 'staking a claim?'"

"They are letting you know that they are available to you," said Cort.

"Available...available for what?"

"Marriage."

Devon looked at him, astounded. "Whatever gave them such an idea?"

"Mrs. Wainwright, it may have escaped your notice that there are 20 men for every woman here, and they find you a very desirable choice. They are waiting for you to choose one of them for a husband."

"Well, I do not want a husband," she replied with certitude.

"Then I'm afraid you shall have to endure their attention until you do."

"Dear God…I can never leave the house again," she cried.

"In that case, you might as well enjoy your last minutes of freedom and have that cup of coffee with me."

Devon glared at him. "I don't find any humor in the situation, Marshal. Good day."

She was walking away, when she spied another miner coming towards her and quickly turned back to Templeton.

"I think I will have that coffee after all, Marshal, if you promise to see me home afterwards."

Cort looked over her shoulder to see what had changed her mind and cracked a smile.

"You're going to have to find a way to deal with the matter," he said, guiding her to the restaurant. "I can't be your guard every time you want to leave your house, Mrs. Wainwright."

"Then do something," she demanded. "You are the marshal."

"What would you have me do?"

"Charge these men with harassment or something."

"Have any of them been disrespectful or threatening towards you?" asked Cort.

"No, but they are an annoyance."

"I can't arrest someone for being an annoyance, Mrs. Wainwright. By that yardstick, we might find you in jail."

Devon glared at him again. "I do not find that humorous either."

CHAPTER TWELVE

A Larger Plan

Templeton sat at his desk in a pensive mood. Coffee with Mrs. Wainwright the previous day had gone fairly well. It would seem that they had come to a truce in an unspoken agreement to avoid certain subjects—her aunt and Matthew Chandler.

When she wasn't being morally indignant or outraged, Cort was surprised to find that she was actually bright and witty. And even when she was in one of her snits, he found her somewhat amusing in the face of her naiveté. He shook his head. For someone so sheltered from life, she was certainly opinionated on matters with which she had little or no knowledge or experience.

For reasons he had yet to comprehend, he felt compelled to watch out for her. Perhaps it was because she was so incredibly naïve, or maybe it was because she was Sadie's kin. Whatever the reason, he resigned himself to the fact that he was stuck with her until she returned to Boston, which he was fairly certain would be soon now that she knew every bachelor in town was trying to court her.

A man dressed in black walked into the office then. His face was craggy and weathered, his eyes squinty, and he walked bowlegged, all indicative of one who spends long hours on the trail.

"Are you Marshal Templeton?" he asked in a gravelly voice.

"I am," responded Cort. "Who are you?"

"U.S. Marshal Tom Clayman. I'm here to pick up the prisoners."

"Do you have papers?"

The man grunted. He pulled aside his coat to display a badge pinned to his vest and a gun strapped to his hip, and he took out two folded sheets of paper from his vest pocket and dropped them on the desk.

Templeton picked up the papers and looked them over. One was a federal warrant for custody of the prisoners; the other was proof of the marshal's identity. His eye shifted to the prisoners. They were standing at the doors of the cells with an air of expectancy.

"The papers seem to be in order," said Cort. "The key ring is over there hanging on the wall."

As the federal marshal started toward the key ring, Templeton quietly took out his revolver from the desk drawer. The chair creaked as he slowly rose to his feet. The man went still. He moved aside his coat, slowly slid his gun from the holster and turned. An explosion of gunshots rent the air.

Outside, Brett and Bridget were walking to the restaurant when they heard the shots. The color drained from Sanger's face.

"Bridget, get Doc Morse," he said and tore off across the street to the jail.

Bridget ran to fetch the doctor, then ran to the house. When she burst through the front door, Nettie came hurrying from the kitchen.

"Gracious, girl, what in heaven's name—"

"Where is Miss Devon?" panted Bridget.

"I'm right here," said Devon, quickly descending the stairs. "What's wrong?"

"Oh, miss, there was a shootout at the jail. I heard someone say that Marshal Templeton was shot twice."

"Oh, dear Jesus, no!" cried Nettie.

"Brett and me was across the street when we heard shots come from the jail—"

Nettie grabbed Bridget by the shoulders. "Is Cort alive?"

"I-I don't know," said Bridget beginning to cry.

Devon rushed out the door, not stopping to take her coat. She ran to the jail and stopped short at the entrance at the sight of a body lying lifeless on the floor in a pool of blood.

Brett was there looking pale and shaken, and she looked at him wide-eyed. "That's not—"

"No, ma'am. That ain't Cort. He's at the doc's. I'm waitin' on the undertaker to come."

Devon turned and ran the distance to the doctor's office next to the barber shop. When she burst into the waiting room, it was empty.

"Doctor!" she called out.

"In here," he yelled back.

She opened the door and rushed into the back room. Cort was sitting on the surgeon's table, and she breathed a sigh of relief.

"Bridget said there was a shootout at the jail—" Her eyes went from the bloody shirt lying on the table to the bloody gash on Cort's right upper arm. "Dear God," she gasped.

"It's just a scratch," said Cort, grimacing as the doctor dabbed away the blood with antiseptic.

The doctor, a gruff looking man with gray bushy eyebrows, grunted. "It's a little more than a scratch. The bullet went through. The shooter didn't get his pound of flesh, but he got an ounce of it."

"Bridget said you were shot twice," said Devon.

The doctor pointed to the bruise above Cort's heart.

"The badge deflected the bullet," explained Templeton in his typical, low-key fashion.

"The sun was sure shining on you today, son," said the doctor with the shake of his head.

"What happened?" asked Devon.

"The federal marshal who came to take custody of the prisoners wasn't really the federal marshal," said Cort.

"Who was he?"

"Don't know yet."

"How did you know that he wasn't the real federal officer?" she questioned.

"He had a revolver holstered on his hip like a shooter…and I know Marshal Clayman." Cort's jaw tightened. "There was blood on the custody papers. The shooter probably shot him."

The doctor applied an antiseptic salve to the marshal's wound and wrapped a cloth bandage around it.

"Come back to see me in a couple of days to make sure there is no infection," he instructed. "I know it's probably useless to tell you this, but take it easy, Cort—at least for the day. You lost some blood."

When Templeton got off the table, he swayed dizzily. Devon rushed to steady him, and he put an arm around her shoulders until his head cleared.

"Told you," said the doctor.

As they stood there, Devon became uncomfortably conscious of the fact that not only was she in the company of a half-naked man, but also that her arm was around his waist and her hand touched his bare skin.

It seemed like an eternity to her, but it was only a few seconds before Cort removed his arm and she moved away from him.

"Doc, hand me my shirt," he said.

Cort grimaced as the doctor helped him into it.

"Where are you going?" asked the doctor as Templeton started for the door.

"Back to the office. Brett is alone."

"Brett can handle things. If the muscle was damaged, you won't be able to shoot with that arm for awhile, and that bruise on your chest is going to be painful for several days. You need to go home and rest."

"The office *is* my home, Doc."

The doctor shook his head again as the marshal walked out.

He looked over at Devon. "You look as though you could use a drink."

"Thank you, but I don't fancy hard liquor," said Devon.

"Then, I can use one. Hope you don't mind."

"No…please."

The doctor took out a bottle from a cabinet and poured himself a drink.

"I've been out of town making my rounds of the homesteaders. We haven't met. I'm Bartholomew Morse. Everyone calls me Doc. I'm guessing you are Sadie's niece I've been hearing so much about."

Devon nodded. "I'm Devon Wainwright. Are you going to tell me how wonderful my aunt was, too?"

The doctor's eye narrowed. "Apparently you don't share that opinion."

"She was the town madam and most likely a prostitute before that," Devon replied dryly.

"According to the Bible, Mary Magdalene was a prostitute."

"What is your point, Doctor?"

"Judge a person by his good works, Mrs. Wainwright, instead of by his sins."

"That depends upon which one tips the scale, don't you think?"

"No, it depends upon what is in one's heart. And I can tell you truthfully, Mrs. Wainwright, your aunt had a good heart."

"Maybe that isn't enough, Doctor."

"What is?"

"I don't know…perhaps to know that she didn't have a choice."

"How do you know that she didn't?" questioned Morse.

"It is true that I didn't know my aunt," admitted Devon, "but she was a member of a respectable family with wealth and privilege before she threw it all away. She had a choice, doctor."

The doctor studied his drink for a moment before downing it. "There are choices and then there are choices, Mrs. Wainwright. Out here, you will learn that life is not always black and white. Most times, it is pretty gray."

Templeton returned to the marshal's office.

When he walked in the door, Sanger jumped up from his chair in surprise. "Cort, what're ya doin' here?"

"Where should I be, Brett?"

"In a room at the hotel resting. You just got shot."

"Don't have time for that. The doc patched me up." Templeton dropped his mangled badge on the desk. "Have the blacksmith make me a new one?"

"Yeah, sure." Sanger picked up the shield and stared at it, registering just how close his mentor had come to death. "I thought you was dead for sure when I seen ya layin' there."

Cort put his hand on the young man's shoulder. "Well, I'm not dead, and we have a job to do. Tell Jasper to gather some men and search for Clayman. There might be a chance he's still alive. Then send a wire to the U.S. Marshal's office in Pueblo telling them what happened."

Brett nodded and palmed the badge. "Oh, Mrs. Wainwright come tearin' in here all upset. I told her you was at Doc's."

"I saw her. She came charging in there, too."

"Thought she was gonna have the vapors when she saw all that blood and the body on the floor," said Sanger.

Cort chuckled. "She is a mite squeamish."

As Brett continued to show a reluctance to leave, Templeton assumed a more commanding air. "Best be on your way now, Deputy. I'm fit enough."

"Yes, sir—but I'll be back as soon as I can."

Templeton breathed a sigh of relief when Sanger walked out the door. He felt more discomfort than he wanted to let on.

"Hagen sure ain't gonna be happy 'bout you killin' his hired gun, Marshal," commented Jacks. "He paid a lot of money for him."

Templeton turned to the prisoner. "Who was he?"

"Hollister…Dan Hollister…out of Texas."

"Never heard of him. Why did Hagen need a hired gun?" asked Templeton. "What's he planning?"

"What makes you think Hagen is plannin' something?" questioned Jacks.

"He wouldn't be trying to break you two yokels out of jail. Misfits are a dime a dozen out here."

"Hey, who you callin' misfits?" protested the other prisoner. "Me and Jacks got a skill."

"Shut up, Shorty!" Jacks rose from his cot and wrapped his hands around the bars. "Don't get in the way, Marshal. Hagen will make you regret it. Be smart and let us out of here. This ain't no business of yers."

"Hagen's gunman tried to kill me. That makes it my business," said Templeton. "If Hagen has bigger plans, he shouldn't have tried to rob the stagecoach."

He walked over to the desk and had just eased into his chair when Matt Chandler strode into the office.

Templeton inwardly groaned. "What do you want, Matt?"

"I heard about the commotion. Thought you could use this," said Chandler, setting a bottle of whiskey on the desk.

At any other time, Templeton would have refused it, but he could use a stiff drink right now. The surge of adrenalin was wearing off. The bruise above his heart hurt like hell, and his arm was beginning to throb.

Templeton nodded. "Thanks."

Chandler glanced at the bloodstained sleeve of Cort's shirt. "How bad is it?"

"Just a scratch."

"A scratch doesn't leave that much blood. That's your shooting arm, isn't it?"

"Doc says I'll be fine in a couple of weeks."

"You are tangling with Billy Hagen. Do you have a couple of weeks?"

Cort eyed Chandler narrowly. "Are you worried about something, Matt?"

The gambler shrugged. "It's bad for business when the town marshal gets killed. If you need help, you know where to find me."

When Chandler left, Cort uncorked the bottle and took a big swig of whiskey. As the sedative effects of the liquor began to take hold, Devon came to mind. The woman was full of surprises. They annoyed the hell out of each other, yet she came running into the doctor's office when she heard he'd been shot. He could still smell the fragrance of lilac in her hair from when he had leaned on her to steady himself.

He grunted and took another gulp of whiskey. He couldn't get sidetracked now.

A half hour later, Brett returned. "I sent the wire, and the blacksmith will have a badge ready tomorrow. Here, I picked up a shirt for ya. Hiram just got a new supply of 'em in. I charged it to the town. I figured they owed ya one."

Templeton took the shirt from his deputy. "Thanks. What about the search party?"

"Jasper has three men. They'll be ready to leave within the hour. Why don't you go in the back room and get some sleep?"

Templeton nodded and got to his feet. "Stay alert."

In the back room, Cort changed his shirt and lay down on the cot, instantly falling asleep.

When he awoke, he winced as he moved to get up. He gave himself a few minutes to pull himself together before walking into the outer office. He couldn't show any signs of weakness around the prisoners.

Brett was sitting outside the front door, and Cort went to join him.

"You look better," said Sanger. "How are ya feelin'?"

"I've dealt with worse," said Templeton. "How long was I asleep?"

"Three hours. Everything is quiet." Brett paused. "Jasper found Clayman. He was dead. Looks like he was ambushed. His horse was nearby, and his rifle was still in the saddle holster. The body is at the undertaker's."

Templeton ran a hand across his face. "Too bad. He was a good man."

Brett nodded. "I notified Pueblo. Clayman had no family that he claimed. They said to bury him here."

"Are they sending someone to pick up the prisoners?" asked Cort.

"Yeah, two this time, but it may be another week or so. I don't get it," said Brett. "All this trouble over these two yokels…gang members are a dime a dozen."

"There is something else going on," said Templeton.

"What?"

"I don't know yet. Until we do, we have to keep a sharp watch. You and Jasper get some rest. I'll take the watch tonight."

"Are you sure you're up to it?"

Templeton nodded. "I have to be. Hagen will strike again."

* * * * *

The members of the gang exchanged uncertain glances as Hagen eyed each one of them, his dark gaze becoming increasingly darker as it moved down the line. He stopped in front of one of the outlaws.

"You told me the stage was transportin' $25,000 in currency, and now two of the men I need for this next job are sittin' in jail, and my hired gun is killed tryin' to break them out."

He suddenly picked up a bottle from the crude wooden table and threw it against the wall of the shack in an outburst of rage. "I told you I didn't want a federal marshal killed! Now we'll have the whole damn Army down on our tails!"

"That was Hollister's doin', Billy. I told you he was crazy," said one of the gang members.

"This weren't our fault, Billy," spoke up another defensively. "I saw Templeton carry out the cash box to the stage driver myself. He was onto us and made a switch."

Hagen leveled his gaze on the outlaw. "How do you suppose that happened, Rix?"

The outlaw shrugged. "Templeton is a tricky son-of-a-bitch. He just figures things out. This weren't our fault," he repeated.

"Are ya sayin' it's mine?" questioned Hagen, a dangerous inflection in his tone.

"No, but Pete told ya he was on board. Maybe ya shoulda planned better."

The mercurial leader suddenly grabbed the man by the neck and pistol whipped him. As the outlaw lay half-conscious on the ground, Hagen viciously kicked him. The others took a step back as he fixed blazing black eyes on them again, daring anyone to make a similar suggestion.

"None of this would have happened if it wasn't for Templeton," said a third member. "He's the problem."

"Then take care of him!" snapped Billy.

"How? Christ, Billy, he outshot Hollister."

"Why not wait until the federal marshals pick up Jacks and Shorty and ambush them on the way back to Pueblo?" suggested another outlaw. "We're being blamed for killing one marshal, what's a few more?"

Hagen pounded his fist on the table. "I want Jacks and Shorty out of jail *now* before they tell Templeton somethin' they ain't supposed to be tellin' him."

"What do you want us to do, Billy? Templeton will be ready and waitin' for us now."

Hagen thought for a moment, and a sinister smile spread across his dark features. "Tell him we'll make a trade."

CHAPTER THIRTEEN

Boundaries

Devon descended the stairs and was met by Bridget in the foyer.

"This just come for you, miss," she said, holding out a small, black velvet box.

Devon regarded the delivery with a mixture of surprise and bewilderment. "Who is it from?"

"I believe Mr. Chandler, miss. It was his man who delivered it."

Devon opened the box to find exquisite pearl drop earrings with diamond studs. Enclosed was a note: *Until next time*.

"Oh, Miss Devon, they're beautiful," breathed Bridget.

Devon pursed her lips and snapped the box shut. "You will return them forthwith."

Bridget looked at her mistress nonplussed. "Why, miss?"

"A lady does not accept gifts from men to whom she is not engaged, married, or closely related." She handed the box to Bridget. "Off with you now before Mr. Chandler gets the wrong idea."

Bridget soon returned, box still in hand, with another message. "Mr. Chandler said he won't take back the earrings unless you return them yourself at dinner this evening," she relayed.

Devon's chest heaved with anger. She snatched the box from her companion's hand. "Bring me my coat and hat, Bridget."

Chandler sat at his table in the corner of the saloon going over the inventory of the bar, when he became aware of a sudden, unnatural silence. The piano player had stopped playing and all conversation had ceased. He looked up, surprised, when he saw Devon standing in the doorway. Her appearance there was as much out of place as an unbeliever in church.

All eyes followed her as she walked over to Chandler, her features set in a tight line.

He stood up and smiled. "Devon, what are you doing here, not that you aren't welcome—" His eyes narrowed. "Is something wrong?"

She slammed the box on the table. "My favors are not for sale, and neither is my company," she informed him. With that, she turned on her heel and stormed out of the saloon.

Chandler took a moment to gather himself, then picked up the box and slipped it into his coat pocket. Belle stood on the stairs, her lips curled up in a smug smile. The handful of miners who sat drinking and gambling held their breaths. This was the only saloon in Blue Springs. And they feared that the embarrassment of the scene might anger the proprietor enough to order them out.

Chandler looked around the room, and a smile spread across his face. "The lady has a temper to match her red hair, eh, boys? Bartender, drinks for everyone."

Laughter broke out. The piano began to play again, and the look of satisfaction faded from Belle's face.

Devon walked swiftly down the boardwalk, surprised and relieved that Chandler hadn't followed after her. Though she was still angry enough to handle another confrontation with him, she didn't want one. It was too exhausting, particularly when she still wasn't sleeping well.

She had just passed the gazebo in the square when she heard her name called and turned to see an attractive woman with black hair, dark eyes, and an olive complexion.

"You think you are being clever, don't you, Mrs. Wainwright?"

Devon blinked in surprise. "I beg your pardon?"

"Matt is interested only in the chase. You are just another Jenny to him."

Devon regarded the woman closer. "I saw you at the saloon."

"I'm Belle Waters."

"You are Matt's business associate."

Belle smiled. "Among other things. A word of warning, Mrs. Wainwright. He always comes back to me."

"If you are that certain of him and of yourself, Miss Waters, I don't think you would have followed after me to tell me this. Excuse me."

Belle's features hardened and her eyes glittered as Devon went on her way.

When Devon walked into the house, her mood was at odds with a settled mind.

"Did you see Mr. Chandler?" asked Bridget. "Did you return the earrings?"

Devon took off her hat and coat and handed them to the young woman. "Yes, I did. I walked into the saloon and—"

"You went into the saloon!" exclaimed Bridget. "Miss Devon, whatever would your mother say?"

Devon gave a sigh of annoyance. "She won't say anything. She won't hear of it. Where is Nettie?"

"In the kitchen."

Devon walked into the kitchen where Nettie was busy preparing a stew.

"Nettie, I wish a word with you," she said.

Nettie turned from the stove. "What about, missy?"

"Jenny."

Nettie looked startled for a moment. "How did you hear about Jenny?"

"Matt—Mr. Chandler—told me about her."

Nettie's brows drew together in a frown. "Did he now? What did he tell you?"

"That she worked for my aunt in her 'establishment' in Baltimore, that both Mr. Chandler and Marshal Templeton courted her, and she chose Mr. Chandler," said Devon. "Unfortunately, he went off to war before they could marry, and he later learned that she had died in childbirth."

She looked Nettie in the eye, determined to know the truth. "Why do you and the marshal continue to blame him for something that was beyond his control?"

The older woman wiped her hands on her apron. "It wasn't beyond his control."

"How so," quizzed Devon.

"Jenny was orphaned and come to Miss Sadie desperate for work like they all did. She was a pretty little thing…sweet, innocent. Miss Sadie saw that she wasn't made for the business and put her to work runnin' errands, helpin' the girls with their dress, and helpin' me to keep house."

"Matt was from Virginia. How did he come to know of my aunt's establishment in Baltimore?" asked Devon, impatient to cut to the chase.

"I'm gettin' to that," responded Nettie shortly. "Matt Chandler used to come to Baltimore with his father before the war to factor their cotton, and they would stop by Miss Sadie's salon. Later, Matt met Cort at West Point, and the two of 'em visited the salon together when they had leave. Cort saw Jenny on one visit and became sweet on her. As soon as he made his interest in her known to Matt, Matt set out to win her first."

Nettie shook her head. "Matt hasn't changed a bit. Everything is a game to that boy, and he always has to win. The trouble is everybody else loses too much when he does."

"Go on," said Devon.

"Matt used that silvery tongue of his to seduce Jenny," continued Nettie. "I'm guessin' you've experienced it a few times yerself or ya wouldna be defendin' him."

"Never mind me," replied Devon sternly.

"We all tried to warn Jenny, but she wouldn't hear it," said Nettie, giving Devon a pointed look. "Then, she discovered she was with child. Matt promised to marry her in the parlor the following week."

Nettie smiled, a bittersweet smile, as she recalled that day. "The child dressed in her finery. Sadie closed the salon that night. The girls wore their Sunday best and decorated the parlor with flowers and ribbons. There was such excitement."

Nettie paused for a moment. "The cook and me prepared a fine reception, and Miss Sadie brought out her best champagne. The preacher arrived, and we all sat waitin'. One hour passed, then two, then three…Jennie tried to make excuses for him, but we all knew Matt wasn't comin'."

"Maybe something delayed him," suggested Devon.

Nettie snorted derisively. "Something delayed him all right. Cort sent a wire the next day sayin' that Matt had gone south to join the Confederacy."

"It was a difficult and emotional time, Nettie. Young men felt duty bound to—"

"Matt never had a sense of duty or honor in his life," scoffed Nettie. "For months, Jenny waited to hear from him. When no word came, she fretted night and day that he was dead or a prisoner. The birth come on early…she and the child died." Nettie shook her head in disgust. "Word never did come from Matt."

Devon fell silent for a few moments. "I'm sorry," she said.

"Cort is private with his feelin's, but he really cared for that girl, missy. Havin' Matt in the same town has opened old wounds and thrown salt into 'em."

"What about Belle Waters?" asked Devon.

Nettie scoffed again. "That woman is a viper. You keep yer distance from her, missy. She worked for your aunt for a spell 'til Miss Sadie turned her out. When Matt came to Blue Springs and bought the saloon, Belle took up with him and opened her own business."

"Does she and Mr. Chandler have a…a personal relationship?" inquired Devon.

"Belle has always fancied him her man if that be yer meanin'."

"Does Mr. Chandler see it that way?"

"Matt don't commit to no one but himself, missy."

Devon sighed. "What happened with Jenny was a long time ago, Nettie. It wasn't right what Matt did, but they were both young. There was a war. Perhaps he has changed. Perhaps you judge him too harshly."

"I'm seein' him right clear, missy. You better start doin' the same before it's too late. Don't you be fooled by him, too."

"Thank you, Nettie, but I am capable of making my own judgments."

As Devon walked out of the kitchen, Nettie shook her head, doubtful. Devon Wainwright might be a widow and older, but she was Jenny all over again—a babe in the woods where Matthew Chandler was concerned.

The next day, Nettie opened the door to find the object of her scorn standing on the doorstep. "What do you want?" she questioned sourly.

"And a good day to you, too, Nettie," responded Chandler with a bright smile. "Is Mrs. Wainwright at home?"

"She's busy."

"Nettie, I can speak for myself," said Devon, coming to the door. "Please go and help Bridget with the wash."

Throwing the gambler a disdainful look, the older woman walked away.

Devon stepped outside and closed the door. "Mr. Chandler, why are you here?" she asked stiffly.

Mr. Chandler. He raised a brow at the formal greeting. He had thought he had given her enough time to get over her anger, but it would appear that he had some fences to mend.

"I have come to apologize," he said. "I did not mean to offend you, Devon. In my line of work, I don't often meet a woman with principles out here."

Devon regarded him closely. He seemed contrite both in countenance and in voice. She nodded. "I accept your apology, Mr. Chandler, but if we are to remain friends, you must remember that I will not accept gifts or orders of any kind from you or from any other man."

"I understand," he said. "If you say that you accept my apology, I must ask that you prove it as people too often say it without meaning it."

She looked at him warily. "And how must I do that?"

His lips curved up in a disarming smile. "Have coffee with me at the hotel now and call me Matt again. I have an aversion to Mr. Chandler."

Devon sighed, finding it difficult to stay angry with him. "I'll get my hat and coat."

CHAPTER FOURTEEN

Miss Pearl

Templeton sat at his desk trying to figure out Hagen's game and the outlaw's next move.

"Did ya hear about Mrs. Wainwright?" inquired Sanger as he cleaned his gun.

"Not lately," replied Templeton, distracted.

"She sure gave Chandler what for. Marched right into the saloon and gave him a piece of her mind."

Cort glanced at his deputy. "Mrs. Wainwright walked into the saloon? Must have been one hell of a rule Chandler violated."

"Bridget said he sent a gift of earrings to her that cost a pretty penny. When Mrs. Wainwright sent Bridget to return them, Chandler said he would accept them only from Mrs. Wainwright at dinner that night. Well, Bridget said the missus stormed out of the house, went straight to the saloon, and told Chandler to stick them earrings where the sun don't shine."

Templeton gave the young man a skeptical look. "I doubt Mrs. Wainwright said that."

"Well, maybe she didn't say it just like that," admitted Sanger. "But that sure enough was what she meant. Crowley was there. Accordin' to him, she said her favors weren't for sale, and she marched out of the saloon before Chandler could say a word. Everybody expected Matt to run after her or to be in a temper, but Crowley said he just laughed and ordered drinks for everyone. Figure that."

Templeton frowned. He figured it very well. Devon was in Chandler's crosshairs.

"Has Mrs. Wainwright been seen with him since?" he asked.

"Yeah. Bridget said he came to the house and apologized as pretty as ya please, and off she went to the restaurant with him," replied Sanger.

Templeton's frown deepened.

A young boy came running into the office then. "Marshal! Marshal Templeton!"

"Easy, boy. Settle yourself down and catch your breath," said Cort. "You're Jake Wheeler's youngest, aren't you?"

The boy nodded. "I'm Adam."

"What has you on fire, Adam?"

"I was on my way to school," the boy puffed. "A man stopped me…said he'd skin me alive if I didn't give ya this note straightaway."

Cort took the note from the boy and read it. "What did this man look like?" he asked.

"He had a scar down his face and looked really scary."

"You did well, Adam." Cort looked at his deputy. "Brett, walk this young man to school. Then, tell the mayor to quietly gather the town council together for a private meeting."

"Yes, sir. What's the note say?" asked Brett.

Cort inclined his head towards the boy. "Later," he replied.

Brett nodded, taking the hint. "Come along, Adam. The teacher is probably wondering where you are."

As Brett ushered the boy outside, Cort walked over to the rifles hanging on the wall to take inventory.

At one o'clock, the mayor convened the town council in Frank Stilwell's back office. "What's going on, Cort? Why did you ask for the meeting?"

Templeton handed the note to him.

The mayor read it. A shadow of concern crossed his face, and he passed the note to the other members.

"What does Hagen mean 'his men for the town'?" he asked.

"I can only assume that he is planning a raid unless we release the prisoners," replied Templeton.

A murmur of alarm went around the room.

"So, as long as these prisoners remain in our jail, we are all in danger," stated a member of the council. "The note calls for the prisoners' immediate release. We can't sit here and wait another week for federal marshals to pick them up."

"What else can we do?" questioned another councilman.

"Wire the county sheriff and have him escort the prisoners to Pueblo," suggested Stilwell.

"I already did that," said Templeton. "He and a posse are tracking some train robbers in Lake County. By the time he returns and refreshes his posse, the marshals will be here."

"What about wiring the governor for troops?" asked the mayor.

"Troops from Fort Lyon won't arrive any sooner," said Cort.

"What other choice do we have?" the exasperated mayor demanded to know.

"Marshal Templeton can deputize some men and take the prisoners to Pueblo," suggested a third councilman.

A fourth argued against it. "They can't leave. The town will be defenseless if Hagen strikes."

"What about forming our own posse and going after Hagen before he can strike?" proposed Stilwell.

"Hagen has someone passing him information," responded Cort. "He will wait until we leave, then hit the town and take the prisoners while we are chasing our tails."

The mayor anxiously swiped a hand across his face. "Any other ideas?"

"Let Hagen have his men," said the third councilman.

"If we do that, we'll be seen as easy pickings for every outlaw who comes around here," retorted Stilwell.

"Then, gentlemen, I suggest that we stand ready," advised Cort.

"How?" asked another councilman.

"First off, we take inventory of all the ammunition and guns in town. Then I suggest you all start practicing your aim."

This brought the crisis into sharper focus. The councilmen looked at each other and a tense silence descended over the room.

"What should we tell the townspeople?" asked the mayor.

"Tell them we are taking precautions after the recent jail break attempt," replied Cort. "No need to alarm everyone just yet."

For the rest of the day, Templeton and his deputies discreetly canvassed the town for a tally of guns and ammunition and to get an idea of who were the best shots. Throughout the night, they kept vigil, but nothing occurred.

As the second day slid into the third without incident, all those familiar with the situation were feeling the strain of waiting for Hagen to make his move.

"Maybe he isn't coming," said the mayor, anxiously pacing the floor of the marshal's office.

Cort sat calmly cleaning his revolver. "He's coming, George."

"Why hasn't he done anything then?"

"He's playing with us. One thing that Hagen and I learned in the war is that anticipation of a battle can be more unnerving than being in the battle." Cort eyed the mayor meaningfully. "After a while, some men begin to unravel under the pressure and make rash decisions."

The mayor bristled. "I'll be at the saloon."

Deputy Sanger grinned as the mayor stomped out of the office. "I guess George wasn't in the war."

Cort snapped the barrel of his revolver shut. "Don't look so smug. Neither were you. And if you have never experienced battle, it can make you overconfident. That is just as dangerous. Get Jasper and take another turn around town…make sure nothing looks suspicious."

"Yes, sir."

As Sanger left the jail, Templeton turned his attention to the information he had collected on the prisoners, trying to figure out what big job the outlaws were planning. What was he missing?

Just then, the telegraph operator walked in. "Marshal, I just got an answer from one of those wires you had me to send out on the prisoners."

Cort took the wire and scanned it. "Demolitionists for the Union Pacific Railroad…. Thanks, Calvin. If anything else comes in, let me know straightaway."

The telegraph operator nodded and hurried off.

Cort stood up and walked over to the jail cells and looked at the prisoners who were lounging on their cots. "You've been found out, boys. What does Hagen want you to blow up?"

Jacks and his cohort slowly sat up and exchanged glances.

"Don't know what yer talkin' about," said Jacks.

Cort studied the prisoners for a few minutes, then went to the wall where a large map of the Colorado Territory hung and reviewed it closer.

The smelting of ore was done in neighboring Blackhawk, but the agents who brokered much of the silver conducted business in Central City. Thus, the banks with the most cache of money were located there. If Hagen was planning to rob a bank, why would he need two demolitionists? wondered Cort. It had to be something more than that for the outlaw to take the risks he was now taking.

Templeton glanced over at the prisoners. "Anybody can blow up something," he remarked. "What makes you so different?"

"We can blow the side of a mountain without causing a ripple," bragged Shorty.

"A mountain, eh."

"Yeah. We know how to place a charge just so as to—"

"Shut up, Shorty!" snapped his cohort.

Templeton smiled. "Thanks, Shorty, that's all I need to know."

"You don't know nothin'," shouted Jacks.

Templeton smiled again and turned away from the prisoners.

"Templeton! Templeton, what do you know? You don't know nothin'!" Jacks continued to shout.

Cort didn't answer. He still had no idea what they were up to, but he played a good game of poker.

Later that afternoon, the stage pulled into town and stopped in front of the hotel. Four gentlemen and a lady stepped out. The woman was blonde, beautiful, and statuesque. Her nature was vivacious, and she was fashionably dressed. It was obvious that she had captivated her fellow passengers, and they were quite disappointed when she diplomatically refused their escort. She looked around her for a moment to get her bearings, then strode purposefully across the street to the marshal's office.

Brett sat on a chair balanced on two legs and nearly tipped over backwards when she walked through the door.

"No need to get up, gents," she said.

When she sashayed over to Templeton and perched provocatively on the edge of his desk, Sanger's jaw dropped.

Templeton grinned. "You're a long way from Denver, lady."

"I came all this way just to see you, sugar," she responded in an intimate, seductive tone.

Brett jumped to his feet and loudly cleared his throat.

"Pearl, this is Deputy Sanger," said Cort. "Brett, meet Pearl Donovan. She runs the best parlor house in Denver."

"Salon, honey," she corrected him. "Didn't Sadie teach you anything?"

"Pleased to meet ya, ma'am," said Brett.

"Likewise, Deputy." She gave him a playful smile and a wink, and Brett visibly melted.

As the deputy continued to stare at her with a silly lopsided grin on his face, Templeton rolled his eyes. He stood up and took his coat and hat off the peg.

"How about something to eat, Pearl? If you just came in on the stage, you must be hungry."

"I never turn down anything from a man," she responded saucily.

Templeton put on his coat and set his hat. "Brett, hold down the office until Jasper comes in. I'll be at Rosie's if you need me." When the young man didn't respond, Cort snorted. "Brett! Did you hear me?"

Brett jumped. "Yes, sir. You'll be at Jasper's until Rosie comes in."

Templeton sighed and ushered Pearl through the door. "Mind turning down the charm a bit, Donovan? I need my deputies alert right now."

Pearl gave him her famous pout. "He's cute, but if you insist."

They crossed the street and entered the restaurant. Cort led her to his table by the window.

"Two specials, Rosie," he called out.

Rosie nodded and disappeared into the kitchen.

Cort pulled out a chair for Pearl and seated himself across from her.

"Sadie has built quite a town," said Pearl, looking around her. "I'm glad she lived to see her vision taking shape. It's too bad she didn't live long enough to—well, never mind."

She looked at Templeton. "You look well, Cort. Handsome and stoic as ever. You were always my favorite, you know. If I were a one-man woman, I would have snagged you a long time ago."

Templeton smiled. "Pretty sure of yourself, aren't you?"

"Actually, yes." She looked at him closer. "You always were the serious type, but you used to be more fun back then. What happened?"

"War puts a mark on a man."

"War or Jenny?" inquired Pearl.

Cort didn't answer.

"Why are you here?" he asked, definitively changing the subject.

"I told you. I came to see you. And since I couldn't be here for Sadie's funeral, I thought I should give my condolences to her niece in person."

"Nettie wired you, didn't she?"

"Cort Templeton, when did you become so suspicious?"

"You read like a book, Pearl. You always have."

Pearl gave a huff of irritation. "Only to you. So what if Nettie did wire me? What is wrong with you, Cort? You are supposed to be watching out for this girl. Instead you let her fall prey to Matt Chandler."

"Mrs. Wainwright is a grown woman. She can handle herself."

"According to Nettie, she's a babe in the woods."

"Nettie put a lot of information into that wire, didn't she?" quipped Templeton.

Pearl refused to be sidetracked. "Come on, Cort. You know how Matt operates. To put it in terms you can relate to he throws out a line and hooks his fish. If the fish resists, he lets out some more line, plays it for a little while, then reels it in with that smooth Southern charm."

Templeton snorted at the analogy. "I have warned Mrs. Wainwright against him, but she has a mind of her own. If she doesn't choose to take my advice, there is nothing more I can do."

Rosie's helper served their order and moved on to the next table.

"I hear Mrs. Wainwright is very pretty," remarked Pearl, cutting off a piece of beefsteak.

Cort knew where this was going and immediately moved to head her off. "We are like oil and water, Pearl, and Mrs. Wainwright has made it quite clear that she is not looking for a partner. Neither am I. Now, can we drop this? I have my hands full at the moment."

Pearl frowned. "Nettie said you were injured in a shooting."

"I'm mending. Christ, Nettie must have paid a fortune for that wire."

"Never mind that. What happened?" quizzed Pearl.

Templeton briefly explained everything, ending with Hagen's ultimatum.

"Sounds as though this Hagen is planning something big to go to so much trouble to get his men released," commented Pearl.

"My thought exactly. I think he and his gang are planning to blow something, but I can't figure out what."

"A bank?"

Templeton shook his head. "It doesn't fit. Two demolitionists seem like overkill for a bank or even a train robbery."

He furrowed his brow, nonplussed. "Hagen keeps to the easy robberies like stagecoaches and trains. What kind of payday would cause him to hire a gunman and be on the hook for the killing of a U.S marshal?"

"What about the Denver Assay Office?" suggested Pearl.

Cort shook his head. "The Assay Office just melts the miners' gold dust and nuggets into coins and gold bars for them."

"It does more than that," said Pearl. "It buys gold and silver for the U.S. Treasury. At any given time, hundreds of thousands of dollars in gold and silver bullion are stored there."

Templeton looked at her in surprise. "Are you sure? How do you know?"

"It's amazing what a madam learns in her salon," responded Pearl with a twinkle in her eye. "And the ingots are stored in two big vaults with cast iron doors and those new time locks."

Cort was astonished by her scope of information. "When do you return to Denver?"

"I haven't decided. Why?"

"I need you to carry a note to Marshal McCaughey."

"Mac? Sure. I know him well. He's a good man," said Pearl. "But why not send him a wire?"

"Someone in town is passing information to Hagen. I can't chance whoever it is learning the contents of the wire," replied Cort.

"You have no idea who the informant is?"

"Not yet. New people have been coming into town. Any one of them could be Hagen's man."

"Maybe I can find out something for you while I'm here," offered Pearl.

"Don't go looking for trouble," warned Cort. "I have enough of that…. If you are planning to visit Mrs. Wainwright, a word of warning. She was not happy to find that her aunt was the madam of the town. She still hasn't made peace with it."

"Perhaps Mrs. Wainwright needs a history lesson," said Pearl.

Cort looked doubtful. "Once she has her mind set to something, she's not likely to change it."

"Well, she can't be too upset. Sadie left her quite a legacy," noted Pearl.

"She has declined it," Cort informed her.

Pearl looked at him in disbelief. "You're joking."

"She says it's tainted."

"But she is living in the house, isn't she?"

Cort chuckled. "She made a deal with Frank Stilwell to rent it, provided she could make 'proper' changes."

"Well, fiddle-dee-dee. If she feels so strongly about the matter, how is it that Matt is in her good graces? He has girls working at the saloon. How does Mrs. Wainwright square that?"

"The girls work for Belle Waters. Chandler just rents them rooms," replied Templeton.

"That's shading things, isn't it?"

"Mrs. Wainwright has a curious sense of logic."

"So it would seem," Pearl responded dryly.

"Matt has another advantage," said Cort. "He was part of the privileged class before the war. He knows the ways of polite society."

Pearl sighed. "When he turns on that Southern charm, I can see how he must seem like an oasis in the midst of a desert of misfits to her—present company excepted."

"Mrs. Wainwright and her companion did come with a different vision of the West," admitted Cort.

"No, don't tell me…the dime novels."

Templeton nodded. "It didn't help that she was on the stagecoach that Hagen held up," he added, omitting his own hand in the matter. And he went on to tell her about Devon's misfortunes with the miners on her first night in town.

Pearl laughed. "I guess she hasn't had the best introduction to Blue Springs. Under the circumstances, I'm surprised she is still here."

"Well, it seems that Mrs. Wainwright has a problem," said Templeton.

"What kind of problem?"

"According to Brett, who has taken a keen interest in her companion, Mrs. Wainwright's husband left her with more debts than money when he died. If she returns to Boston, in order to maintain her position and lifestyle, she will have to marry again, which she has no interest in doing. I gather the first marriage didn't go so well."

"Huh. If she doesn't accept her inheritance, what's she going to do for money?" asked Pearl.

Cort shrugged. "I guess we'll see just how morally indignant she continues to be."

Pearl shook her head. "Poor Sadie. This isn't the way she had planned for things to go." She paused with another thought. "Cort, something isn't right about Sadie's death. You know as well as I do that she didn't take drugs. She hated them and dismissed any of her girls who used them even to sleep. She couldn't have been high on opium when she fell down the stairs."

"The doc said laudanum was in her champagne and a vial of it was next to the glass."

"Then someone else put it there. Come on, Cort, you've known Sadie for a long time. Did you see any change in her in the months before her death?"

Templeton lowered his voice. "I'm still looking into the matter, Pearl but quietly."

"Then you do think she was murdered."

"I can't say that either."

"What *are* you saying?"

"I haven't made a determination yet."

"Why not?"

"Look, Pearl, I admit that the facts surrounding Sadie's death don't add up, knowing her as we did. But I haven't found a motive for murder or anyone who had something to gain by Sadie's death."

Pearl moodily pushed the food around on her plate with her fork. "Sadie and I often exchanged letters. She told me about her vision for the town. I always meant to visit but never seemed to find the time. I should have."

"We all take time for granted until it runs out," said Cort.

"Did you know Sadie was planning to close her salon?"

Templeton nodded. "Stilwell told me."

"Things are booming again. Maybe someone wasn't happy about her closing the salon," surmised Pearl. "Most of her girls were no longer the Baltimore girls. She had problems with a few of them."

"Still, I can't imagine any of them would kill her over that," responded Cort.

Pearl hesitated. "Did Frank tell you why she was closing her salon?"

Templeton nodded again. "Sadie kept her secrets close, didn't she? When did she tell you?"

"She wrote me just before she died. The irony is beyond words, Cort. It shouldn't have happened this way."

"A lot of things shouldn't happen the way they do. That's life.... Pearl, did Sadie own expensive jewelry?" he asked in afterthought.

"Yes. She loved good jewelry and was fond of emeralds and diamonds. She had several nice pieces."

"Where did she keep them?"

"In a wooden box in her bureau drawer. Why?"

"It would appear that her jewelry was stolen."

"Well, there's your motive then," said Pearl. "The box wasn't stolen, was it? It had little worth, but it was of particular value to Sadie."

"The box is there. Mrs. Wainwright found it on top of the bureau. Did Sadie have any more secrets I should know about?"

"I don't think so. Why?"

"Mrs. Wainwright said the drawers had been searched. Any idea what someone might have been looking for?"

Pearl shrugged. "More jewelry?"

"I don't think so," said Templeton. "I have a feeling there is another piece to this that I'm not seeing."

"Cort, if any of this has to do with Sadie's death, Mrs. Wainwright could be in danger."

"I'm keeping an eye out, Pearl."

They finished their meals, and Cort walked her to the hotel.

"Care to join me in my room tonight for drinks and a little relaxation—for old time's sake?" she asked, her manner and tone enticing. "With Sadie's girls gone, there must not be much opportunity for you to…unwind."

Templeton smiled. "It has been a while," he admitted ruefully. "But as tempting as your invitation is, the hotel manager would frown upon me visiting a lady in her room at night."

"But you're the marshal," said Pearl.

"Especially because I am the marshal," replied Cort.

"Don't tell me that you have to uphold morality, too?"

"Just appearances."

Pearl sighed and shook her head "Then I guess you will have to make a trip to Denver."

Cort grinned. "I expect so."

"Well, if I can't sway you, perhaps I can be persuasive to someone else on another matter. Where is Sadie's house?"

"At the far end of the street past the square…the large house. You can't miss it," said Templeton with a chuckle. "There's a sign out front."

CHAPTER FIFTEEN

A Lesson in Life

"Miss Devon, there be a lady waitin' in the parlor to see ye," announced Bridget.

Devon stopped putting away clothes in the chest of drawers and turned to her. "Who is it?"

"I don't know, but she's real pretty."

"Bridget, haven't I told you to always get a name?"

"Yes, ma'am, but she did not offer one, and I did not want to seem discourteous."

"It is not being discourteous to inquire as to who is calling. What does she want? I am busy."

"She did not say. She just asked to see you."

Devon gave a huff of annoyance. "Oh, very well. But next time, get a name and the purpose for the visit."

"Yes, ma'am."

Devon descended the stairs, not much in the mood for visitors. When she entered the parlor, she was surprised to find a mature woman of sophistication and style surveying the room.

"I am Mrs. Wainwright. I understand you wish to see me," she said.

Pearl turned and smiled. "I'm Miss Donovan."

Devon regarded her guest closer. The woman was older but still stunningly attractive. Devon instantly recognized her as one of the Baltimore girls in the photograph. Though she had a touch of rouge on her cheeks and lips, she didn't look like a painted lady, and she most certainly didn't look like a faded rose.

"Pearl!" exclaimed Nettie, rushing excitedly into the parlor. "Bridget told me you was here." She turned to Devon. "This be the Pearl I was tellin' ya about, missy."

"So I gather," replied Devon, surprised by Nettie's demeanor. She had never seen the woman so animated about anything or anyone—except Matt Chandler and not in a good way.

Nettie returned her attention to the visitor. "It's good to see ya, honey."

Pearl gave the little woman an affectionate hug. "It's good to see you, too, Nettie."

"How long ya stayin'?"

"For a few days," replied Pearl. "I came to meet Sadie's niece and to extend my condolences. I'm sorry I wasn't able to be here for the funeral. I was in New York on a buying trip, and…well, I must confess that I didn't want to remember her that way. Sadie was too full of life to suddenly have none."

"I know, honey. The girls and me left the house right after the funeral. It wasn't the same without Sadie." Nettie inclined her head toward Devon. "She's a chip off the old block, ain't she?" she remarked with a touch of pride.

Pearl smiled. "Yes, she looks very much like Sadie."

Devon stiffened. "I may have a resemblance to my aunt in appearance, but I assure you that I share none of her proclivities."

Pearl regarded the young woman for a few minutes. "Nettie, would you please leave us alone?"

Nettie nodded. "I'll be in the kitchen."

As Nettie left the room, Pearl turned to Devon. "You don't know much about your aunt, do you?"

"She operated brothels. What more do I need to know?" questioned Devon shortly.

"That they were not brothels or bordellos for one thing. They were salons, parlor houses of the highest order. There is a difference," said Pearl.

"Whatever you call them, women sold their favors, Miss Donovan. Any other distinction makes no matter to me," retorted Devon.

"These women provide a valuable service, Mrs. Wainwright."

"I beg your pardon?"

"If men visit their beds, they are not so often visiting the beds of wives who find no pleasure in the act. For those men who exercise skill, where do you think they learned it? It has been a long-standing practice for fathers to bring their sons to parlor houses and bordellos to be initiated."

Devon stared at Pearl, too shocked to form a response, the twist in logic confounding her.

"Did you know that your aunt and her Baltimore salon were instrumental in helping the Union win the war?" continued Pearl.

Devon raised her brow in surprise. "My aunt was a spy?"

"You can say that. Maryland didn't secede from the Union, but Baltimore was a hotbed of Southern sentiment, and, throughout the war, Confederate officers frequented the salon," explained Pearl.

"Early on, Sadie realized that she was in a position to help the Northern cause, and she instructed us girls on how to extract vital information from these officers. She then passed it on to the Union command in Washington City. It was a dangerous business. If found out, we could have been hanged, but your aunt was very clever."

"Clever or not, she put you all in harm's way," said Devon.

"It was our choice, Mrs. Wainwright. In war, one does what one can with the talents one has. I daresay your aunt and we girls were responsible for helping to save many a day for the North with ours.

"That is laudable…I suppose," Devon grudgingly allowed. "But other women found ways to be useful to the Union cause without putting their bodies to such use."

Pearl fixed a level gaze on Devon. "Forgive me, Mrs. Wainwright, but during the war, you were safely tucked away in Boston. You have no idea what it was like to live in or near a war zone for four years. You cannot know to what extent you would go to survive."

Devon was silent for a long moment as she remembered the young men she had known, had grown up with, who had come home maimed, in a box, or had not come home at all. And she remembered the anguished cries of the mothers, wives, and sweethearts when the names of their loved ones appeared on that certain list outside the post office. That had been traumatic enough for her.

"You are right, Miss Donovan," she said at length. "I have no right to sit in judgment of actions taken by you and others at a such a time. But the war is over. How can you excuse your actions now? I cannot imagine how a woman possessing even a small amount of self-respect can engage in such a business."

"Women of poor circumstances don't have great choices, Mrs. Wainwright."

"My aunt didn't grow up in poor circumstances," argued Devon. "She did not need to make that choice."

"Are you sure about that?" questioned Pearl. "I understand that she was turned out by her father—your grandfather—without so much as a penny. What would you have had her do—starve?"

"No, I would have had her decide to obey her father and observe the conventions and rules of polite society."

"As you have?"

"Yes."

"Has that made you happy?"

Devon didn't answer.

"It may surprise you to know that your aunt—but for one regret— was happy, Mrs. Wainwright," continued Pearl. "She lived her life her way, not according to the dictates of a society that acknowledges women as little more than slaves to men. There is something to be said for that."

"Perhaps—if she hadn't forfeited respect to do so," replied Devon stubbornly.

"That is a matter of opinion, Mrs. Wainwright. She was beloved by the people of this town, was she not?"

That was a fact that Devon couldn't dispute. It was brought home to her time and time again, and she quickly changed the subject.

"You must have money enough to go elsewhere and start a new, more reputable life. Why do you choose to continue to bear the stigma of this business, Miss Donovan?"

"Why do you choose to be bartered, Mrs. Wainwright?"

Devon was taken aback "I beg your pardon?"

"Did you choose your first husband?"

"No."

"Did you love him?"

Devon hesitated. "No."

"Let me guess. The marriage was arranged by your parents. He had money and name that enhanced your family's position in society, and he was probably much older than you."

"Miss Donovan, I fail to see how—"

Don't you see, Mrs. Wainwright, you were sold, and I gather that you will be sold again if you return to Boston. And the fact that you married for gain and may do so again, I believe, makes you a gold digger of sorts into the bargain. Where is your self-respect?"

Devon stared at Pearl speechless for a second time.

Pearl smiled. "To answer your question, I stay in this business, Mrs. Wainwright, because it brings me a great deal of money, and money is power, power is influence—and I get sexual gratification on my own terms."

Devon, again, could proffer no response.

"Women don't start out to choose this business, Mrs. Wainwright. Society chooses it for them when it leaves them with so few resources," continued Pearl. "But, if a woman is smart, she can make it work to her advantage."

Devon drew herself up and lifted her chin a notch, imitating her mother's most imperious bearing. "Good day, Miss Donovan. Nettie will show you out."

Her tone was cool and dismissive, but inside she was filled with anger and confusion as she strode out of the room and hurried up the stairs, her black and white world not so black and white.

Nettie joined Pearl at the door. "Well?" she inquired.

Pearl shook her head. "Cort said she was stubborn. But I think I have given her enough to think about. Nettie, Cort told me that Sadie's jewelry is missing."

"That's what the missy said."

"When did you last see it?" asked Pearl.

"The morning she died. She had me to fetch a necklace from the box. The jewelry was all there."

"Which necklace did Sadie ask you to get?"

"The pearl and emerald one," replied Nettie.

"Was she wearing it when you found her?"

Nettie furrowed her brows as she thought about it. "When the girls and me come home to find Miss Sadie lyin' there like that, we was in such a tizzy—" Her eyes suddenly widened. "No…she couldn't have been wearin' the necklace. I would have seen it when I laid her out in the parlor for the wake."

"Did you check her box after that?"

"No, I didn't think there was a need to," replied Nettie. "Later, it didn't seem right to touch her things. After the funeral, the girls and me left the house. You think someone pushed Miss Sadie down them stairs to steal her jewelry?"

"Cort is considering the possibility."

"I knew that weren't no accident," Nettie responded angrily.

"Until he figures it out, keep a close eye on things here for anything that might seem strange," advised Pearl.

Nettie looked at her in consternation. "Why? Is the missy in danger?"

"We don't know yet, but something isn't right."

"I'll keep an eye out," promised Nettie. "Do you want a cup of tea or coffee? Ain't seen ya fer so long."

Pearl gave the little woman a hug. "Another time, I promise. Right now, I have an old acquaintance to see," she said, a steely glint coming into her eyes.

Matthew Chandler was lounging against the bar when Pearl walked unabashedly into his saloon. He straightened to his full height, and a smile spread across his features as she strolled over to him.

"The saloon was abuzz about a beautiful blonde who stepped off the stage this afternoon. I never dreamed it was you," he said. "You look good, Pearl."

"It must be the good life I live," she returned pertly.

"I heard you have a fine parlor house in Denver that rivals Mattie Silks. I figured to look you up one of these days."

"You heard wrong. My house is better than Mattie Silks," corrected Pearl. She glanced at the woman who hovered around Chandler. "Who are you?"

The woman glowered at her. "Belle Waters."

"Sadie wrote me about you," said Pearl. "She turned you out. Laudanum, wasn't it?"

Belle's black eyes glittered with anger. "How dare you! I don't know who you are but—"

Pearl turned to Chandler cutting her off. "I want a word with you, Matt—in private."

"You bitch!" shrieked Belle.

Chandler chuckled. "Easy, ladies. No need for a cat fight here. Go see to your girls, Belle."

"Matt—"

"Leave us, Belle. Miss Donovan and I have some old times to catch up on."

Belle glared at Pearl and flounced off.

Chandler signaled to the bartender. "Bring a bottle to my table," he ordered.

"Make that your best whiskey, not that swill you serve to your customers," interjected Pearl.

Chandler grinned. "You heard the lady."

He escorted Pearl to his private table and pulled out a chair for her.

"Still the gentleman," she commented, sitting down.

"Always for a lady." He took a seat next to her.

The bartender approached then and set a bottle and two glasses on the table and departed.

"What are you doing in Blue Springs?" asked Chandler, pouring drinks for them.

"I might ask you the same thing," responded Pearl. "I couldn't believe it when Sadie wrote me that you had slithered into town."

Chandler smiled. "You always did put all your cards on the table. You haven't changed a bit, Pearl."

"Neither have you, Matt. You're still the same charming snake you always were." She picked up her glass, tested the whiskey, and gave a nod of approval. "What are you doing here? This is Cort's and Sadie's town."

"I didn't know they were here. You might say that it was the hand of fate that brought me."

Pearl scoffed. "I might if it were anyone but you. Why have you stayed?"

Chandler shrugged. "The town holds promise, and I see opportunity. Sadie, Cort, and I made a truce to co-exist, and we have all profited." Chandler lifted his glass to her. "To old friends."

"We're not friends—old or otherwise," she said.

"You are a hard nut to crack, Pearl." He took out a small, ornately engraved silver case from his vest pocket and opened it. "Cheroot?"

Pearl took one. He followed suit and snapped the case shut.

"I thought about leaving Blue Springs a few times with families moving in," he continued, finding a match and lighting their cigars. "The town was getting dull."

"So leave."

Chandler blew smoke from the cigar and smiled. "It is getting interesting again."

"Mrs. Wainwright is off the table, Matt."

"Nettie didn't waste any time, did she?"

"I'm warning you. Stay away from her," said Pearl. "You are not going to be allowed to break her heart the way you did Jenny's."

Chandler sighed. "We were young…a war was coming…things happened."

"Jenny was playing for keeps, Matt. You weren't, and the war gave you an excuse to run away." Pearl eyed him closer. "Tell me, if Cort hadn't loved her, would you have made a play for her?"

When he didn't answer, she gave a snort of disgust. "I thought so. Cort offered to marry Jenny to save her from the stigma of being an unwed mother and the child from being a bastard, but she declined. She held out hope that you would come back for her—until hope killed her…. You couldn't write Jenny one letter, Matt—not even to tell her that you were still alive?"

Chandler had no response and stared at the glass of whiskey in his hand.

"In case you're interested, Jennie and your son are buried in the Baltimore Cemetery," said Pearl.

Chandler looked at her.

"Yes, Matt, you had a son."

Chandler threw back his drink. For the first time, he felt a deeper sense of contrition about the matter. Knowing that he had had a son made it more than just a regrettable event in his past.

"People change," he responded soberly. "I'm not that young man anymore, Pearl. I like Devon. I enjoy being with her. Is it so hard to believe that I might be ready to settle down?"

Pearl gave a short laugh. "If you think that, honey, you are fooling yourself. You and I are alike, Matt. We aren't capable of making that kind of commitment. It's not in our character." She inclined her head toward Belle who watched them closely. "Just ask her?"

"Belle and I are business partners," maintained Chandler.

Pearl laughed again. "Was that before or after she was the next notch on your bed post? You may have done with her, but she is not done with you."

She drank the rest of her drink, stubbed out her cheroot, and rose to leave. "Watch your back, Matt. One day you are going to jilt the wrong woman."

CHAPTER SIXTEEN

The Game Changes

Cort entered the office. "I have the watch tonight, Brett. You can ask Miss Ryan to dinner."

Brett looked at him in surprise. "How did you know I was hoping to take Bridget to dinner?"

"Powers of observation."

"What?"

"You have a haircut and a shave, and you are wearing a new shirt."

Brett grinned sheepishly. "Oh. How long is Miss Donovan stayin'?"

"She hasn't decided yet."

"How many women you got, Marshal?" Jacks shouted from the cell.

"Can you spare one?" shouted the other prisoner. "I'll take the yeller-haired one. It's been a while." He laughed and rubbed his crotch.

Brett angrily started for the cell, but Templeton pulled him back.

"Ignore them."

"Bastards," murmured Brett under his breath. He turned to Cort. "Maybe Hagen was all talk and ain't comin'. You did best his gunman."

Templeton shook his head. "No, he's coming for them. Whatever he's planning, these two are key to it."

"I'm tired of sittin' here waitin' for 'em," groused Brett.

"Then figure out Hagen's source of information."

"How do I do that?"

"Someone must have noticed something out of character—" Cort stopped as something Pearl had said leaped to mind, and he started for the door.

"Where ya goin'?" asked Brett.

"To the saloon."

Cort walked into the bar, took a seat at a table, and ordered a whiskey. For the next hour and a half, he watched the stairs to see who went up on the arm of a saloon girl. There were the usual miners, but no one and nothing stood out.

For the next few days, Templeton posted Brett and Jasper at the saloon on alternating watches. They didn't understand the reason for the duty, but they didn't protest it. Neither had anything to report.

Cort ran a hand across the back of his neck, stymied. "You're sure you and Jasper didn't miss anything?"

Brett shook his head. "Just the usual goings-on, unless you count seein' Calvin Ford sneak up the stairs," he added with a laugh. "Turns out he's a regular. Who would have thought it—him bein' so pious and all?"

Cort suddenly came out of his chair. "Damn! Why didn't I see it before?"

Sanger looked at him in surprise. "What?"

"He's the source of Hagen's information, Brett."

Sanger was incredulous. "Calvin?"

"Think about it," said Cort. "He sees every wire that goes in and out of town."

"Yeah, so?"

"Pearl reminded me that a lot of information flows through parlor houses and brothels."

Brett's jaw dropped when he realized what Cort was saying. "So that's why you had Jasper and me watchin' the girls in the saloon. Hells bells, I can't believe that Calvin would help an outlaw."

"I doubt that he realizes he is," remarked Cort. "He's probably just a lonely guy that someone saw a way to use. Does Calvin see the same girl each time?"

"He seems to favor Josie."

"Buy her a couple of drinks. Try to find out who she reports to and what her instructions are, but don't raise any suspicions. And, Brett, keep it quiet. I don't want Calvin to be unfairly marked for this."

"Yes, sir."

* * * * *

Devon came out of her suite and was starting down the hall when she heard crying coming from Bridget's room. She stopped and tapped on the door. When she received no answer, she opened it to find Bridget lying on her bed in tears.

"Bridget, what is it? What's wrong?" asked Devon.

"Oh, miss, you were right about him," said Bridget, sniffing back tears and wiping her eyes. "He's not to be trusted."

"Who?"

"Brett—I mean Deputy Sanger."

"Whatever has he done?"

Bridget sat up and blew her nose. "I was comin' from the butcher shop, and…well, I peeked in the window of the saloon—just to see what it was all about. And I saw him."

"Deputy Sanger?"

Bridget nodded, dabbing at tears.

"Well, there is nothing unusual about that. Men go in there to drink and play cards," said Devon, sitting down beside her. "I've seen Marshal Templeton walk in there upon occasion."

"Brett wasn't in there for a drink. I saw him with one of those…those women," she sobbed.

"Oh. Well, he was probably just talking to her."

Bridget emphatically shook her head. "That was no talk as I've ever seen. She was sittin' on his lap and…and he was whisperin' in her ear."

"I'm sure there is a good explanation," said Devon. But she couldn't possibly imagine what it could be. "I promise you I will get to the bottom of this."

Cort was leaning back in his chair, his feet resting on the desk, when Devon marched into the office. He lowered his legs and stood up.

"Mrs. Wainwright, what can I do for you?"

"You can keep your promise, Marshal," she replied crisply.

"What promise is that?"

"The promise that you would keep your deputy in hand. I should have known better."

Cort looked at her, his brow furrowing in confusion. "Mrs. Wainwright, what are you talking about?"

"Mr. Sanger…his behavior, of course," she replied. "Bridget is in tears. I will not have her heart broken, Marshal."

Just then, Brett had the misfortune of walking in.

Devon turned on him. "You! You should be ashamed of yourself!" With that, she stormed out of the office, slamming the door behind her.

Jacks burst into laughter. "This is better'n one of them theatre plays, ain't it, Shorty?"

"Knock it off, boys, or you won't get supper tonight," warned Templeton.

Brett looked at Cort in bewilderment. "What did I do?"

"Did you and Miss Ryan have a disagreement?"

"Not that I know about. She was fine when I last saw her. What did Mrs. Wainwright say?"

"Just that Miss Ryan is upset abut something, and Mrs. Wainwright isn't going to let you break her heart."

Brett searched his mind for some incident of a misunderstanding.

"I don't get it," he said.

"Welcome to the workings of a woman's mind," quipped Templeton. "It usually makes little sense to a man."

"He's got that right," chimed in Shortie.

"Shut up!" yelled Brett.

"Never mind him. Did you find out anything at the saloon?" asked Cort.

"Yeah. Josie said that Belle always wants to know what the men talk about with the girls. She probably passes stuff on to Chandler."

The deputy eyed the door. "Uh, Cort, do you mind if I take myself over to see Bridget?"

Templeton sighed. "Yeah, go on, but don't expect to get a clear explanation. It seems a man is expected to know the sin he committed, and it only angers a woman more if she has to tell him."

* * * * *

It was near to midnight by the time Cort finished his walk around the town and checked in with Jasper at the lookout. All was quiet and he returned to the office to relieve Sanger.

Suddenly, a rock came crashing through the window. The prisoners jumped up from their cots, and Cort and Brett reached for their rifles. Cort picked up the rock and untied the paper wrapped around it. Written on it was a warning: *Free the prisoners or the rest of the town is next.*

Templeton doused the light. "You stay with the prisoners. I'm going outside to have a look around."

Brett nodded. "Be careful."

Cort cautiously moved outside.

"The school is on fire!" yelled a townsman, frantically ringing the fire bell.

People came running from their homes in their nightclothes as flames lit up the sky.

Pearl emerged from the hotel. Spying Cort at the end of the street, she walked up to him. "What's happening?"

He handed her the note. "It looks like Hagen just showed his hand."

She read it and glanced up at the smoke billowing in the air. "I guess I leave on the stage tomorrow then."

"Sorry. I know you expected to stay longer."

"To save Sadie's town, I'd leave tonight if I could."

"You are clear about the plan?"

Pearl nodded.

"I'll hold the prisoners long enough to give you time to get to Pueblo," said Templeton.

There was the clang of a bell as the horse-drawn, steam-powered fire truck came speeding up the road.

Devon stood in the fire brigade line along with Nettie and Bridget passing buckets of water, as everyone fought to keep the fire from spreading to the rest of the wooden structures in town.

At one point, Devon saw Cort and Pearl together. She was surprised at first, then realized that, of course, they would know each other if Pearl had been one of Sadie's girls. She felt a flash of anger. Had he had a hand in Pearl coming to visit her? The woman next to Devon nudged her to keep the line moving, and Devon returned her attention to the task at hand.

It was nearly dawn when the townspeople wearily sought their beds for a few hours of sleep. Luckily, there had been no wind. In the end, only the school lay in a pile of smoldering ash. As it had stood apart from other buildings and homes, there was only slight damage to a couple of nearby businesses.

The town stirred again just before noon. The acrid smell of smoke still hung in the air.

The mayor rushed into Cort's office. "People are wondering on the cause of the fire," he said. "Can't blame it on lightning. What should I tell them?"

"The truth," replied Cort. "Now that Hagen has made his move, we need to form a plan. Call a town meeting for this afternoon."

"I'd rather have a tooth pulled. People get angry when they're scared," fretted the mayor.

At two o'clock, people began filing into the saloon, curious as to why a town meeting had been called.

"I want to thank Mr. Chandler for allowin' us to meet here since the school has burned down," said the mayor. "When the theater is finished in the spring, we'll hold our town meetings there."

"Get on with it, George!" yelled an agitated voice. "What's goin' on? How did the fire start last night? There weren't no lightnin'."

"Simmer down, Floyd. I'm gettin' to that."

Haltingly, the mayor told them about Hagen's ultimatum.

Murmurs of alarm sounded around the room.

"Our lives are in danger, and you didn't tell us!" exclaimed an outraged citizen.

"We didn't want to needlessly alarm the town until we knew if Hagen was really a threat," said the mayor.

"Well, it turns out that he is. What're ya gonna do about it?" demanded another man. "The next time, it could be our homes…we could be burned alive in our beds."

"What if there's a wind the next time?" interjected Teddy the livery stable owner. "The whole town could be wiped out."

"I'll tell ya what we're gonna do about it. We're gonna release the prisoners," broke in the butcher. "They ain't worth my house and business gettin' torched."

"Yeah, let 'em go," shouted others. "Let the federal marshals track em' down."

"If we let them go, Hagen will know that he can make any demand he wants by threatening to burn down the town," responded the mayor.

"We'll cross that bridge when we come to it," retorted Floyd. "For now, I ain't losin' everything I got on account of two prisoners."

There followed an outburst of conflicting opinions.

The mayor repeatedly pounded a gavel on the table. "Settle down, people. Settle yourselves down."

It had no effect, and he looked desperately to Templeton. When Cort walked to the front of the room, his commanding presence calmed the crowd.

"The mayor is right. We can't give in to blackmail," he reiterated.

"You got a plan, Marshal?" asked the butcher.

"Tomorrow, Deputy Sanger and I are taking the prisoners out of Blue Springs to a place where deputy marshals from Pueblo will take custody of them," said Cort. "Until then, I want all able-bodied men to arm themselves and take up positions on the top of buildings and at entrances to the town. Get together and set up shifts.

"The rest of you observe the curfew and stay off the streets," he continued. "Whatever business you need to transact, do it now. If you notice anything suspicious, report it."

The people were still unsettled but felt more reassured that the marshal had everything under control. And tasked with lending a hand in the matter, they redirected their anger from fear to a determination to safeguard their town.

As the crowd dispersed, Brett walked up to the marshal. "Cort, you know the feds ain't sendin' marshals tomorrow to meet us. Why'd ya tell 'em that?"

"I want the word to get back to Hagen," he replied.

"Why? He'll either strike before we can take the prisoners out of town or ambush us on the way."

"I know. We're going to be one step ahead of him. I'll explain later," said Cort at the look of confusion on his deputy's face.

Templeton left the saloon. He saw Pearl coming out of the hotel and strode over to her.

"How did the meeting go?" she asked.

"People are angry and ready to fight. How about you? Are you ready to go?"

Pearl nodded. "The stage leaves in 15 minutes."

He took the satchels from her and escorted her to the stagecoach.

"Put these in the boot," he said, handing the bags to the driver. "The lady is catching the train in Canon City to Pueblo."

When Cort turned to her, she gazed up at him. "Remember, you owe me a visit in Denver."

Cort smiled. "I'll remember."

"If only I were the marrying kind," she said with a wistful sigh. "You wouldn't stand a chance you know."

"Maybe I'm not the marrying kind either," he replied.

She cocked her head to one side. "No, I believe that you are. You just haven't met the right woman yet—or maybe you have and just don't know it."

"I'm not looking, Pearl."

"That's what they all say until that certain lady appears."

"Drop it," said Templeton. "I have more serious concerns." He helped her into the stagecoach, closed the door, and surreptitiously passed her two notes. "Put these in a safe place."

Pearl slipped them inside the top of her bodice. "Nobody gets in there unless I allow it, honey."

Cort chuckled. "Remember, when the stage stops at the home station, tell Silas Webster to wire one message to Marshal McCaughey," he instructed. "Take the other note to the U.S. Marshal's Office in Pueblo. Make sure that at least three deputy marshals get on the train to Denver with you. The office is short-handed and will probably resist sending anyone based upon my gut instinct. How persuasive can you be?"

"I should think you would already know that," she replied with a saucy smile.

Templeton's hand rested on bottom of the window, and she placed her gloved hand over top his, her flirtatious manner turning serious.

"Be careful, Cort."

"Always am."

Devon started to leave the general store when she saw the marshal in intimate conversation with Pearl. She quickly stepped back inside the store and watched them through the window. They obviously shared a close relationship. Considering Pearl's profession, she wondered just how close it was.

"Did you forget something, dear?" asked Mrs. Walker.

Devon jumped. "No—yes." She looked around her and picked up the closest item. "I forgot to buy soap."

"Bridget bought some yesterday," Mrs. Walker reminded her.

"Oh…yes…well, we need more," said Devon. "Please put it on my bill."

She saw the stagecoach pull out then and hastily departed the store, figuring the marshal would return to his office. She figured wrong.

"Mrs. Wainwright," he called out.

Devon cringed and stopped. His long strides brought him quickly alongside her.

"Mrs. Wainwright, you shouldn't be on the streets," he said. "There is no telling how or when Hagen will strike again."

"I am on my way to the house now," replied Devon. She paused. "I saw Miss Donovan leaving on the stage. You both wasted your time, Marshal."

As she hurried off, Cort stared after her in puzzlement. But he had more important things to worry about now. It wasn't the first time that she made no sense to him, and he was certain it wouldn't be the last.

An hour before midnight, Templeton raked a tin cup across the cell bars to rouse the prisoners.

"What the hell?" grumbled Jacks, rubbing his eyes.

"Get up," said Cort. He dropped handcuffs threw the bars to them. "Put these on."

The prisoners eyed each other and picked up the cuffs, reluctantly locking them around their wrists.

"Where're we goin'?" asked Shorty.

"For a little ride," replied Cort.

He unlocked the cell doors and motioned them out with his revolver. After checking to make sure their cuffs were tight and locked, he ordered them outside.

"You said we was leavin' in the mornin'," said Jacks.

"A change of plans, boys."

The prisoners moved to the door and hesitated, exchanging uncertain glances, until Cort prodded them outside.

Sanger was already mounted on his horse and holding the reins of two other horses.

Deputy Hale came forward. "What do you want me to do, Marshal?"

"Make sure everyone on the night watch stays alert in case I'm wrong about this, Jasper. If anyone asks, you don't know anything."

Jasper nodded. "You can count on me."

Templeton nudged Shorty and Jacks again with his gun. "Mount up."

Their wrists cuffed, the prisoners awkwardly did as they were told.

Templeton swung himself atop his horse and took the reins of Jacks' horse from Brett. Quietly, the two lawmen led the prisoners out of town. The sentries atop the buildings nearby watched with curiosity but said nothing.

When they were far enough out of town, Cort led the party off the road to a large ponderosa pine tree.

"Get down," he ordered the prisoners.

"Why? What're ya gonna do?" asked Shorty, becoming increasingly nervous. "You ain't gonna shoot us, are ya?"

"Heh, he can't shoot us," said Jacks. "He's the law."

"I said get down," said Cort.

Hesitantly, they climbed down from their horses. Sanger dismounted and took out a rope from his saddlebag.

"Hey, what're ya gonna do with that?" cried Jacks.

"You can't hang us. We got rights," whimpered Shorty.

"Shut up and put your backs against the tree," ordered Brett.

The prisoners relaxed when it became clear they weren't going to be dangling from the end of a rope and did as they were told. But when Sanger began winding the rope around them, tying them securely to the trunk of the tree, they began to have grave misgivings again.

Brett tested the tension of the rope and the knot. "They ain't goin' nowhere, Cort."

Templeton looked at the prisoners. "You better hope that Hagen finds you before a wild animal or the federal marshals do."

"You can't do this!" shouted Shorty, struggling against the rope.

"Best not make noise, boys. It might attract a bear or a mountain lion," cautioned Brett.

"You can't do this!" repeated Shorty in a hoarse whisper.

"Why not?" quizzed Brett.

"Yer lawmen," broke in Jacks desperately.

Templeton smiled. "Didn't you ever hear of frontier justice?"

Sanger mounted his horse and grabbed the reins of the prisoners' horses.

"If Hagen finds you first, tell him to stay out of my town," said Cort.

As they rode off, Sanger burst into laughter. "That ought to scare the bejesus out of them. Do you think Hagen will find them?"

"If his informant got word to him, he has to ride past them on his way into Blue Springs," said Cort. "This way, Hagen will get what he wants and spare the town, and as far as the townspeople will know, we didn't give in to the blackmail of an outlaw. When we get to town, we'll pick up fresh mounts and ride north."

Brett looked at Templeton in surprise. "Why? Where're we headin'?"

"Unless I miss my guess, Hagen and his gang will take the Tennessee Pass to Denver?"

"Why?"

Briefly, Cort explained what he and Pearl had figured Hagen's grand plan to be.

Sanger was incredulous. "So that's why Miss Donovan left town so fast. Geez, Cort, it makes me wonder if you weren't an outlaw once yourself. You sure think like one."

"Don't be too amazed," said Templeton. "If I'm not right and Hagen has some other scheme in mind, then we'll have lost the prisoners, and Hagen will have gotten away with whatever it is he's really planning."

An hour elapsed. To the prisoners tied to a tree, it seemed a lifetime. Each growl of a mountain lion or howl of a coyote sounded more threatening to them, and they struggled uselessly against the ropes.

"If I get my hands on Templeton or that deputy of his, I'll make 'em pay good for this," snarled Jacks.

"Not if we get eaten first," whimpered Shorty. At the sound of another growl from a mountain lion, he let out a cry of alarm. "It's gettin' closer."

"What're ya doin'? You pissin' yerself, Shorty?"

"I heard it keeps animals away."

"It attracts 'em, ya jackass."

"Shit." Shorty quickly scuffed dirt over the puddle of urine at his feet. "How d'ya know?"

"An old mountain man said."

As the growling intensified, the two men struggled frantically against the ropes. Suddenly, they heard horses approaching.

"Help!" cried Shorty. "Help! Over hear!"

"Shut up!" snapped Jacks. "They may be the marshals."

"I don't care."

When a cougar let out another loud growl, both men began to shout at the top of their lungs.

The horsemen stopped, and the riders cautiously walked their horses in the direction of the prisoners' cries.

"That you, Jacks?" called one of the men, peering through the darkness.

"Quentin! Over here," shouted Jacks. "It's me and Shorty."

"Can't see ya fer the scrubs. Why don't you come out?" asked the robber, suspicious.

"Because we're tied to a goddamn tree!"

Billy Hagen motioned to Quentin. "Check it out."

"Could be a trap, boss."

"Then we'll find out, won't we?" sneered Hagen. "Check it out."

The outlaw hesitated, then slowly dismounted. Cautiously, he skirted the scrub trees and approached the pine tree with his gun drawn. When he came upon his fellow outlaws, he burst into laughter and holstered his revolver.

"What the hell happened to you two?"

"Stop laughin' and untie us!" barked Jacks. "I'm gonna kill Templeton and that deputy of his."

"Hurry up," pleaded Shorty. "There's a mountain lion closin' in."

"All clear," Quentin shouted to the others. "Lord Almighty, Shorty, did ya piss yerself?"

"Shut yer pie hole," snapped the outlaw.

Quentin took out his knife and was cutting the ropes, when Hagen and the rest of the gang rode up. Hagen glared down at the pathetic scene from atop his horse.

"They have double lock handcuffs on," said Quentin. "What do we do about it, boss?"

"Find a rock and smash the link. We'll take care of the cuffs later," replied Hagen, clearly unamused by the situation.

"Templeton thinks he's smart. We outta torch the town anyway," suggested another gang member.

"He has men all around town armed and waitin' fer ya" said Jacks. "And federal marshals are on their way from Pueblo."

Hagen grunted. "We'll deal with Templeton later. Right now, we have something more important to do. Bring the extra horses around."

Cort watched tensely from atop a ridge for any sign of the outlaws in the predawn hour. They should have appeared before this. His theory was either wrong or the gang had stopped to take vengeance on Blue Springs, in spite of the false threat of federal marshals on their tails.

He was considering sending Brett to check on the state of the town, when Sanger called out: "Riders comin'. Is that them?"

Templeton took out his spyglass and peered through it. His mouth curved up in a smile. "It's them."

* * * * *

Hagen and his men stole into Denver beneath a new moon and furtively made their way to the Assay Office in the dead of night.

Despite reports that the two-story, brick structure was the most substantial building in Denver, it wasn't difficult for Jacks to jimmy the lock on the door with his crevice tool. The gang quickly entered the first floor and went to the vaults.

Two lanterns were lit, and Jacks and Shorty each went to work on a vault. They forced the crevice tools between the doors and the seals to create a gap wide enough to sprinkle just the right amount of black powder to blow the doors with the least amount of damage and noise. As Jacks and Shorty prepared to ignite the powder, the gang heard the distinctive sound of the cocking of firearms and looked around them.

"Up here, boys."

The outlaws looked up startled and stunned to find a dozen men pointing rifles down at them from the second floor. Other lawmen suddenly appeared to block the door.

Marshal McCaughey stepped forward. "Drop your weapons on the floor," he ordered.

One of the gang members pulled out a gun and got off a shot before being felled with a dozen bullets.

"Any others for the undertaker?" questioned McCaughey.

There was a clatter as the outlaws quickly dropped knives and guns on the floor. Federal marshals came forward then to handcuff the robbers and take custody of them.

"We've been waitin' for you boys," said McCaughey. "Which one of you is Billy Hagen? Marshal Templeton sends you his regards."

"I'll kill that son-of-a-bitch!" shrieked Hagen. "You tell Templeton he's a dead man…a dead man!" he shouted as he was led off.

CHAPTER SEVENTEEN

The Ladies' Auxiliary

Devon opened the door to find four women standing on her porch. Two she recognized from the barn raising—Mrs. Tillotson and Mrs. Andrews.

Mrs. Tillotson stepped forward as the leader. "Mrs. Wainwright, we are from the Ladies' Auxiliary. Might we have a word with you?"

"Of course. Please come in, ladies."

The ladies stepped into the foyer, and Devon closed the door. As she led them into the parlor, they looked around with great interest.

"How lovely," murmured one.

"Yes, quite tasteful," agreed another in surprise.

Mrs. Tillotson turned to Devon. "We heard you had made changes, Mrs. Wainwright. I would never guess this had been a brothel," she declared with marked approval. "Not that I was ever inside of one," she quickly added.

Devon smiled, inwardly amused. She didn't bother to mention that, in the interest of time and money and as Nettie had assured her that nothing untoward had occurred in this room, she had done nothing more to the parlor than remove the card table and rearrange some of the furniture.

"Please sit down, ladies," said Devon. "What can I do for you?"

When they were all comfortably seated, Mrs. Tillotson introduced the other two ladies, Mrs. Bell and Mrs. Greenway.

"Mrs. Wainwright, we have a great favor to ask of you," she said, getting down to business.

"What is that, Mrs. Tillotson?" inquired Devon.

Mrs. Tillotson glanced at the other ladies, and they gave her a nod of encouragement.

"Well, with the school having been destroyed by those outlaws," she began with more confidence, "the children have nowhere to go to continue their learning. Your house is so large, and now that you have purged all traces of its prior life, we had hoped to prevail upon you to allow the teacher to set up classes here."

Devon blinked in surprise. "You want to set up a school…here?"

"Oh, it would only be until the school can be rebuilt in the spring," Mrs. Andrews hastily assured her. "As the children just started the school year, it would be a shame to have their lessons interrupted for so many months."

"There is no other public building that would do?" asked Devon.

"I'm afraid not," said Mrs. Bell.

Devon frantically searched her mind for another alternative. "What about the church?"

"The church is not convenient to the children, particularly once winter sets in. And none of us have houses large enough to accommodate the students," explained Mrs. Greenway.

"How many students are there?"

"Currently, there are 14 students," replied Mrs. Tillotson. "They range in age from six to 13 years of age."

Devon sat in numbing silence, trying to figure out how to extricate herself from this situation. In the absence of any immediate rejection of the idea, the ladies took her to be in agreement and jumped up excitedly from their seats.

"We knew you would want to continue your aunt's benevolence to the town," twittered Mrs. Andrews.

Devon's eyes widened. "But I didn't—won't parents object to their children being taught in a house of dubious reputation?" she sputtered.

"The Ladies' Auxiliary will vouch for its new cloak of respectability," Mrs. Greenway assured her.

"The children are well-mannered, and the new teacher Miss Primrose will keep them well in hand," interjected Mrs. Bell. "They won't be a bother to you at all, Mrs. Wainwright. You are doing a wonderful service to the community."

As the ladies lingered and eyed each other, Devon sensed there was more. "Is there something else?" she asked reluctantly.

"Well, now that you mention it," said Mrs. Tillotson, seizing on the opportunity, "Miss Primrose had living quarters in the school. Since it was destroyed, she is homeless."

"And the town is paying for Miss Primrose to stay at the hotel now, which is quite costly," added Mrs. Andrews.

"I'm sorry," said Devon. "I don't have an abundance of funds at the moment, but I will be happy to make a donation."

"Actually, Mrs. Wainwright, we were hoping that you might allow Miss Primrose to room here until the school is rebuilt—for a modest rent, of course," said Mrs. Tillotson.

Caught off guard again, Devon took too long to respond.

"Wonderful!" exclaimed Mrs. Tillotson clapping her hands together. "The marshal was right, ladies. He said Mrs. Wainwright would help us in our hour of need. We'll tell Miss Primrose she can move in here and resume classes on Monday next."

"That will give us time enough to gather together the needed materials," said Mrs. Bell. "Mrs. Walker said the store can donate paper and pencils. I see that you have yet to furnish the dining room, Mrs. Wainwright. No matter." She turned to Mrs. Andrews. "Minnie, your husband is a handy carpenter. Perhaps he can fashion a long table with benches."

As the women continued to take mental measurements and make plans for transforming her living room and dining room into classrooms, Devon looked on helplessly.

Finally, the ladies left, and she dropped into a chair. When Bridget and Nettie returned from shopping a short time later, they found her staring off into space.

"Miss Devon, are you well?" asked Bridget, her brow drawn with concern. "Has something happened?"

Devon looked at her. "I think our residence just became a school and a boarding house."

* * * * *

A few days later, Devon walked down the stairs to find two men carrying a makeshift blackboard into her dining room. It was a large piece of flat board painted black and mounted on a hastily constructed stand.

Later that the afternoon, the delivery boy from the general store arrived with a box of paper, pencils, and a couple of small slates. More slates and a real blackboard were on order, he reported.

Four days after that, Mrs. Andrews' husband delivered a crude trestle table and two long benches. Meanwhile, Bridget and Nettie readied one of the empty bedrooms for Miss Primrose.

The following Monday, Devon opened the door to find the teacher and her students on the front porch. As the students filed into the entry and parlor, they let out various exclamations of amazement.

"We ain't never seen a house as fine as this," cooed one 11-year-old girl. "It is so beautiful."

While the girls continued to admire their surroundings, the four oldest boys admired Devon.

"Miss Primrose ain't gonna have no trouble gettin' me to come to school now," one commented in a low voice.

The other boys snickered and bobbed their heads in agreement.

Miss Primrose clapped her hands to demand the students' attention. "The older children aged 10 to 13 take your seats on the benches in the dining room—girls on one side, boys on the other. The younger children shall find seats in the parlor and write the stories that have been assigned. Hurry now."

As the students moved to take their places, Devon joined Nettie and Bridget in the kitchen.

"It's gonna be a long winter," grumbled Nettie, giving the bread dough another punch. "What was ya thinkin', missy?"

Devon couldn't rightly say.

Throughout the morning, Devon could hear students reciting numbers and reading the stories they had written as she passed through the house. When the children got a little rowdy, she sought refuge in her suite. Dear Lord, how was she going to put up with this until spring? she wondered. She gave a laugh of relief when she suddenly remembered that she wasn't intending to remain in Blue Springs that long anyway.

The teacher rang the bell for lunch. While the children returned to their homes for the midday meal, Miss Primrose moved her modest possessions from the hotel into the room that Nettie had set aside for her.

Devon had just poured herself a cup of coffee, when the teacher came into the kitchen.

"I hope you find your room comfortable, Miss Primrose."

"Oh, yes, very much so. Thank you for the use of your home, Mrs. Wainwright. It is very generous of you."

"The Ladies' Auxiliary can be quite…persuasive," replied Devon, searching for the right word.

Miss Primrose smiled. "Yes, I have experienced their 'persuasion,' and it is how I now find myself in the position of schoolteacher. Miss Rigby left rather abruptly, and another teacher cannot be assigned here for several months." She sighed dejectedly. "I fear I am not up to the task."

Devon felt sorry for the plain, bespectacled woman. "I can imagine it is not easy to hold the attention of 14 children of varying ages."

"Indeed. And it has been made more difficult now with all the readers having been lost in the fire," said Miss Primrose. "Some families have donated books that they brought with them from the East, but I'm afraid cookbooks hold little interest for children. And the Bible is read so often in homes and in the church, I fear the students' ability to read passages from it comes more from memorization."

Devon thought for a moment. "Miss Primrose, I might have an idea that may be of help."

"I would be grateful for any suggestions, Mrs. Wainwright. What is your idea?"

"Dime novels."

"Yes, I am familiar with them. They are quite popular in the East."

"I know that they are not classic literature by any definition," said Devon, "but I guarantee you they will captivate the students and encourage them to want to read."

The teacher's eyes lit up. "Why, yes, I do believe you are right, Mrs. Wainwright. But how can I procure these novels?"

"My companion brought several copies with her," replied Devon. "I am sure she will be happy to lend them to you. And while you are teaching the older students math and English, perhaps Bridget can read some of the more appropriate stories to the younger children to keep them occupied."

"That would be wonderful."

As Devon had predicted, the students were enthralled with the dime novels and were eager to learn to read them. Bridget proved to have a talent for artistic narration.

When it became known that Devon was adept at playing the piano, she was pressed into service to provide a music session as an added inducement for the students to mind the teacher and their studies.

Devon was unenthused and skeptical about the value of it, until she saw how much the children loved to sing and how the prospect of a song fest brought them to order. One boy even brought his harmonica to accompany her on the piano.

When some of the older students seemed prone to be tardy or to play hooky after the lunch hour, Devon suggested to Miss Primrose that the children bring their lunches and eat there. Devon also moved the music class to the end of the school day. As the school settled into a stricter, more orderly routine, the students proved to be much more manageable.

CHAPTER EIGHTEEN

Outlier

Cort entered the restaurant for lunch. He spied Devon at a table finishing her meal and reading the town newspaper and walked over to her.

"Good afternoon, Mrs. Wainwright."

Devon looked up at him, her manner guarded. "Good afternoon, Marshal."

"I understand that you are to be commended," he said.

"For what?" asked Devon.

"For allowing the children to be schooled in your house until a new school can be built."

"It is not my house," Devon replied stubbornly, "and I didn't have much of a choice in the matter."

"Mrs. Tillotson and her band of ladies can be a formidable force when they want something," admitted Cort.

"Indeed…especially with help from you, Marshal."

"How's that, Mrs. Wainwright?"

"The ladies said that when they conferred with you, you told them I would be happy to help them in their time of need."

Templeton cracked a smile. "No, Mrs. Wainwright, I told them that it never hurts to ask for help. They made of it what they would."

"It didn't occur to you to try to dissuade them from wanting to use my house in the first place?"

"You just said that it wasn't your house," he reminded her. "Perhaps the town council will agree to pay you some rent toward your rent."

The irony was not lost on Devon, and her chest heaved with irritation.

She glanced down at the newspaper. "I believe you are to be commended as well, Marshal."

"How so, Mrs. Wainwright?"

Devon pointed to the front-page story with the banner headline heralding his part in foiling the robbery at the Denver Assay Office.

"You are a hero, Marshal."

A look of displeasure passed over his features. "The story is overblown like the dime novels you like to read. I was doing my duty."

"You are much too modest," she replied. "Most men would jump at the opportunity to toot their horns."

"Tooting one's horn draws trouble, particularly out here." He touched the brim of his hat. "Good day, Mrs. Wainwright."

As he strode over to his favorite table by the window, Devon arched a brow, surprised by his reaction. Apparently, the marshal was uncomfortable with any praise or recognition. How curious, she thought. Everyone had a streak of vanity in him or her.

She tucked the newspaper under her arm and rose from her chair. From his place, Templeton watched her move gracefully across the room to the door. When she walked outside, he continued to observe her through the window. His brows dipped into a frown as Matthew Chandler approached her.

Rosie appeared to pour Cort a cup of coffee, and her eye followed his gaze. "Miss Sadie must be turning over in her grave," she remarked.

By the time Templeton returned to the office, he was not in the best of moods. Brett was waiting for him with news that would not improve his disposition.

"Hagen escaped," reported Sanger. "It just come over the wire."

Templeton looked at his deputy in disbelief. "How the hell did that happen?"

"Two deputy marshals were taking him from the jail in Canon City to stand trial in Pueblo. He got the slip on 'em and jumped off the train. Cort, ya know he's gonna come after ya. Marshal McCaughey said Hagen threatened to—"

"I know what Hagen said, Brett. It doesn't mean that he will. If Hagen is smart, he'll head for Mexico."

"Hagen ain't smart," said Sanger. "You know as well as me he'll be out for revenge. He could raise another gang."

"Keep it quiet for now, Brett. No need to panic the town."

"Yes, sir."

Cort eyed him meaningfully.

"I won't tell Bridget," the deputy promised.

The next day, Devon emerged from the bank and was strolling down the boardwalk, when she heard the distant sound of gunshots coming from behind the marshal's office and jail. Cautiously, she walked down the alley to the back of the building and was surprised to find Colt practicing his shooting.

Devon could see that he was having difficulty raising his injured arm and holding it steady enough to hit the target of cans. He clenched his jaw as more shots missed, and he stopped to massage the muscles in his arm and flex his hand. Devon realized now why he was so quick to decline any attention that might draw the notice of shooters seeking notoriety.

She ducked back when Cort turned to pick up a bag of grain and continued to watch as he used it as a weight to build strength in his arm. Knowing that he wouldn't appreciate an audience, she quietly left to go about her business.

CHAPTER NINETEEN

No Olive Branch

The town was abuzz, the excitement contagious as everyone gathered in the square for the Harvest Festival. The festival had become something of a tradition over the last three years, providing an opportunity to further build community. Even people from the surrounding farms traveled to town to take part.

Tables had been set up in the town square to hold the various foods volunteered from household pantries and gardens. On a separate table, women proudly displayed their preserves, cakes, and pies to be judged by a select panel. Children competed in games, the ladies gossiped, and the men played horseshoes. And, for one day, everyone could set aside the tedium of his or her life. Over it all, Cort kept a careful watch for any threat.

Sanger walked up him to take the duty.

"I'm guessing you haven't made up with Miss Ryan yet," said Cort, noting the glum expression on his deputy's face.

"She still won't talk to me—not even to tell me what I did," complained Brett. "She said I should know, and if I didn't, then I must not think it was wrong." He paused. "Does that make any sense to you?"

The corners of Cort's mouth curled up in amusement. "You have a lot to learn about women. Take her some candy and beg forgiveness."

"For what? I don't know what I done?"

"It doesn't matter. You'll find out later."

"But Mrs. Wainwright won't let me near Bridget."

"I might be able to help with that," said Templeton, spotting Devon coming down the street with her companion. "Watch for your chance."

As Brett looked on, Cort approached the two women.

"Ladies," he greeted, touching the brim of his hat. "Mrs. Wainwright, may I have a word with you?"

Devon hesitated. "Well…I suppose. What do you wish to speak to me about, Marshal?"

He took her arm and deftly steered her away from Bridget. "I have been looking into your aunt's missing jewelry. It would seem that your instincts were right. Nettie, Frank Stilwell, and Pearl Donovan all agree that your aunt was very fond of fine jewelry. They say that Sadie possessed several pieces of high value."

"So her jewelry *was* stolen," said Devon.

"Or sold."

"Sold?" Devon regarded Templeton with surprise. "Why would my aunt sell her jewelry? She was very wealthy."

"There were lean times when the gold played out. Sadie had already invested much of her fortune in rebuilding the town. Maybe she needed more money," conjectured Cort.

"Wouldn't Nettie know if my aunt had sold her jewelry?" questioned Devon.

"Not if Sadie hadn't told her."

"But Nettie said the jewelry was still in the box when she left the house after the funeral," noted Devon.

"No, Nettie said that she hadn't touched the box after Sadie's death," corrected Cort. "She just assumed the jewelry was still there."

"Well, if my aunt had sold the jewelry, why were the drawers rifled?"

Cort shrugged. "Either someone didn't know the jewelry had been sold or he was looking for something else."

"Or maybe some of the jewelry had been sold and the rest stolen," suggested Devon tongue-in-cheek.

"Yep, that too."

She looked at him with a measure of exasperation. "Marshal, what *do* you know?"

Cort looked over her shoulder to see that his deputy and Miss Ryan were talking. By the looks of it, he had to stall Devon a little longer.

"Frank not only represented Sadie in her legal affairs, but he was also a close friend and confidant," continued Cort. "He didn't know anything about Sadie selling her jewelry either but recollected that Sadie had taken a trip just before her death. Nettie also recollected that Sadie had mentioned some earrings and a necklace were missing. When Nettie told her to make a report to me, Sadie said she would take care of the matter herself."

"That's proof that her jewels were stolen then, probably by one of her 'girls,' and that's why she wanted to handle the matter quietly," surmised Devon. "I can't imagine it would have been good for business."

"Maybe. It could just as easily have been one of the customers," suggested Cort.

Devon massaged her forehead. "This is all too confusing. You are giving me a headache, Marshal."

Cort looked over her shoulder again to see that Bridget and Brett had disappeared and took it as a sign that his job was over.

"Answers will surface sooner or later, Mrs. Wainwright. Enjoy the festival."

Devon watched him walk away, perplexed. The exchange seemed odd to her and his departure a bit abrupt. She shrugged. She had given up trying to figure him.

She looked around for Bridget. The girl materialized behind her in a high mood, her eyes bright, her cheeks pink.

Devon eyed her with suspicion. "Bridget, where were you?"

"Oh miss, Brett explained everything," gushed Bridget. "It was just a misunderstandin'. He was following the marshal's orders."

Devon raised a brow, but before she could respond, Penny Johnson appeared to sweep her into the festivities. The next time Devon looked for Bridget, she found that her companion had vanished again. She would have to exercise tighter control over matters, she decided.

As twilight fell, many were reluctant to let the happy day end. Streetlamps were lit, and three men brought out fiddles and a harmonica and struck up the lively tune "Oh, Susannah." People immediately paired up to dance the polka in the street.

Cort watched as Chandler moved Devon through the dance steps. When the musicians followed up with a popular waltz, Cort tapped him on the shoulder, and he gracefully bowed out with a tight smile.

"You surprise me, Marshal. I would not have pegged you for a dancer," said Devon as Cort took her in his arms and smoothly led her into the waltz.

"I guess you could say it was an unspoken part of the curriculum at West Point," he replied. "Deputy Sanger and Miss Ryan appear to have resolved their differences," he noted as they danced by.

Devon frowned. "Bridget is entirely too trusting. Mr. Sanger had the nerve to tell her that he had been acting on your order the day she caught him in the saloon with that hussy."

"He was," said Cort. "Brett is telling the truth."

Devon looked at him in surprise. "Why would you issue an order like that?"

"Hagen had a spy in town. We had to divine who it was."

Devon gave a derisive laugh. "You must tell me, Marshal, how spending time in a saloon with a saloon girl accomplishes that end."

"A lot of information passes through there, Mrs. Wainwright. Shall I explain?"

Devon realized his meaning and felt the heat of a blush on her cheeks. "That won't be necessary," she replied primly. "Were you successful?"

"We discovered how information flowed to the source."

"But not the source."

Cort glanced over at Chandler who was keeping a close eye on them. "I have my suspicions."

She paused with a thought. "Mr. Templeton, to what lengths did Mr. Sanger have to go to glean such knowledge for you?"

"He bought the girl a couple of drinks, Mrs. Wainwright."

"Bridget saw her sitting on his lap, Marshal."

"He had to play the part. Nothing happened, Mrs. Wainwright. Brett did not betray Miss Ryan's trust.

Devon eyed Cort skeptically. "Perhaps not by a man's standards."

"Not by any reasonable person's standards, Mrs. Wainwright," he countered, returning her gaze.

Devon bristled at the inference.

"Well, I hope the mission was worth the hazard," she commented facetiously. "Do I have your assurance that Mr. Sanger will not be under orders to repeat such behavior?"

"Brett will carry out orders as I require him to in the line of duty," answered Cort.

Devon huffed with annoyance. "That is not a 'yes' or a 'no.'"

"At some point, you have to have some trust, Mrs. Wainwright.

The song ended and Cort released her.

Calvin came hurrying over to them then. "This telegram just come in for ya, Marshal. It's from the federal marshals' office in Pueblo. Hagen was sighted near Canon City. Thought you'd want to know," he said, eager to atone for previous misdeeds.

Cort let out a sigh when he saw Devon react. "I can read the telegram for myself, Calvin."

The telegraph operator took note of Devon then and swallowed hard. "Ma'am," he acknowledged. "Sorry, Marshal, I know you said to keep it quiet."

"Be more careful, Calvin," Templeton warned sternly.

"Yessir, Marshal. Yessir, I surely will." The operator practically fell over his feet in a hurry to be gone.

Devon rounded on Cort in alarm. "Hagen is not in jail?"

Cort hesitated. "He escaped while the marshals were taking him to stand trial in Pueblo City."

Apprehension flooded her face. "Hagen has sworn vengeance on you. How will you protect yourself? You can't—" She stopped short.

Cort's eyes narrowed. "Can't what, Mrs. Wainwright? Finish your thought."

Devon took a deep breath. "I saw you practicing your shooting," she confessed. "And during the dance, I noticed you held your right arm lower."

"I assure you I am up to the task, Mrs. Wainwright," he replied firmly. "There is a $2000 bounty on Hagen's head. Hunters and federal marshals are on his tail. He will be found. Unless or until there is a threat, I expect your silence on the matter."

Devon nodded. "Of course, but—"

"The discussion is closed, Mrs. Wainwright. Now, might I tell my deputy that he has found favor with you?"

"He has more to do to demonstrate that his intentions are honorable, Mr. Templeton."

"But Matthew Chandler doesn't?"

Devon stiffened. "You are being unfair, Marshal."

"Check in the weeds, Mrs. Wainwright." Cort bid her a good evening and walked off.

Devon gave a huff of exasperation. She simply did not know what to make of this man.

Chandler came over to her. "You appear to be unsettled, my dear. What did Marshal Templeton say to upset you?" he asked, curious.

Devon looked at him, vexed. "Mr. Templeton was just being Mr. Templeton."

The fiddlers struck up a new tune, and Chandler extended his hand. "Shall we…to soothe your troubled spirit?"

"I'm sorry, Matt. I am not in the mood. I would like to leave now."

Chandler could see there was no dissuading her. As he escorted her from the festivities, he and Cort locked eyes for a moment in a combative gaze.

A Good Day

Brett restlessly drummed his fingers on the desk.

Cort glanced up from his newspaper and glared at the deputy.

"Sorry," mumbled Sanger.

"What's the problem, Brett? You have been moping around here all morning."

The young man sighed. "It's Bridget."

"I thought you had mended things with her at the festival."

"I did."

Templeton put down his newspaper. "Then what is bothering you?"

"Mrs. Wainwright. She hardly gives Bridget and me a minute to ourselves, Cort. Every time I try to get Bridget alone, she pops up."

"Did you try talking to her?"

"Yeah, but she gives me that look of hers and all thoughts fly out of my head."

Templeton laughed. "You have no fear of facing down a gang of outlaws, but you are afraid of a woman?"

"It ain't funny, Cort. My grandmother called it giving the evil eye. Ask Jasper. He sure enough keeps his distance from Mrs. Wainwright." Brett leaned forward, his manner pleading. "You have a way with her. Can't you talk to her?"

"She doesn't cotton to me any more than she does to you, Brett."

"Maybe not, but you ain't afraid of her and she, at least, listens to you—sometimes."

Cort sighed. "All right, I'll have a talk with her, but I'm not promising anything."

Brett's face brightened. "When?"

"Can't say. One thing I have learned about Mrs. Wainwright is that you have to pick your time well."

Two days later, Nettie poked her head in the door of the marshal's office. "Cort, Mrs. Wainwright is in a fair mood today. You asked me to let ya know."

"How fair is her mood?" asked Templeton.

"About as fair as it's gonna get. You best get yerself on over there afore somethin' puts her out of it. It ain't hard to do ya know."

"Thanks, Nettie."

Cort stood up and reached for his hat and coat. He looked at Brett who regarded him with high hope. "You stay here until I get back," he ordered. "The last thing we need is for Mrs. Wainwright to think that we are plotting behind her back."

Brett nodded. "Yes, sir."

Devon was passing through the foyer, when she heard the knock on the door and peeked out the window. She drew back with a gasp. The marshal was standing on the porch, and a panic rose up inside her. She wasn't mentally prepared to see him.

When he knocked again, she stood stock still, praying that he would go away. Miss Primrose was busy teaching a math lesson to the older children, Nettie had gone out to the store, and Bridget was elsewhere in the house. There was no one but her to answer the door.

Cort knocked a third time with more insistence, and it was clear that he was not leaving. Devon patted her hair and pinched some color into her cheeks. Taking a deep breath, she opened the door.

"Marshal," she greeted with wide-eyed surprise. "What are you doing here? Is something amiss?"

Cort smiled to himself. He had seen her at the window and heard the falter in her voice, and he knew that he had knocked her off balance, if only a bit. But a bit was all he needed.

"Didn't Dr. Morse tell you?" he asked.

Her face screwed up in bewilderment. "Tell me what?"

"I'm taking some supplies out to the Johnson house. He thought as how it would be good if you came along, since you and Penny have struck up a friendship and this being a bad time of the year for her."

"Dr. Morse didn't say anything to me about it," said Devon.

"He must be getting forgetful in his old age."

"Why is this a bad time for Penny?"

"She lost the child two years ago today. The doc thought some female companionship might help her with the doldrums," explained Cort.

"Oh, yes. Penny told me about her loss." Devon hesitated. "I'd like to go…but Nettie hasn't returned yet, and I shouldn't leave Bridget alone."

"Miss Ryan isn't alone. You have a house full of kids in there and Miss Primrose. And I am sure that Nettie will be back soon," said Cort. As Devon continued to waver, he added: "Penny sure would be cheered by your visit."

"Well, if you think that I can be of some help to her, I suppose I should go," she relented. "I just need a few minutes to tell Bridget and fetch a hat and coat."

"I'll wait out here," said Cort.

Devon raced up the stairs calling for Bridget and ran into the bedroom suite.

Bridget rushed in moments later to find Devon in a tizzy. "What's amiss, Miss Devon?" she cried.

"He just showed up—out of the blue," said Devon, pacing the floor.

"Who?"

"Marshal Templeton. He can't just drop in without warning."

"I don't understand, miss."

"He has come to drive me to the Johnson farm to cheer up Penny—this being a bad time for her. He said Dr. Morse was supposed to have told me, but he didn't. What am I to do?"

Bridget breathed a sigh of relief. "Calm down, miss. You like Mrs. Johnson. 'Tis just a trip to visit with her. 'Twill be a pleasant afternoon."

"But I must travel with the marshal. I-I'm not prepared, Bridget."

"You look fine, miss."

"No, no, I mean I have not the presence of mind."

Bridget looked at her in bewilderment. "Miss?"

"Never mind," said Devon. "Please fetch me a lavender compress, quickly."

The front door opened 15 minutes later, and Devon walked out in a calmer frame of mind.

As Cort guided her to the buckboard wagon, she raised a brow. "We're traveling in this?"

"Only way to transport supplies, Mrs. Wainwright."

The seat was higher than in a buggy and, as she considered how best to climb up to it, he put his hands around her waist and lifted her up. The action surprised her, and she quickly moved to settle herself.

The seat was wooden, hard and uncomfortable, and the low rail gave little back support or sense of security. When he climbed up beside her, she found there was little space between them. It most certainly was not built for the comfort of travel.

He clicked the reins, turned the wagon around, and they started off. As they drove out of town, Devon was silent, struggling to keep her seat each time a rut in the road jostled her against him. Cort glanced over at her and suppressed a smile. She was gripping the side rail for dear life, and he could see how uneasy she was. The wagon hit a deeper rut, and she grabbed hold of his arm.

"If I had to guess, I would say you have never ridden on a buckboard before," he remarked. "You'll have to get used to it. It's a staple out here."

She let go of him. "The list seems to be getting longer of things I must get used to," she replied dryly.

"Maybe because you haven't experienced life."

"Of course, I have," retorted Devon. "I've traveled abroad—"

"That's not what I mean. I am talking about real life," said Cort. "You have led a sheltered life…servants tended to your every whim and money bought you anything you wanted. You don't know what it means to live on the edge of existence."

"You make it sound as though that is a bad thing."

"Not necessarily, but you are not living in the real world. You are insulated from it, which I suppose is not a problem unless you are forced to travel outside your life of privilege."

"Just what do you consider to be the real world, Mr. Templeton?"

"The world of the masses, Mrs. Wainwright."

Devon bristled. She wasn't sure if he was being critical of her or not. "You know nothing about me," she replied defensively. "I've had my crosses to bear."

"Apologies, ma'am. While money can buy ease and privilege, I guess it cannot always buy happiness."

"What is that supposed to mean?" demanded Devon.

"You didn't have an agreeable marriage."

She glanced at him sharply. "Why would you think that? Did Bridget say something to Mr. Sanger?"

"Information flows both ways, I suspect," replied Templeton, giving her a pointed look.

Devon looked away. "Perhaps we should both have a talk with our employees."

Silence fell between them, but the marshal's remarks continued to grate on her.

"You are right…about my marriage," she said at length, bitterness creeping into her tone. "My husband was 12 years older than I. He was controlling, domineering, and demeaning—just like my father and grandfather. For 10 years, I lived under that man's thumb. I didn't realize how small and weak he was until after he died."

"You can't judge others by your experience," said Cort, surprised by the confession. "Miss Ryan has a right to make her own judgments about Brett."

"Mr. Sanger's character is not my only consideration, Marshal. The life of a lawman is dangerous and sometimes short-lived. It wasn't that long ago that you were shot," pointed out Devon. "And now that outlaw is on the loose…who knows what may happen? Bridget is more than a companion to me. I have an obligation to protect her against disappointment and heartache."

"No one can be protected from life, Mrs. Wainwright."

"Maybe, but precautions can be taken to make some outcomes less certain and life less tragic," argued Devon.

Court looked at her. "To what sacrifice? If one makes determinations out of fear of what may or may not happen, that person may find it a very disappointing life, Mrs. Wainwright. A life untried is a life unlived."

Devon bristled that he should lecture her. "Perhaps you should look in the mirror, Marshal. Are you really living your life, or are you just making substitutions for Jennie?"

The remark hit home. Pearl had said much the same thing to him.

Silence fell again as uncomfortable truths hung over them wishing for no more exposure.

When Cort drove into the Johnson farmyard, Emmett came out of the barn and hurried over to greet them. He put a hand to the brim of his hat. "Mrs. Wainwright, 'tis right nice to see ya."

Devon smiled. "Thank you, Mr. Johnson."

"It's Emmett, ma'am."

The young man looked at Templeton. "What brings you out here, Cort, not that ya ain't always welcome?"

"Thought I'd save you a trip to town," replied Templeton. "I brought your supplies."

"'Tis a blessin' fer sure. An axle broke on one of the wheels of my wagon. Ain't had time to fix it."

"I'll give you a hand with it. Mrs. Wainwright came along to visit with Penny."

"I thank ya kindly fer comin', ma'am. My Penny could do with some female companionship. She be in a low mood today."

The door suddenly opened, and two little tow-headed boys ran out. "Uncle Cort, Uncle Cort," they shouted excitedly.

Cort climbed down from the wagon and lifted up one in each arm. "Do you know any little boys who like candy?"

"We do," they answered in unison.

"Have you been minding your mama?"

They nodded their heads vigorously.

"We been real good, Uncle Cort," said five-year-old Harper. "Ain't we, Tim?"

The three-year-old giggled. "Real good," he repeated.

"All right then." Cort set them on the ground and pulled out a bag from his vest pocket and handed each of them a piece of licorice candy.

Penny stood in the doorway holding the toddler. "Cort Templeton, you spoil them boys too much. And where's your manners? Help Miss Devon off that wagon."

"I can manage," Devon assured her.

She was trying to divine a way to climb down gracefully when Cort swung her down from the seat. The action was so quick and unexpected, she let out a cry of surprise, and he had to steady her when he set her on her feet. As when he had hoisted her into the wagon, the move was more expedient than presumptuous, but she wished he would give her some warning.

Penny impatiently waved everyone inside. "Come on in here and sit yourselves down. I'm just about to lay out the midday meal."

"Oh, we don't want to intrude," said Devon.

"Ain't no bother at all," replied Penny. "Ain't everyday we get visitors."

"No use arguin' with her," said Emmett.

Cort, Devon, and Emmett filed into the house.

"Miss Devon, you can mind Emma, whilst I set up the table," said Penny, plopping the apple-cheeked toddler in Devon's arms.

Startled, Devon looked helplessly about as she awkwardly held the child. She had no experience with babies or small children. In her circle of friends in Boston, nannies were employed, and children were rarely seen or heard. She looked down to find large blue eyes staring up at her with an air of expectancy, and Devon felt a moment of panic as the toddler started to fuss.

Cort watched in amusement. "Children like motion," he said.

Devon looked at him wondering how he would know, but she followed his advice and the child quieted as she moved about.

"Emmett, call them boys in to eat," Penny instructed her husband. "Cort, you sit there next to Miss Devon."

Cort looked at Emmett and grinned. "Bossy as always."

"Some things ain't never gonna change," the young man responded with mock resignation.

Much to Devon's relief, Penny swooped the child from her arms and settled the toddler in a highchair.

Emmett beckoned the boys, and they noisily entered the cabin. At a stern look from their mother, they quickly quieted.

"Are your hands clean?" she asked.

The boys held out their hands for inspection, and she nodded her approval.

When all were settled around the table, Penny gave a nod to her husband to proceed.

"Let us all join hands with this offering of gratitude," he said.

Penny took Devon's left hand. Devon looked at Cort to her right and hesitated, but he showed no such reticence. His large hand engulfed hers, and she felt a sense of well-being wash over her. When the prayer ended, Cort released her hand, and the sensation ceased.

She glanced sideways at him. He didn't seem to have noted anything unusual, and she was mystified as to why such an insignificant act should affect her as it did. It was utterly bizarre to her.

Penny ladled out the stew and passed around a plate of biscuits and a pot of apple butter.

"Mighty good, Penny," remarked Cort after tasting a spoonful of stew. He looked at Emmett and winked. "Glad to see she finally learned to cook. You were nearly down to a shadow."

"Cort Templeton!" exclaimed an indignant Penny. "You'll keep a civil tongue in yer head, or you'll get none of that apple pie you're always hankerin' for."

"Yes, ma'am."

Devon echoed Cort's compliments to the cook. The stew was delicious, the biscuits light and flaky, and the apple butter sweet. And she marveled at Penny's efficiency. It seemed miraculous to her that, even though Penny had had no expectations of visitors, there was plenty of food to go around.

The conversation throughout the meal continued to be light and bantering with a sprinkling of wit, and Devon was sorry when it came to an end.

"Emmett, I'll give you a hand fixing that wagon wheel now," said Cort. "I'm sure the ladies would like some time to talk."

The men stood up and took their hats and coats off the row of pegs next to the door.

Cort turned to the boys. "If it's okay with your mama, why don't you fellows come, too?"

The boys looked hopefully at their mother. "Can we, Mama? Can we go with Papa and Uncle Cort?" begged Harper.

"All right, but don't be gettin' in the way," Penny lectured them.

She barely had the words out of her mouth before the boys jumped up from their seats and ran over to join the men.

"Emmett, you watch that they don't get hurt now," she yelled to her husband as the group departed the house. "I can't be losin' another child," she added in a low, somber tone.

Devon reached over and gave Penny's hand a gentle squeeze to comfort her.

Penny smiled and wiped a tear from her eye. "The Lord took my Liza away, but he left a blessin' in her place," she said, looking lovingly at Emma. "Loss is a part of life, but it don't make it easy. You would know that since you lost your husband."

Devon hesitated. "I'm afraid that my loss was not so heartfelt."

"Oh…well, whatever the circumstances, life is about new beginnings, too," said Penny. "Why just look at you. You come all the way from Boston to Blue Springs. Miss Sadie was all about second chances. That's how come she built this town."

Devon smiled. She didn't have the heart to tell her new friend that her second chance wasn't working out so well and that her stay was only temporary.

She rose to clear the table—something she never would have considered doing in Boston—but Penny stopped her.

"The dishes can wait," she said. "I don't often get to visit with another woman. Emmett and me don't get into town much, and it gets a mite lonely out here. I wish Cort would finish that house of his."

Penny eyed Devon meaningfully. "It would be real nice to have a neighbor close by."

"Oh…no, you have the wrong idea," said Devon, realizing her train of thought. "Mr. Templeton and I are merely acquaintances."

Penny smiled. "That's what I used to say 'bout Emmett when I was first sweet on him 'til I found out that he was sweet on me."

"No really, the marshal and I have not a sweet thought for each other," Devon assured her new friend. "Quite the opposite, I fear."

"That ain't what I saw at the fall festival," insisted Penny with a twinkle in her eye. "Cort never dances and believe me plenty of women have tried with him." She giggled. "Just ask him about the Barley sisters."

"The dance didn't mean anything," said Devon.

"Maybe…maybe not, but I seen how he looks at ya when ya ain't lookin'," continued Penny. "I seen it at the festival, and I seen it right here today."

Devon laughed. "I think that your imagination is running away with you. Marshal Templeton wouldn't know a sweet thought about a woman if it jumped up and bit him. And if he did think it, he would say so. He is the most plain-spoken man I've ever met."

"Cort is a private man," admitted Penny. "Most times his actions are his words."

"Indeed." Devon looked around her. "You have a lovely house, Penny," she said, seeking to change the subject. But rather than changing the subject, her comment only fueled it.

"Cort helped us to build it," said Penny. "He was an engineer in the war, you know. He told us how to position the house and how to design the rooms to keep warm in the winter and cool in the summer. Here, I'll show you."

She lifted Emma out of the highchair and led Devon on a tour through the one-story house. The house was small but well-built and laid out in an efficient manner. She could see Cort's hand in the design.

She could also see Penny's hand in the decor. It wasn't elegant but it was bright and cozy. Gingham curtains hung from the kitchen windows, lace curtains hung in the parlor, and muslin curtains in the three bedrooms. A large, patterned rug lay on the floor of the open parlor and a braided rug in the kitchen. There wasn't much furniture, but what there was of it was comfortable and practical.

Penny looked about her beaming with pride. "I never dreamed I would have a house so fine as this."

Devon had to smile to herself. In her world in Boston, this would have been little more than a caretaker's cottage. And she marveled that Penny could be so happy with so little.

"Emmett and me, we owe Cort much," continued Penny. "He's the godfather of our children, you know."

Devon blinked in surprise. "I never would have imagined it."

"Ain't no one else I'd trust my babies with," said Penny, an emotional catch in her voice. "Cort is a good man."

"How does one ever truly know a person?" asked Devon. "Some people are very good at hiding their low character and faults."

"You look to their actions," Penny replied soberly. "A body true to hisself never falters."

Once again, Devon was struck by the wisdom of such a simple person.

At a shout from the men, the women walked outside to the porch. The wind was whipping up and the air was turning colder. Penny pulled her shawl around Emma.

"Feels like winter is comin' on," she said.

"The wagon wheel is fixed," said Cort. He looked at Devon. "We best be getting back to town now. Looks like a storm may blow up."

As Devon made her farewells and thanked the Johnsons for their hospitality, Cort pulled out the bag of licorice candy and divided the rest of the pieces between the boys.

"Best put them in your pockets before your mama sees," he whispered with a conspiratorial wink.

They giggled and quickly hid the candy in their pockets.

"Cort Templeton, ya better come back soon," said Penny. "We don't see near enough of ya."

"I will if you serve up stew and another apple pie like that," he replied.

"Only if you bring Miss Devon with you," she countered.

Cort glanced at Devon. "Well now, that will be up to her."

When he lifted Devon onto the seat of the wagon, this time she was prepared for it, and buoyed by a pleasant visit, she was in a charitable mood. He climbed up beside her. With a final wave to the Johnsons, they drove out of the farmyard.

As they rode in silence, Cort caught Devon's sidelong glances on him. She seemed amused about something.

"What did you women talk about?" he asked, effecting a casual air.

"Things," replied Devon.

He looked at her. "What things?"

"Oh, the house, life…you."

Cort snorted. "It appears to me there are more interesting topics to talk about than me…. What did Penny say?"

"She said that you are godfather to her children. I wouldn't have thought you to be so paternalistic," remarked Devon.

"It puts to rest a fear for her. Penny grew up in an orphanage," explained Cort. "Neither she nor Emmett have any folks to speak of. I know how it feels to lose parents at a young age. But I had an uncle who cared about me and saw to it that I got an education and a firm footing in life. I figure I can do the same for someone else if need be."

"That is very commendable of you, Mr. Templeton. And do not say that you are just doing your duty, or I will no longer find it commendable."

"They are good people," he responded.

Devon had to smile to herself, recognizing that it was probably the most self-effacing response he could find.

"Penny wants you to finish your house and provide her with some female companionship," continued Devon.

Templeton grunted. "It's a common refrain of hers."

"She also said that I should ask you about the Barley sisters…something about a dance."

Cort harrumphed and clicked the reins. "I see that I need to have a talk with Penny about boundaries."

Devon suppressed a giggle, smug in the knowledge that she had finally shaken his reserve.

CHAPTER TWENTY-ONE

Gone Fishing

Over the next few weeks, Devon settled in, despite her intentions to leave soon. She felt comfortable in the house and with the towns-people. They were welcoming, nonjudgmental. It didn't matter whether she had on the right dress for the right time of day, or took supper at precisely eight o'clock, or used the right fork and spoon. And she found it freeing, which presented quite a conundrum for her. As she relaxed into the less restrictive lifestyle, she found herself more and more in opposition to the strict code of etiquette that had been ingrained in her from birth.

The only fly in the ointment was that Nettie had been called away to tend to her ill sister. She had been gone for only four days before Devon was forced to admit that she missed the gruffly attentive wom-an's culinary skills.

Chafing at the unexpected expense of her and Bridget having to take their meals at the restaurant, Devon decided to try her hand at baking one day. It didn't end well. Two weeks later, she was still liv-ing down the alarm she had caused in the town.

Thus, when she announced to Bridget that they were going to try cooking again, a look of panic flooded the young woman's face.

"Oh, Miss Devon, I don't think that is a good idea. After the last time, Marshal Templeton said you wasn't ever to cook again."

Devon dismissed the marshal's order. "Fiddle faddle. He was being overdramatic. The oven got a little too hot is all."

"You forgot to open a draft. Smoke filled the whole house, miss," Bridget reminded her. "If the marshal hadna come by when he did, I shudder to think—"

"Never mind, Bridget. Mistakes teach."

"Miss Devon, you never even boiled water before, and I ain't done much more than that. Can we not wait until Nettie returns?" pleaded Bridget.

Devon waved aside her companion's concerns. "Heaven knows how long that will be. Cooking can't be that difficult. You've helped Nettie before. You should be able to remember what she did. There are only a few cans of beans and some jars of pickled beets and preserves in the pantry, so you will have to go to the general store and to the butcher."

"What shall I get, miss?"

Devon thought for a minute. "We haven't had eggs in a long time. Not even the restaurant is serving them. I am sick of porridge…bacon and beef steak, too…. Get a chicken at the butcher but make certain he dresses it. I am not about to do what one must do to make it ready for the pot," she said with a grimace. "And there must be some fresh vegetables to be had. We just had a fall festival."

Bridget returned an hour later largely empty-handed, except for a pumpkin, squash and some ears of corn in her basket.

Devon looked at her in surprise. "Did you forget what I had asked you to buy?"

"No, ma'am."

"Where are the eggs and the chicken, then?"

"Ain't no eggs right now."

"Why not?"

"Mrs. Walker said chickens don't lay much in the winter and eggs is hard to come by. And the butcher said as how chickens ain't good to eat now, as there's not enough sun for them to thrive."

Devon let out a sigh of frustration. "Oh, very well. What *did* the butcher have?"

"He had lots of veal and beef steaks. The ranchers are decreasing their herds for the winter."

"What else did he have?"

"Mutton."

Devon wrinkled her nose."

"He has pickled pork and salt pork," offered Bridget.

"I am sick of that, too. Has the butcher no fresh ham?"

"Hogs ain't killed and butchered 'til the weather gets colder. He said he's goin' huntin' tomorrow and may have a turkey or some venison in a few days."

Devon was incredulous. Of course, she was aware that fruit and vegetables were seasonal, but she had no idea that there was a season for meat as well.

"What shall we eat then?" she wondered aloud.

"What we been eating—at the restaurant," replied Bridget on a hopeful note.

Devon huffed. "Oh, very well. Can we at least manage to boil water for tea?"

"Yes, miss."

Bridget prepared the stove and put on the tea kettle.

"Miss Devon, I heard them noises again last night. Did ye not hear them?"

Devon hesitated. "No…not last night."

The teacher entered the kitchen then. It was Saturday—a half day of school—and the students had just left.

"Miss Primrose, would you care to share a cup of tea with us?" asked Devon.

"No, thank you, Mrs. Wainwright. I've come to say that I am leaving to visit a friend. I expect to return tomorrow afternoon."

"Oh. Well, a day away from here will be a nice respite for you," said Devon. "Miss Primrose, have you heard any strange noises at night?"

Miss Primrose looked at her in bewilderment. "Noises? What kind of noises?"

"Bridget claims to have heard disturbances coming from inside the walls on a couple of occasions and again last night."

"No, I have not heard anything, Mrs. Wainwright."

"I am not imagining it," insisted Bridget.

"It might be mice or rats inside the wall," suggested Miss Primrose.

Devon and Bridget looked at each other, the very idea horrifying them.

"Squirrels, rats, mice, and even snakes may seek shelter there or in the attic when the weather turns cold," the teacher continued unhelpfully.

"Oh, miss, I won't sleep a wink tonight," fretted Bridget.

"I would suggest getting some traps," said Miss Primrose. "But be careful. They can snap off a finger if not set correctly. Well, I'm off now. I shall see you tomorrow."

As the teacher departed the kitchen, Bridget turned anxiously to Devon. "Oh, miss, what shall we do?"

Devon sighed. She didn't want to take this course of action, but as she saw it, she had no choice.

Brett jumped to attention and swallowed hard when Devon walked into the office.

"Mrs. Wainwright…w-what can I do for you?"

Devon scanned the room. "Where is Marshal Templeton?"

Brett let out his breath in relief that she wasn't there to see him. "The marshal is off fishin', ma'am."

"Fishing? Who fishes this time of the year?"

"Cort says it's the best time. The water is low and clear, and there ain't many fishermen around. He'll be back in a few days."

"A few days!" exclaimed Devon. "I can't wait that long. I have a matter that needs to be dispensed with now. Where can I find him?"

"I don't think that is a good idea, Mrs. Wainwright. The marshal is real serious 'bout his fishin'. He won't take kindly to bein' disturbed."

"His duty is to keep the populace of this town safe, is it not?"

"Well, yes, but—"

"No 'buts,' Mr. Sanger. Bridget and I have need of his protection straightaway."

Brett looked at her in consternation. "Are you and Bridget in danger?"

"I dare say that we are."

"I'm in charge, Mrs. Wainwright. How are you threatened?"

"Please take no offense, Deputy, but I mean to speak to the marshal about this matter."

Brett hesitated. Cort would be mad as hell, but she was insistent, and her manner was urgent. If Bridget was in danger—

"Cort is fishin' downstream of town near the turnoff to his house," he quickly told her.

"Thank you, Mr. Sanger."

Devon hurried to the livery stable and rented a horse and buggy. Before long, she was traveling the road along the river. She discovered the marshal at the spot where the deputy said he would be, standing in the middle of the river in three feet of water. She reined in the horse and climbed down from the buggy.

"Marshal," she called out. "Yoo-hoo…Marshal Templeton."

When he looked over at her, she waved her arms. Even at this distance, she could sense that he was not thrilled to see her. She could almost hear him groan. But Devon would not be deterred from her mission. She saw a path and quickly made her way down the rocky bank to the water's edge.

"Marshal…"

Cort ignored her. He had told Brett not to tell anyone where he was, but it would seem that his deputy still had difficulty standing his ground with this woman, he fumed.

"Mr. Templeton, I must have a word with you," she yelled.

"Talk to my deputy!"

"I can't. I am in need of *your* assistance."

Templeton suddenly felt a tug and quickly moved to set the hook. He could tell it was a good size trout and excitedly began to play it. "Not now, Mrs. Wainwright."

Undeterred, Devon stepped across some rocks and negotiated her way closer to him. "Marshal—"

"Go away!"

Cort fought to keep hold of the fish. All of a sudden, he heard a splash and a scream, and he turned his head to see that Devon had fallen into the water.

The water wasn't deep, but the current was swift, and she was rendered helpless by the weight of her sodden skirts. Cort hesitated for a split second torn between keeping his fish or saving her.

Uttering a heartfelt oath, he dropped his rod and quickly waded through the water to grab hold of Devon as the current dragged her closer to the riffle. Dismally, he watched his coveted rod sail over the rapids and disappear down river along with his fish.

He hauled Devon to the bank. The water and air were cold. When she began to shiver, he took off his coat and put it around her shoulders. Wordlessly, Cort removed his waders and put on his boots. Holding his fishing equipment—or what was left of it—in one hand, he took her firmly by the arm with the other hand and propelled her up the path to the buggy.

If Devon didn't know that he was furious before, she knew it now when he threw his gear on the floor of the conveyance. Wisely, she held her tongue and scrambled to take her seat. He climbed in next to her, picked up the reins, and turned the horse and buggy around to take the path to his house.

"Mr. Templeton, I—"

He raised a hand. "Do not speak, Mrs. Wainwright."

"But—"

"Do-not-say-a-word."

When they arrived at the house, he got out of the buggy, walked onto the porch, and opened the door. She climbed down from the conveyance and hesitantly followed him inside. She had never seen him so angry.

He stooped down and started a fire in the fireplace. When it was robust enough, he stood up and turned to her. "If you don't want to risk getting pneumonia, you'll take off your clothes and lay them out on the floor to dry," he instructed. "There is a blanket on the cot you can use to cover up. I'm going out to take care of the horse. You will have 15 minutes."

When the door closed on him, Devon debated whether she really needed to take such drastic action. But she was cold and began to sneeze and decided that Cort was probably right. She took off his coat and quickly worked to separate herself from her dripping wet garments, undressing down to her chemise, corset, and drawers.

The drawers were wool and would take forever to dry, but she wasn't about to compromise her reputation any further by removing them. She had just finished laying out her articles of clothing before the fire, when Cort returned, his mood not much improved.

She reached for the blanket and pulled it around her. "I don't know what you are so angry about," she said. "I'm the one who is wet and may catch my death of cold—and my coat and dress, which are of no small value, are ruined. All you lost was a stick that can be easily replaced."

Cort's thin thread of control snapped. "That was not a stick!" he roared. "It was a J.C. Conroy fly fishing rod and reel. It came all the way from New York and took me months to come by it."

Devon blinked in surprise. She had not expected such an eruption over a piece of wood.

"And I did not lose just a rod," he continued to rail. "I was about to reel in a Greenback Cutthroat trout of no small dimension! What is so all fired important that you could not wait for me to return to town?!"

Devon swallowed hard. "Mice," she replied lowly.

Cort stared at her. "You cost me a highly valued fishing rod and a prize fish because of mice?!"

"Well, Bridget was hearing noises at night, and Miss Primrose thought as how it might be rats or mice in the walls," Devon hurried to explain.

"She said the cold brings them in, and now Bridget is afraid to go to sleep on account of some people in tenements in New York City were gnawed to death in their sleep by rats," continued Devon, her words tumbling over each other. "So, I need for you to investigate and set some traps or something."

"I am not your handyman!" snapped Cort. "There are any number of men in this town who would be happy to oblige you."

"But you are an engineer and—"

"It does not take an engineer to set traps for rodents, Mrs. Wainwright. Besides, I doubt that your noise comes from rats in the walls. Houses make noises. They creak as they settle."

"All the more reason why I need an engineer," argued Devon, further risking his wrath. "Bridget is most emphatic that the sounds she hears are not those of a settling house. And, if you were friends with my aunt, you would be the one most likely to determine the cause."

"And how is that, Mrs. Wainwright?"

"Well, I would imagine you were a frequent visitor and thus quite familiar with the residence."

Cort caught the inference in her remark and was hard pressed to check his temper. He was convinced now that she was being neurotic. It didn't fit with her personality, but the hint of a suggestion of the presence of mice, rats, or snakes was known to send sensible women into hysterics. For this nonsense, he lost his rod and his fish?!

"Mr. Templeton," Devon continued tentatively, "there is more. I haven't said anything to Bridget about this. She is upset enough as it is, and I don't wish to alarm her further. But, of late, I have also heard sounds and sensed some strange things in that house."

"Like what?" he demanded to know.

"I have felt a…well, I have felt a presence there."

Cort didn't think it possible to be any more surprised by her, and he looked at her in disbelief. "Are you telling me, Mrs. Wainwright, that you think there is a ghost in the house?"

"I know how it sounds," said Devon. "But something is there I tell you. Things have disappeared, and I've heard footsteps on the stairs a few times. When I go to look, there is no one there."

She looked up at him with troubled blue eyes, and he could see that she didn't take the matter lightly. As she stood there shivering beneath the blanket, wet strands of hair framing her oval-shaped face, she looked more like a bedraggled waif in need of care than the fire-breathing dragon of Brett's description.

"All right. I'll check out your house," relented Cort. "In the future—"

"Yes, I know. You are not my handyman."

It was nearly twilight by the time they returned to town. Cort drove the buggy up to the house. Devon stepped out of it and was walking through the gate, when Bridget came running out the door.

"Miss Devon, I've been so worried…" Her voice trailed off and she came to a halt at the sight of Devon's disheveled appearance and crumpled, water-stained clothes. "Miss Devon, what happened to you?" she cried in alarm when her mistress stepped onto the porch.

Devon sneezed and walked swiftly passed her into the house. Noting the stony expression on the marshal's face, Bridget raised a brow and hurried after her mistress.

When Templeton walked into the marshal's office, Brett took his feet off the desk and jumped up.

"How was the fishing?" he asked cheerfully. His smile faded when Cort glared at him.

"I lost my Conroy as I was about to hook a Greenback Cutthroat trout of good size. That's how it went, Brett."

Sanger looked at the marshal in confusion. "How did you lose your Conroy?"

Instantly, he knew it was the wrong question to ask as the expression on Cort's face turned darker.

"Oh," he murmured. "I take it Mrs. Wainwright found you. I'm sorry, Cort. I know I shouldna told her where you was, but you know how intimidating that woman can be—and she said that she and Bridget were in danger, and she wouldn't talk to no one but you."

"They hear house noises, Brett."

"Yeah, I know. I was worried and went to check on Bridget after Mrs. Wainwright went lookin' for ya. She's terrified it might be rats in the walls. I checked out the house from attic to basement. There weren't no sign of any rodents as I could find, but I set a couple of traps to make Bridget feel better. I told her that it was probably just the wind makin' the house creak."

"No doubt. Still, Mrs. Wainwright is insisting upon an inspection from an engineer."

"Why?"

"She says she has been experiencing other kinds of incidents as well."

"Like what?"

"Missing items…the sound of footsteps on the stairs."

Brett's eyes widened. "Sweet Jesus! She has a ghost?"

Cort snorted. "More likely she has an active imagination. Keep this to yourself. Mrs. Wainwright doesn't want to upset Miss Ryan any more than she is, and I don't want the town to think these women are crazy."

Over the next few days, everything seemed to have settled down. Miss Primrose had returned, and school had commenced. Neither

Bridget nor Devon heard any more noises or experienced any further strange occurrences. Cort had gone through the house and had found nothing suspect. He hadn't said it, but Devon could detect it in his tone and manner that he thought she and Bridget had overreacted to some settling noises.

* * * * *

Brett spied Bridget coming out of the general store.

"Bridget, hold up," he called.

She smiled and waited as he dashed across the street to her.

"If you are inviting me to lunch, I accept," she said.

Brett looked at her in surprise. "You usually have to hurry back."

"The students have decided to put on a Christmas concert, and Miss Devon is busy selecting music. Are you free?"

He gave her a roguish grin. "For you, every time."

Bridget's cheeks took on a rosy hue. "Brett Sanger, you need to attend church more often," she said with a giggle.

"Did you ever find out what happened between the marshal and Mrs. Wainwright?" he asked as they walked arm-in-arm to the restaurant.

"No. Miss Devon won't discuss it, and she has forbidden me to speak of it to anyone, though I don't know what it is I'm not supposed to speak of," replied Bridget. "Did Marshal Templeton tell you anything?"

"Nah. All I know is that she caused him to lose a fine fish and, even worse, his fishing rod." Brett shook his head. "There ain't no gettin' them two together after that. Cort is still hoppin' mad about it."

"Well, that's just plain silly. Marshal Templeton can buy another pole."

"It ain't just any fishin' pole, Bridget. It was a Conroy. They make the finest rods for fly fishing in the country. Cort takes fishin' serious like. Nobody messes with his stuff."

Bridget came to a halt outside the restaurant. "How do you know that it wasn't the marshal's fault that he lost his pole?"

"Ha! Not a chance," said Brett. "The Conroy was sacred to Cort. Besides, you know how Mrs. Wainwright can be."

Bridget stiffened. "What I know, Brett Sanger, is that Miss Devon is right. Men are boys who need to grow up." She pulled her arm free and marched off.

"Where ya goin'? What about lunch?" he called out.

"Eat it yourself!" she shouted back.

Cort looked up in surprise when Brett stormed into the office and threw his bowler across the room in a fit of pique. "Women!" he exclaimed. "I'm done with 'em."

Devon was just as surprised when Bridget strode furiously into the house loudly proclaiming the same sentiment about men.

It was a few days before Devon and Cort were able to piece together what had caused the falling out between the young people. Bridget was so upset Devon decided she needed to do something about the matter.

Cort was about to pour himself a cup of coffee, when Devon walked purposefully through the door. She was obviously on a mission, and he smothered a groan.

"Mrs. Wainwright," he greeted guardedly. "Coffee?"

"No, thank you," she replied.

He set the coffee pot back on the stove and walked over to her.

"What can I do for you?" he was reluctant to ask. Posing the question usually had the effect of opening a can of worms. "Are you hearing more noises?"

Devon ignored the facetious note in his tone. "No, Mr. Templeton, I am here about the disagreement between my companion and your deputy. I am sure you are aware of it."

"I am certain they'll mend things," said Cort.

"Perhaps, but, in the meantime, Bridget is…well, she is useless in her duties."

"As is my deputy," admitted Cort. "What is your point?"

"Understand that I still have doubts about Mr. Sanger's suitability for Bridget, Mr. Templeton, but you lectured me to step back and let them find their own way, and that is what I am trying to do. Unfortunately, you and I appear to be at the root of their recent rift, so I suppose it falls to us to fix it."

He eyed her warily. "What do you have in mind, Mrs. Wainwright?"

"Quite simply, you and I need to bury the hatchet concerning the-uh-incident at the river. I will tell you that I am sorry you lost your fishing stick—"

"Rod."

"Rod," she amended. "And you will apologize for making me fall into the river."

"How did I make you fall into the river?" he questioned.

"Well, if you hadn't ignored me when I called to you that day, I wouldn't have had to pick my way across the stones to gain your attention, which caused me to fall into the river and you to lose your stick—rod. So, you can see the fault is yours, Mr. Templeton, but I am willing to accept a share of the blame for Bridget's sake."

Cort stared at her. Never had he met anyone capable of piercing his careful control with such twisted logic.

"How very generous of you, Mrs. Wainwright, particularly when it is you who is completely at fault," he replied.

Devon blinked in surprise "I beg your pardon?"

"You trespassed upon my day and caused your own mishap, setting into motion the entire 'incident,' as you call it."

Devon's brow went up. "You are the marshal," she pointed out tersely. "It is your duty to protect the citizens of this town, of which I am one, and I was in need of your service that day. I am not to blame that you decided to put a day of leisure ahead of your duty."

Cort folded his arms across his chest in an uncompromising stance. "Tell me, Mrs. Wainwright, how many times did you and Miss Ryan hear these noises?"

"Three, maybe four times."

"Yet, you said nothing to me or to my deputy then."

"Well, no. We didn't want to appear odd."

"You didn't mind appearing odd when you trespassed upon my day of leisure. What was the emergency then?" he demanded to know.

Devon stood her ground. "With talk of rats and snakes in the house, I thought there cause enough for concern that should not go unaddressed for another day."

"Have you or Miss Ryan heard noises since then?"

"Well, no."

"Have you found any rats in the traps?"

"Miss Primrose says not," Devon admitted. "But Bridget and I did not imagine those sounds, and it was not the sounds of a house set- tling. Nor did I imagine those 'other things,' strange as they may seem," she added defensively. "And things have disappeared."

Cort continued to regard her with skepticism. "Brett and I have been through every inch of that house and found nothing suspicious, Mrs. Wainwright."

Devon drew herself up. "I am not the kind of woman who imagines things, Marshal." She paused, reluctant to invite more skepticism. "I—I have felt that I am being watched when I walk down the hall upstairs."

She looked up at him, daring him to belittle her fear or to chalk it up to flights of fantasy. Strangely enough, he didn't do either. He could relate to such an instinct. It had saved his life upon occasion during the war.

"I'll tell Jasper and Brett to keep a close eye on the house and to frequently inspect the premises."

Devon nodded. "Thank you. Regarding our other matter, Marshal, do we have a truce?"

Cort was silent. Everything still rankled him about the matter from the loss of his rod to her refusal to accept full responsibility for the incident.

"Marshal, do we have an agreement?" she asked again.

"We have no agreement on the truth, Mrs. Wainwright, but I will agree to a truce on the facts," he replied.

Devon looked at him, wary. "What facts?"

"That I lost my fishing rod, and you fell into the river."

"What is the difference?"

"As a lawman, I have come to realize that people can view the same truth differently. Facts, however, are indisputable—even to you."

Devon considered that for a moment. "Well, I suppose that shall have to suffice."

She bit her lip, a sign that Cort came to recognize when she was bothered.

"Is there something else weighing on you, Mrs. Wainwright?"

She gave a little self-conscious laugh. "I-I've just been a little jittery with all the strange occurrences lately...and that outlaw is still out there."

Cort took his hat and sheepskin coat from the peg. "It is getting dark. I'll see you home."

She was readily agreeable to the idea. "Yes, thank you."

They walked down the street. The air was refreshingly cold and crisp. It was quiet. They didn't talk. But it was one of those seemingly inconsequential times that held one in the moment, a moment the mind would choose to hold in its memory banks for no apparent good reason.

Devon glanced over at Cort, once again struck by the differences between him and Matthew Chandler. Matt was fun, witty, charming. She liked being with him. He made her laugh and lightened her mood.

But Cort Templeton was who people went to with their problems. He was steady, intuitive, stalwart. Notwithstanding the fact that he was a lawman, one felt a sense of trust and security in his presence—including her, and she felt herself relax for the first time in days.

"You have an unusual first name," she remarked.

"It's short for Cortland—a family name," he replied. "My name is John Cortland Templeton, but I've been called Cort for as long as I can remember. I suppose to distinguish me from my father whose name was also John. What about you? Devon isn't a common name."

"The name comes not from anything as illustrious as a family name, which if you knew my mother, would surprise you," said Devon with a wry smile. "I am named for a county in southern England where my mother visited a seaside resort. Apparently, it had made quite a favorable impression on her."

"It suits you," remarked Cort, matter-of-factly.

Devon glanced at him, not sure if that was a compliment or not.

They arrived at the house then. She expected him to leave her at the gate, but he walked her up to the door. Both reached for the doorknob at the same time, and his large hand covered hers. She pulled her hand away, but it was another one of those small moments that resonates. One couldn't say why exactly. It just did.

When Cort opened the door for her, she looked up to thank him for walking her home, but her gaze became locked in his and the words didn't come. For a moment, she thought he was going to kiss her, and, in that instant, he had entertained the thought. But then he touched the brim of his hat and bid her a good night—discretion being the better part of valor.

Devon entered the house feeling relieved, confused, and ultimately disappointed.

CHAPTER TWENTY-TWO

Ghost in the House?

Devon groaned and ran a hand across her forehead. She had a thumping headache. She appeared to have slept the sleep of the dead but awoke unrefreshed and groggy. It had been much like this for the past three days. Bridget complained of the malaise as well, but Miss Primrose seemed unscathed. Thus, Devon concluded that she and Bridget still must be suffering the effects of the high altitude.

She donned a skirt and blouse and twisted her hair into a coil, pinning it in place at the nape of her neck, more and more, adopting the casual, more practical fashion of the other women in town.

When she went to the bureau to get her watch pin, Devon wrinkled her brow, perplexed. She was certain she had put it there when she had undressed for bed last night. She looked around the room and didn't find it. Something else gone missing for the marshal to be skeptical about, she thought irritably. A small part of her was beginning to wonder if, with so many things on her mind, she was misplacing items.

Devon left the suite. As she walked down the hall, she slowed to a stop. The hair on the back of her neck rose. It was that unmistakable feeling again of being watched. Then she heard a creaking sound. She looked around her, but nothing seemed untoward, and she continued on to the staircase. She started to place a hand on the banister, when she suddenly felt dizzy and closed her eyes. In the next instant, she was sailing through the air.

Bridget and Miss Primrose heard her scream and ran into the foyer. When they found Devon lying half conscious and moaning on the landing midway down the staircase, Bridget and the teacher rushed up the steps to her.

"Miss Devon," cried Bridget. "Miss Devon, are you alright?"

"Don't move her. Get the doctor," said Miss Primrose, when Devon didn't respond. "Hurry!"

Bridget ran down the stairs and out the door.

As the children ventured into the foyer to see what had happened, Miss Primrose firmly instructed them to return to their studies in the parlor.

Dr. Morse arrived and hurried up to the landing. Devon had lost consciousness now, and he was in the process of doing a cursory examination when Cort rushed in with Bridget close behind him. Miss Primrose stepped aside and went to calm her students.

"Miss Ryan said Mrs. Wainwright had an accident," said Cort.

The doctor looked up. "She appears to have fallen down the stairs. It's good you are here. I need you to carry her up to her bed so I can conduct a better examination."

Cort took the stairs two at a time up to the landing.

When he bent down to pick Devon up, the doctor cautioned him. "Try not to jostle her. I won't know if she has any broken ribs until Miss Ryan gets the corset off her. Can't chance a punctured lung if she does."

Cort carefully lifted her in his arms and carried her up to her suite, laying her on the bed with as little movement as possible. She was pale and still.

Bridget sniffed back tears. "Shouldn't you try to wake her, Doctor?"

"Not yet. I need you to remove Mrs. Wainwright's blouse and corset."

Bridget hesitated and looked at Cort.

"I'll wait outside in the hall," he said.

While he waited, he walked over to the staircase and checked out the carpet runner. There were no loose edges, and if she tripped before taking her first step on the stair, the carpet couldn't have been at fault. The runner stopped with the last step.

When Cort returned to the suite, Dr. Morse was coming from the sleeping room. "How is she?" he asked. "Is she awake?"

"Yeah. The young lady is very lucky," replied the doctor. "She has a nasty bump on the head and a sprained wrist but no broken bones as I can find. I told Miss Ryan to keep an eye on her for a few days to make sure she doesn't have a concussion. She'll be feeling mighty sore and bruised for awhile."

"Can I talk with her?"

"Yeah, but don't stay long. I'll stop in tomorrow." The doctor paused and gave Cort a meaningful look. "Seems like we've been down this path before. First, Sadie and now her niece."

Cort nodded. He had been thinking the same thing. "I'll keep a close watch on her."

The doctor left, and Cort walked into the sleeping room. "Miss Ryan, I would like to speak with Mrs. Wainwright alone."

Bridget hesitated. "It isn't proper for a gentleman to be in a lady's room with her alone, sir."

"It's all right, Bridget," intervened Devon. "Tell the children that I am sorry to miss the music lesson today."

Bridget glanced at Cort, still uneasy with the impropriety, and reluctantly left the room with the promise—or warning—that she would be back soon.

When they were alone, Cort pulled up a chair next to the bed and sat down. "Miss Ryan is quite the protective bulldog."

"One of the duties of a lady's companion is to safeguard her mistress' reputation. Bridget takes her job quite seriously," said Devon with a touch of humor in her voice.

"So it would seem," remarked Cort. "What happened, Mrs. Wainwright?"

Devon put a hand to her head and winced. "I don't know. I became dizzy as I was about to descend the stairs."

"You became dizzy?"

"I haven't been feeling well of late…Bridget, too. I think we must have mountain sickness again."

"Do you remember anything more?" asked Templeton.

She started to shake her head when a strange look came over her face. "I think someone may have pushed me down the stairs."

"Did you see anyone?"

"No, but I heard a noise in the hall—a creaking sound."

"Like a door opening?"

"I can't say for certain."

It was obvious she was tiring.

Cort stood up. "I'll leave you to rest now. Perhaps you'll remember more tomorrow."

When Templeton returned to the office, Brett was waiting for him.

"How is Mrs. Wainwright?" he asked.

"She'll be pretty sore, but there are no broken bones."

"You have that look," said Brett.

"What look?"

"The look that says somethin' ain't right."

Cort took off his coat and hat and hung them on the peg. "Mrs. Wainwright thinks that someone may have pushed her down the stairs."

"Who? A student playing a prank?"

"She doesn't know. She heard something but didn't see anyone."

Brett wrinkled his brow, baffled. "There ain't nowhere to hide. If someone was there, Mrs. Wainwright would have had to see him, especially in daylight. I s'pose someone could have come out of one of the rooms and crept up on her."

"She mentioned before she felt that someone was watching her when she walked down the hall," recounted Cort.

"But we searched that house from top to bottom. Unless—" Brett's eyes widened in wonder. "Do you think it was the ghost?"

Cort snorted. "There is no ghost, Brett."

"But miners claim to see the ghost of that prostitute who was strangled some years back."

"Miners see a lot of strange things after a few drinks," replied Templeton dryly. "Mrs. Wainwright also mentioned that she and Miss Ryan have been feeling unwell of late."

"Yeah, Bridget said she wakes up feelin' tired and out of sorts in the mornin'. But she says she feels better in a few hours. Must be an illness goin' around."

"Maybe. Send a telegraph to Nettie. Find out when she's coming back," said Cort.

CHAPTER TWENTY-THREE

A Score to Settle

The next afternoon, Templeton went back to the house and met Chandler coming down the steps from the front porch.

"What brings you here?" inquired Chandler, his eyes narrowing with suspicion.

"I might ask you the same thing," said Cort.

"I heard about Devon's accident," he replied. "I came to see that she is all right. Why are you here?"

"Routine investigation."

"Why are you investigating a fall down the stairs?"

"Perhaps you should talk with Mrs. Wainwright," said Cort.

"I did. She said she tripped and fell." Chandler leveled a hard gaze on the marshal. "I intend to marry Devon. If you think something else is at work, I want to know of it."

"That is between you and Mrs. Wainwright," said Cort.

He sidestepped the gambler and walked up the steps to the porch in a dour mood now. Matt Chandler had that effect on him, and the man's announcement that he intended to marry Devon only fueled his aggravation. Now, he would have both Nettie and Pearl on his back to do something to thwart it.

Bridget opened the door to him. When Cort entered the house, he heard a chorus of children singing and moved to the doorway of the parlor. The students were practicing a song for the Christmas concert. Their performance was animated, the enjoyment plain to see on their faces as they made their way through an arrangement of "One Horse Open Sleigh."

Cort was surprised by how good they sounded. And he watched as Devon, a bandage wrapped around her sprained wrist, accompanied the students on the piano while another student played a harmonica. Sometimes she rose from the bench to wave a hand to direct them while continuing to play the melody on the piano with the other hand. Cort had never guessed that she was musically inclined.

When the song ended, she smiled, and her eyes shone with pride. "Very good, students. Tomorrow, we shall take up 'Silent Night.' Now, it is time to go back to your studies."

The children groaned and reluctantly began to disperse.

Cort entered the parlor. "I didn't know there was so much talent in Blue Springs," he remarked.

Devon looked up at him unguarded, her features luminous. At this moment, she reminded him of Jenny, and he felt a tug on his heart.

"Yes, the children have worked very hard," she said, pulling him back from the past.

"I would say that the teacher has a good deal to do with it," replied Cort.

Devon blushed and gave a self-conscious laugh. "Thank you, sir."

She got up and began to gather the students' sheets of music.

"How long have you played the piano?" he asked.

"Since I was a child," replied Devon. "Playing a musical instrument well is a prerequisite to being a lady in Boston society. Did my aunt play the piano, or was it just a prop?"

"Sadie played very well," he replied. "She employed a pianist, but she often played and sang for the guests herself."

Devon was silent for a moment as she digested another piece of information about her aunt that she hadn't known.

"Some of the students are quite musically gifted," she said. "I've decided to use part of my aunt's money to purchase a couple of guitars and violins to develop their talents."

"Fiddles," corrected Cort.

"What?"

"Out here, we call violins fiddles."

"Oh. Very well…fiddles then. What do you think?"

"I think Sadie would approve."

Devon stiffened. "I do not seek my aunt's approval, Marshal."

"Your pardon, Mrs. Wainwright. I think it a good idea."

Devon nodded and let him off the hook. "I can give piano lessons, but I'll need to find people able and willing to teach the other instruments."

"I'm sure you won't have any trouble. From what I've observed, you can twist an arm as well as any of those ladies in the Auxiliary."

Devon laughed. "I shall take that as a compliment, sir. Why are you here, Marshal?"

"I came to see if the night passed without incident," he replied.

"Yes, I believe so. I experienced nothing strange, and Bridget didn't mention anything out of the ordinary."

"How are you feeling?"

"Stiff and sore and my sprained wrist makes it difficult to play the piano, but I'm well."

"Any headaches or blurred vision?"

"You sound like the doctor. My head still hurts from the bump but no headaches or blurred vision." She frowned. "Bridget and I are still plagued with this pesky mountain illness though."

Cort knew that mountain illness could not be the cause of her discomfort after all this time, but he said nothing. Until he could get to the root of the matter, he didn't want to alarm her any further.

He glanced over to see that Miss Primrose was eyeing them as she passed out books to the students. She looked away then and commenced the lesson.

"Has Miss Primrose had any complaints?" asked Cort.

"No, none that she has mentioned," replied Devon.

"I'll have Brett and Jasper continue to keep a close eye on the house," said Templeton.

"Thank you, Marshal. I must confess to still feeling a bit uneasy…. Is there something else?" she asked when he was slow to leave.

Cort hesitated. "I-uh-ran into Chandler leaving the house."

"Yes, he heard about the accident and came to see if I was sound."

"I gathered you hadn't told him that you thought you were pushed down the stairs."

"Good heavens no," said Devon. "He was quite solicitous—too much so. If he thought me to be in jeopardy, I fear he would be constantly underfoot."

Cort felt buoyed that there seemed to be a crack developing in their relationship.

"But I suppose I shouldn't be too cross with him," continued Devon, dashing his hope. "Matt has generously offered me the use of his establishment for the children's concert."

"Why not have the concert at the church?" suggested Cort.

"The dance hall has a stage and is more conducive to performances," she replied, her tone indicating that the matter was settled.

"Forgive me, Mrs. Wainwright, but there was a day not so long ago when you wouldn't have considered such an offer," he pointed out.

"Yes, yes, I know. I seem to be doing a lot of things I wouldn't normally do since coming to Blue Springs, Mr. Templeton."

"I am not sure how the ladies of the town are going to feel about stepping foot inside a dance hall and saloon or allowing their children to perform there," noted Cort.

"They don't seem to have a problem sending their children to school in a house that was not so long ago a bordello," countered Devon. "And the ladies don't seem to have a problem with attending court trials and town meetings in the saloon."

"You have a point," conceded Cort. "But human nature isn't always logical."

"Well, perhaps, it won't be such a hard line to cross if the establishment doesn't look like a dance hall and saloon."

"What would it look like, Mrs. Wainwright?"

"A concert hall, of course."

As she launched into the changes she would make to disguise the venue, Cort was fairly certain that Chandler hadn't intended for her to close his business for a day to transform the place into a concert hall, but he refrained from further comment on the subject.

"Nettie is returning next week," he informed her. "Got a wire from her this morning."

Devon's face lit up. "Oh, I shall tell Bridget at once. The restaurant is becoming tiring, not to mention an onerous expense. And neither Bridget nor I have enjoyed a good pot of tea in this house since Nettie left. The drink always comes out with a bitter taste…. How difficult can it be to steep a proper pot of tea?" she mused aloud." Devon laughed. "I never imagined I would miss that woman."

Cort chuckled. "Nettie has that effect."

Templeton looked across the room. All the children seemed to be well engaged. Some were writing and drawing, while Bridget read to a group of younger children in a far corner of the room. Miss Primrose was teaching math to the older students. His gaze rested on her for a few more minutes before returning to Devon.

"I'll send over Brett or Jasper to escort you ladies from the restaurant tonight and to check the house before leaving."

"Thank you, Marshal."

When Cort returned to the office, he was in a pensive mood. He looked at Brett. "You might want to clean up later. You are escorting Mrs. Wainwright, Miss Ryan, and Miss Primrose home from the restaurant this evening."

Brett jumped up from the desk. "Yes, sir. I should probably get a haircut and—"

"I said later. You'll have plenty of time for that." Cort took off his hat and coat and sat down at the desk. "What do you know about Miss Primrose?" he asked at length.

Brett scratched his head. "Not much. Just that she took over as the teacher after Amanda Rigby left."

"How long has she been in town?"

"I don't know. A lot of people been comin' into the area, and she ain't someone as you would notice, if you know what I mean."

Cort knew exactly what his deputy meant. He put the teacher's age near 40. She was plain with wire-rim spectacles, conservative in manner and dress—an unassuming spinster who blended into the background.

"Brett, go talk to the ladies in the Auxiliary. Find out what they know about Miss Primrose—where she came from, when she came to Blue Springs."

"Why?"

"Just curious…. Did you telegraph Pueblo City marshals' office?"

Brett nodded. "There ain't been any sightings of Hagen. Probably went to ground for the winter like ya figured."

Cort sat down at the desk, thoughtful. "You said that Belle wanted to know everything the Johns told her girls."

"Yeah. Accordin' to Josie, Belle said information was gold. You sure put a stop to that." Brett chuckled. "Your talk with Calvin put the fear of God in him. He ain't been to the Golden Nugget since."

"Belle and Hagen are only links in a chain," said Cort.

The school day finally ended; the children were gone. Devon and Bridget prepared to make the walk to the restaurant for supper and were in the foyer putting on their hats and coats.

"Miss Primrose, will you soon be ready to leave?" Devon called up the stairs.

Miss Primrose appeared at the top of the staircase. "I'm sorry, Mrs. Wainwright. Please go on without me. I am not feeling well."

"Oh. Shall I have the doctor call on you?"

"No, no. I fear I must be suffering the same malaise as you and Bridget. I have a dreadful headache. I'm sure I will feel better tomorrow."

"That is strange," remarked Devon. "It usually strikes Bridget and me in the morning upon awakening. Perhaps you just need some rest. The plight of the schoolteacher can be stressful. We'll bring you back some supper."

As Devon and Bridget stepped onto the porch, they clutched their cloaks tighter and bowed their heads against the wind.

"I don't think I shall ever get used to this wind and dust," grumbled Devon, putting a hand to her hat to hold it in place.

"It will be better when the snows start," said Bridget.

Devon glanced at her companion in annoyance. Sometimes she wanted to strangle the girl for her optimism. "No, Bridget, it will not be better. If we are lucky, it will just be tolerable."

Once comfortably seated inside the restaurant, Devon was in a better mood. The menu offered more variety this evening, and her disposition only improved with her meal. She found the meat pie quite tasty and the chocolate cake and tea very much to her liking.

"Honestly, Bridget, I don't know why we cannot seem to brew a pot of tea like this ourselves," she commented, pouring them each a second cup.

"Perhaps it has something to do with the tea we are using," suggested Bridget.

"I purchase it from the general store. Mrs. Walker said it is what everyone else uses. I shall ask Rosie what her secret is."

"I see that you have recovered from your accident, Mrs. Wainwright. One should take better care on the stairs," said a female voice.

Devon grimaced and glanced up at Belle Waters. "Thank you for your concern," she replied, facetiously.

She was about to look away in a sign of dismissal, when her eye caught the emerald and diamond brooch pinned to Belle's jacket.

"Miss Waters, I can't help noticing your brooch. It is quite lovely. How did you acquire it?"

The fixed smile on Belle's face wavered slightly. "I'm glad you like it, Mrs. Wainwright. It was a present from Matt. Good evening, ladies."

When Belle walked away, Bridget made a face. "That woman can curdle cream. Miss Devon, are you alright? Ye look a wee bit pale."

"Bridget, that brooch Belle is wearing...I am certain that my aunt was wearing one just like it in a photograph I viewed of her."

Bridget looked at Devon in perplexity. "There kenna be two—" Her eyes suddenly widened. "Oh miss, do ye think Mr. Chandler stole yer aunt's jewelry? I kenna imagine him to be a thief."

"Apparently, we don't know Mr. Chandler as well as we thought," said Devon, recalling all the warnings from Nettie and Cort not to trust him.

"He seems to enjoy giving jewelry to women, doesn't he? The diamond earrings he tried to give me probably belonged to my aunt, too," she added cynically.

"We should tell the marshal, miss."

Devon nodded. She paid the bill, and they were preparing to leave, when Bridget gasped. "Miss Devon, Mr. Chandler just come in. What'll we do?"

"Turn away," said Devon, putting up a hand to shield the side of her face. "Maybe he won't notice us."

"He's coming this way," squeaked Bridget.

"Don't look," whispered Devon.

Both girls jumped at the sound of his voice.

"Devon...Miss Ryan. I see that fortune finds me this evening as well," he said.

Devon looked up at Chandler with a strained smile. "Good evening, Matt. I'm surprised to see you here when you have such a wonderful cook."

"Variety is the spice of life," he quipped. "May I join you, ladies?"

"Bridget and I are just leaving," said Devon, her tone a bit brusque.

Chandler regarded her quizzically. "Is something wrong, Devon? You seem on edge."

"It has been a trying day, Matt."

"Well, perhaps I can make it better. Permit me to see you ladies home. I have something to discuss with you in private, Devon."

"I believe Miss Waters is waiting to dine with you," she said.

Chandler looked across the room to see Belle watching them and smiled to himself, taking Devon's churlish mood to be a touch of jealousy.

"It is merely coincidence that finds Belle and me here at the same time," he assured her.

"I wouldn't want to delay your supper, Matt."

"Food is of no consequence, my dear, when I can be in your company."

"Madam, did you forget? Marshal Templeton is sending a deputy to walk us to the house," Bridget reminded her mistress. "He should be coming any minute now."

Chandler smiled. "Even better. The deputy can escort Miss Ryan, and I can escort you, Devon, and we can have that private talk."

"I would prefer that we talk at another time, Matt. "I am feeling tired and intend to retire early this evening."

Chandler regarded her more intently. Something was definitely off with her. "Of course, my dear. I shall leave you to your evening."

At the marshal's office, Brett pulled out his watch and checked the time. "Bridget, Miss Primrose, and Mrs. Wainwright must be finished with their supper by now. They been in the restaurant for over an hour. I'll go and see if they're ready to leave."

Cort nodded absently, still trying to put together a puzzle with pieces that didn't seem to fit. Brett's investigation into Miss Primrose yielded little information. When it came right down to it, the ladies in the Auxiliary knew very little about their teacher. When the woman had offered to fill in until a new teacher arrived, they didn't look a gift horse in the mouth.

"Brett, tell Miss Primrose to step in here. I would like a word with her. I'll walk her home afterwards."

"Sure thing."

Brett donned his hat and coat and pulled open the door. As he walked out, there came a volley of rifle shots. Cort grabbed his gun from the drawer, doused the light, and ran outside. Bullets whizzed past him, and he dove behind a barrel.

"Get off the street!" he shouted to by-standers.

People screamed and darted for cover.

"Brett, are you hit?" called Cort, searching the darkness for any sign of the shooter's whereabouts.

Brett groaned. "Yeah. Sure hope it ain't my gut."

"Hold on," said Cort. "Don't move."

As he started to make his way to Sanger, shots whizzed past him again, holding him at bay. Then the firing ceased. Calculating that the ambusher was stopping to reload, Templeton darted across the street rapidly firing his revolver into the alley from where he had seen smoke from the rifle fire. When he stopped to reload, he heard the sound of a horse gallop off.

After several minutes of tense silence, people hesitantly emerged from the saloon and other buildings.

Inside the restaurant, Devon rushed to the window, elbowing her way through the patrons to get a clear view. When she saw a crowd gathering in front of the marshal's office, her heart dropped.

"No, no…dear God, not again," she whimpered to herself.

Bridget came up behind her. "What is it?"

"I don't know. Wait here," said Devon.

"But Miss Devon—"

"Bridget, stay here," she repeated firmly.

As Devon raced across the street to the jail, the sickening feeling at the pit of her stomach intensified. "What happened?" she asked an onlooker.

"The marshal and Deputy Sanger were ambushed. Someone said that one of 'em is dead," he reported.

Devon blanched. Desperately, she pushed her way through the crowd to the front and nearly swooned with relief when she saw Cort. He appeared to be unhurt and was kneeling beside his deputy, who lay deathly still. Devon's heart lurched.

Dr. Morse came running up to the scene and stooped down to examine Brett. Someone held a lantern high, and Devon could see that the deputy's coat was soaked with blood and that he was unresponsive.

When the doctor stood up, she grabbed his arm. "Is he…is he dead?" she asked haltingly.

Morse shook his head. "No, but close to it." He turned to some onlookers. "Get this man to my office…quickly. Mrs. Wainwright, come with me. Since Nettie isn't here, you will have to assist me."

Devon paled. "But I can't. I have never done anything like this. I don't know what to do."

"If you want this young man to live, you'll learn," he responded tersely.

Devon heard Bridget cry out and turned to see her running up to the scene. The men were carrying Brett away, and Devon quickly moved to intercept her, enfolding her in her arms before she could get any closer.

"Is that Brett? Is he dead? Someone said he's dead," she cried, struggling to break free. "Let go of me! I have to go to him."

Devon gave her a little shake to focus her attention. "Bridget, listen to me. Brett is alive, but Dr. Morse needs my help. Go home and wait there."

"No! I'm coming, too. I have to be with him."

"Mrs. Wainwright!" shouted the doctor. "Now, if you please."

Devon looked at Bridget. "All right, you can come, but you must calm down and stay out of the way."

Bridget choked back sobs. "I promise."

Hand-in-hand, they ran down the street to the doctor's office and rushed inside. Bridget reluctantly remained in the outer room. Devon entered the back room and shut the door.

Brett was lying unconscious on the table, looking pale. Templeton stood to one side, his features grim.

"Cort, light all the lamps. Mrs. Wainwright, take off your coat and roll up your sleeves," ordered the doctor. He handed her a bottle of liquid labeled as antiseptic. "Rinse up to your elbows in that bowl, and don't touch anything after you do."

Cort and Devon quickly set about their tasks. When everything was ready, Devon watched tensely as the doctor opened Brett's coat and vest. She had to look away for a moment at the sight of so much blood. Everything was so saturated it was difficult to know the color of the clothing.

Dr. Morse cut away the shirt and the union suit to reveal two bullet wounds—one at the edge of the ribs on the right side and the other on the lefthand side at the waist—Devon's stomach churned.

She started to move away, but Cort clamped a hand over her shoulder to stay her. "Buck up, Mrs. Wainwright. Brett's life depends upon it."

That was a terrifying thought to Devon. No one had ever depended upon her for anything of significance before, most certainly never for a life. And she looked up at him with fear and uncertainty in her eyes.

"You can do this," he said.

Devon closed her eyes to draw strength and took a deep breath. When she met his gaze again, she nodded that she was ready, and Cort removed his hand from her shoulder.

"How bad is it, Doc?" he asked tensely.

"Can't say as yet," replied the doctor. "We have to get this bleeding stopped. The boy has lost a lot of blood. Mrs. Wainwright, fetch those cloths over there and hold them tightly against the wounds."

Devon sucked in her breath as blood seeped through the coverings to stain her fingers.

"More pressure," instructed the doctor. "That's it. Cort, help me get these clothes off Brett."

Cort helped Morse strip the young deputy to the waist. Brett moaned a few times, and his eyes opened once when they had to jostle him to cut around the top of the long johns to remove the covering.

"These damn union suits don't make a doctor's job easy," he muttered. "Pressure, Mrs. Wainwright…keep the pressure on."

"What are you waiting for, Doc?" demanded Templeton, when the doctor made no further movements.

"Patience, son, patience," responded Morse. "The bullets aren't going anywhere, but if we don't stem the bleeding first, it won't make a tinker's damn. How are we doing, Mrs. Wainwright?"

Devon lifted the cloth. "It seems to be ebbing."

After several more tense minutes, Dr. Morse rinsed his hands and surgical instruments with the antiseptic. "Never let anyone near you if you have an open wound without doing this first, Mrs. Wainwright," he lectured. "I learned this in the war from a brilliant doctor. Nobody believed him that unsanitized instruments and dirty hands posed more of a threat than bullets until they saw how few cases of infection he had. Made a believer out of me…. Now to work."

Devon stepped aside when the doctor approached the table. He removed the cloths, wiped away the blood, and cleansed the wounds with the antiseptic.

"Looks like we are in luck with this one," he said. "The bullet went through the flesh on his left side…just missed the intestines. But this other one—" He frowned. "This one on the right could be a problem. It may have damaged the liver."

Devon had to look away again as the doctor gently probed the hole with his finger. Morse grunted and reached for a long, thin instrument with a small porcelain ball on the end.

"Cort, hold Brett down in case he starts to come around again. Don't let him move. Can't risk that bullet going deeper."

Cort went to the head of the table and put his hands on his deputy's shoulders. "Go ahead, Doc."

The doctor carefully threaded the instrument into the wound.

"I've hit something," he said. He slowly twirled the instrument. "If this is the bullet, the knob will have lead markings on it. Never cared much for the French, but this is a handy little instrument they make. They call it the Nelaton probe…named after some doctor who invented it—"

"Doc…" said Cort, his tone impatient.

"Sorry. I find talking eases the tension."

Morse removed the probe. Brett started to stir and moan, and Cort increased the pressure of his hands on Brett's shoulders.

"Mrs. Wainwright, fashion that piece of cloth into a cone and place the open end over Brett's nose and mouth. Then slowly administer chloroform a drop at a time to the tip of the cone until he passes out," instructed Morse.

Devon did as she was told.

"What does the probe say?" asked Cort.

The doctor looked at the ball. "It's the bullet, and it isn't in as deep as I feared. Brett's coat probably slowed it some."

When Brett was still, the doctor reached for the forceps. "Cort, hold that lamp higher."

Slowly, Morse inserted the long, thin, serrated blades into the wound and deftly pulled out the bullet. He probed the wound further with his fingers for debris.

The doctor gestured to Devon, and she cleaned away more blood.

He picked up a magnifying glass and peered into the bullet holes. "They look clean, but only time will tell. No telling what a bullet can pull in with it. All it takes is a strand of thread from a shirt or a tiny piece of debris stirred up by the other shots to cause an infection."

Morse poured antiseptic into the wounds, suctioned them to decrease the risk, and applied dressings. "Cort, give me a hand with the bandage."

Templeton helped the doctor wrap a bandage around Brett's chest to hold the dressings in place.

"Well, that's all we can do for now," he said. "There may be some bruising to the liver. We'll need to keep a close watch."

He walked over to a basin to wash his hands again. "How's the arm, Cort…still pain you to lift it?"

Cort glanced at Devon and moved closer to the doctor. "Some," he acknowledged in low voice.

"Keep working to strengthen it. How's your aim?"

"I'm fine, Doc," said Cort, his brusque tone cutting off further inquiry of it.

Morse nodded and passed a hand wearily across his face. "I need someone to sit with Brett for a while. I've been up these past two nights waiting for the Ferguson baby to make his entrance into the world. I have to get some sleep."

"Bridget and I will sit with Deputy Sanger," said Devon, leaving Brett's side.

She looked at Cort. "Is this one of those instances in life I shouldn't try to protect Bridget from?" she asked sharply. "Sometimes the cost of doing nothing is too high, Marshal." With that, she strode from the room.

Morse went to a cabinet, took out a bottle of whiskey and poured two drinks. "What was that all about?" he asked, handing a glass to Templeton.

"She isn't in favor of Brett courting Miss Ryan. She thinks his job is too dangerous," replied Cort. He swigged his whiskey. "I should have foreseen this, Doc."

Morse snorted. "How?"

"I knew Hagen was out there and had sworn vengeance against me. I underestimated his determination to make good on the threat. And Brett paid the price."

"Brett knows the cost of being a lawman, and he isn't dead," said Morse, refilling their glasses. "How do you know it was Hagen? It was dark out there. Did you see him?"

Cort shook his head, his features taut. "I know it was him. Ambush is his style."

"Are you going after him?"

Templeton nodded. "At first light."

Bridget rushed in then. She came to an abrupt halt and gasped when she saw Brett lying on the table still and pale and the bloody clothes and cloths lying about.

"He's just under the influence of chloroform," the doctor assured her.

He pulled up a chair for her, and she sat down and took Brett's hand. As she gazed at him, her lower lip quivered with emotion.

Cort finished his drink and went to the reception room to talk with Devon. He found it empty and returned to the treatment room.

"Miss Ryan, where is Mrs. Wainwright?" he asked.

"She went to the house to tell Miss Primrose what has happened," replied Bridget, her eyes fixed on Brett.

"Didn't Miss Primrose accompany you to dinner?"

"She said she wasn't feeling well and stayed back."

Cort looked at Morse. "I'm going back to the office. Let me know if anything changes with Brett."

The doctor nodded.

As Templeton walked back to the office, a little voice inside his head became more insistent that something wasn't right.

Jasper came running up to him. "Marshal, how's Brett?"

"Doc thinks he has a good chance," said Cort. "Miss Ryan is with him now."

Jasper shook his head. "I shoulda been there."

"It was your night off, Jasper. If you had been there, you might have been shot, too. You're my only deputy. I need you to be vigilant."

"Was it Hagen?"

Templeton nodded. "I'm sure of it."

"What do you want me to do?"

"Go to the office and wait for me," instructed Cort. "I'm going to Mrs. Wainwright's house to check on her and Miss Primrose."

"Yes, sir."

Cort crossed the street and hurried to the house. He leaped up the steps to the porch and knocked on the door. When no one answered, he opened it and walked inside. The house was quiet.

"Mrs. Wainwright, Miss Primrose," he called out.

When he was met with silence, he made his way through the first floor. Finding no one, he vaulted up the stairs, continuing to call out. When still no one answered, the uneasy feeling increased. One by one, he checked the rooms. There was no sign of either woman.

Cort returned to the kitchen. There was an unfinished cup of tea on the table. Remembering that Devon had complained about the tea, he picked up the cup and took a sip from it. The drink tasted sweet and bitter.

His eye went to the sugar bowl. He put a dab of sugar on his finger and tasted it. He could detect the same distinctive bittersweet flavor that was in the tea. Laudanum.

It was usually mixed with alcohol or honey to make it more palatable. Lacing it with the sugar probably masked the bitter taste just enough to not raise suspicion. When the sweetener was put into the tea, it would make it seem that whatever bitterness was detected was from the tea itself. Mrs. Wainwright and her companion were not suffering an illness. They were being drugged!

Cort grabbed the bowl of sugar and returned to the doctor's office. He found Bridget still sitting anxiously beside Brett.

"Any change?" he asked.

Bridget shook her head.

"Brett is young and strong," said Cort. "He'll survive this." He looked around the room. "Where's Doc?"

"He went upstairs to sleep."

Cort hesitated, reluctant to stress Bridget any further, but he needed answers. "Miss Ryan, Mrs. Wainwright and Miss Primrose were not at the house. Do you know where they might have gone?" he asked.

Bridget looked up at him in surprise. "No. They should be there this time of night."

"Did Miss Primrose usually have tea with you and Mrs. Wainwright?"

"We drank a cup every night together before goin' to bed. We talked about the day and the children."

"Did you and Mrs. Wainwright put sugar in your tea?"

"Yes."

"Did Miss Primrose?"

"No. The bitterness of the tea didn't bother her. She said she liked strong tea—Marshal, is something wrong?" she asked in alarm. "Has something happened to Miss Devon and Miss Primrose?"

"It is probably nothing to worry about, Miss Ryan." Cort set the sugar bowl on a table. "When Doc comes down, ask him to test the sugar."

"Marshal Templeton, if anything happens to Miss Devon—" her voice cracked, and her eyes filled with tears.

Cort could see that she was close to the breaking point, and he put a hand on her shoulder. "You look after Brett, Miss Ryan. I will find Mrs. Wainwright and Miss Primrose."

His deep voice was reassuring, and Bridget took comfort from it. Cort wished he felt as confident as he sounded, but he took heart in the fact that he found no blood anywhere.

Cort picked up a lantern at the office and returned to the the house. He searched the grounds and found wagon tracks at the back of the property near doors to a root cellar. A rusty padlock on the doors was broken. His eyes narrowed as he surveyed the area. It was strange to have the entrance to a root cellar this far from the house. This must be a storm shelter, he decided.

Cort entered the house through the back door. He took another quick look around the kitchen. Finding nothing more, he went upstairs and walked into Devon's suite. He could smell her fragrance and felt a twisting in his gut. He made a closer check of the other rooms and found nothing to explain the women's absence.

Cort walked into the hall, the walls of which were covered with wallpaper and decorative molding. When he approached the staircase, his eye caught site of something on the wall. He held the lantern closer and saw that a fragment of material was caught on a nail a foot above the floor.

Cort peered closer and could make out a barely perceptible crack. The molding and wallpaper were cleverly concealing a door, he realized. He pushed on it in a few places before he felt the panel give way and shoved it open. Lifting the lantern high, he entered a small area and saw a staircase. This was obviously where Devon's "ghost" had come from. The question was who was the ghost?

Cort descended the stairs to a tunnel and realized it was an area that was walled off from the rest of the basement. If he hadn't been so quick to dismiss Devon's complaint of noises, he would have noticed that the dimensions of the basement were smaller than they should have been when he had checked out the house, and he cursed his lack of attention.

There were signs of recent use. Cort could see footsteps in the dirt, and it appeared as though one person had been dragged through the passage. His heart lurched. Had Devon or Miss Primrose been hurt? His mind went to the half-finished cup of tea, and he concluded that Devon must have been drugged. He followed the tunnel to where steps led up to the outside doors.

This wasn't a storm shelter. It was a secret passage for the more fastidious clientele who wished to come and go from the parlor house without notice. Sadie had had one in her Baltimore house. Templeton had never guessed that she had one built into this house and wondered why she had never mentioned it to him.

Cort pushed open one of the cellar doors and stepped up into the yard. He looked at the broken padlock again. Sadie must have sealed the passage at some point. Who had unsealed it—why and when?

He looked at the wagon trail again. It led north out of town. He flexed his gun hand, his features set in a grim line as a picture came into clearer focus.

CHAPTER TWENTY-FOUR

Old Enemy, New Ally?

The doors crashed open, and Cort walked grim-faced into the Golden Nugget Saloon. All activity stopped. Everyone went still and a tenseness fell over the room.

Cort looked at the bartender. "Where's Chandler?"

After a moment's hesitation, the man answered, "Upstairs."

All eyes followed the marshal as he vaulted up the steps.

Chandler was going over the day's receipts in his suite with Belle, when Cort kicked open the door and strode in.

The gambler jumped up from behind his desk. "Hells bells, can't you knock, Templeton?!"

"I don't have time for niceties, Chandler. Mrs. Wainwright is missing? Where is she?"

"I don't know—what do you mean she's missing?"

"Come off it, Matt. I know Hagen is responsible, and you're his spy in town. Where did he take her?"

Chandler was taken aback. "Hagen took Devon? Cort, I have nothing to do with that outlaw."

"I figured it out, Matt."

"Figured out what?"

"That the telegraph operator liked to visit one of Belle's girls. That Belle instructed Josie to pump him about the content of the wires he sent and received, then passed the information on to you. You passed it on to Hagen. That's how Hagen always knew when there was a cash box on the stage."

"Whoa, Cort, you're wrong," said Chandler, alarmed at the accusation. "I swear to you I have no connection to Hagen." He turned to a wide-eyed Belle. "What have you been up to, Belle?"

"N-nothing," she stammered.

She gasped when he grabbed hold of her arm and pulled her forward. "Who did you pass the information on to, honey? It sure as hell wasn't me."

Belle shrank from him. "I-I didn't know she was spying for Hagen. Honest, Matt, you have to believe me."

"Who, Belle?"

"I met her when I was comin' from Doc's one day. He wouldn't give me any more laudanum," whimpered Belle. "I was in a bad way. She said she would give it to me whenever I needed it in exchange for information that was going around town."

"You said you were off that stuff."

"I tried, Matt. Honest I did."

"What is the woman's name?" asked Cort impatiently.

Belle shook her head. "I-I don't know. She never said. I didn't ask. She said not to ask questions."

Chandler took her by the arm again. "What does the woman look like?"

"I never saw her face," Belle hurriedly replied. "She always wore a veil over it. She said she was hiding a scar and that's why she lived away from town. People made fun of her in other towns."

"Where did you go to meet her?" quizzed Templeton.

"In a cabin—the old Shipman place. But she isn't there anymore. Please, Matt, you're hurting me," cried Belle.

Chandler unhanded her, and she retreated to a far corner of the room.

"The woman, whoever she is, must have thought you were getting too close and left town," surmised Chandler.

"No, she just changed disguises," said Cort.

"What do you mean?"

"I'm certain that Belle's 'friend' is Miss Primrose."

Chandler looked at the marshal in astonishment. "The schoolteacher? How do you know?"

"She's missing, too. No one seems to really know anything about her, and I found evidence that she's been drugging Miss Ryan and Mrs. Wainwright at night."

"Good God!" exclaimed Chandler. "Why?"

"I discovered an escape passage in the house," explained Templeton. "Sadie had one in her Baltimore establishment."

Chandler nodded. "I remember."

"My guess is Hagen has been using the passage to hide out in the house," continued Cort. "Miss Ryan and Mrs. Wainwright were drugged to keep them from hearing him move about."

Chandler was incredulous. "That outlaw has been in the house all this time without Devon knowing it? If we didn't know of this passage, how did Hagen learn of it?"

Cort looked at Belle. "You used to work for Sadie. You must have known about the passage, Belle. Is that one of the things you told this woman about?"

Belle paled. "I-I don't know. I sometimes don't remember after I've taken some...some medicine." She rubbed her forehead in confusion, trying to recall. "Miss Sadie sealed it a long time ago when she caught gents sneaking out without paying."

Templeton started for the door.

"Where are you going?" asked Chandler.

"To the Shipman place. I found wagon tracks at the house heading for the road in that direction."

"Wait. I'm coming with you."

"I don't need your help, Matt."

"Don't be a fool, Cort. Hagen will be waiting for you if he's there. You don't know if he has recruited more gang members."

"He doesn't know that I have figured the connection."

"Maybe so, but he knows you will figure him for the shooting of your deputy and will come after him," pointed out Chandler. "Why do you think he took Devon?"

Cort hesitated. He knew Chandler was right, and, at this hour of the night, it would take too long to raise a posse.

"I'll get some provisions from the store," he said. "Meet me out front with the horses. Ted knows my horse and saddle."

Cort banged on the door of the general store. Before long, a light went on in the upstairs living quarters and traveled down to the store.

"Hiram, open up."

The store owner peeked cautiously around the edge of the drawn shade, then quickly unlocked the door and opened it.

"Marshal? What's amiss?" he asked in confusion.

"I need some provisions for the trail," replied Cort.

"Now? It's the middle of the night."

"I can't wait until morning, Hiram. Mrs. Wainwright has been abducted."

The proprietor's mouth dropped open. "Who would do such a thing to that nice, pretty lady?"

"It's a long story, and I don't have the time right now."

"What do you need?" asked Hiram, hurrying behind the counter.

"Canteens, beef jerky, biscuits, a bag of oats, and two boxes of shells for the '73 Colt and Winchester."

"Is Jasper raising the town for a posse?" inquired the shopkeeper as he picked the order.

Cort shook his head. "There's no time. Matt Chandler is coming with me."

The store owner raised a brow. Everyone in town knew there was bad blood between the two men. "Anything else?" he asked.

"Yeah. Can you make me up two bedrolls—just tarp and blankets?"

Hiram nodded. "Sure thing."

Chandler was waiting with the horses. They filled the saddlebags with provisions and tied the bedrolls to the back of their saddles.

"Hiram, tell Jasper what has happened and to raise a posse if I'm not back in two days," instructed Templeton.

The shopkeeper nodded. "I'll tell him, Marshal."

With grim purpose, Chandler and Templeton mounted up and galloped off.

CHAPTER TWENTY-FIVE

Miss Primrose

Devon slowly came awake at the sound of voices raised in argument.

"I told you not to bring her," a woman was saying. "She'll slow us down. You know Templeton will come looking for you."

"Maybe for shootin' his deputy, but not for kidnappin' the woman," retorted Hagen smugly. "He'll be searchin' for you. Ya said as how he was gettin' suspicious of ya. He'll think you took her. I wonder which one of us he'll come for first?"

The woman snorted. "What reason would I have to take her?"

"Lawmen collect grudges. Maybe ye're workin' with someone Templeton sent to federal prison."

"Like you?" she shot back sarcastically. "Maybe I'll tell the marshal that you kidnapped the both of us when he catches up with you. I can be very persuasive in case you haven't noticed."

"Shut up and start packin' the supplies," the outlaw snarled.

"Billy, listen to me. There is no one to connect us to this place. By the time Templeton finds her here, we can be out of the territory."

"Snow has likely closed the passes. We'll need her for bargaining."

"That was real smart of you," the woman quipped in a derisive tone. "You couldn't have waited until the spring thaw to try to shoot Templeton?"

"He was gettin' too close...always at the house. It was only a matter of time until he discovered the tunnel and that you weren't no schoolteacher."

Devon groggily sat up on the cot and looked about her in confusion. "Where am I? What has happened?" When her eyes focused on Hagen, she recoiled in fear. "Y-you're that outlaw."

"See, Alice, even she knows me," he gloated.

Devon's attention was drawn to the woman. The glasses were gone, the hair and dress were different, the figure was slimmer, and she appeared younger, but there was something familiar about her.

Devon wrinkled her brow in bewilderment. "Miss Primrose? Is that you?"

Billy laughed. "She ain't Miss Primrose, and she ain't no schoolteacher. This here is Alice Graham."

"I-I don't understand," said Devon.

"She was my eyes and ears in town."

Devon looked at Alice in disbelief. "You're the spy? But why?"

"Billy and me been together for a long time. We met on a wagon train coming West after the war," said Alice, dropping all pretenses.

Devon scoffed. "And you decided to rob stagecoaches?"

"It's a damn sight easier an' more excitin' than farmin' or workin' a claim," interjected Billy. "When mining companies started transportin' payrolls through Blue Springs, Alice figured a plan to learn the schedules."

Devon regarded Alice intently, trying to reconcile the image of a ruthless outlaw with that of the diligent educator. "Perhaps you should have tried acting," she remarked. "Why did you pretend to be a schoolteacher?"

Alice shrugged, her manner matter of fact. "My source of information was becoming unreliable. I needed to move into town without raising suspicion. When I heard that the schoolteacher left, I saw my opportunity."

"Then why burn down the school if—" Devon stopped mid-sentence as the reason came to her. "You burned it down so you could move into the house."

"The lady wins a prize." Alice laughed. "It took some skill to convince those silly women in the Ladies' Auxiliary that a former bordello was the perfect solution to a temporary school. It was their own idea to have you take me in as a border. I couldn't have planned it better."

"Why my house?" questioned Devon.

"The secret passage."

"What secret passage?"

"The one that your aunt had built inside the house so persnickety gents could come and go without notice."

Devon rubbed her forehead, struggling to put all the pieces together in her woozy mind. "The footsteps…the noises—" she looked at Billy. "That was you Bridget and I heard in the house. You stole all the items that have gone missing."

Billy smiled, pleased with his cleverness. "Right under yer noses. That's when Alice started druggin' yer tea at night, so's you wouldn't hear nothin' no more. Couldn't have ya runnin' to Templeton, raisin' suspicion, every time ya heard somethin'."

Devon turned her attention back to Alice. "But you drank the tea, too. I watched you pour it from the same pot."

"I didn't use the sugar. It was laced with laudanum. That's why the tea tasted bitter to you," she explained.

Billy's eyes darkened. "I'd like to see Templeton's face when he finds out I was there the day he searched the place. I shoulda killed him then."

Devon shuddered thinking of all the times that he was in the house listening, watching her, and she never knew.

She turned an accusatory eye on him, "You pushed me down the stairs, didn't you?"

"You was becomin' a problem," said Billy. "And with you gone, Alice could buy the house. The tunnel is a good place to hide from the law and to store the loot…. Only it didn't work out that way," he added, suddenly becoming irritated. He pulled Devon roughly to her feet. "Alice, get them supplies together."

"I only agreed to bring her to buy us time, Billy. We are not taking her with us," she declared.

The outlaw glowered at her. "And I say that we are. She's Templeton's woman."

"That makes her all the more dangerous to us. It's bad enough that you shot his deputy. Isn't that revenge enough?"

"It won't be enough until Templeton is dead," responded Billy in a voice so menacing it sent a chill down Devon's spine. "He has busted my plans for the last time."

"You'll jeopardize the cause," said Alice. "Mr. Goodnight won't be happy about that."

"I can take care of Mr. Goodnight."

She scoffed "You don't know who he is. If you cross him, you won't see him coming—"

Alice suddenly cried out when Hagen viciously slapped her across the face. "Shut yer mouth, woman! Fill that bag with some food and get the canteens."

"I'm not spending the rest of my life in prison or looking over my shoulder just because you have a vendetta against Templeton," she retorted, holding a hand to her bruised cheek.

"Then I guess you'll be the one stayin' behind."

Alice looked at him, incredulous. "After all I've done for you—I'm the brains behind your gang."

"Yeah. And they're all in jail," he sneered. "Maybe you and Templeton are workin' together."

"You bastard!" she spat, lunging at him.

There was a struggle and a deafening explosion, and Devon stared in horror as Alice slumped to the floor.

Hagen looked from the revolver in his hand to his woman lying on the ground. "She shouldna reached for the gun," he said, his voice devoid of emotion.

* * * * *

Cort and Chandler galloped along the river, following the wagon tracks by the light of a moon three-quarters full. A light snow began to fall as the sun peeked above the horizon.

Cort reined in the horse. "The tracks leave the road here. This is the old Shipman place."

He took out a spyglass and scanned the area. In the distance, he saw the cabin shielded by scrubs. "The wagon is out front."

"Do you see anyone?" asked Chandler.

"No. It looks quiet," observed Cort.

"Maybe they're sleeping. We can take them by surprise."

Cort shook his head. "Billy is paranoid. He'll be watching. If he sees anyone coming, Mrs. Wainwright could get hurt. I'm not taking any chances, Matt."

Templeton peered through the spyglass again. "It doesn't look as though anyone is there. I don't see any horses. Just in case Hagen was clever enough to hide them, we'll come in from the north. There are no windows on that side."

They circled to the north side, then dismounted and slowly made their way up to the cabin.

"Cover me," said Cort.

Chandler nodded and trained his rifle on the house, watching tensely as Templeton darted up to the porch. Cort pressed himself against the wall, listening for any sound of movement, then edged to the window and peered in. He suddenly holstered his gun, kicked open the door, and rushed into the cabin with a sense of urgency.

Surprised and alarmed, Chandler ran up to the dwelling. When he entered the cabin, he stopped short at the sight of Cort kneeling over the still form of a woman lying on the floor in a pool of blood.

"Sweet Jesus," he murmured. "It's not—"

Cort shook his head. "It's Miss Primrose."

Chandler let out a sigh of relief. "Is she alive?"

"Just barely," replied Cort. "She's been shot. Hand me that blanket."

Chandler brought him the blanket.

As Cort covered her, Alice moaned, and her eyes fluttered open. "Billy shot me. It hurts."

"Hang on," said Cort. "We'll get you to the doctor. Where did Billy take Mrs. Wainwright?"

"As…As-pen Ridge," she whispered raggedly.

"Whereabouts?" pressed Cort.

"Cabin…mine…" She drifted into unconsciousness.

"What does she mean?" queried Chandler.

"I think she's talking about a miner's cabin. There's an abandoned mine and some cabins in the area. Hagen must be heading for one of them," said Cort. "Make a bed in the wagon, Matt. You're going to have to take Miss Primrose back to town."

Chandler looked at him. "What are you going to do?"

"Go after Hagen."

"Cort, you can't go up there alone. We'll take the woman back to town, get a posse together—"

"There's no time for that, Matt. The snow will cover Hagen's trail before long."

"You know Miss Primrose isn't likely to make it to the doc's," noted Chandler.

"Maybe, but we can't leave her here to die alone," said Cort. "She may have a chance if you take her into town."

Chandler followed Cort outside. He pulled out a bottle of whiskey from his saddlebag. "Here you might need this. It's the good stuff," he said, handing it to him.

Cort put the bottle in his saddlebag. "You always did have a different sense of priorities, Chandler."

"Someone has to remember the important things," he quipped. He untied the bedroll from his horse. "You might need this, too."

Cort secured the extra bedroll to his mount and swung himself into the saddle.

"Find Devon. Bring her back safe," said Chandler.

Templeton nodded and galloped off, a determined glint in his eye.

CHAPTER TWENTY-SIX

Desperate Measures

Now that the shock was wearing off, Devon knew moments of increasing despair. How would Marshal Templeton possibly find her? Had he even discovered that she was missing yet? How long would it be until he figured out that Hagen and Miss Primrose—Alice Graham—were working together?

There was no reason for him to suspect Miss Primrose of anything. He might think her a victim, too. Even more worrisome to Devon was the dispassion that Billy Hagen had shown at the death of a woman who had been his lover and fellow conspirator for several years. How much easier would it be for him to kill her?

Desperately, she looked for some way to escape him, but he kept a tight hold on the reins of her horse. Added to that, Devon was fighting the effects of the opiate that still remained in her system from the drugged tea, as well as the effects of the altitude as they climbed higher into the aspen forest.

At a clearing Hagen stopped and dismounted. "Get down," he ordered.

When she didn't respond fast enough, he pulled her roughly from the horse.

"Start walking…that way," he said with the point of his finger.

They walked single file northeast. The cold air, higher elevation, and the restriction of her corset made it difficult for Devon to breathe. Her lungs burned as she struggled to take in air, and she stumbled and fell to her knees. He yanked her to her feet, and she wobbled again.

"Stop. I have to rest," she said, breathing heavily.

Hagen hesitated. "You got two minutes."

It had stopped snowing, but the clouds continued to block out any warmth from the sun. Devon had no coat, hat or gloves, and her shoes were not weather protected. She sank to the ground cold and wet.

Billy removed the saddlebags and bedrolls from the horses and hid them under a fallen tree.

When he shooed the horses away, Devon cried out. "No! Why did you do that?"

"You'll see," he said.

He yanked her to her feet and took out a Bowie knife.

Devon shrank from him, her heart beating hard against her chest. "Please…please don't kill me," she pleaded.

Hagen laughed harshly. "I ain't gonna kill ya—yet. I want to do that in front of Templeton."

He grabbed hold of her hand, and she cried out as he slashed the knife across her palm. Blood dripped from it, staining the snow crimson.

He pushed her ahead of him. "Start walking. Keep your hand down. Let the blood drip as you go."

They trudged through the snow and had gone only a short distance before the cold restricted the blood flow from her wound. The outlaw stopped to slash her other palm. By now, Devon was numb to all thought and sensation, and she hardly felt the blade slice across the inside of her hand.

Hagen stopped again to cut a bough from a pine tree and directed her to turn around and walk back the way they had come but, this time, paralleling their tracks.

"Don't try anything funny," he warned. "There are animals around here looking for their next meal, and they can smell your blood."

As though to punctuate his warning, there came the screech of a mountain lion all the more terrifying for the echoing effect of the canyon. He laughed when she looked around her wide-eyed with fear.

Hagen gave her a shove to start her moving. "Don't mess up those other tracks."

As they walked back, Hagen brushed away their returning footprints with the pine bough, and Devon realized that he was creating a false path.

Finally, they came to where they had first stopped. While Billy retrieved the saddle bags and bedrolls, Devon sat down on a limb of the fallen tree and reached under the layers of petticoats to tear off strips of material from the bottom of one of her skirts.

"What're ya doin'?" barked Hagen.

"Making bandages to bind the cuts on my hands. I wouldn't want wild animals to smell the blood," she responded facetiously.

He snorted impatiently. "Be quick about it."

"I can't tear the material. I need your knife," said Devon.

"You ain't gettin' my knife. How big a fool do ya think I am?"

"I dare not say," she muttered.

"Watch yer mouth, woman!" Hagen pulled out his knife and made slashes in her petticoat, cutting off several strips for her.

Her fingers were so stiff she had difficulty wrapping her hands.

"Hurry up," barked Hagen.

When Devon finished, she pocketed the excess material.

Hagen yanked her to her feet and shoved the bedrolls at her. "Carry these."

He picked up the saddlebags, and they started out in the same way as before with her in the lead and Hagen following behind, brushing out all signs of their trail with the pine bough. As they passed a bristlecone pine tree, Devon took out a strip of cloth from her pocket and draped it across a branch while Hagen's back was turned. She covertly repeated the gesture on two more trees before running out of material.

Presently, they came to a log cabin built into the side of the ridge. Hagen opened the door and pushed her inside. It was crude with homemade furniture—a table, two chairs, and a bunk bed—but at least, it was protection from the elements—and there was a fireplace.

She collapsed onto a rough wooden chair, tired and numb with cold. "Thank God we can make a fire."

Billy looked at her and sneered. "Do you think I brushed out our tracks for fun?"

"The marshal doesn't know where to look for you. Even if he finds Alice, she's dead and can't tell him anything," said Devon.

"Templeton has the help of the devil. I don't know how, but he'll find his way here, and I sure as hell ain't gonna make it easy for him."

Devon wished she could believe that, but her hope that the marshal would find them had disappeared when Hagen shot Alice, and she considered how many things he would have to tie together to figure out where she was.

"You let the horses go. How do you expect to leave?" she asked.

"The horses will find their way here. If they don't, I'll use the marshal's after I kill him."

Devon's teeth began to chatter. "If we don't light a fire, I'll freeze to death."

Hagen wavered for a minute. She was right. The likelihood of the marshal tracing them there was low, but the marshal was no ordinary man. He seemed to have senses not normal to a person. Billy was still wondering how Templeton had found out about the gang's plan to rob the Denver Assay Office.

"Mr. Hagen—"

"No fire!" he snapped.

"What if the marshal doesn't come?" Devon asked hesitantly.

He looked at her. "You're pretty enough. Maybe I'll keep you around for company."

Devon flinched at the thought. "I would rather die first."

"You best reconsider that. There are a lot of ways to die a painful death, honey, and I know 'em all."

His head bent against the swirling snow, Cort crossed the river at a low, narrow point and rode hard into Browns Canyon.

He had picked up the hoof prints from two horses that he figured Hagen and Devon were riding. The snow was coming down harder, and he pushed his horse as much as he could to cover the ground before the trail was completely obscured.

A few miles into the canyon, Cort saw where Hagen and Devon had taken the north-south trail to the aspen forest. The steep incline was getting slippery. One side of the trail dropped down precipitously to a gulch, and Cort was forced to dismount and walk.

Leading his horse, he came to a broad meadow and an outcropping of rocks. There were signs of a disturbance in the snow. They must have stopped here to rest, he concluded. Luckily, it had stopped snowing, and he could make out a trail of footprints and followed them. He furrowed his brow when he saw the tracks of horses running off in another direction. Something must have spooked them.

As he continued to follow the footprints, he saw the droplets of blood on the snow and all manner of emotions ran through his mind as he feared the worst—something bad had happened to Devon.

He tamped down his concern and forced himself to view the scene through a more analytical eye. There wasn't enough blood to indicate that she had been shot or grievously injured, he determined after following the footsteps a little while longer. And who was to say that this was her blood?

Cort took out his spyglass and surveyed the area but could see no signs of any dwelling or shelter, nor was he familiar with any in the area. They couldn't survive the cold without shelter once the sun set. Something didn't add up. As he thought about it, it came to him that this was a false path. Hagen and Devon must have been on the horses.

He turned back to the resting point. The horse tracks were heading higher up the ridge. Again, Cort knew there was no shelter up there. He hunted the area.

He bent down to study the tracks closer. They weren't deep enough for horses carrying riders and saddlebags. Another false trail. A grim smile slowly crossed his features. Hagen was trying to delay him until nightfall in the event that he had discovered the outlaw's trail.

Cort stood up and looked around him. There were cabins widely scattered about the slope to the west. Hagen would be heading to one of them. But which one? Alice Graham said a miner's cabin, he recalled, or that was what he had interpreted her to have said.

Cort moved northwest toward an old silver mine, looking for any sign that indicated Hagen and Devon had come this way. What if he was wrong? He will have wasted precious time. He couldn't bear to think what she might be enduring at the hands of Hagen.

He was reconsidering his course when his eye caught site of something hanging off a bristlecone pine. He walked up to it and lifted a piece of material off the branch. He took out his spyglass again and spied strips of material on two other trees, pulling him in a direction where he knew there to be one of the cabins. Cort breathed a sigh of relief. Devon had to be fairly sound to have had the presence of mind to leave a trail.

Dusk was falling. The cabin was dark and cold.

Devon gave up all hope of being rescued. If she looked at the situation objectively, she wondered why she had had any hope at all. The marshal wasn't some superhuman as Billy's paranoid mind might think. He was just a man.

Billy peered intently out the window.

"He's not coming," said Devon, dispirited. "With Alice dead, he has no way to know where we are or even that you are the one who abducted me. I don't care what sixth sense you think he has."

Billy didn't answer.

"If you want to face Marshal Templeton so badly, why did you make a false trail?" she questioned. "And why did you try to ambush him outside his office?"

"Shut up!" growled Hagen.

Devon cocked her head. "You're afraid…you're afraid to go up against him in a fair fight, aren't you?"

Billy turned and approached her menacingly. "I ain't afraid of no one."

"Then why did you bring me, if not to use as a shield to hide behind when he catches up with you—"

Hagen backhanded her across the face, nearly knocking her from the chair. "Shut up, or I'll shoot you where you sit," he snarled.

Devon put a hand to her bruised cheek and lip, dazed.

From outside came the growl of a mountain lion and the terrified whinnies of a horse followed by the horrible sound of a life and death struggle, pushing Devon closer to the breaking point.

"Well, one horse ain't comin' back," remarked Billy, impassive.

He gazed out the window.

"Not even Templeton can stay out there at night without lighting a fire," he murmured. "Then, I'll know where you are."

Devon glanced at him. "You don't know if he's coming. How long can *you* go without sleep or a fire waiting for him—one day, two days, three?"

Billy turned his head to glare at her. She didn't care if he hit her again or not. She was past caring about anything.

The wind picked up, and the cabin made moaning, scratching sounds, intensifying the strain on both their nerves. Something hit the window, and Billy swiveled his gaze to it, straining to see into the gathering darkness.

Devon checked the lantern on the table. It still had oil in the font. "Can't we at least have some light?"

Billy ignored her. He cautiously opened the door and walked outside. There wasn't a fire to be seen anywhere, no smell of smoke in the air. Maybe the woman was right. Maybe the marshal wasn't as smart as he thought.

He returned inside and threw Devon a match. "Light the lantern."

With shaking hands, she removed the chimney and lit the wick before he changed his mind. When she set the chimney back in place, she wrapped her hands around it for any warmth it could afford.

Hagen pulled up a chair and sat down at the table. Devon watched, listless, as he took out his knife and idly carved something into the top of it.

She shivered with cold. "I don't have an overcoat. Please light a fire."

Billy gave her a dispassionate glance.

"If I freeze to death, the marshal will hold you responsible," she continued. "You know him. He'll hound you to the ends of the earth. You won't know when, but he *will* come for you like a ghost in the night."

"I told you to shut up!" growled Billy.

He raised a hand to strike her again, when a thud sounded outside. He stopped midair and rushed to the window. A tree limb had fallen on the ground.

"All right, light a fire—a small one," he growled. "No more of yer bellyachin' then."

Devon was almost giddy over being allowed so small a pleasure that she had always taken for granted.

"I need wood and a match," she said.

Hagen looked around the cabin. He went over to the bunkbed and kicked at the frame until the wood splintered. "Use that." He gave her another match from his coat pocket.

Never having had to do it before, Devon awkwardly worked to start a fire as she had watched a servant do. Luckily, the pieces of wood were dry enough that they easily caught. When she threw on larger pieces, smoke began to billow from the fireplace.

"You stupid woman!" screamed Hagen, shoving her aside to put out the fire. "Open the door!"

Coughing and wiping tears from her eyes as smoke filled the cabin, Devon pulled open the door and ran outside. She cried out when she was grabbed from behind and pulled around to the side of the cabin. It had happened so fast her first thought was that she was being dragged away by a bear.

When she twisted around to see what had her in its grip, she gave a cry of joy and threw her arms around Cort. He held her for a moment before setting her from him. When she started to speak, he put a hand to her mouth to silence her.

Hagen ran out of the cabin coughing and sputtering. "Where are you, woman!" he bellowed. He fired wantonly into the air. "Get back here or I swear I'll make you regret it. There's nowhere to run. Either I find you or that mountain lion will."

He walked several feet from the cabin and peered into the darkness. There was dead silence. At the crunching sound of footsteps on snow, he whirled about.

"Who's there? Show yourself."

"It's me, Hagen."

Hagen gasped. "Templeton?"

As Cort appeared, the outlaw stared at him in disbelief. "No, it can't be. There weren't no fire."

"I sheltered in a mine near by," said Cort. "I've been watching you."

Hagen burst into laughter that bordered on the maniacal. "I got ya good, Templeton. I killed yer deputy and took yer woman."

"And now I have both her and you," responded Templeton. "I would say that I'm the winner, Hagen."

Standing on the side of the cabin, Devon heard two shots. Her heart in her throat, she tore around to the front, and she sobbed in relief when she saw Cort standing there, revolver in his hand, unscathed.

Her eyes shifted to Hagen who was moaning and cursing as his blood stained the snow.

"Ya near to blew my arm off, ya bastard!" he screamed.

"You're lucky it's dark. I was aiming for your heart," said Cort. "Deputy Sanger sends his regards. He'll most likely make a full recovery. You got nothing for your trouble, Billy."

The outlaw scooped up his revolver from the ground and ran off into the night.

"He's getting away," cried Devon.

"He won't get far without a horse," said Cort.

As they started back to the cabin, Devon stumbled and swayed, all her energy suddenly deserting her. Cort put an arm around her, attributing it to the ordeal she had been through as she leaned weakly against him.

There came the growl of a mountain lion followed by a gun shot then. Minutes later, came a second shot. Cort stopped, perplexed. Something didn't sound right to him, but he didn't have time to ponder it as he felt Devon sinking to the ground.

"I can't walk any further," she murmured. "She started to take off her jacket."

Cort looked at her nonplussed. "What are you doing?"

"I'm hot," she murmured, lying down in the snow.

He knew what that meant. Alarmed, Cort scooped her up in his arms and hurriedly carried her into the cabin. It was still a bit smoky, but much of it had cleared away. He laid her on the floor and took off his hat and gloves.

She was barely conscious, and he could feel that her clothes were wet. Running a hand beneath her jacket and blouse, he felt that her skin was cold to the touch, but she was hardly shivering. Cort frowned. It was an indication that her body temperature was dangerously low. When he saw that her color was taking on a grayish pallor, he knew that hypothermia had set in.

Templeton took off his coat and covered her with it, then quickly cleared away the brush that he had placed atop the chimney to smoke out Hagen and built a roaring fire.

He stooped down and shoved up the sleeves of her jacket, unbuttoned her blouse at the wrist and rolled up the sleeves to rub some circulation into her arms. She rallied, but he couldn't keep her awake.

His jaw clenched when he noticed the bruises on her face and saw the bandages wrapped around her hands; he would deal with that later. For now, he had to get some warmth into her. Cort suspected that she was also severely dehydrated from the thin air.

He left the cabin to retrieve the supplies that he had stashed behind the dwelling. When he returned, he pulled off her wet boots and pushed aside the covers to peel off her jacket and skirt. Her breathing was shallow, and he opened her blouse and removed her corset. The constriction of one's lungs at such a high elevation was a prescription for trouble in any case.

Moving quickly, he unrolled the bedrolls, unfolded the tarps, sougans, and blankets and made a pallet near the fire, then lifted her onto it. She rallied enough that he was able to get her to drink a few swallows of water before she lapsed into sleep again. He knew that it was a sleep she might not awaken from at this point, and he gently shook her. Her eyes fluttered open, then closed.

Cort figured the outside temperature to be 15 degrees below freezing by now and not much warmer inside the cabin. The water in his canteen was half frozen. He pulled out the bottle of whiskey Chandler had given him, poured some into the canteen, and set it near the fire. He felt Devon's arm. She was still ice cold and had stopped shivering altogether.

"Damn," he murmured.

Cort stoked the fire and made another pallet next to her, then knelt down beside Devon to unwrap the blankets from around her and remove the rest of her clothing. Steeling himself against the cold, he took off his own clothes and lay down beside her. He turned her on her side so that her back was to him and brought her tightly against him. Cort sucked in his breath when her cold body touched his, and he quickly pulled the heavy quilts and blankets over them, tucking the covers around and under them. Frequently, he ran a hand over her to stir the circulation.

Finally, her body began to warm. She stirred a few times and fell back to sleep, this time more from exhaustion than from the dangerous sleep of hypothermia, he decided. Satisfied that she was out of danger, he allowed himself to fall off to sleep as well. At one point, Devon turned and snuggled against him, and it just seemed natural that he should put his arm around her.

Near dawn, Devon roused. She felt warm and cozy and was loath to stir from her nest. She suddenly jerked awake and lifted her head, fearful. "Hagen...where's Hagen?"

"Easy," said Cort. "He's gone."

She looked at him and the bedding in confusion. "Why are we..." She quickly moved away from him, taking more than her share of the covers. "Oh, good heavens!" she exclaimed at the realization that they were both unclothed. "What—How—Did you—"

Her face turned beet red, and she had no idea what question to ask first. Each one seemed just as damning as the next, and she didn't know if she really wanted to know the answers. How could she have been unaware of her clothes being removed—of any of this?

Cort had been awake steeling himself for her reaction. "Relax, Mrs. Wainwright. Nothing happened," he calmly assured her.

Devon looked at him incredulous. "What do you mean nothing happened? We are both in a state of undress!"

"Indeed, madam, and it is cold. These blankets are only so wide. Do you mind?"

Seeing that he was half uncovered, Devon lay back down and moved a little closer to allow him more covering, more for her sensibilities than for his comfort.

She lay stiffly on her back, staring up at the ceiling. "Explain yourself, Mr. Templeton," she demanded furiously.

"It was all for good reason, Mrs. Wainwright. Instead of excoriating me, you should be thanking me."

Devon turned her head and looked at him, flabbergasted. "Thanking you! Thank you for what...ruining my good name?"

"For saving your life."

"I am grateful that you rescued me from that horrible outlaw, but gratitude does not extend to...to this!" she exclaimed. She raised herself up on one arm. "Grateful or not, I most certainly would not have given you leave to...to—why can't I remember anything?" she cried in exasperation.

"Calm yourself and lie down, Mrs. Wainwright, you are letting in cold air," said Cort.

She let out a huff and lay back down, all the more infuriated by his persistence in treating the situation so casually. The incident with the miners had been bad enough, but this was the most scandalous situation she had ever found herself in, and there was nothing in the rule book to tell her how to extricate herself from this gross infraction with her dignity and reputation intact.

"If you will allow me to explain," continued Cort, "I'm not talking about saving you from Hagen, although you owe me for that as well."

"What *are* you talking about?" she snapped.

"Your body temperature had fallen so low last night you were very close to freezing to death. The condition is called hypothermia," explained Cort. "You don't remember anything because you had fallen unconscious. Using my body heat was the only way I could warm you enough before you slipped into a coma and your heart stopped."

Devon reddened again at the idea of lying so close against him unclothed, but she did remember having felt very cold at one point. To hear that she had been so close to death without any other memory of it was both shocking and sobering to her, and she was silent for a long moment as she processed the information.

"Still, it seems to me that a man without ulterior motives would have found another way," she insisted testily.

"Madam, lying next to you was like lying next to a block of ice. I assure you it did not incite me to entertain any thoughts other than warming you—and there was no other way. The sacrifice was all mine."

"Ha! Somehow, I doubt that, Mr. Templeton."

"I don't know what you are fussing about, Mrs. Wainwright. I have seen you half clothed before, as have several miners in the town," he reminded her.

Devon stiffened. "A gentleman would not have recounted that," she responded primly.

"My point is, Mrs. Wainwright, the removal of a few more articles of clothing is of no consequence."

Devon looked at him again. "Of no consequence—it is certainly of consequence to me! We are not all created equal, sir."

"True, but from what I have observed, you have nothing to be ashamed of," Cort assured her.

Devon's jaw dropped. "That is not what I meant," she sputtered. "This just isn't done. A woman of my station is not seen in such a state by a man, let alone by a man to whom she is not married."

"Are you telling me that you and your husband never came together unclothed?"

"We were properly attired in night clothes."

Cort regarded her with surprise. "You only engaged at night?"

"Of course. When it was properly dark."

He let out a laugh. "That must have been exciting."

Devon bristled. "It is not supposed to be exciting. And I do not think this an appropriate subject for discussion."

"You do have a lot to learn about real life, Mrs. Wainwright."

"I wouldn't expect you to understand polite society," she retorted.

"Polite society is a euphemism for hypocrisy."

"It establishes a standard of civility, Mr. Templeton."

"For whom?" questioned Cort. "Polite society is an elite group of men who devise rules that preserve their power and circle of exclusivity…rules, I might add, that they selectively do not observe themselves when it doesn't suit them."

"You sound like Pearl Donovan."

"She is a victim of it," said Cort. "But whatever you may think of Pearl's ways, she exploits the system to her benefit—as did your aunt. You, on the other hand, allow the system to exploit you by refusing to accept your aunt's legacy and marrying against your will."

He could feel her bristle again, but she didn't return argument.

"The status quo of the elite is not a friend to any woman, Mrs. Wainwright."

"Thank you for your insights," replied Devon, her tone dripping with sarcasm. Intellectually, she knew there was truth to what he said, but she wasn't near ready to admit it. "Where are my clothes?"

"Drying by the fire."

She gathered a blanket around her and moved to get up. When she was greeted with a teeth-chattering chill that took her breath away, she quickly lay back down and burrowed beneath the covers again.

"It is cold," she said.

"Yep," he responded.

"You should get up and get dressed and stir the fire."

"Ladies first," he replied.

"That will not do, Mr. Templeton."

"Why is that, Mrs. Wainwright?"

"Well, because I know that I will not peek when you get up, but, as men cannot be trusted, you most certainly will peek if I go first."

Cort turned his head and looked at her. There was that crazy logic again, and it was all he could do to keep from bursting out laughing. He knew human nature pretty well. But knowing the ordeal that she had been through, he decided not to test her further. Cort sighed and shoved aside the blankets and rose.

Devon greedily gathered his share of the blankets around her and covered her head. But after a few moments, she couldn't resist the overwhelming temptation to pull the covers down just enough to sneak a look.

Her eyes widened as she took in the long, muscular body as he dressed. She had been married for 10 years, and though she had never viewed her husband in his natural state, she was quite certain that he had never looked anything like this.

As he pulled on the union suit, Cort glanced up just as she pulled the covers back over her head, and his lips curled up in a knowing smile. He was rarely wrong about human nature.

When Cort was dressed, he stirred the fire. "I'm going out to get more wood and to take care of the horses," he said.

Devon pulled the covers from over her head and looked up at him in surprise. "Where are the horses?"

"There is an abandoned mine just down the slope. I have my horse and one of Hagen's horses stabled there."

"I think the other one was killed by a mountain lion," she said, soberly recalling the sickening sounds of the attack.

"I saw," replied Cort. He pulled on his coat and gloves and set his hat. "I suggest you make use of this time to get dressed—and leave off the corset. The air is thin here. It will be difficult for you to breathe as it is. The corset will make it even more so."

When he opened the door, snow blew in, and Devon shivered beneath the blankets. She continued to lie there for several minutes after he left before she found the fortitude to brave the cold.

Stiffly, she got to her feet, wrapped a blanket around her, and collected her clothes. Shaking from the sub-freezing temperatures, Devon quickly donned the various articles of clothing. She was just pulling on her wool jacket when Cort returned with rotted wood timbers from the mine and fed the fire, stoking it to greater heat.

"How is Deputy Sanger?" she asked.

"Holding his own when I left," replied Cort.

He fetched a canteen from among the provisions. "You're probably dehydrated. You need to drink," he said. "Take small sips. You have to rehydrate slowly."

Devon took the metal container from him and did as he directed. She made a face. "The water tastes funny."

"I put whiskey in it to keep the water from freezing." When she hesitated to drink more, he added, "It will help with the mountain sickness." It wasn't true, but he figured the whiskey might help her to relax. He could tell, she was still feeling the effects of her ordeal.

He took out some dried beef and biscuits. "Hungry?"

Devon nodded. It was well over 24 hours since she had last eaten.

"How did you find me?" she asked.

"It's a long story. Eat first," said Cort.

Devon hungrily devoured the food. It was the simplest meal she had ever eaten, but the salty strips of dried meat and dense cracker-flavored biscuit tasted so good.

Cort noticed the crude carving in the top of the table. It was the letters KGC inside a circle. "Did Hagen do this?" he asked, drawing her attention to it.

Devon nodded.

"Did he say anything about it?"

"No. Does it mean something?"

"It was a symbol for the Knights of the Golden Circle," replied Cort.

"What's that?"

"An organization that was formed in 1858 to ensure the continuation of slavery in the South," he explained. "During the war, they were so effective in committing acts of espionage and raising money, arms, and men for the Confederacy that Lincoln called them the Fifth Column."

Cort's brows dipped into a frown. "There are rumors that the group is organizing again to overthrow the federal government in another civil war, but the reports haven't been taken seriously."

Devon looked at him. "Maybe they should be," she said. "I overheard Miss Primrose telling Hagen that he was endangering the cause if he didn't leave me behind. They must have been members of this group."

Cort's consternation increased. "Did they say anything else?"

Devon thought for a moment. "Miss Primrose said that Mr. Goodway…Goodright…no, Mr. Goodnight—that was his name—would not be happy."

"I don't know of anyone in town with that name," said Cort. "It is most likely a false name. The organization had an elaborate hierarchy and system of secret codes. Members went to great lengths to conceal their identities. Few of them were ever exposed during or after the war." He paused with a new thought. "If the KGC has resurfaced and Hagen and Alice Graham were part of it, then the KGC has been actively recruiting."

"But Hagen is an outlaw," said Devon.

"He fought for the Confederacy and has a blind hatred for the federal government. That's all that matters to them," replied Templeton. "Besides, most of the mines are owned and financed by northern banks and financiers. Hagen's payroll robberies are viewed as strikes against the Union."

Devon was incredulous. "The war has been over for years."

"It will never be over for the South," responded Cort with a note of bitterness in his voice.

"How dangerous is this group now?" asked Devon.

Templeton shook his head. "It's hard to say. Hatred is a powerful force."

In the light of day, he took closer notice of the bruises on her cheek and lip. When he raised a hand to examine her face, she instinctively flinched.

"Easy now. I just want to take a look." He gently placed a hand under her chin and turned her face. "Hagen's handiwork?"

Devon nodded. "He didn't like what I said."

Templeton lifted one of her hands and unwrapped the dirty bandage, then unwrapped the other hand. His jaw clenched at the sight of the gashes across her palms.

"Hagen slashed them to leave blood on a false trail for you," she said.

"I saw the trail," acknowledged Cort. "He wanted to make sure that I followed it. Hagen rode with Bloody Bill Anderson during the war. It's a delaying tactic used in guerilla warfare…let the enemy chase you until nightfall, then you know where they are and how many they number by their campfires," he explained.

"Did you follow the trail?" asked Devon.

"Not far. It wasn't long before I figured it to be a ruse."

"How?"

"I knew there to be no shelter in that direction. I hunt up here and know the location of the mine and cabins in the area," said Templeton. "I wasn't sure which cabin Hagen might be heading to though until I saw the strips of material you left on trees. That was good thinking. Otherwise…" he paused. "Otherwise, I would not have found you in time to make a difference."

Devon looked at him, still dubious. "How close to death was I…really?"

Cort solemnly met her eye. It was all the response she needed. And she was struck by the thought that, in the few months she had left Boston, she had come face-to-face with her own mortality twice when it had never been a consideration to her before.

Templeton took out the bottle of whiskey from his saddlebag and poured some of the liquor over the cuts on her hands. "Can you work your fingers?"

Devon grimaced as she tried to flex them. "They're stiff, but I think so." She looked at him in alarm. "Will I be able to play the piano?"

"There doesn't appear to be any permanent damage, but there may be some weakness for awhile. If there is numbness or tingling, wait until it subsides and work your fingers every day. Don't suppose you would know where I might find more bandages?" he inquired with the lift of his brow.

Devon lifted her top skirt to reveal a tattered petticoat underneath. "I think there might be a few more left here."

Cort took his knife and cut off some strips. "How's your wrist?"

"Truth to tell I forgot all about it," said Devon. "I believe the bandage helped.... I didn't think you would find us, but Hagen was convinced that you have some other worldly sense."

"It would appear that he had more faith in my prowess than did you," quipped Cort, bandaging one of her hands.

"How could you possibly have figured everything out?" she asked in wonder.

Cort told her how he had found the drugged tea, the contaminated sugar, and the secret passage and realized that the schoolteacher was in league with Hagen.

"How did you track us to that other cabin?" she quizzed.

"It turns out that Miss Primrose was supplying Belle with drugs in exchange for information. Belle said that was where they had met. I saw the wagon tracks heading from your house in that direction and figured to find you there," explained Cort."

Devon looked at him astonished and confused. "Belle was involved, too?"

"She was an unwitting dupe."

"Hagen killed Miss Primrose," relayed Devon soberly. "I'll never forget the expression on his face as he looked at her lying on the floor. She had been his companion for years, and he felt nothing.... I was seriously ill with a fever once. My husband had looked at me the same way."

"She wasn't dead when I found her," said Cort. "She told me where Hagen was heading with you."

Devon looked at him in surprise. "She's still alive?"

"She was in bad shape," he replied, bandaging Devon's other hand. "Matt took her back to town in the wagon."

"Matt was with you?"

"He insisted on coming along. Do you know how to ride?"

She nodded.

Cort put out the fire and pulled out a sougan before rolling up the bedrolls. "Wrap this around you to keep you warm," he said, handing her the heavy quilt. "And take my gloves. They'll protect your hands and make it easier to handle the reins."

Cort packed up the remaining provisions, threw the saddlebags over his shoulder, and picked up the bedrolls. They were walking out of the cabin, when she stopped and turned to him.

"Mr. Templeton—"

"I know, Mrs. Wainwright. We shall never speak of what occurred here."

It was near the end of the day when Cort and Devon rode into town.

Jasper rushed out of the marshal's office to meet them. "I was just about to get up a posse and come lookin' fer ya. Did ya get Hagen?"

"Yeah. A mountain lion finished the job. I left him up on the slope," said Cort.

"A mountain lion… jeez." The deputy shrugged. "He deserved it."

Templeton dismounted and lifted Devon down from her horse. He unfastened his saddlebags and threw them over his shoulder.

"Jasper, take the horses back to the livery stable," he said. "I'm going to walk Mrs. Wainwright home."

"Yes, sir."

"How is Brett?"

Jasper grinned. "I'd say he's makin' out pretty good. He's got that pretty Miss Ryan waitin' on him hand and foot at the house."

Devon raised a brow but was too tired to question it.

"What about the woman Chandler brought in?" asked Cort.

"Miss Primrose?" Jasper shook his head. "She didn't make it."

Sighting the marshal's return, people came streaming into the street. When they saw the bruise on Devon's face and her bandaged hands, they were horrified to imagine the ordeal this lovely, young woman must have suffered at the hands of the outlaw who had shot their deputy, killed their school mistress, and tried to kill their marshal.

Devon assured everyone that she was fine and was overwhelmed by their show of concern and gratitude that she was safely returned. That so many people cared was astonishing to her.

Mrs. Walker wiped away a tear. "We knew you'd bring her back to us, Marshal."

As others heaped praise on him, Cort responded in his usual self-deprecating manner that he was just doing his job. "Mrs. Wainwright deserves the credit," he said. "She left a trail for me to follow. Now, I think Mrs. Wainwright could do with some rest."

"Amen to that," said Mrs. Walker. "You can tell us everything later, dear."

The townspeople were just dispersing, when Chandler came out of the saloon and rushed across the street to them. "Cort, thank heavens you're back. I was about ready to join Jasper's posse. Devon, are you alright?" he asked, passing a solicitous eye over her.

Devon responded by slapping him soundly across the face to the shock of both men.

"Marshal, I want Mr. Chandler arrested," she said, further stupefying them.

"On what charge?" asked Cort.

Her blue eyes flashed with anger. "Robbery. He stole my aunt's jewelry."

Chandler stared at her dumbfounded. "Devon, I-I would never do such a thing," he stammered.

"No use denying it, Matt. I saw Belle wearing a brooch that my aunt was wearing in a picture. She said that you gave it to her."

Chandler looked helplessly at Cort. "It isn't true. I swear it."

"Mrs. Wainwright, I think Belle was lying about Matt giving her that brooch," intervened Templeton.

Devon was unconvinced. "How else would she get it?"

"I suspect that she was the one who stole your aunt's jewels," said Cort.

"How?"

"She worked for your aunt in the salon until Sadie turned her out for stealing and drug use," explained Cort. "She knew about Sadie's jewelry. I think she returned to the house and stole the jewelry after Sadie's death."

"I don't like the woman, but I never would have thought her to be a thief," remarked Devon.

"There is no end to what drug addicts will do to feed their habits." Cort looked at Chandler. "Where is Belle?"

"I don't know," he replied. "She was gone when I returned to town."

"I'll send out a notice to the sheriffs in the surrounding counties," said Templeton. "Maybe Belle is the one who pushed you down the stairs, Mrs. Wainwright."

Devon shook her head. "No, Hagen confessed to that. He said I was becoming bothersome."

"You were pushed down the stairs? Devon, why didn't you tell me?" quizzed Chandler.

"I didn't know if I had imagined it at the time. I owe you an apology, Matt. I'm sorry for accusing you of stealing my aunt's jewelry."

"I understand how it might have looked that way, my dear, but I do wish you had had more trust in me," he chided lightly. "Well, no matter. I'll see you home. Now that the air is cleared, I have something important to discuss with you."

"I don't want to talk now, Matt. I just want a hot bath and a comfortable bed. The marshal will walk me."

Chandler glanced askance at Templeton, but he saw that Devon was in a prickly mood and didn't argue the matter. "Of course, dear heart. Forgive me. You have been through a terrible ordeal. I will call on you when you are rested."

As Cort walked Devon down the street, he could feel Chandler's eyes following them. "You'll regret it," he commented.

"Regret what?" she asked peevishly.

"Marrying, Matt. That's what he wants to discuss with you."

"Why should you care, Marshal?"

"Maybe I don't want to see you make another mistake, Mrs. Wainwright."

Devon glared at him. "Thank you for your concern. But I am quite capable of handling my own affairs."

Cort raised a brow, and even as she made the statement, Devon realized how hollow it sounded in the face of recent events.

When they arrived at the house, she handed him his gloves and walked through the gate.

Bridget came running out the door. "Miss Devon! I've been so worried. Are ye all right?"

"I am fine, Bridget, and Hagen is no longer a threat to us," said Devon.

"It must have been terrible for ye, miss."

"Yes, it was most unpleasant. I really do not want to talk about it now."

Devon was about to start up the steps to the porch, when Cort called out to her. "Mrs. Wainwright, you forgot something."

She stopped and turned around. "What?" she asked impatiently.

He reached inside his saddlebag and took out her corset.

Devon quickly retraced her steps to Cort and grabbed the garment from his hand.

As she passed by her wide-eyed companion, she warned sternly: "You shall never speak of this, Bridget."

Bridget nodded dumbly.

CHAPTER TWENTY-SEVEN

Coexisting

Devon felt as though she had been swept up in the funnel cloud of a tornado as the next several days swirled around her giving her little room to breathe.

There was a steady stream of well-wishers.

The mayor, the town council, and the women from the Ladies' Auxiliary were among the first to visit, chagrined and horrified at having been duped by a mad woman and placing Devon and the children in harm's way. After assuring them that she didn't hold them responsible for the kidnapping, Devon agreed to continue schooling the children until another teacher could be found.

Women brought her preserves, and her students gave her homemade gifts. Penny Johnson came to town to see for herself that Devon was all right. And men stopped to pay their respects to her before making their way upstairs to visit with Brett.

Her ordeal was not something Devon wished to discuss, but tiring of everyone's curious questions, she finally agreed to an interview with the editor of the newspaper to put the matter to rest once and for all—or so she thought.

Three weeks later, she opened her door to find a half dozen strange men encamped on her porch. Immediately, they began peppering her with questions about the kidnapping. Devon was so astounded her automatic response was to shut the door on them.

"Bridget!" she shouted.

Bridget quickly appeared from the kitchen. "Yes, miss?"

"Fetch the marshal." As Bridget started for the front door, Devon stopped her. "No, no, go out the back door."

"What's amiss, ma'am?" asked Bridget, alarmed by her mistress' behavior.

"We are besieged, Bridget. Hurry!"

Bridget looked out the window to see the men on the porch and rushed to the back door, the past experience with the miners still fresh in her mind.

Fifteen minutes later, Devon heard Cort outside and watched from the window as he made the reporters leave her porch. Her relief was short-lived, however, when they went only as far as outside the fence.

When Cort came to the door, she opened it and pulled him inside.

"Who are those men? Were did they come from?" she asked.

"They're reporters from Eastern papers and writers of dime novels," replied Templeton. "They happened to be in the area covering the latest silver discovery when they heard about your story."

"How?"

"How does any story of interest spread?"

"Well, make them leave town," demanded Devon.

"I can't, Mrs. Wainwright. They have rights as journalists. All I can do is charge them with trespassing if they don't stay outside your gate."

"But they have to leave," fretted Devon. "The longer they stay in town the more likely they are to uncover the fact that my aunt was a madam and this house a...a—"

"Salon," furnished Cort.

She glared at him. "Yes, a salon."

Another thought even more disturbing came to her. "Oh good heavens, what if they come to know that we stayed the night on the ridge. What if they begin to wonder what occurred in the cabin? You said they make things up. My reputation will be in tatters. What am I to do?"

"If you ignore them, they will soon move onto another story," said Cort, unconcerned.

Devon wasn't about to take that chance. That afternoon, she invited the reporters into the parlor and, drawing on her training, staged her best performance.

Seated royally on the settee and dabbing at her eyes, she proceeded to tell them how traumatizing the experience had been and how difficult it was to have to relive it again. If they could please consult the article in the *Blue Springs Journal*, as she had nothing more to add, she would be eternally grateful for their courtesy, she said with glistening blue eyes and a tremulous smile.

Those with artistic ability furiously sketched this beautiful, fragile, distressed damsel as she spoke. By the end, the hardened reporters were falling all over themselves professing their deep desire not to add to her discomfort and promising to honor her privacy. Devon smiled smugly to herself, certain that the matter was closed.

But as is the nature of reporters, in finding one avenue closed to them, they soon find another. In questioning the townspeople, they found a more compelling story when they learned about the history between the taciturn marshal and the ruthless outlaw.

Templeton's shooting of Hagen's hired gun and his thwarting of the jail break, the ambush, the foiling of the payroll and Denver Assay Office robberies were the stuff of legends, and the marshal emerged for reporters as a larger-than-life-hero who, against all odds, rescued his fair lady from the hands of a killer who had kidnapped her in an act of vengeance.

Cort soon had his hands full when the focus of attention turned on him. Reporters invaded his office and dogged his heels for interviews and comment. His refusal to give them either only added to his mystique and appeal as the strong, silent hero, fueling their interest all the more.

While Devon was relieved that the reporters' spotlight had largely turned from her, neither she nor Chandler was pleased that she was being touted as the marshal's "fair lady." The idea of such a romance, however, caught the interest of the townspeople who decided they rather liked the thought. Several times, Devon had to disavow Mrs. Walker and other ladies of the notion, but it was plain to see that some ideas die hard.

When Templeton walked into his office one day to find Jasper holding forth with reporters, it was the last straw for him.

"Get out!" he ordered the reporters.

He didn't have to say it twice. At the scowl on his face and the rumble of anger in his voice, the men scrambled to leave.

When he slammed the door on the last one, Cort turned to his deputy. "I don't want to find you or Brett talking to reporters," he warned.

"I don't know what the harm is," mumbled Jasper.

"The harm is that these stories will bring to town every two-bit gun slinger looking to make a name for himself. And the sooner people stop feeding these reporters information, the sooner they will leave."

Three days passed before the reporters finally departed town, armed with sufficient facts and a fertile imagination, and Blue Springs settled into the normal routine of life again.

It was taking longer for Devon to move on. While her wrist and hands may have healed with no lasting damage, her psyche remained an open wound. Nightmares plagued her. She was having difficulty setting aside her ordeal with Hagen, as well as the horror of the shooting of Deputy Sanger and the marshal's shoot out with the hired gun.

Just as distressing to her on another level was that Marshal Templeton had seen her in her natural state. She tried to remember that he was a pragmatist, solely motivated by a sense of duty—even in a circumstance such as this. Still, he was a man, and she felt awkward in his presence. Unfortunately, she couldn't avoid him on his frequent visits to the house to check on his deputy's progress.

Cort was aware that Devon was trying to distance herself from him. She began sending Bridget to the door to admit him. This morning, it was one of her students. Bridget must be busy, he thought with a wry smile, as he climbed the stairs.

He was walking down the hall to Brett's room, when Bridget tearfully ran out and darted past him. Cort sighed at the thought of another problem.

"What is upsetting Miss Ryan?" he asked, entering the room.

Brett rose stiffly from the bed. "I asked her to marry me," he replied.

"That's usually cause for celebration," said Cort.

"She said 'no.'"

Templeton regarded the downhearted young man in bewilderment. "Why?"

"Mrs. Wainwright is fixin' to move back East as soon as a new teacher is found," said Brett. "She thinks it is too violent here."

"Oh," murmured Cort. "After all she has been through, I suppose you can't blame her for feeling that way. Miss Ryan doesn't need to leave, too."

"That's what I told her, but she said she can't abandon Mrs. Wainwright. Bridget feels beholdin' to her."

Brett looked at him, and Cort easily read the entreaty in his deputy's face.

"I'd like to help, Brett, but it doesn't sound as though Mrs. Wainwright is in the mood to listen to anything I might have to say right now. With a little more time, she'll get past this and settle in."

The young man shook his head. "I don't think so…. Please, Cort, just try talking to her."

Cort thought for a minute. "Perhaps someone with a direct line to a higher power might be more effective."

Devon was seeing the last of the students out the door at the end of the day, when Pastor Clemmons came down the stairs.

She gave him a warm smile. "Pastor Clemmons, how nice to see you. I didn't know that you were here visiting with Deputy Sanger."

"I have been trying to calm troubled waters," he said.

"What do you mean?" asked Devon.

"Bridget didn't tell you?"

"Tell me what?"

"Brett proposed to her."

Devon looked at him in surprise. "No, she didn't mention it."

"She has refused him because she said that you are leaving soon, and she feels compelled to accompany you out of a deep sense of loyalty," explained the pastor.

"Oh…I see. Well, maybe she doesn't want to marry Mr. Sanger," suggested Devon.

The pastor smiled. "I think we both know that is not the case. I am hoping to convince you to remain in Blue Springs."

Devon shook her head. "I'm sorry, Pastor Clemmons. After everything that has happened, I cannot stay."

"What about Bridget?" asked the pastor.

"I feel a sense of responsibility for her. I believe it is best for her to return East with me," replied Devon. "We do not belong here. This is not a world that we know and understand."

"You mean it is not a world that is black and white."

"It is better to have strict societal rules if that's what you mean. Otherwise, order breaks down. There are too few boundaries out here, Pastor."

"Some people might call that freedom," he countered.

"I call it lawlessness, sir. I've seen and experienced the results of it. Mr. Sanger is a lawman. The next time, he might not recover from his wounds. I don't want Bridget to go through that heartbreak."

The pastor sighed. "Sometimes bad things happen, and it doesn't matter where you are, Devon. You could just as easily get sick or suffer a carriage accident in Boston as here. And your class and society rules don't protect you from violence any better in the 'civilized' East. I seem to recollect a famous society murder in Boston in 1849—George Parkman. It gained national attention. Perhaps you know of it. It was quite brutal."

"I was only five years old at the time, but, yes, I am familiar with the story," said Devon.

"I also remember that a young socialite was kidnapped in New York City a few years ago and held for ransom," continued Clemmons. "And both the New York and Boston police departments have been charged with corruption and political influence peddling. Boundaries are not impenetrable, Devon. Laws, no matter how many or how strong, are only as good as the people enforcing them."

"How do you know so much about the East?" she asked.

"I had a church in New York City and saw the politics and corruption firsthand," replied the pastor. "When I read your aunt's advertisement in the paper seeking a pastor to shepherd the people of a fledgling town called Blue Springs, I came straightaway. And I haven't looked back."

Devon was silent for a moment. "How does one get past the occurrence of something bad? How can one forget acts of violence?" she asked in a low, quiet tone.

Clemmons put a comforting hand on her shoulder. "One focuses on the good in his life and does for others. One does not hide away. No one cheats death, Devon. When it is time, it is time, and none of us can know when or how that day will come. Until then, God has granted us the gift of life. The sin would be for us not to live it to its fullest—or to deny another the right to do so, however well intentioned."

Devon caught the thinly veiled accusation. Cort had said much the same thing to her.

*****

Devon looked over the students, mentally taking attendance this morning. "Where is Virginia?" she asked.

"Her took ill," said one of the girls.

"*She* took ill," corrected Devon. "Is it serious?"

"No, ma'am. Her mother thinks it's just the sniffles."

Devon recalled then that the little girl had been coughing, sneezing, and rubbing her eyes for the past few days.

"Very well," she said. "Let us begin."

The day progressed smoothly. Out the corner of her eye, Devon saw the marshal cross the foyer to the stairs to check on his deputy. Not long after, Bridget announced that there was another visitor at the door.

"Who is it?" she asked.

"Mr. Chandler, miss."

Devon sighed. She knew why he had come, and she was running out of ways to avoid him and the question he wanted to ask her.

When she walked into the foyer, Chandler took off his hat and smiled. "Beautiful as always," he observed, kissing her on the cheek.

Devon gave him a tepid smile. "Hello, Matt. I'm sorry. I'm busy right now."

"I know. Every time I come you are busy no matter the time. Don't these kids get a play break or something?" he asked with some annoyance. "All I want are a few minutes alone with you, Devon."

"Can it not wait until after school, Matt?"

"Only if you promise to have dinner with me—no interruptions."

Devon sighed again. "All right, I promise."

As Chandler turned to leave, there came another knock on the door. With mounting irritation, Devon opened it to find Dr. Morse on her doorstep.

"I suppose you're here to see Deputy Sanger," she said.

The doctor strode past her into the house. "No, I'm here to see you."

There was an urgency in his tone and manner that Devon didn't find comforting. "What is it? Has something happened?" she asked apprehensively.

Just then Cort came down the stairs, his pace slowing when he saw Chandler, and the two men regarded each other with the same lack of enthusiasm.

"Hello, Matt."

"Hello, Cort. Didn't expect to see you here."

Templeton looked at the doctor. "You here to see Brett, Doc? I hope you'll declare him ready to get back to work soon."

"I'm not here about Brett," said the doctor. "Mrs. Wainwright, you have a student named Virginia Waller."

Devon nodded. "She is ill today and not in attendance."

"I know. I just saw her," said Morse. "There is a possibility that she may have the measles."

"Oh, I am sorry to hear that," said Devon.

"Until I know for sure, I am quarantining your house. The students will have to remain here for a few days."

Devon's eyes widened in disbelief. "You can't be serious."

"I'm afraid so."

Templeton chuckled. "Looks like you and Miss Ryan will have your hands full, Mrs. Wainwright."

He walked to the door and opened it.

"Where do you think you're going, Cort? I said the house is quarantined," repeated Dr. Morse. "No one comes in or leaves, including you and Matt."

Templeton laughed. "You can't quarantine me. I'm the marshal."

"Try me."

The humor disappeared from Cort's face. "Doc, I'm already down one deputy."

"Things are quiet. Jasper can handle whatever needs to be handled," said the doctor, standing firm.

Devon joined Cort in vigorous protest against the quarantine until the doctor raised his hands and shouted: "Quiet…the both of you! I'm sorry, but that's the way it must be for a few days. I'll notify the students' parents."

"Doc, I will not be stuck in a house full of kids with two women who can't cook," insisted Cort.

Devon glared at him. Doc was more sympathetic.

"I'll have food sent over from the restaurant," he promised.

When Morse left, Chandler remarked cheerily: "Look on the bright side. We can all get to know each other better." He looked at Devon. "And you and I will be able to have that discussion," he said with a wink.

Devon closed her eyes and inwardly groaned.

"Cort and I can also help you with the students," continued Chandler. "I can teach them some card tricks—"

"Like how to make one disappear," interjected Cort.

"I run a clean game, Templeton."

As the two men started to fling barbs, Devon clapped her hands for silence.

"This is not your saloon, Matt, or your jail office, Marshal. This is a school and there are children here," she sternly admonished them.

"Yes, ma'am," they answered, somewhat contrite.

The day was long and nerve-wracking for Devon. The quarantine created yet more excitement and disruption on the heels of the reporters for the students, and they were unruly. Any attempt at formal education this day went out the window.

Added to this, she found the marshal and Chandler annoyingly underfoot. She would sidestep one only to turn around and come face-to-face with the other. She finally took Chandler's suggestion and put him and the marshal to work to keep the students entertained.

The younger children gravitated to Chandler, enthralled by his flair for showmanship and card tricks, while the older students were drawn to the more serious-minded Templeton as, after some coaxing, he began to recount some stories of his more humorous adventures as a lawman. Devon stopped to listen a few times, surprised to find that he actually had a knack for storytelling.

Finding sleeping accommodations for all the unexpected guests was not so easy. With the wounded deputy occupying one room, there was a shortage.

She divided the children and put the boys in one room and the girls in another. The marshal and Chandler would have to share Nettie's room, she informed them. They started to object, but Devon officiously cut them off in no mood to indulge their grievances with each other.

"The children are camping on the floor. You may move in an extra bed from the boys' room," she said. "Look on the bright side. You shall have a chance to get to know each other better," she added, echoing Chandler's words with a waggish smile.

The two men glanced at each other and grimaced.

"I suppose we can endure for one night," grumbled Chandler.

"Oh no, gentlemen, if it is determined that Virginia has the measles, I'm afraid you shall have to endure for at least seven days," Devon informed them, taking great satisfaction in the stunned expressions on their faces.

When the children were finally settled for the night, Devon and Bridget retired to their rooms. Left to their own with nothing to do, Cort and Chandler turned in as well.

"I'll take the bed by the window," said Templeton.

"Fine," responded Chandler.

They undressed and fell into their beds.

"I never knew kids could be so exhausting," groaned Chandler. "I can't get a minute alone with Devon."

Cort grunted. "She is not going to marry you, Matt."

"How would you know?"

"I think I have come to know her pretty well."

Chandler smirked. "You still call her Mrs. Wainwright. How well can that be?"

Cort smiled. "You might be surprised," he murmured under his breath.

Held captive, along with the very men from whom she sought distance, Devon awoke the next morning with little enthusiasm for the day. She rose from the bed and dressed, dismally wondering how she was ever going to get through the week.

As she descended the stairs, her spirits rose with the pleasing aroma of coffee and food in the air. She smiled and rushed into the kitchen only to find Templeton standing at the stove cooking.

Her smile faded. "I thought Nettie had returned."

Cort turned his head to her. "Sorry to disappoint you. Hopefully, this will be almost as good. Rosie sent over a pot of porridge for your students," he said, indicating the pot warming on the stove.

"There are some biscuits and sweet roles on the table," he continued. "I thought the rest of us could do with something more filling. I found some cans of beans, potatoes, onions, and dried beef in the pantry, but not much else. I sent a list back with the errand boy."

"Hagen was pilfering food," said Devon. She walked over to the stove and looked at the hash in the pan. "It smells good. Where did you learn to cook?"

"Trial and error. If you're a bachelor or spend much time on the trail, you had better know how to cook. Also, Penny took pity on me and gave me some tips."

He glanced at her. "Maybe Penny can give you a few so people don't have to worry about you setting their town on fire."

Devon raised a brow at the jibe but decided not to engage. She needed to conserve her energy for the day.

"Coffee?" he asked.

She nodded, and he poured her a cup, then dished up a plate of food for her. She sat down at the table and tasted the hash.

"It's good," she pronounced with some surprise.

"You can tell Penny that I wasn't such a hopeless cause," said Cort, sitting down across from her with a plate of food.

"How did you find Matt last night?" she asked as they ate.

Cort snorted. "Annoying. The man snores. I buried his body in the back yard."

Devon laughed. "As outrageous as that sounds, nothing would surprise me in this town. But you must be mistaken, Marshal. Gentlemen do not snore. It is against the code."

"I rest my case," said Cort. "Matt, is no gentleman."

Devon giggled. "You are irreverent, sir."

At that moment, Chandler strolled into the kitchen, surprised to find Devon and the marshal sharing a light moment.

"I didn't hear you get up, Cort," he remarked, pouring himself a cup of coffee.

"The marshal cooked breakfast, unless you prefer porridge," said Devon.

"The marshal is a man of many talents," responded Chandler, his eyes shifting back and forth between her and Templeton. He had the feeling that he had interrupted something.

Bridget entered the kitchen then. "The students are awake, Miss Devon."

Devon instructed Bridget to set up a serving line for the porridge in the kitchen. "The children can sit at the table in the dining room and eat," she said.

"I'll take some hash and coffee to Brett," said Cort. "We have some matters to discuss now that he is up and about."

The next three days went much the same as the first, with Templeton and Chandler helping out where they could. But, unwilling to leave anything to chance, Chandler made sure to rise in the morning with the marshal. For Devon's part, with the men in the house, the students tended to mind her and Bridget more, so she had to be grateful for that.

A noticeable tension had arisen between Bridget and Brett, and there was an air of despondency about them that Devon tried to attribute to the strain of the quarantine. But in her heart of hearts, she knew the real reason, and she struggled over what to do about it. She was certain that the marshal was aware of it, too, and was surprised that he didn't try to intervene in the matter.

On the fourth day, the doctor arrived to announce that Virginia did not have measles and that he was lifting the quarantine. "You are all free to leave," he announced.

Everyone met the news with various degrees of enthusiasm with the children being the least eager to leave. It had been something of an adventure for them and a respite from the chores at home. Cort and Brett, on the other hand, practically ran out the door with Chandler following close behind.

Leaving Bridget in charge of vacating the children, Devon took the doctor aside. "May I have a word with you, Dr. Morse?"

"Of course, Mrs. Wainwright."

He followed her into the kitchen, and she poured them coffee.

"Please sit down," she said, handing him a cup.

"You look as though there is something on your mind," observed the doctor, taking a seat at the table. "Are you feeling well? You had quite a harrowing experience and then to be saddled with unexpected guests for a few days…I imagine it has been quite a strain."

"I'm fine." She sat down across from him. "Doctor, hypothetically speaking, if someone were suffering from hypothermia, what would that person be experiencing?"

"Well, it depends on how advanced the hypothermia is," he replied. "If it is severe, the person will stop shivering."

Devon looked at him nonplussed. "Why? I should think that to be a good sign."

"On the contrary, Mrs. Wainwright. Shivering is the body's attempt to warm itself. If the body temperature is too low, it can no longer do so."

Morse stopped to take a sip of his coffee.

"The person may also experience confusion, drowsiness, a weak pulse, and shallow breathing," he continued. "Once the person slips into a state of unconsciousness, it is certain death unless action is immediately taken to increase the body temperature and stabilize the heart rate."

"Action like what?" inquired Devon.

"Wet clothes should be removed and the person covered in layers of blankets, and, if a fire is possible, the patient needs to be placed as close to it as is safely possible," explained Morse. "If the patient doesn't seem to be warming, more drastic action must be taken."

Devon was silent for a moment. "What would you consider to be drastic action?" she asked.

"Well, I would say skin-to-skin contact with someone."

When a bright pink suffused her cheeks and she looked down at her cup, the doctor smiled, putting together what might have transpired on that ridge in Browns Canyon.

"Is there anything else you wish to know?" he asked.

Devon shook her head. "No. Thank you."

Dr. Morse strolled into the marshal's office later that afternoon.

"Have you got a drink in that drawer?" he asked, dropping wearily into a chair.

Cort took out a bottle of whiskey and two tin cups from his desk and poured each of them a drink.

"To what do I owe the pleasure?" he inquired, sliding a cup over to the doctor.

"A long day," replied the older man, taking a swig of the liquor. "I-uh-had an interesting conversation with Mrs. Wainwright this morning," he remarked casually.

Templeton eyed the doctor with more interest. He had come to recognize the man's understated approach when he had something of a sensitive nature to discuss.

"What did she say?" asked Cort.

"She wanted to know about hypothermia—hypothetically speaking," said Morse.

When Templeton made no response, the doctor continued. "How do you know so much about hypothermia?"

Cort leaned back in his chair and took a sip of his drink.

"I was on a government expedition to the Rockies after the war to map the area," he replied. "It was cold. One of the men became ill—tired, listless, dazed. We attributed it to the altitude sickness and told him to sleep it off. The next morning, he didn't wake up. A doctor arrived that afternoon with the second half of the expedition and said the man had died from hypothermia."

Cort shook his head. "Henderschott had survived the war only to freeze to death on top of a mountain." He quaffed his drink, still amazed by the irony of it. "It affected the rest of the men so much they were afraid to go to sleep, so the doctor educated us on the subject."

He looked the doctor in the eye. "I know what it means when a person stops shivering, the breathing becomes shallow, and he slips into unconsciousness—hypothetically speaking."

Morse nodded. He threw back the rest of his whiskey and stood up. "I let Mrs. Wainwright know that the right treatment was applied, hypothetically speaking," he said with a twinkle in his eye. "I don't know if it made her feel any better, but at least she knows. Thanks for the drink."

When the doctor left, Cort considered what Morse had told him. He was well aware that Devon was uncomfortable in his presence and figured it went back to what had occurred in the cabin on the ridge. He was wondering how much that might have contributed to her wanting to return East and what he could do about it, when Jasper walked into the office.

"Some men brought Hagen's body in," he said. "They was huntin' on the ridge when they come across it."

"How bad is it?" asked Cort.

Jasper scratched his head in bewilderment. "Well, animals got at him, but Doc says that ain't what killed him. He was shot first."

"Yeah, I know. I shot him in the arm," said Cort. "But that wouldn't have killed Hagen."

"That ain't it, Marshal. Hagen was shot in the back with a rifle."

Templeton came forward in his chair. "Where is the body?"

"At the undertaker's."

When Cort walked into the undertaker's prep room, he saw Hagen's mutilated body on the table.

"I wondered how long it would take you to get here," said Dr. Morse. He cocked his head to one side. "You don't seem surprised."

"I was when Jasper first gave me the news," said Cort. "Then, I remembered something. When Hagen ran off after I shot him, I heard a mountain lion and a gun shot. I figured Hagen was scaring the animal off. A few minutes later, I heard another shot. I thought, at the time, that second shot sounded different, but I had to tend to Mrs. Wainwright and forgot about it."

"Someone else was up there on that ridge," said the doctor. "Couldn't have been anyone in Hagen's gang. They're all in jail. Who else would it be?"

"Maybe Mr. Goodnight," murmured Cort thinking aloud.

"Who?"

Cort took the doctor aside. "Doc, keep this under your hat. You've heard of the Knights of the Golden Circle?"

Morse nodded. "They were disbanded after the war."

"They just went underground. It looks like they are regrouping," said Cort.

"The devil you say. How do you know?"

Templeton recounted the conversation Devon had overheard between Alice Graham and Hagen about Mr. Goodnight and of Hagen's etching of the KGC symbol in the top of the table in the cabin on the ridge.

The doctor let out a low whistle. "They almost won the war for the Confederacy.... How do they expect to fund another one?"

"I think they've been recruiting disaffected Confederate soldiers to steal for the cause," said Cort. "I'm certain that's why Hagen and his men were robbing the Denver Assay Office. That gold would have purchased a lot of guns if they had been successful."

Dr. Morse nodded. "If that is the case, Mr. Goodnight must not have been happy when Hagen botched the robbery."

"And Hagen became too much of a liability when he shot Brett and kidnapped Mrs. Wainwright," added Templeton.

"Do you know who this Goodnight is?" asked Morse.

Cort shook his head. "According to Mrs. Wainwright, neither did Hagen nor Alice Graham. If the KGC operates anything like it did in the old days, we may never know. Goodnight could be anyone."

"Sounds like he's tying up loose ends," surmised the doctor. "With Hagen and the schoolteacher dead and Hagen's gang in jail, maybe Goodnight's plans were thwarted enough that he has moved on."

"Maybe." But Cort didn't sound convinced.

* * * * *

Devon sat quietly in the parlor while Matthew Chandler delivered his proposal of marriage on bended knee, calling up every ounce of Southern charm in his arsenal.

Admittedly, she was touched by it, but at the end, she shook her head. "I'm sorry, Matt, I cannot marry you."

He looked nonplussed. "Why? Is it because of what Cort and Nettie have said about me?"

"No, it is not that," said Devon. "I had one marriage. I have no wish to experience another."

Matt was silent for a minute as he regrouped. He sat down on the sofa beside her and took her hands in his. "Devon, I know that you had an unpleasant experience with your first marriage, but I am not like your husband—and I am not like that young man anymore who treated Jenny so shamefully."

"I know, Matt, and I do like you, but my answer is still 'no.'"

Chandler imagined that he detected a waver of doubt in her voice and felt confident in his ability to overcome her resistance.

"You will find me quite insistent," he warned lightly.

"My answer will be the same, Matt."

"We shall see." He kissed her on the cheek and stood up. "I'll let myself out."

Devon breathed a sigh of relief when she heard the front door close on him. Matt was tenacious. She knew he wouldn't give up easily, but, at least, she had cleared the first hurdle. With that task out of the way, she had one other loose end to tie up, and she called Bridget into the parlor.

"Is something amiss?" asked Bridget in consternation.

"Yes, Bridget, there is. You have not been forthright with me."

The young woman looked alarmed. "Oh, Miss Devon, I didna say a word about the marshal and your corset. No, miss, I didna…not to Brett or to anyone. I swear it."

Devon shifted uncomfortably. "That is not what I am referring to, Bridget. Before the quarantine, it was brought to my attention that Deputy Sanger had asked you to marry him."

"I told him 'no,' miss," the young woman quickly assured her.

"Why?" asked Devon. "Do you not wish to marry him?"

"Oh, yes, miss, with all me heart. But I kenna leave ye."

"You don't have to choose between us, Bridget."

Bridget looked at her mistress in bewilderment. "I do na understand, miss."

"If you love Mr. Sanger and truly want to marry him, you must do so," said Devon.

Bridget blinked in surprise. "Miss Devon, did ye just say—"

"Yes, Bridget, I said that you should marry Mr. Sanger."

The young woman put her hands to her face. Tears sprang to her eyes, and she nearly jumped for joy. "Oh, Miss Devon, does this mean that ye be stayin' in Blue Springs?"

Devon hesitated. "I cannot say, Bridget, but whether I stay or not has nothing to do with you."

Bridget, again, looked nonplussed. "Where you go, I must go."

"No, Bridget, not anymore," replied Devon. "Make no mistake. I am touched by your devotion to me, and I highly value your loyalty, company, and service, but you are not enslaved or indentured. You must live your life for yourself, not for me. Now, does Mr. Sanger have suitable housing for the two of you?"

"We never really talked about it," said Bridget.

"A deputy does not make much money," noted Devon. "There are more than enough bedrooms upstairs. If you and Mr. Sanger are agreeable, I propose that we take two adjoining rooms and make a suite of them, such as mine. I'm sure the marshal will help you with the conversion.

"In lieu of rent," she continued, "I will benefit by having a lawman living in my house for security and a handyman for maintenance. The arrangement will benefit us all. Have you a suitable gown in which to be married?"

"I-I don't know," replied Bridget, overwhelmed.

"No matter. My aunt had several lovely gowns. I'm sure we can find one suitable for your wedding."

"Oh, Miss Devon, I don't know what to say."

"I do. Go and inform Mr. Sanger that you will accept his proposal and that you have my approval and blessing," instructed Devon. "But tell him that if he does anything to make you unhappy, he shall have to deal with me."

Bridget laughed and wiped away tears of happiness from her eyes. She started to run out of the room, then turned back and hugged Devon. "Thank ye, miss."

As she ran out of the room, Devon smiled and wiped away a tear of her own. Pastor Clemmons was right. Sometimes, it did help to do something for someone else.

CHAPTER TWENTY-EIGHT

No Peace

Nettie finally returned to Blue Springs, not at all pleased to learn of all the excitement she had missed. The students had resumed their regular school routine with the measles scare behind them. Bridget and Brett were excitedly planning a Christmas wedding, and, in addition to teaching, Devon was busy putting together the holiday concert. Everything was back to "normal."

Devon awoke this morning feeling particularly uplifted. It was a bright, crisp, sunny day. Christmas was around the corner, raising everyone's spirits. The preparations for the concert were going well. Everything was wonderfully ordinary…. Then came the authoritative knock on the front door.

"Hold yer horses," yelled Nettie as the knocking became more impatient. "I'm comin."

She opened the door to see a well-dressed older woman of obvious sophistication. Already, Nettie didn't like her.

"What's so important ya gotta knock down the door?" she asked in a tone and manner that didn't bode well for the visitor.

The woman bristled. "I wish to see Mrs. Wainwright," she said, looking down her nose at Nettie.

"She's busy now. Ye'll have to come back."

"I will see Mrs. Wainwright now," the woman haughtily declared.

"No, you won't," said Nettie.

With a huff of indignation, the woman pushed her way into the house. "Who do you think you are? You are just a servant," she trilled loudly. "How dare you address me that way?"

At the commotion, Devon excused herself from the children and hurried into the foyer.

"Mother!" she exclaimed, shocked and dismayed. "What—why are you here?"

Mrs. Toller snapped open the *Boston Herald* newspaper that she held in her hand. "This is why I am here."

Devon groaned as she read the headline: BOSTON SOCIALITE KIDNAPPED BY OUTLAW IN COLORADO TERRITORY; SAVED BY TOWN MARSHAL.

"It is the talk of Boston. As I've had no word from you, I had to travel here myself to know of your situation," Mrs. Toller admonished her daughter. "And such a god-awful trip it was. A stagecoach is not fit transportation for decent people," she rambled on. "Can you imagine I was expected to spend the night sleeping on the floor at this way station?! I had to pay the proprietors to use their bed. And what they offered for a water closet—well, there are no words to explain the crudity of that!"

"You shouldn't have come, Mother. You know how newspapers exaggerate. I'm fine."

"It would seem that you aren't fine," said Mrs. Toller as the students emerged from the parlor to peer curiously at the guest. "You have a house full of children and the rudest servant I have ever encountered."

"I ain't a servant," retorted Nettie.

"You answered the door. That makes you a servant," declared Agatha Toller crisply.

Devon recognized the dangerous glint in Nettie's eyes and quickly stepped between the two women.

"Children, Nettie, this is my mother Mrs. Toller from Boston," she said.

As a murmur of awe passed among the students, Devon's mother cast a critical eye over them. "Who are all these children, and why are they here?"

"They are students, Mother. I am teaching them until a new teacher can be found."

"Here? Isn't there a school? What happened to the other school-teacher?"

"The school was burned down by outlaws," replied one of the younger students.

"And our teacher helped Billy Hagen kidnap Mrs. Wainwright," interjected another.

"And Marshal Templeton saved her," finished an older girl with a romantic sigh.

Mrs. Toller's eyes swiveled to Devon. "Apparently, the newspaper wasn't exaggerating. I told you this was no fit place for a young wom-an of your breeding. I insist that you return to Boston with me immediately."

"I'm sorry, Mother, I cannot leave."

"Surely you don't mean to stay," said Mrs. Toller in astonishment. "You have experienced for yourself that it isn't civilized here. You are lucky to be alive and unscathed."

"Mother, we will discuss this later," said Devon, conscious of the students' eyes on them.

"No, we shall discuss this now, daughter."

"I don't know how long I will remain here, Mother, but I am not returning to Boston at this time," replied Devon firmly.

"How do you expect to live?" quizzed the older woman. "A Toller doesn't toil."

"I have an inheritance," Devon reminded her mother, failing to mention that she was refusing to accept it.

Mrs. Toller scoffed. "I saw your sign out front. At least you don't intend to keep running a boarding house."

An older boy sniggered. "This weren't no boarding house. It was a—"

"School is dismissed for the day," Devon announced, quickly cutting him off. "We will resume your studies tomorrow. No homework."

The students let out a whoop. They quickly gathered their hats and coats and darted around Devon's mother to dash out the door.

"Well, I never!" huffed Mrs. Toller with indignation. "Those children need to be taught some manners."

Nettie smirked. "Maybe ya shouldna planted yerself in front of the door."

Mrs. Toller raised a brow and turned her attention to the annoying little woman. "You may take my bags upstairs. The others will arrive shortly."

"I told you. I ain't no servant," said Nettie.

"Then what are you?"

"I look after things here as a favor to Miss Sadie."

"Who is Miss Sadie?" demanded Mrs. Toller impatiently. "I thought this was my sister's house."

"Sadie is the name that Aunt Clarissa used here," explained Devon.

"Why? Why would she use another name?"

"Probably to forget the past and start a new life, Mother."

"I never heard of such a thing. Well, who is going to carry my bags upstairs then?" queried Mrs. Toller.

"Why don't you try doin' it yourself," suggested Nettie snidely.

Devon's mother glared down her nose at Nettie but saw that she was not going to get anywhere with this low-born creature. She looked around her. "Where is Bridget?"

"She's running errands. Mother, I don't really have servants. Things are different out here. We do for ourselves and each other," explained Devon.

Mrs. Toller dismissed the idea with the wave of her hand. "Nonsense. A Toller always has servants. It would appear that I have come in the nick of time. You have quite forgotten yourself, daughter."

"This ain't Boston, lady," interjected Nettie.

When her mother and Nettie began to argue again, Devon threw up her hands and fled the house.

Marshal Templeton was sitting at his desk looking through some warrants, when Devon walked in and dropped dejectedly into the chair. She had been doing her level best to keep a distance between them, but her mother trumped any difficulties she had with the marshal at the moment.

"Trouble?" he asked, surprised to see her.

"Not until an hour ago," she replied dismally.

Cort had an idea what the source of her problem was.

"Had an encounter with your mother myself," he said.

Devon looked at him, hesitant to ask. "Under what circumstance?"

"She created quite a ruckus when she got off the stage…insisted that I arrest a passenger for ungentlemanly conduct," replied Cort.

"What did he do?"

"It seems that Mr. Farlington took a few too many sips of whiskey from his flask and fell asleep. When the coach rolled into town, he fell against your mother and his hand dropped into her lap," explained Cort. "The poor man had to see Doc Morse for a few stitches and a broken nose. If he presses a complaint, I may have to arrest your mother for assault."

"Oh no," groaned Devon. "Shouldn't this man bear some of the blame? If he hadn't been drinking none of this would have happened. Isn't there some law against that?"

"It is a breach of stagecoach etiquette for a passenger to get drunk but not a crime. It is left to the driver to deal with the situation," said Templeton. "Usually, the passenger is put out at the next station if he proves to be unruly."

"Well then, the driver is at fault," maintained Devon.

"The driver says that Mr. Farlington was a model passenger until after they left the last stop, at which time, Mr. Farlington claims he was finally driven to drink by your mother's incessant complaining."

Devon snorted. "I know Mother can be difficult, but isn't that a stretch?"

"Actually, I would have thought it to make perfect sense to you," responded Templeton.

Devon ignored his remark. "I'm sure the other passengers will bear witness to the fact that the man was out of line."

"The other passengers are taking his side, Mrs. Wainwright."

Devon propped her elbows on the desk and put her head in her hands. "This is a nightmare," she moaned.

Cort pulled out the bottle of whiskey. "This might help," he said, pouring a small amount into a cup.

Accustomed to fine cut crystal, Devon looked questioningly at the tin cup for a second, then sighed and reached for it. This was the Wild West, and she was sitting in a jail office. How far her expectations had dropped.

She took a sip of the liquor, grimacing at the taste. "Doesn't any-one in this town have a good wine?"

"I'm afraid you will have to make do with whiskey or beer."

Devon forced down a few more sips before shoving the cup away.

"Chandler has wine in his private stock," Cort commented off-handedly.

"That is not an option," responded Devon shortly. "Every time Matt sees me, he pesters me to marry him. Why do men assume that all women want to get married?" she asked in annoyance.

Cort shrugged. "I suppose because most women do."

"Well, I don't," she flatly stated.

"If I have learned anything, Mrs. Wainwright, it is that life is shaped by events—most times beyond our control. In the blink of an eye, anything can change."

"In these past few months, Marshal, I've had a lifetime of change. I will accept no more." Devon rose from the chair. "I should get back to the house before my mother and Nettie kill each other. It's like being in the eye of a storm with those two."

A look of panic suddenly swept across her features. "Good heavens! Bridget doesn't know that Mother is here. I must warn her not to let it slip that Aunt Clarissa's boarding house was a brothel," she said, rushing out the door.

When Devon returned to the house, she was surprised to find that all was quiet, in spite of the fact that her mother's trunk and bags still remained in the foyer.

When Nettie appeared, she asked tentatively: "Where is my mother?"

Nettie snorted. "In the bathin' room. There ain't much to her likin' 'bout the house, but she sure likes that part. Been in there for better part of an hour. She ain't stayin' here, is she?"

Devin sighed. "I don't know."

"Well, she ain't gettin' my room," grumbled the housekeeper.

"Has Bridget returned yet?"

Nettie shook her head. "She probably heard your mother was here."

Devon ignored the comment. "When Bridget comes in, warn her not to say anything about this having been a—a salon. I'll be in my suite."

The housekeeper again shook her head, this time in dismay. "Miss Sadie is turnin' over in her grave," she muttered.

For the next few days, Devon balanced the responsibilities of teaching school, overseeing the remodeling of two bedrooms into a suite for Bridget and Brett, and acting as a buffer between Nettie and her mother.

This afternoon, she sat in the kitchen enjoying a rare moment of silence and a cup of tea. The students and workers had just left for the day, and her mother was visiting the general store. Devon prayed that she and Bridget would still be welcome patrons.

She was about to pour a second cup of tea, when Mrs. Toller stormed into the house. "Devon! Pack your bags. We are leaving this godforsaken place immediately," she shouted.

Devon cringed. With a heavy sigh, she set the teapot down and went to see what had upset her mother this time.

"What's amiss, Mother?" she asked resignedly, walking into the foyer.

"This town—and I use the word loosely—is unsafe for a woman of decency," Mrs. Toller ranted.

"Has something occurred?" inquired Devon.

"Well, I should say so!" exclaimed the older woman. "I was openly accosted on the street by a ruffian. Where are the police in this town?"

"Mother, calm down and tell me what happened."

"I was coming out of the store—which, by the way, is woefully inadequate—when this man, who most certainly was not a gentleman of class, approached me to ask if I was married. Can you imagine such impertinence? Why, I had to take my cane to him."

Nettie had come from the parlor to hear the conversation and rolled her eyes.

"Mother, he meant no disrespect," said Devon.

Mrs. Toller stared at her daughter, incredulous. "No disrespect— the man accosted me."

Devon took a deep breath and attempted to explain about the uneven ratio of men to women in the West and that, when a woman arrives new to town, it is not uncommon for single men seeking wives to approach her about her availability.

Agatha Toller was dumbfounded. "How could that man possibly think that I, a member of Boston society, would have any interest in him? He was obviously a ne'er-do-well."

Nettie snickered. "Some of them 'ne'er-do-wells' is miners that probably got more money than you in gold."

Mrs. Toller glared at her. "No man of real wealth is without manners," she returned haughtily. "I don't expect someone like you to understand that."

"Lady, why don't you take that stick out of your—"

"Nettie!" exclaimed Devon.

There was a momentary halt to hostilities before Mrs. Toller and Nettie began arguing again. Devon was shouting above them to stop, when Matthew Chandler strolled in.

Agatha Toller broke off in surprise at the appearance of a bona fide gentleman.

"I let myself in," he said. "I hope I'm not interrupting anything." He flashed Mrs. Toller a disarming smile and took her hand with a gallant bow. "You must be Devon's mother. I see where your daughter gets her beauty."

Nettie made a face and went off to the kitchen, muttering.

"Well, thank goodness there is one person in this town who knows manners," tittered Mrs. Toller. "Devon, who is this nice, gentleman?"

"This is Mr. Chandler, Mother."

"Matthew Chandler," he interjected.

"Perhaps you will join us for tea in the parlor, Mr. Chandler, now that those children are gone for the day," invited Mrs. Toller.

"Matt probably has other things to do, Mother."

"Actually, I don't," responded Chandler. "I am pleased to accept your kind offer, madam." He held out his arm to Devon's mother. "May I?"

Mrs. Toller gave a little laugh. "You may."

Devon's jaw dropped as Chandler and her mother walked arm-in-arm into the parlor like long lost friends.

She strode into the kitchen in a snit. "Nettie, bring tea to the parlor. It seems that my mother has finally found someone she likes in this town."

Nettie snorted. "Two peas in a pod them two."

"No spiking the tea with a physic," warned Devon.

She left the kitchen and was crossing the foyer, when she was shocked to hear her mother giggling like a schoolgirl.

"I had always heard about that famous Southern charm," Mrs. Toller was saying as Devon entered the parlor. "After meeting you, Mr. Chandler, I dare say the claims are not exaggerated. What a shame that you people had to start that horrible war."

"Mother!" admonished Devon.

Chandler didn't flinch. "I must agree with you, Mrs. Toller."

"I am surprised to hear you say that," she replied. "Southerners are quite touchy on the subject."

Chandler smiled. "If I learned anything from the war, madam, it is better to bend with the wind."

"Charming and a philosopher, too. What is your education, Mr. Chandler?"

"West Point, madam."

"West Point…very fine, indeed. What a pity you went over to the other side."

"Mother, please," said Devon. "The war is over. People don't wish to discuss it."

"Oh, very well," her mother huffed. "Mr. Chandler, how make you a living now, sir?"

"I own a business establishment, madam."

"What kind of business establishment?" she pressed.

"A dance hall and saloon," he answered forthrightly.

Devon braced herself for the storm, but her mother remained surprisingly measured.

"I do not approve of such an establishment, Mr. Chandler."

"It is temporary employment," he replied. "I intend to sell my holdings in Blue Springs and invest my resources in commercial gold mining operations in California."

"I see. Where in California?" quizzed Mrs. Toller.

"The Sacramento area."

"Your choice of investment seems rather tenuous, Mr. Chandler."

He smiled. "Not so, Mrs. Toller. There is new technology now and new deposits are being discovered every day. Add to that, there is talk that the government may be switching back to the gold standard to end the depression. I needn't tell you how that will increase the value of gold."

"How very clever of you, sir. What holds you here?"

"Your daughter, madam. Alas, she cannot see her way clear to accepting my proposal of marriage. Perhaps you might convince her."

Mrs. Toller's gaze swiveled to Devon. "Is this true? You have refused his proposal?"

Devon wanted to leap across the room and slap Chandler. "Yes, Mother."

"Mr. Chandler is a most charming and attractive man. You are not getting any younger, daughter. If he possesses generous resources and the keen mind to invest them in a more reputable business that will take you away from this backward town, why would you decline his offer?"

"Because, Mother, I do not wish to marry again. Matt knows that he is not the issue."

"Well then, I dare say nothing is written in stone, sir," declared Mrs. Toller giving Chandler a smile of encouragement.

CHAPTER TWENTY-NINE

More Than One Truth

"I'm tellin' ya, Cort, I thought Mrs. Wainwright was fearsome, but that mother of hers wins the prize," said Brett. "As much as I want to marry Bridget, I ain't lookin' forward to livin' in the same house with that woman. How long do ya reckon she'll stay?"

"My guess is as good as yours," replied Templeton, perusing the newspaper.

"That ain't encouragin'," grumbled Sanger.

Frank Stilwell walked into the office then clearly agitated.

"Cort, I just got back into town. Is it true that Mrs. Wainwright's mother is here?"

Cort set aside the newspaper and looked at his deputy. "Brett, why don't you see the blacksmith about a new set of manacles?"

Sanger glumly nodded. He grabbed his hat and coat and left the office.

"What's wrong with him?" asked Stilwell.

"The same thing that is wrong with you," replied Cort. "It would seem that Mrs. Toller has everyone on edge."

"What do you think that woman is doing in Blue Springs?"

"She saw the story about Mrs. Wainwright's kidnapping and came to fetch her back to Boston," said Templeton.

Stilwell ran a hand across his face. "What do you think we should do?"

"Nothing. Let it play out, Frank."

"What if it doesn't, and Mrs. Wainwright leaves?"

"Then she leaves."

"Hello, gentlemen. I hope I'm not interrupting anything," said Chandler, striding into the office.

"This seems to be a popular place today," quipped Cort. "We were discussing Mrs. Wainwright's mother being in town."

Chandler smiled. "Ah, yes…lovely woman."

"I don't believe that is quite the impression she is leaving with others," remarked Templeton.

Chandler shrugged. "One has to know how to handle a strong woman." He looked at the attorney. "Frank, do you mind if I speak to Cort in private?"

Stilwell hesitated, not yet finished airing his own issue. "Yeah, sure. I'll talk with you later, Cort."

When the attorney left, Chandler sat down.

Templeton's eyes narrowed. "Something on your mind, Matt?"

"What happened up on the ridge, Cort?"

"What are you getting at?"

"Devon has changed since her return. She's more distant, quieter."

"The hours she spent with Hagen were terrifying to her, Matt. She didn't know what he was going to do from one minute to the next…if she was going to live or die. She just needs some time."

"That's not what I mean," said Chandler. "Did something happen between the two of you? She seems to act differently with you now."

"As opposed to what?"

"There was always friction between you before. Now, I sense a…a camaraderie of sorts."

Cort shrugged. "She tried to avoid me as much as she did you during the quarantine."

Chandler stiffened at the inference. "Devon was overwhelmed. I wouldn't make an assumption," he warned. He stood up to leave. "By the way, Mrs. Toller is going to be staying for awhile. She is having Devon connect the other two rooms into a suite for her."

"Why should that interest me?" asked Templeton.

"She is in my corner."

"That might not work to your benefit," commented Cort.

Chandler's eyes narrowed. "What do you mean?"

"Nothing…. I wouldn't think a woman like Mrs. Toller would approve of her daughter marrying the owner of a dance hall and saloon."

"I assured her it was temporary. I have decided to move to California to invest in a business opportunity when Devon and I marry."

"Have you told Mrs. Wainwright that?"

"She knows."

"And yet she hasn't said 'yes' to you," observed Cort. "It seems to me that she isn't in a hurry to leave Blue Springs."

"It's just a matter of time," said Chandler as he walked to the door.

"Matt," called Templeton, "when did Alice Graham die?"

Chandler turned to him. "I don't know exactly. She died on the way into town. Doc can tell you better."

"Did she say anything more?"

Chandler shook his head. "She never became conscious after you left the cabin. Why?"

"Just curious. Hunters brought in Hagen's body."

"Yeah, I heard. A mountain lion got him."

"That's not what killed him," said Cort, watching the gambler closely. "He was shot. Someone else was on that ridge. The gunman was probably hoping a wild animal would mutilate the body enough that it wouldn't be noticed."

"It appears someone did you a favor then," remarked Chandler, his features expressionless.

"Maybe, but I think it more likely that someone was doing Mr. Goodnight a favor."

"Who is Mr. Goodnight?"

"I thought you might be able tell me," said Cort.

"Why would I know?" queried Chandler.

"As the proprietor of the Golden Nugget, you hear things, notice strangers."

"Never heard the name. Where did you hear of it?"

"Mrs. Wainwright."

Chandler was visibly surprised. "Devon? How did she hear it?"

"She overheard a conversation between Alice Graham and Hagen when she was held captive," replied Templeton.

"What sort of conversation?"

"Just that Mr. Goodnight wasn't happy with the way things were going. I suspect there is a larger story here than just the tale of a robber."

Chandler was pensive for a moment. "I'll let you know if I hear anything."

He left the office then, passing Brett on his way in.

"What was he doin' here?" asked Sanger.

"Nothing important," replied Templeton.

Cort leaned back in his chair more disturbed than he let on about Matt Chandler's plans to marry Devon and whisk her off to California. He suspected Mrs. Toller's motivation for getting her daughter to leave Blue Springs, but what was Chandler's? Why was Matt so hell bent upon marrying Devon? For the love of her? As desirable a woman as Devon might be, Cort wasn't buying it.

* * * * *

Devon dismissed school and hurried to the general store just as she had every day for the past week.

"Mrs. Walker, is it here yet?" she asked. "I fear that time is not a friend."

The shopkeeper's eyes twinkled merrily. "Today, my dear, it is." She went behind the counter, took out an elongated box, and opened it. "I believe it is as you ordered it."

Devon smiled. "It is perfect. Mrs. Walker, I should like to keep this between us."

"My lips are sealed," the shopkeeper replied with a conspiratorial wink. "I haven't even told Hiram. The man can't keep a secret to save his soul." She paused. "Is…is your mother expectin' to come to the store today?"

"No, I don't believe so," replied Devon.

The shopkeeper breathed a sigh of relief.

Armed with her special package, Devon strode out of the store and came to an abrupt halt when she spied Pearl Donovan coming out of the marshal's office. She quickly turned to duck back inside the store, but she was too late.

"Mrs. Wainwright…hello," called Pearl.

Devon turned around and gave a tepid wave of her hand, hoping that would be the end of it. But Pearl quickly crossed the street to her.

"How nice to see you again, Mrs. Wainwright."

"Miss Donovan, what brings you to Blue Springs…again?" questioned Devon, unenthused. "If you are here about my aunt…"

Pearl smiled. "No, I brought a Christmas present for the marshal. I wanted to make sure that he received it in time. I understand that you and the children are performing a Christmas concert. Cort says it promises to be quite good. Perhaps I shall delay my return to Denver to attend."

"It is just a simple performance," said Devon. "I doubt it is worth postponing your trip. Besides, Mr. Walker tells me that, according to his bones, it is going to snow soon and make travel more difficult."

Pearl smiled. "Well then, I would say that gives me all the more reason to stay. Have a good day, Mrs. Wainwright."

As Devon watched Pearl walk down the boardwalk to the hotel, it was all she could do to keep from stamping her foot in vexation. The woman annoyed her to no end. The observations Pearl had made on that first visit to her still rankled, perhaps because Devon knew a few of them to be true.

Once she had thought about it, Devon realized that she did feel as though she had been bartered and that it was probably the basis for the resentment she still felt over her marriage. And she had to admit that Pearl was right about money empowering women. She had certainly felt empowered enough to defy her mother after learning about her inheritance. But Devon drew the line at being called a gold-digger.

She returned home in a sour mood only to find the house in an up-roar. Her mother was lying on the couch in a state of hysteria, and Bridget was attempting to calm her by applying a lavender-scented compress to her forehead.

"What has happened?" she asked in alarm.

Nettie snickered. "One of the workers told her that this weren't no boarding house."

Devon moaned. "Oh, dear God."

Over the next couple of hours, Devon worked to calm her mother, but her mother wasn't to be calmed.

Agatha Toller furiously paced the floor of the parlor. "How dare that woman! How dare Clarissa shame the family name like that!" she ranted. "If anyone hears about this in Boston—it was bad enough when she said she was running a boarding house in a lawless Western town. To find out that she was actually running a bawdy house—it is too much to bear," she wailed, dropping into a chair.

Devon rolled her eyes heavenward and prayed for fortitude as she had done so many times since her mother's arrival.

"Mother, please. Get hold of yourself. I was just as shocked as you when I learned of it. But it is not as bad as you think."

Her mother stopped crying and looked at her in disbelief. "How can you say that? Our name will be ruined."

"No one in Boston will know of it, Mother. Aunt Clarissa changed her name to protect the family."

"I knew there was something suspicious about that. Why didn't you tell me?"

"Because I knew you would react this way," said Devon.

"Well, how should I react? I've just been told that my sister was the madam of a bordello, and God only knows how she rose to that," cried Mrs. Toller. "How can you live here with that stain on our name? We must leave for Boston immediately."

"I told you. I cannot leave, Mother. I have a concert to put on. The children have been practicing for weeks, and I'll not disappoint them or the townspeople."

"Who cares about a silly concert in this wretched place?"

"Everyone," replied Devon. "They don't see much entertainment."

"How can I hold my head up when everyone knows what my sister was?"

"People have a different attitude here, Mother. Sadie—Clarissa—helped a lot of people. She was highly regarded and still is—"

"How can you defend her?" demanded Mrs. Toller.

"It is how the townspeople see her that is important, Mother."

Mrs. Toller rose from the chair, her features set in a determined line. "Very well, Devon, put on your concert if you are so insistent. But afterwards, you will either return to Boston with me and marry Mr. Birdwell, or you will marry that nice Mr. Chandler and go to California with him. More than ever now, you must have the protection of marriage."

With that, Agatha Toller swept from the room, sidestepping Nettie with a glare.

Nettie's lips quivered with amusement as she entered the parlor. "Thought you could use some tea, missy," she said, setting a tray on the table. "You ain't gonna do neither of them things what yer mother said, are ya?"

Devon sighed heavily and put a hand to her forehead. "Both my mother and Mr. Chandler are forces to be reckoned with and neither take 'no' for an answer."

"Well, I hope ya don't leave, missy. I kinda got used to havin' ya around—and the children would miss ya even when ya ain't teachin' 'em no more."

Devon looked at Nettie, surprised and touched by the woman's rare moment of sentimentality. "Thank you, Nettie."

"I reckon the marshal would be right sorry to see ya go, too."

"I think the marshal will be very happy to see my mother and me leave town," replied Devon with a wry smile.

"Maybe yer mother, but not you, missy."

Devon remained skeptical. "I saw Miss Donovan in town," she mentioned casually. "She and the marshal seem to be quite close. She came all the way from Denver just to deliver him a Christmas present."

"Pearl and Cort go way back together. Ain't nothin' they wouldn't do for each other. They was always Miss Sadie's favorites."

"How is it that they never married then?" questioned Devon.

Nettie laughed. "Them two...ain't a chance. Cort is a one-woman man. Pearl ain't a one-man woman. And neither one is gonna change. They understood that about each other a long time ago. What they got between 'em is trust and respect. Ain't many ya can say that about. Well, I best be about my chores."

"Wait," said Devon. "Tell me more about my aunt."

A smile transformed Nettie's features. "Miss Sadie was as beautiful as she was pure of heart. Everyone loved her. Ain't no one she wouldn't help who deserved helpin'. During the cholera epidemic some years back, she took in miners and nursed 'em. That's how come miners have a special feelin' for her. She was smart, too, and she had a wicked wit that could tear a body down to size whoever he was. And oh, how she loved music. She could sing like a nightingale."

"If she was so smart and pretty, how could she have chosen a life like this?" asked Devon, still struggling to understand.

Nettie shrugged. "She didn't choose it. It's what was left to her, and she made the best of it. In the end, she lived her life the way she wanted."

"As what…a prostitute and a madam? How is that a life to be proud of?"

Nettie's features hardened and she drew herself up. "Don't ever talk against Miss Sadie like that again," she responded sharply. "Ya don't know nothin' 'bout her life and what she suffered. Ya ain't got no right to sit in judgment of her."

Devon stared after Nettie, stunned, as she stormed out of the room.

It took a few hours and considerable finesse for Devon to mend fences with Nettie. It wasn't that Devon felt the need to apologize for maligning her aunt. It was, after all, the way she felt. But she needed to maintain peace in some corner of her house.

School was in recess when Agatha Toller strode imperiously into the house the next day and ordered: "Bridget, pack my bags."

Devon looked at her mother in surprise. "Are you returning to Boston?"

"Good heavens no, but I cannot continue to live in this bawdy house."

"This is no longer a parlor house, Mother. And I have redecorated it."

"It doesn't matter if you replaced every board, Devon. A residue of tawdriness will forever hang over this property."

"Where are you going then?"

"To the hotel. I just met a lovely woman of class and high standing who is visiting from Denver."

Devon nearly gasped aloud, and she shot Nettie a look of warning when she heard her snicker.

"She is staying at the hotel," continued Mrs. Toller. "And she suggested that I do the same. She assured me that it is a dwelling of quality and above reproach in reputation. I have a boy coming to collect my bags. Do not try to talk me out of it, Devon."

"Ain't no need to worry 'bout that," muttered Nettie.

Devon closed her eyes and took a deep breath to regain her equilibrium. She didn't want to even consider what her mother's reaction would be when Agatha Toller discovered who her new friend really was.

* * * * *

There was an air of excitement as townspeople streamed into the dance hall and saloon for the children's holiday concert. Devon noticed that her mother was not among them. She wasn't surprised, in spite of the transformation that she had made to the place to override any misgivings women might have about attending or allowing their children to perform in such an establishment.

The Golden Nugget sign had been replaced with one renaming it the Concert Hall. The bottles of liquor had been removed and the bar covered with boughs of Douglas fir. Pine boughs decorated with ribbons and ornaments made by the children were hung strategically about spreading a fresh scent of pine throughout the venue.

When everyone was seated, the children took their places on stage, and a hush fell over the audience. The hall was filled to standing room only, and Devon noticed that even miners were in attendance.

As the children looked out over the sea of faces, however, they froze when Devon started to play the piano, and there were a few awkward minutes of silence. Then Devon began to sing in a clear, melodious voice, and the children gradually joined in. The concert goers' reaction was so enthusiastic that the children lost their stage fright and sang their hearts out for the rest of the concert. Those playing instruments also turned in laudable efforts.

Toward the end, attendees were invited to join in and sing, and they did so to great participation. Devon noticed that a few miners had even been moved to tears as songs brought to mind memories of faraway homes and families.

When the concert was over, the townspeople filed out with their children, imbued with the holiday spirit. Devon was surprised and greatly moved by the magnitude of their appreciation for what she had thought to be such a small act.

She turned to Chandler. "Thank you, Matt. It was generous of you to allow the concert to take place here. I know that it cost you some profit."

He took her hands in his. "It matters little if I have made you happy, my dear."

Devon smiled. "More importantly, you have made the townspeople happy."

"It's Christmas Eve. Why don't you join me in my quarters for a glass or two of wine?" he suggested. "Can't let all this holiday spirit go to waste."

Devon laughed. "As tempting as your offer is, I must decline. Bridget and Deputy Sanger are getting married tomorrow. I have many things to attend to yet, and I should stop by the hotel to take supper with my mother."

"Of course."

"Matt, you are welcome to attend the wedding, you know," said Devon.

"Thank you, but I believe this to be a personal event where my absence would be more appreciated," he replied. "Shall I walk you to the hotel?"

Devon shook her head. "I have another matter to take care of first."

"Then, I shall give you this now." Chandler reached into his pocket and pulled out a small box with a ribbon tied around it. "I know that you are averse to accepting gifts from me, but it is my hope that you can accept this one in the spirit of Christmas."

At the frown on her face, he quickly assured her, "It is but a small token."

Devon took the box, untied the ribbon, and lifted the lid. It was a tortoise shell comb inlaid with Mother of Pearl. "Oh, Matt, it is lovely. Yes, I do believe I can accept it—in the spirit of Christmas," she added with a smile. "Thank you."

When Devon left, Chandler joined Templeton at the bar. "Looks like I won the bet," he said.

Cort coolly regarded him. "What bet is that?"

"It's the first snowfall, and Devon is still here."

"What do you want, Matt?"

"Just your acknowledgement that I have won," replied Chandler.

Templeton snorted. "I don't think Mrs. Wainwright is still here because of you."

"We'll see." Chandler took out a cheroot and lit it. "I noticed that Pearl is in town."

"So?"

"Devon's mother has moved into the hotel. Rather a coincidence, don't you think?"

"Careful, Matt, you're starting to sound paranoid."

Chandler regarded his perceived rival with suspicion. "What's your game, Cort?"

"You're the one who plays games, Matt."

Chandler smiled. "You always did hold your cards close to the vest." His smile disappeared. "Tell Pearl to keep her stories of me to herself, or Mrs. Toller is going to find out who her new friend is," he warned.

The two men locked eyes for a moment before Chandler moved away.

Cort left the saloon and strode across the street to the jail in a heavy mood. He was one of the few who wasn't feeling the holiday spirit, and his conversation with Chandler hadn't helped.

When he opened the door and walked into the small clapboard building, Templeton's eye was immediately drawn to a long, narrow box on top his desk. Nonplussed, he walked over to it and warily lifted the lid. A smile spread across his features as he gazed down at the Conroy fly rod and reel. He picked up the note and read: *To catch the fish that was lost. Merry Christmas.*

Devon walked to the house from the hotel no longer feeling the high energy of the concert. Her mother had been amiable enough throughout supper, finding the establishment somewhat to the level of her standards, but her mother's ultimatum still hung heavy over Devon's head.

When she opened the door and entered the foyer, Nettie emerged from the kitchen, a twinkle in her eyes and a smug smile on her face. Devon raised a brow, wondering if the woman had been taking a few nips of something stronger than tea.

"Did Bridget come in?" she asked.

"She come in an hour ago and took herself to bed," said Nettie, "though with all them butterflies in her stomach, I ain't sure she's gonna do much sleepin'."

Devon eyed the older woman closer. "Are you feeling all right?"

Nettie's smile broadened. "Fit as a fiddle. A package was brought for ya. It's upstairs in yer room."

"What kind of package? From whom?"

Nettie chuckled. "You'll see."

Her curiosity piqued, Devon quickly climbed the stairs and went to her suite. When she opened the door, she saw a large basket on the table. She walked over to it and lifted the lid and was astonished to find that it contained four bottles of imported French wine.

Her first thought was that Chandler had sent it. Her brow knit in perplexity, however, as she looked at the note. It just read *Merry Christmas.* It wasn't in Chandler's handwriting. Devon was familiar with that from other notes he had sent her. And the note wasn't signed. Matt would have signed it. Then, too, there was Nettie's strange behavior.

Devon suddenly recalled her complaint to the marshal that there was no good wine to be had in this town, and she looked at the note again. "No…it couldn't be," she murmured, awed by the thought. She was about to dismiss the idea, when she remembered Pearl saying that she had come to deliver a Christmas present for the marshal. Devon smiled as she realized what Pearl had meant.

CHAPTER THIRTY

A Different Prospective

Good cheer permeated the air inside and outside of the little church as the townspeople filed in for the Christmas Day service and the added excitement of a wedding.

Devon sat next to her mother. "Smile, Mother, it's Christmas."

Mrs. Toller looked about her at the crude dwelling and simply dressed parishioners and sniffed. It was a far cry from Boston.

Pearl slipped into the pew in front of them beside Nettie and Bridget and twisted around to greet Devon and her mother. "Merry Christmas, ladies."

Mrs. Toller's face brightened. "Miss Donovan, I am heartened to see another of refinement and taste among this sea of mediocrity."

Pearl gave her a smile of forbearance. "Indeed. And how did you find your gift, Mrs. Wainwright?"

Devon smiled, feeling more charitable toward the woman. "It was very well chosen, Miss Donovan—and quite a surprise I must admit."

"Cort was most specific in his instruction," said Pearl.

Devon looked over at him He sat with Brett in a pew on the other side of the aisle. She was surprised to see him in a suit of clothes, white shirt, and tie instead of the plain shirt, leather vest, and boots he usually favored. He looked quite the handsome gentleman, and she felt a fluttering in her stomach.

Pastor Clemmons took his place at the pulpit then and all turned their attention to the service.

At the conclusion, the preacher announced that the nuptials of Bridget Ryan and Brett Sanger would now take place, and Devon and Cort stood up to accompany the couple to the front of the church as their witnesses.

It was nothing like the dull, impersonal wedding ceremony that Devon's had been. It was thoughtful, loving, and heartfelt, and she could hear sniffles from the ladies in the congregation as the young couple recited their vows. She struggled to hold back a tear or two herself.

When Pastor Clemmons pronounced the couple man and wife, they looked so happy Devon felt a twinge of envy. Bridget fairly glowed and Brett looked relieved and proud. Devon glanced at Cort and found him glancing at her.

After the preacher announced that there would be a reception at the hotel restaurant, the couple walked down the aisle to the door, beaming and nodding at well-wishers along the way. Cort held out his arm to Devon, and they followed after the newlyweds.

Outside, Bridget and Brett climbed into a buggy decorated with ribbons and bells, while Cort guided Devon to another buggy. The sun shone bright, and the weather was crisp and cool as everyone made their way to the restaurant in high humor.

Devon looked over at Cort, a twinkle in her eye. "Something quite extraordinary occurred last night, Mr. Templeton."

"What is that, Mrs. Wainwright?"

"When I returned home, I discovered a basket of the most exquisite French wine in my suite, and I must confess to having partaken of a glass or two."

"It was to your liking, then?"

"Indeed, I have tasted none so fine since leaving Boston. I don't suppose you would know anything about how it came to be?"

"Perhaps it was the same spirit who brought me a Conroy fly rod and reel," he suggested.

"And was it to your satisfaction?" she asked.

He gave her a smile that warmed her. "Very much so, madam."

The reception was gay and lively. Rosie had laid out a nice spread. Nettie had made a wedding cake. And the newlyweds were toasted with hard apple cider. When all had partaken of their fill of food, tables were moved aside, a couple of men took out fiddles, and people began to dance. Even Mrs. Toller, after bemoaning the lack of elegance of an Eastern wedding, was soon tapping her feet as she availed herself more than once of the tasty hard cider.

"Lovely wedding," commented Pearl approaching Devon. "Bridget and Brett look to be a happy couple."

"Yes. I hope their happiness isn't fleeting," replied Devon. "I had sought to spare Bridget the disappointment of marriage, but, alas, I fear that she was blinded by the notion of romance."

"Rest assured, Mrs. Wainwright, I don't think the marriage bed will be a disappointment for her. I have an instinct about such things."

Devon blushed. "I'm sure you do, but that is not the only disappointment in marriage, Miss Donovan."

"You don't believe in romance or love, Mrs. Wainwright?"

"Romance is a fantasy, a foundation for deception. And love, if present at all in a marriage, is fickle," replied Devon. "I should think that, in your profession, you would know a woman can trust in neither."

"With some men I might agree with you, Mrs. Wainwright. But I believe that romance is the foundation for love, and love is steadfast when you have the right man...a man like him, for instance," said Pearl.

Devon followed Pearl's eye to Cort. When he caught her gaze on him, she became flushed and quickly looked away.

"I-I have guests to see to. Please excuse me, Miss Donovan."

Pearl smiled. "I'll be at the hotel if you wish to talk further."

"Rest assured I won't," said Devon.

As she hurried off, Nettie came to stand beside Pearl. "Her and the marshal got some things to figure out," she remarked.

"Only if they decide that they want to figure them out," responded Pearl. "They're both as stubborn as mules."

Nettie snorted. "They better decide soon. Chandler and Mrs. Toller are determined to have their way."

It was dark when the newlyweds slipped upstairs to a room in the hotel for their first night together and guests began to depart.

Cort came up to Devon. "I'll walk you home," he said.

He put her cape around her shoulders and guided her out the door, giving her no room to object. She had been preoccupied about something for much of the celebration, and he was curious to know of it. He had noticed Pearl talking with her earlier. That was never a good sign.

The night was quiet, and they walked in silence. Light from the streetlamps and the moon reflected off newly fallen snow, and there was something in the air that invited introspection.

Despite her efforts to dismiss them, Pearl's words buzzed in Devon's head. She glanced up at Cort. She couldn't imagine him the romantic type, but he was steadfast...somewhat considerate...trustworthy. He had kept her secrets and conducted himself in such a way as to spare her as much embarrassment as possible.

"Well, now that the broom has been jumped, perhaps I will have a deputy with his mind on the job," said Cort, breaking the silence.

Devon laughed. "I know what you mean. Bridget has not been very useful herself these past few weeks." She knit her brow in concern. "They haven't known each other very long. How can they possibly know if they will be happy together?"

"They can't. But they'll never know if they don't take the chance," replied Cort, thinking that to be the source of her distraction at the reception. "I wouldn't worry about them. Two people know when they belong together. They make each other happy, and there is a feeling of trust."

"Like the trust between Miss Primrose and Billy Hagen?" questioned Devon cynically.

"They were two twisted people and like attracts like," said Cort. "On the other side of the coin, look at Penny and Emmett Johnson…Ruth and Hiram Walker."

"What about Mrs. Tillotson, Mrs. Bell, and Mrs. Andrews and their husbands?" countered Devon.

Cort thought for a moment. "Bulldogs get along quite well with Chihuahuas."

Devon burst into laughter at the image. Cort found it a pleasing sound and so infectious he had to laugh as well. It was one of those moments that on the surface was silly. Below the surface, it was cathartic, and, in that moment, they were suspended in a place where emotion edged out reason.

Their laughter stopped and the air crackled with expectancy. Devon raised her face to his. It made no sense; it made perfect sense. Cort's arms went around her, and he leaned down to press his lips to hers in a light caress that evolved into a kiss of deeper desire.

When they parted, neither spoke as each worked to process the event. It came as such a surprise they didn't know quite what to do with it. Neither felt that it deserved an apology. Thus, they did what came natural to them. Cort opened the gate for her and bid her good night; Devon bid him good night and avoided his eye.

As he watched her hurry to the house and let herself in the door, Cort was wondering what had just happened. There were other instances when the thought had flashed in his mind that he might like to kiss her, but there was always the consideration of where to go from there once that line had been crossed, and, in his pragmatism, he had let those moments pass. This one, however, had hung suspended over them demanding to be addressed. He and Devon were from two different worlds. The odds were against them, thought Cort. And it vexed him how forces seemed to persist in bringing them together anyway.

* * * * *

Bridget and Brett moved into their new suite in the house, and over the next few days, Devon filled her hours with teaching and various other chores trying to keep her mind off Cort's kiss.

It had filled her with warmth and stirred something inside her she had never felt before, not that she had much experience. Her husband had never kissed her that way. Matthew Chandler's kisses actually had been her first, and it had been a new sensation, but she realized now that they didn't move her in the same way that Cort's kiss had. Matt's were light and flirtatious; Cort's had held a feeling of depth and sincerity.

Penny had said that Cort's actions spoke louder than words. But what was he saying? The basket of wine Devon had considered to be a gift of friendship—of sorts—for, as with Nettie, she wasn't sure what her relationship was with the marshal. Now with the kiss, what was she to intuit from that? Her emotions were in such a quandary this was one of those times that she wished his words would be louder than his actions.

Bridget was fair to glowing as she flitted about the house dispensing with her duties, and Devon noticed that Brett had a spring in his step when he left the house in the morning and an eagerness when he arrived home in the evening. They all barely made it through dinner before the newlyweds were excusing themselves to rush off to their suite for the night.

When Devon would later pass by their rooms, she heard giggling and laughter and the sound of the bed jingling, and she couldn't help feeling envious of the intimacy they shared and more than a little curi-

ous as to what pleasurable sex—if there really was such a thing—
actually entailed.

She walked into her suite this night feeling particularly lonely and
miserable. She poured herself a glass of wine and sat down on the settee, hoping the wine would raise her spirits and help her to see her
way clear through the confusion and conflict she felt. But thoughts of
Cort—his kiss, the events in the cabin, their small moments of intimacy—and Pearl's words refused to allow any resolution. She set down
the glass, stood up with an air of determination, and strode from the
room.

"Where are you going?" asked Nettie as Devon breezed past her on
the stairs.

"Out to see someone," said Devon.

Nettie shook her head and continued to climb the stairs to her
room. The young mistress had been acting mighty strange these past
days.

Pearl answered the knock on her door and smiled, not at all surprised to see her visitor. "Come in, Mrs. Wainwright."

Devon hesitated uncertainly on the threshold before stepping inside, her earlier determination fleeing her. "I thought you might have
returned to Denver by now."

"I decided to extend my stay," replied Pearl, closing the door.

Devon looked around the hotel room, not really seeing the plush
furnishings as she tried to come up with a comfortable explanation for
her visit. None came to mind.

"Please sit down," invited Pearl.

Devon wavered for a moment. "I-I shouldn't have come. I'm sorry
to have bothered you," she said and turned back to the door.

"Mrs. Wainwright, stop. What is it that troubles you so much?"

"It is nothing of importance, Miss Donovan."

"It was important enough to bring you here," said Pearl.

Devon turned to her. "It isn't supposed to be pleasurable," she blurted out.

"What isn't? Sex?" When Devon cringed and reddened, Pearl smiled. "Forgive me, Mrs. Wainwright. I see that you are as uncomfortable with the word as you are with the idea."

"The subject is not discussed in my circle," replied Devon stiffly.

Pearl smiled again appreciating the irony of the visit even if Devon didn't.

"What is it that is so confounding and distressing to you about sex, Mrs. Wainwright?"

"Can you not use that word please?"

Pearl rephrased the question. "What disturbs you so much about a man and a woman engaging in acts of intimacy, Mrs. Wainwright?"

Devon took a deep breath. "It is not supposed to be pleasurable," she primly repeated. "Yet women who are not of loose morals appear to find it so with their husbands. I don't understand how this can be possible, or how decent women could seek it out with all good conscience. The act is degrading."

"Perhaps that was your experience, Mrs. Wainwright, but with the right partner, I can assure you that it is indeed pleasurable and not, in the least, degrading. Every part of the body comes alive. The heart races, every cell is ignited, every nerve is touched and every fiber of one's being is felt."

Pearl paused and regarded Devon closely. "I dare say you would find it a most exhilarating experience with a man like Cort were you to avail yourself of the opportunity—should one arise."

Devon's face reddened again, and she became flustered. "I-I assure you, Miss Donovan, that I would not entertain much less indulge in such a...such an impulse," she stammered, indignant. "For you to make such a suggestion is insulting."

"Why? You are a widow, not some young ingénue, and you can trust Cort."

Devon stiffened. "Finding pleasure in the act—if possible—especially outside the bounds of marriage is incompatible with what it means to be a lady," she responded starchily. "There is a code of conduct to be observed in such matters. It's what distinguishes a lady from a…a—"

"Woman like me?"

Devon nodded.

Pearl smiled, not in the least offended. "One thing I have learned is that societal codes are arbitrarily written and arbitrarily observed, Mrs. Wainwright. Hypocrisy abounds. I dare say that, were you to scratch below the surface, you might be amazed by the behavior of many of your society ladies."

"Be that as it may," acknowledged Devon, recalling a few whispered rumors, "there must be some moral standards established and women have an obligation to uphold them, or else there is wantonness and a breakdown of society and civilization."

"I hardly think that a woman's enjoyment of sex—intimacies—most certainly within the confines of a loving relationship whether married or not will lead to a breakdown of society or civilization," remarked Pearl dryly. She paused. "Do you honestly believe that it is a woman's duty to carry that cross, to always be unhappy, to never express her needs or desires?"

"Women are gatekeepers of civility and morality. Sometimes we must make sacrifices for the greater good," insisted Devon.

"You tried martyrdom once, Mrs. Wainwright. What greater good was served by it? Certainly not yours. Do not men have some responsibility in the matter?"

Devon had no response, and her shoulders slumped as the fight went out of her.

Pearl studied her for a long moment. The dictates of Devon's upbringing and training clearly were not aligning with her burgeoning desires.

"Mrs. Wainwright, what do you really want for yourself?"

"I don't know," responded Devon dismally. "In any case, it doesn't matter what I want. My course is charted."

"How do you mean?" asked Pearl.

Devon sat down heavily in a chair. "You were right when you said that society does not provide for women without means, and I fear that I am about to be numbered among them, for I will soon be without funds myself. As I certainly cannot open a bordello and seem ill-suited to any other means of supporting myself, I see no choice but to marry again." She gave a slight smile. "I guess that does make me a gold digger of sorts."

"Who would you marry?" questioned Pearl.

Devon shrugged. "I like Matthew Chandler well enough. At least he would be better than Mr. Birdwell."

Pearl gave a cynical laugh. "Honey, Matt is a woman's dream and that is all that he is. He may be attractive, polished, charming, and fun to be with, and I have no doubt he will treat you well enough. But you will wake up one day to find him gone. In the end, your situation will be as it is now, and you will be seeking yet a third loveless marriage."

"If you are thinking about Jenny, she and Matt were very young, and the country was on the verge of war. He is older now, more mature," said Devon in his defense.

Pearl scoffed. "Is that what he tells you? The fact is that Matt loves women and leaves them when he begins to feel tied down. He is incapable of making a commitment to anyone. Just ask Belle Waters if you ever see her again." Pearl cocked her head to one side. "You have the money Sadie left you, don't you?"

"I can't accept that kind of legacy," replied Devon. "Besides, there was a time limit. It has probably gone back to the town by now."

"Well, that was pound foolish."

Devon glared at her and stood up. "I am going to accept Matt's proposal and hope that he proves you wrong. I see no other option."

"I can think of another one, Mrs. Wainwright."

"What?"

"You have two other bedrooms unoccupied in that house. Why don't you take in boarders? Then you can still be a lady," added Pearl with a touch of sarcasm.

Devon thought about it for a minute. "Yes, I suppose I could do that. I am renting the house myself. I imagine I would have to get Mr. Stilwell's approval."

"I doubt you will have a problem."

"But two tenants are hardly enough income, Miss Donovan."

"Then petition the town council to hire you on as the schoolteacher," suggested Pearl. "You're educated and have been filling the role for the last several weeks. You should be getting paid for it."

"But Mrs. Tillotson of the Ladies' Auxiliary told me that the position is held to single women," said Devon.

Pearl shrugged. "You are single. You may be a widow, but you are single."

Devon's features brightened. "Yes, you are right. Thank you, Miss Donovan."

"Call me Pearl, honey."

Devon started for the door again.

"Wait, Mrs. Wainwright. There is another matter I wish to discuss with you before you leave."

Devon stopped and turned. "What is that?"

"The matter of your aunt."

Devon stiffened. "I know all I need to know about my aunt."

"If you are going to sit in judgment of her, don't you think you owe it to her to hear her side of the story?"

"Why? What does it matter now?"

"It matters, Mrs. Wainwright."

Devon hesitated. "All right, if I must, I will hear what you have to say, but I doubt you shall change my opinion."

"Perhaps not, but you should know the unvarnished truth, not that of your family's invention," replied Pearl. "Sit down."

Devon heaved a sigh of impatience and sat down again not really of a mind to listen, and Pearl could see that she had her work cut out for her.

"Your aunt's family abandoned her in Paris when she was barely 18 years old, leaving her with few resources," began Pearl.

"My mother is a lot of things," said Devon. "But I cannot believe she would abandon her sister in a foreign country."

"Your grandfather was the ultimate authority on the matter."

"Why? Why would he do such a thing?"

"Your aunt had committed the age-old sin of a society woman. She fell in love with a man her father didn't approve of," said Pearl.

"Nettie told me about the sailor who was lost at sea. I'm sorry, but I still can't see how that would be the impetus for setting my aunt on the path of becoming the madam of a parlor house."

"She had conceived a child with this young man, Mrs. Wainwright."

Devon looked at Pearl, stunned.

"Your grandfather couldn't decide which was the greater transgression—that his grandchild was a bastard or that the father was a lowly sailor," said Pearl.

"My mother said that her sister had been rebellious and something of a black sheep in the family and that she had been turned out before shaming the family name. I had never guessed anything as this," murmured Devon.

"To keep the secret, your grandfather took the family to France. Sadie was confined in Paris for the duration of her increasing time," went on Pearl. "After giving birth, she became ill with childbed fever. When she recovered, she found herself being cared for in a convent. Her parents and sister had returned to Boston. Your grandfather left her a note saying that she was never to come home again. He meant it. He left her with too little money to return."

"How did she make her way?" asked Devon.

"She sang on street corners and in cafes for food and a place to sleep in back rooms. She survived by her wits. One day, Madam Le Bonheur was passing by a café and heard your aunt sing. She was so taken by her beauty and voice that she brought Sadie into her salon to entertain her clients."

"Perhaps she should have stayed in the convent," interjected Devon snidely.

"I think that was your grandfather's intentions. And she did for awhile," said Pearl. "Have you ever been in a convent or know what life is like as a member of the order, Mrs. Wainwright?"

"No."

"It isn't for everyone."

"My aunt was educated. There must have been a teaching position of some sort available or a position as governess perhaps," insisted Devon.

"She had no references. But it is not as you think, Mrs. Wainwright. Your aunt was never a courtesan, only an entertainer."

Devon looked dubious. "Is that what she told you?"

"Sadie never lied. She wasn't ashamed of who she was or of what she did. Understand that a salon in Paris was as much a place for intellectual discourse and entertainment as it was for pleasure," explained Pearl.

"Go on," said Devon.

"Madam Le Bonheur's salon was the most notable of them all. Your aunt's beauty, wit, and song made her a favorite in Paris, and Sadie quickly learned the business," continued Pearl. "When she had saved enough money, she returned to America and, with the help of a benefactor whom she had met on the ship, she set up her own salon in Baltimore."

"What happened to the child?" queried Devon.

"Sadie was told that the baby had died," replied Pearl solemnly. "She carried that loss with her the rest of her life as well."

Devon was moved by this part of the story, having seen how much Penny Johnson still mourned the loss of her infant.

"Nettie said my aunt had many opportunities to marry a wealthy man. Perhaps her life would have been easier had she done so," remarked Devon.

"Would your life be easier, Mrs. Wainwright, had you stayed in Boston and married that man?"

Devon stiffened. "It isn't the same thing."

"No, I guess not. You have never known what it is to love a man."

Devon stood up abruptly. "Good night, Miss Donovan. Thank you for your time."

As Devon walked home, her mind was preoccupied with everything Pearl had told her regarding Clarissa. Devon wasn't surprised that her mother hadn't recounted the full story—family honor above all else. Still, as shameful and scandalous as the situation might have been, the abject cruelty of the family shocked her. For the first time, Devon felt a measure of sympathy for her aunt. She wondered about the sailor. Had he returned her aunt's love, or had she been just a dalliance for him?

Something else Pearl had said weighed on Devon. If she married Matt, would he one day abandon her in California with no resources just as Clarissa's family had abandoned her in a foreign land?

CHAPTER THIRTY-ONE

A Night to Remember?

Devon answered the knock at the door to find Cort standing on her front porch.

"Marshal Templeton." Her brow puckered in bewilderment at the saddlebags slung over his shoulder and the carpet bag in his hand.

"I understand you are taking boarders," he said.

"Well, I'm thinking about it," replied Devon, surprised that he had heard about it so soon. "I haven't asked Mr. Stilwell's approval yet."

"I'll square it with Frank. I'm renting a room. I have no desire to spend the winter in the back room of the jail again. Does $40 dollars a month sound fair?"

Devon was astonished by both his pronouncement and the amount that he was willing to pay. "That is very generous, but a room at the hotel is only $24 a month."

"Tell Nettie I'll expect some meals to go with it," said Cort.

"But what will the townspeople say?" she asked, flustered.

"Nobody will think anything, Mrs. Wainwright. I am the marshal. And, Nettie, Brett, and Bridget will safeguard your reputation," he replied. "I'll take this up to one of the spare rooms."

"You're moving in *now*?"

"Just my belongings. I'll be back later this evening."

Devon was too stunned to speak as he moved past her and up the stairs. She hadn't seen him since the night he had kissed her and had been uncertain how she would feel or what she would say to him when their paths did cross again. She most certainly wasn't prepared for him to move into her house that day. Still somewhat dazed, she was about to close the door, when her mother appeared on Matthew Chandler's arm.

"Mother. I hadn't expected to see you here and at this hour of the morning—or you Matt," said Devon. "The students will be here soon. Nettie has made coffee in the kitchen if you—"

"This isn't a social call, Devon," her mother interrupted sternly. "It is time for you to make a decision. Return to Boston with me or marry Mr. Chandler and go to California."

"Mother, I am not prepared to do either. Sorry, Matt."

"You have no choice, daughter. Your money must be running out now, and I checked with Mr. Stilwell. You refused your inheritance. At least, you learned pride from me. You have no other choice."

Just then, Cort came down the stairs.

"What are you doing here?" asked Chandler, visibly surprised to see him.

"I'm renting a room from Mrs. Wainwright," replied Cort.

Mrs. Toller's mouth dropped open. "Devon, is this true?"

"Uh, yes, Mother, I guess it is."

"I have to get back to the office," said Cort. He touched the brim of his hat. "Always a pleasure, Mrs. Toller...Matt."

As he walked out the door, Agatha Toller's eyes swiveled back to her daughter. "Devon, have you lost your mind? Think how this will look to the town...a man living in your house. Think of your reputation."

"He is the marshal, Mother, and Bridget and her husband and Nettie live here as well. This is not Boston," reiterated Devon.

"I don't care if this is Timbuktu," huffed Mrs. Toller. "You are becoming reckless. What say you, Mr. Chandler?"

"I'll leave you two ladies to discuss the matter," he said and hurried outside to catch up with the marshal.

"Templeton!" he called.

Cort stopped and turned. "What do you want, Matt?"

"Clever move," said Chandler. "Was this Pearl's idea for you to move into the house?"

"Don't know what you mean. Mrs. Wainwright is taking in boarders. I rented a room," replied Templeton matter-of-factly.

"You can't fool an old fooler, Cort. You and Pearl have been trying to get between Devon and me from the start."

"You're sounding paranoid again, Matt."

Chandler blew off the jab. "I told you that I would put a bee in Mrs. Toller's bonnet about Pearl if Pearl interfered."

"Pearl left on the stage this morning," said Cort. "And I think Mrs. Toller will be mad as hell at you for not telling her sooner."

Chandler faltered. "Just don't get in my way, Cort."

Templeton fixed a narrow-eyed gaze on him. "Why are you so intent upon marrying Mrs. Wainwright anyway?"

"Even you can't be that blind," said Chandler with a snort. "Devon is a stunningly beautiful woman. I enjoy being with her.... A man reaches a point in his life when he is ready to settle down."

"Not you, Matt. If you deceive Mrs. Wainwright in any way, I promise you you'll be looking over your shoulder for the rest of your life."

Chandler laughed. "Are you Devon's guardian now?"

"No, Matt, but I will be her sword of justice," replied Templeton.

The steely glint in Cort's eye gave the gambler pause.

At the end of the school day, Devon followed up on another one of Pearl's suggestions and went to see Mr. Stilwell.

When she was ushered into his private office, the attorney jumped to his feet. "Mrs. Wainwright, what a pleasant surprise. Please have a seat."

When she had seated herself, he sat down and looked at her with a measure of hope. "Have you changed your mind about accepting the inheritance?"

"No, Mr. Stilwell, I have not. You are a member of the town council, are you not?" she asked, getting to the point.

"Yes."

"The town council hires the schoolteacher, correct?"

"Yes, with the advice and the consent of the Ladies' Auxiliary. I can assure you that we are doing everything that we can to find a new teacher, Mrs. Wainwright. I am certain that we shall have the position filled soon."

"Mr. Stilwell, you misunderstand me. I want the position," said Devon.

The attorney looked at her in astonishment. "But, Mrs. Wainwright—"

"I know what you are going to say, Mr. Stilwell. You are going to tell me that it is a position given only to single women."

"Why, yes. They are not distracted by families."

"I am a widow, Mr. Stilwell. I believe that makes me single and thus eligible for the position, does it not?"

Mr. Stilwell thought for a moment. "Why, yes, I suppose it might in theory, but—"

"I am educated, and I have taken Miss Primrose's place for the past month. Have there been any complaints?"

"No, none that I have heard, but—"

"Then, I will depend upon you to make my case to the rest of the council. I shall take care of the members of the Ladies' Auxiliary. I believe you all owe me this consideration, Mr. Stilwell, given my harrowing experience at the city council's lack of inquiry into Miss Primrose's character and background.... Oh, and Mr. Stilwell, I shall expect to be recompensed for my time served."

The attorney stared dumbly as she stood up and swept out of the office.

While Devon's actions would make her financially independent enough to stave off her mother and Matthew Chandler for the time being, it brought with it a new set of problems for her. Her mother announced that if Devon was staying in Blue Springs, so would she until her daughter came to her senses. That was bad enough. But Marshal Templeton taking up residence in the house was downright disturbing to her.

Painstakingly aware of him in the room next to hers, Devon paced the floor of her sitting room this night especially troubled. She could not get her rather frank conversation with Pearl about sexual gratification and a woman's right to experience it out of her mind. Everything Pearl had said made sense intellectually. But it cut across everything that had been ingrained in Devon since she was a child about what it meant to be a lady and a member of proper society.

To whom did she owe her allegiance— to Boston society, to her family or, as Pearl had maintained, to herself? Was she being selfish for wanting to be happy instead of doing her duty, as her mother had charged? Or were Pearl's arguments mere justifications for her own poor choices? Yet, she made no apologies for them and seemed genuinely pleased with her life. Devon flopped onto the settee and moaned. Why should being a lady mean having to surrender one's happiness?

As Devon fussed and fumed, Cort was settling in comfortably. He wasn't thrilled about having to pay twice the rent, but he had to hold out an eye-popping offer that she couldn't refuse. Matthew Chandler was not going to win this time, he resolved.

* * * * *

Devon awoke early in the morning and quietly hurried to use the bathing room before the others aroused. With so many people in the house again, she was going to have to make a schedule like she did during the quarantine, she grumbled.

She hadn't slept well and was in a contentious mood. She hoped a hot bath might relax her. When she pulled open the door, she started at the sight of Cort standing at the sink shaving, stripped to the waist.

He turned his head. "Good morning," he greeted, unfazed by the intrusion. "There wasn't any water in my room. I guess you'll have to make a schedule again."

Devon blushed and pulled her robe tighter around her. It seemed a silly gesture in light of the fact that he had seen her in less—much, much less. This moment was tame in comparison.

"I'll tell Nettie about the water," she said, trying not to notice his broad shoulders and muscular chest.

He acted so natural that she felt herself relax, and, instead of fleeing, she continued to wait, watching as he finished shaving.

She liked his eyes, the way they narrowed when he was pensive or dubious about something; she liked the way the sides of his face dimpled in moments of wry amusement; she liked the way his hair curled around the nape of his neck and waved across his forehead to give him a boyish appeal. In short, she was finding little not to like about the marshal these days.

He rinsed and dried his face, then gathered up his shaving implements. "The room is all yours," he said.

"It is New Year's Eve. Will you be joining us for supper?" she asked. "So I can tell Nettie," she quickly added.

"Probably not. Jasper and I are sparing Brett the night shifts to give him time to get used to this marriage business, and I expect this night to be particularly lively in town," replied Cort.

"Yes, Bridget and Mr. Sanger seem to be spending a great deal of time in their rooms," remarked Devon dryly.

Cort smiled. "I figure another couple of days until they get it out of their system. Good day, Mrs. Wainwright."

"Good day, Marshal."

As he moved past her, she could smell the masculine scent of sandalwood.

Cort smiled again when the door closed on him. Chandler was right about one thing. Mrs. Wainwright was beautiful, even at this hour of the morning with her hair unbound and disheveled, tendrils curling about her face. He would like to have kissed her again but now was not the time to overstep himself, he decided. If this morning's encounter was any indication, she seemed to be finding more comfortable ground with him.

The day slipped past quickly for Devon. The students were moderately well-behaved. When they threatened to become unruly, she shooed them outdoors for a short recess or engaged them in a song fest.

Brett, Bridget, and Nettie joined her for supper and, not wanting to spend New Year's Eve alone, Devon pressed them into a couple of rounds of Fox and Geese. In Boston, there would be a round of parties to attend until the wee hours of the morning. The parties, the holiday balls and celebrations, the beautiful gowns—that she did miss.

When everyone retired, Devon felt restless and unsettled. She returned to the parlor and sat down at the piano and began play through the standards, losing herself in the music as she sang. She was in the middle of *Lorena,* a particularly poignant tune, when she noticed Cort standing in the doorway and stopped.

"Mr. Templeton…how goes the night?"

"The troublemakers are fast asleep with drink now. Jasper can handle anything that comes up from here," he said. He gestured at the piano. "Please continue with the song. I would like to hear it if you don't mind."

Devon hesitated, then began the tune again. When she had finished, Cort walked over to her.

"I haven't heard *Lorena* since the war," he said, his mood somber. "General Grant had banned it from the campsites. It made the men so homesick and melancholy he was afraid they might desert or not be able to fight effectively. He was probably right."

"It must have been terrible…the war," said Devon.

"If you can imagine hell, you know only the half of it. Did your husband serve?"

Devon shook her head. "When the Draft Act was passed, my husband paid the fee to exempt himself," she replied with a measure of contempt.

"He wasn't alone," Cort assured her. "One is usually patriotic until he tastes battle and sees the insanity of war. I recall that in one battle a truce was called so that each side could bury the dead and tend to the wounded."

Cort smiled a bittersweet smile as he became lost in the moment. "Soldiers crossed the lines. We played cards with the Rebs, exchanged pictures and stories of our families, joked, sang songs." His smile faded. "Then, the next morning we went back to killing each other. All these years later, I cannot fathom it," he murmured.

"I'm sorry," said Devon.

Cort shook off the memory. "Such it would seem is the nature of man. Good night, Mrs. Wainwright."

"Good night, Marshal."

It was a while before Cort settled down to sleep. He thought he had buried the wounds of war but, apparently, not deep enough.

He had just drifted off, when he heard a soft knock on the door. It might just as well have been a pounding. As a tested soldier and now lawman, he was a light sleeper, always alert to sounds of danger. He threw off the covers and hurried to answer it, anticipating an emergency in town.

It was Devon. She was dressed in her robe and nightgown, and dark red hair tumbled down her back and about her shoulders in loose waves. He could see by the light of the hall sconces that her cheeks were flushed and her manner agitated.

"Has something happened in town?" he asked in consternation.

"No. May I come in, Mr. Templeton?"

Shuttering his surprise, Cort opened the door wider. "Of course."

She took a deep breath and walked into the room.

She was acting strange even for her, and he looked at her quizzically. "Is something amiss, Mrs. Wainwright?"

"No—yes. Please close the door. I wish for privacy."

Cort closed the door, his curiosity further tweaked.

"What can I do for you?" he asked, lighting a lamp.

"All my life, I have done everything I was supposed to do," she said, pacing the room and gesticulating with her hands. "I observed society's rules and abided by the teachings of the church. Oh, I suppose you could argue that I was rewarded with a life of privilege for it, but I have also paid with a regrettable marriage."

She stopped pacing and turned to him. "For 10 years, I felt nothing, Mr. Templeton. Nothing…not so much as a twinge."

Cort regarded her closely. "Have you been drinking, Mrs. Wainwright?"

"Yes, but that is beside the point."

"What is the point, madam?"

"I want to know what it is that makes Bridget so eager to retire for the night with Mr. Sanger and women like Miss Donovan to prefer the life they lead even when they have funds enough to choose another."

"I guess you shall have to ask them," replied Cort, stymied as to where all of this was leading.

"I did ask Miss Donovan," said Devon. "She told me that with the right man, the act can be a rather enlightening experience for a woman." Devon fixed steady blue eyes on him. "I want to know the truth of it, Mr. Templeton."

Cort raised his brows. Not much shocked him, but he was shocked now. "Forgive me, Mrs. Wainwright. Are you…are you asking me to take you to bed?"

Devon took another deep breath. "Yes, Mr. Templeton, I am."

Cort stared at her, trying to wrap his mind around the surreal moment. He had worried about overstepping his bounds earlier with just a kiss!

"And Miss Donovan said that—"

"What does Pearl have to do with this?" he quizzed.

"She made me see things a little differently," replied Devon. "She said that I could trust you to…well, to do it right. And as there is already a degree of familiarity between us, you are the logical choice to satisfy my curiosity."

Normally a man of few words, Cort was struck speechless. And he didn't know if he should feel flattered or not that he was the "logical choice."

"Mrs. Wainwright, you cannot be serious about this," said Cort, finding his voice.

"But I am, Mr. Templeton. How should we proceed?"

"You want to do this now?"

She squared her shoulders and lifted her chin as though about to go into battle. "Yes. I have fortified myself with two—maybe three—glasses of wine. I am ready."

"Mrs. Wainwright, have you given any thought as to how you will feel afterwards. You couldn't look me in the eye for days after returning from Aspen Ridge."

"Yes, it may be a bit awkward for awhile," admitted Devon. "You will have to make yourself scarce, I suppose…perhaps return to your quarters at the marshal's office."

"Madam, I have no intentions of quitting this room," replied Cort firmly. "Have you considered how you will face your guilt for violating your moral code?"

Devon hesitated. "I have," she replied. The uncertainty in her voice told him that she was still, in fact, grappling with the problem.

Cort ran a hand across the back of his neck. What in the hell was Pearl thinking? He didn't want to humiliate Devon by sending her away, but, fortified with wine or not, he couldn't imagine her ready to take such a step. When he looked at her again, he saw that she was regarding him with wide-eyed expectation.

"Mrs. Wainwright, such an engagement requires a stimulus of sorts."

"What do you mean?"

"A raising of the flag," said Cort, trying to explain the matter delicately. At the blank look on her face, he sighed. Her degree of naïveté never ceased to amaze him. "Never mind. I ask you one last time. Are you sure you want to do this?"

She met him with an unwavering gaze. "Yes."

"Very well, Mrs. Wainwright. You shall have to remove your robe and nightgown."

"Why?" she asked.

"Let's just say that it is part of the experiment," said Cort.

"How does that make a difference?"

"Trust me, Mrs. Wainwright, that it does."

"But it is cold," she argued.

He walked over to the little stove and put more wood on the fire. "It will be warm enough for you soon."

He saw the look of indecision flicker across her features. He had figured the order to undress would send her running from the room in a panic. It didn't. Instead, she slipped off her robe to reveal a nightgown of fine lawn with a square neckline trimmed with lace.

"I still don't see the need for this," she muttered.

"You will," said Cort.

The garment was not form-fitting, but the lamp behind her shadowed the lines of a curvaceous body with which he already had, as she had said, a degree of familiarity—and appreciation. Cort swallowed hard.

She stood there waiting, obviously nervous, and he walked over to her and put a hand beneath her chin to raise her gaze to his. Despite her assurance to him that she had thought through her request, he could feel her uncertainty.

Devon fought the urge to flee when his large hands cupped her face and he bent his head to capture her lips in a light, sensual caress that was much like the kiss he had given her before. Just as she began to relax, it changed.

His arms went around her, drawing her closer, and his kiss became more passionate, more intimate. She had no idea how to respond to it. When he dropped a hand to lift her nightgown, she stiffened and broke away.

Her cheeks were flushed, and her chest heaved as she worked to regulate her breathing. Her heart was racing but not from the excitement of prospective lovemaking, but from fear of the unknown.

Cort was certain she was having a change of heart now. And he gave her a few minutes to recover herself. But once again, she surprised him.

"Before going any further," she said, taking a deep breath, "please extinguish the light."

"Isn't that a little like closing the barn door after the horse has bolted?" he inquired dryly.

"With the hypothermia, I was not aware of my state of undress then," replied Devon primly. "Now I am."

"And that makes a difference?"

"Of course. In that instance, it was beyond my control. In this instance, it isn't," she explained.

Cort looked at her, again confounded by her logic, until he suddenly realized that it wasn't actually logic she practiced but a rationalization of events she had a hard time accepting. He extinguished the light.

"I have a condition of my own, Mrs. Wainwright."

"What is that?"

"Once we begin, you must see the act through to its conclusion. And there will be no half-measures," he warned.

Devon wasn't sure what he meant by no half-measures and, again, felt the impulse to flee, but taking another deep breath, she nodded. Still, when he started to raise her nightgown once more, she stayed his hands.

"I should like to get into bed first," she said.

Cort acquiesced. She wasn't a virgin, but he understood he would have to treat her like one, though he had no experience in that area.

Under the security of the covers, Devon slowly removed her gown. In the dark, she could hear him removing his union suit. When the mattress shifted as he got into bed, she moved closer to the edge of her side and pulled the blankets up to her chin. Lying stock still, her heart pounding, she waited for him to make the first move.

Cort didn't try to release her iron grip on the covers. He circumvented it by slipping his hand underneath to lightly stroke her thigh. She jumped at the touch of his hand on her bare skin. She had never felt such a sensation. Her husband had never touched her in such a manner.

She squeezed her eyes shut as Cort traced the curves of her body with maddening deliberation from her thigh to her stomach, and higher, the sensation intensifying. Her face flamed, and she stiffened when he stopped to fondle a full breast and massage the sensitive peak of her nipple. It was too intimate a gesture for her, and it had a sobering effect.

If she allowed him to go any further, she would be shunned by society, her friends, her family, and her church should it become known. Her life would be as shattered as her reputation, never to be fixed again. And she saw herself following in her aunt's footsteps. Was all that she valued worth risking for a few moments of supposed ecstasy taken at the word of a madam and former "lady of the line?"

When she balked, Cort readily guessed her state of mind. "Relax and stop thinking," he said. "Just let yourself feel."

His deep, even voice was hypnotic and calming to her. When he guided her hand to him, however, she recoiled again.

"What are you doing?" she asked, mortified.

Cort sighed. "Madam, it must be a two-way street. Did you never touch your husband?"

"No, of course not."

"And I'm guessing he never touched you."

"It is something that is not done in polite society," she replied defensively.

He brought her hand back to him. "Polite society has nothing to do with it, madam. I suspect your husband preferred to exercise himself and was neglectful of you."

Devon could feel the heat of a blush suffuse her face and was grateful for the darkness that hid her embarrassment at such a discussion.

"Mr. Templeton, I really don't think we need to discuss—"

Cort leaned over and kissed her, cutting short her objections.

The clock in the hall struck midnight then. The church bell rang, and firecrackers exploded loudly in the street.

"Happy New Year," murmured Cort.

As he trailed kisses down the column of her neck, a shiver of delight went through her. When he moved his fingers lightly over her abdomen and down the inside of her thighs to a more intimate area, Devon gasped, torn between feelings of mortification and the desire to continue feeling the pleasure she could never have imagined.

She thought she was prepared for whatever might come this night, but she found that she was totally unprepared for any of it. She had never known what it was to be touched, let alone in such a sensual way, and as he continued to caress her neck and shoulders with his lips while keeping up the play of his hand, she did as he said—she stopped thinking and just let herself feel. And, as she did this, every muscle in her body began to relax, and she drifted away in a haze of bliss.

The next morning, Devon awoke disoriented with a thumping headache, only this time it wasn't from being drugged with opium. As the haze of the previous night's activities began to lift, she looked around her in confusion. She was in her bed, and she was wearing her nightgown. Devon bolted upright. Her robe lay draped over the chair.

Everything looked so normal she almost wondered if she had dreamed everything.

Nettie bustled in then. "You still in bed? You best hurry. The students will be arrivin' soon."

Devon groaned. She threw her legs over the side of the bed and put her head in her hands. "I don't feel very well."

"I don't wonder," remarked Nettie, glancing at the nearly empty bottle of wine on the table. "You're lucky it's Saturday and a half day of school. Here, I'll help you to dress. Then take yourself downstairs and get some coffee into ya."

Devon was all thumbs, and Nettie took over helping her dress. She fussed with Devon's hair then, pinning it loosely at the nape of her neck in a roll.

"I ain't so good at fixin' hair fancy like. I'm sure yer mother'll have somethin' to say about it, but it'll have to do," grumbled Nettie. "Off with ya now. I'll clean up the room."

Devon slowly made her way downstairs and into the kitchen, struggling to hold herself together. The smell of hash cooking on the stove turned her stomach. She poured herself a cup of coffee and sat down. She had managed only a few sips before shoving the cup away.

She was resting her head in her hands, her elbows propped on the table, when Cort strolled into the kitchen. "Feeling under the weather, Mrs. Wainwright?"

Devon could hear the amusement in his voice and lifted her head to glare at him.

"Shall I dish you up a plate of hash?" he asked.

"No!" she snapped. "And stop being so cheerful."

Cort chuckled. "You'll feel better as the day goes on."

As he turned to leave, she jumped up from the table. "Mr. Templeton, wait—"

"No one shall know of last night, Mrs. Wainwright," he assured her, intuiting her request.

"It's not that." She walked over to him. "Mr. Templeton, how…how went the night?" she asked in a hushed voice.

"It was quite memorable," he whispered back. "Why do you ask?"

Devon nervously twirled a loose strand of hair around her finger. "I-uh-I can't seem to remember everything."

Cort held back a grin. "Wine does tend to dull the memory, Mrs. Wainwright, but I hope not the experience. By the way, the mayor said to tell you that the town council voted to give you the teaching position with pay for time served. I don't know what your argument was, but it was apparently effective."

"Guilt always is," said Devon.

"You must be figuring on staying in town then."

"For the time being."

"What about Chandler?" asked Cort.

Devon sighed. "I told him I needed more time."

She sat down and lay her head on the table. As students noisily began to arrive, she groaned.

Templeton smiled. "Enjoy your day, Mrs. Wainwright."

CHAPTER THIRTY-TWO

Mr. Goodnight

Brett poured himself a cup of coffee and set the coffee pot back on the pot belly stove in the office.

"It's a damn sight better havin' you livin' in the house than Mrs. Toller," he remarked. "It sure ain't keepin' Chandler away though."

Cort looked up from perusing the new wanted posters. "What's that?"

"Bridget says that Chandler always seems to know when you ain't at the house and that's when he shows up," said Brett. "He weren't too happy about the town council makin' Mrs. Wainwright the new schoolteacher. Her mother neither. They've been tryin' to convince her to quit."

"I think Mrs. Wainwright has found her strength," said Cort.

"Maybe, but somethin' sure has been stickin' in her craw. Bridget says she ain't been herself the last few days…short tempered an' all. You musta noticed."

Cort smiled to himself. "She has seemed a mite tense."

The door opened then, and a man walked in wearing a duster. He was lean, of medium height, and his weathered face sported a bushy mustache. He shoved back his slouch hat to reveal a broad forehead, low brow line, and intense dark eyes.

Cort slowly rose to his feet. "It has been a long time since I laid eyes on you," he said, his voice toneless, his expression inscrutable.

"Nearly two years, I'd reckon," replied the man, stone-faced.

A long, tense moment followed while Templeton and the visitor took stock of each other. Brett's eyes shifted between them, and he slowly moved his hand to his gun, when the men suddenly smiled and exchanged a hearty handshake.

"Stand down, Brett," said Templeton with a laugh. "This is David Cook the best lawman I've ever known. We worked on a case together when I was with the Rangers and he was sheriff of Arapahoe County. David, this is my deputy, Brett Sanger."

Cook gave Brett a nod of acknowledgment. "Deputy."

Brett's eyes widened. "David Cook…you broke up the Musgrove-Franklin Gang."

"That was a while ago," said Cook. "Got any more coffee in that pot, son?"

"Yes, sir," replied Brett.

Cook looked at Templeton. "Heard how you stymied Hagen's plan to rob the assay office in Denver."

"I had some help," said Cort.

"Hagen escaped on the way to prison. Did you get him?"

"Yep."

"Dead?"

"Yep."

The man nodded. "That's one less wart on society."

Cook wearily sat down on the chair. He took off his hat, laid it on the desk, and gratefully accepted the tin cup of coffee from Brett.

"Can't sit a saddle like I used to. Gettin' too old for this job."

Cort snorted. "You're as old as I am, and being a lawman is in your blood." He settled back into his seat. "Heard you were appointed Major General of the Colorado Militia."

"Yeah. I could use a good man like you in the militia," said Cook, taking a sip of coffee.

"Sorry, David, I'm settled here for the time being."

The lawman smiled. "Wouldn't have anything to do with a certain pretty redhead, would it?"

Templeton let out a sigh of annoyance. "You've been talking to Pearl."

"I might have run across her when I was in Denver," admitted Cook. "I read about your heroics in the paper there. By the time the dime novels get done with you, you'll have every young pup who fancies himself a shooter coming to town to make a name for himself."

"Yeah, I know," said Cort. "What brings you here? I haven't heard of anyone causing mischief in the area."

"I oversaw the transport of a prisoner to Fort Collins who might be of interest to you," the lawman replied.

"Fort Collins…that's over 200 miles from here. And you came all this way just to tell me? Who was the prisoner?"

"Belle Waters."

Templeton's brow rose. "Belle…how the hell did you—"

"Came across her in Denver," said Cook. "Saw the post you put out on her."

"Then you know I have a prior claim on her. She stole Sadie's jewelry."

"Sorry, Cort. The military has priority in this matter. You'll get her when we're done with her."

"How could Belle be of interest to the military?" quizzed Templeton. "What has she done?"

"It's not what she's done," said Cook. "It's what she knows."

"About what?"

"A map that leads to a Confederate gold shipment that disappeared hereabouts at the end of the war."

Templeton laughed. "That rumor has been around for years. Since when does David Cook chase after phantom treasures?"

"This isn't a phantom treasure, Cort. You know I worked counter-espionage during the war."

"Yeah. You formed the Rocky Mountain Detective Association in 1864."

"That's right. In the last months of the war, I was tracking a sizable gold shipment," explained Cook. "I lost track of it in the area of the Royal Gorge. After the war, I let it go. I figured my information had been wrong and didn't think any more about it until Miss Waters mentioned this map."

"Why are you so interested now?" questioned Cort.

"The Knights of the Golden Circle are looking for it. The gold belongs to them."

Cort and Brett glanced at each other.

"By the looks on your faces, I take it you know they have resurfaced and are actively working to stage another insurgency," said Cook.

"Not until recently," replied Templeton.

He explained about Devon's abduction, Hagen and Alice Graham's talk of a larger cause, and Hagen's carving on the table in the miner's cabin.

"I figured something was up then."

"You figured right," said Cook. "The KGC was a major source of funds for the Confederacy. When Lee surrendered, they hid any treasure in their possession with the intention of retrieving it later to mount a future insurrection. They buried caches of jewelry, gold, and silver all over the country and have been adding to them."

He stopped to take another sip of coffee.

"This gold shipment would go a long way toward funding another war—as would have the gold from the Denver Assay Office if Hagen had been able to pull off the robbery."

"If the KGC buried the gold shipment, why can't they find it?" asked Brett.

Cook smiled. "Because someone else found it first and moved it."

"Who?"

"I'll get to that in a minute, Deputy. Ever hear of Mr. Goodnight, Cort?"

"Yeah. Mrs. Wainwright said that Hagen and Alice Graham made mention of that name during her captivity," replied Templeton. "He appears to head the operation they were part of."

"Whatever else Goodnight is doing to further the cause, his prime objective is to recover this lost treasure," said Cook.

Cort frowned. "I haven't been able to turn up anyone with that name. It's undoubtedly an alias."

"How's your friend Matthew Chandler these days?" asked Cook, a glimmer in his eye.

Cort snorted. "I have no illusions about Matt, but don't you think that is a little obvious?"

The lawman shrugged. "He fought for the Confederacy, and you know what they say about hiding in plain sight. What better way to gather information about a lost treasure than as the proprietor of a saloon?"

Brett's jaw dropped. "Holy crap! Matt Chandler is Mr. Goodnight?"

"We don't know that for sure," Templeton warned his deputy.

"And you don't know for sure that he isn't," interjected Cook. "Don't you find it strange that he would stick around given the history between you two?"

"I never trusted that guy," mumbled Brett.

"David, how do you know that this map is real?" asked Cort.

"I don't know for sure," admitted Cook. "But there are a lot of old mines in these parts, and the KGC was known to have hidden stashes in abandoned mines and tunnels. They left symbols on rocks and trees to mark the path to them. It is not inconceivable that someone might have seen and deciphered the symbols or just blindly stumbled upon this Confederate gold, relocated it, and made a map to it."

While Brett was spellbound by the story, Templeton remained skeptical.

"I'll grant you the resurgence of the KGC, David, but this treasure hunt sounds like something out of a dime novel."

Cook was undeterred. "Sometimes you gotta put two and two together. You, of all people, know that, Cort. You do it better than anyone I know."

"Okay, so what is your two plus two?"

The weathered lawman leaned forward in his excitement. "The KGC have this system whereby agents are assigned caches to protect. I'm guessing that when the agents in charge of this cache went to check on it, they found it missing and fanned out into nearby towns and mining camps looking for any information that might tell them where it is."

Cort shook his head. "Sorry, David, that doesn't add up to four for me."

"Now hold on. I'm not done yet," said Cook. "An old miner named Bushy Bill came into town some years back and bragged that he had found a great treasure and flashed some gold coins around."

"It was before my time here. I never heard of the man." Cort looked at Sanger. "How about you, Brett?"

Brett shook his head. "No, sir. I never did."

"He died in the cholera epidemic," said Cook.

"So, you think Bushy Bill's treasure was the KGC's lost gold shipment," concluded Cort.

The major general nodded. "I'd bet my career on it. Sadie and the girls were nursing miners through the epidemic. Miss Waters was workin' for Sadie then and claims Bushy Bill had drawn up a map to the treasure shortly before he died."

"What happened to it?" asked Cort.

"According to Miss Waters, he gave it to Sadie. No one has seen it since. After Bushy Bill died, Miss Waters said a stranger came into town asking about him and this treasure he found. Then lo and behold, Matthew Chandler shows up later, buys the saloon, takes in Miss Waters." Cook raised his hands. "Two plus two equals four."

"If you're right that Matt is Mr. Goodnight, why hasn't he made a move?" questioned Cort.

"The KGC is meticulous and patient. You know how they work. But I think he has made his move," replied Cook.

"How?" asked Brett.

"Well, Miss Waters isn't too pleased about the attention Chandler has been paying Mrs. Wainwright since she came to town."

Brett made a face. "He's courtin' her now. She keeps sayin' 'no,' but he won't stop botherin' her."

The lawman smiled. "Maybe because Mrs. Wainwright is Sadie's heir, and the map was last known to be in Sadie's possession—"

"And if Mrs. Wainwright marries Matt, he'll will have unquestioned access to the house to look for it," finished Templeton. He came forward in his chair. "Brett, fetch Nettie. And make sure that someone is always with Mrs. Wainwright, especially when Chandler is around."

"Yes, sir."

When Brett left to get Nettie, Cook took out a cigar. "Cort, there is something else you should know," he said lighting it and taking a few puffs. "In a slip of the tongue, Miss Waters confessed to being in a confrontation with Sadie when Sadie fell down the stairs. She said it was an accident."

Templeton looked at Cook in surprise. "I had laid that to Billy Hagen."

The lawman shook his head. "Sadie returned early from an outing and caught Miss Waters in her room stealing her jewelry. When she started out to fetch you, Miss Waters tried to stop her. According to her, Sadie lost her balance on the stairs and fell. To make sure it looked like an accident, Miss Waters put laudanum in Sadie's champagne and set the vial next to the glass. I get the feeling there was also a measure of revenge in that act."

Cort nodded. "Sadie had cut Belle loose from her salon because of Belle's drug use. Do you believe her that Sadie's fall was an accident?"

Cook shrugged. "We can't prove otherwise."

"Then make damn sure Belle is returned to Blue Springs to stand trial for her other offenses," said Cort.

"Miss Waters bargained immunity in exchange for information about the map."

"Dammit, David!"

Cook smiled. "Take it easy. I gave her immunity for stealing the jewelry. You can still charge her with accidental death in the commission of a theft. You'll get her returned for a larger crime."

"I'm holding you to that," warned Cort.

"You have my word."

While they waited for Brett to return with Nettie, they reminisced.

"You never forget being in a war, do you?" commented Cook.

Templeton shook his head. "A generation of young men were lost. And there are those who want to risk the next one."

"The war was waged and fought on emotion, not on reason," said Cook. "Southern pride won't allow them to accept that they lost. They'll never stop."

Brett walked in then with a loudly complaining Nettie.

"I don't know what is so all-fired important that it can't wait until—" she stopped when she saw David Cook and smiled broadly. "Mr. Cook, ain't seen you in a coon's age."

Cook grinned. "It's nice to see you, Nettie. I was sorry to hear about Sadie."

"It was a sorrowful day, sir. But it's like they say—when one door is shut, another is opened. I got Miss Sadie's kin to look after now." She looked at Templeton. "What's amiss, Cort? I got a dinner to cook."

"This won't take long, Nettie. During the cholera epidemic, you, Sadie, and the girls nursed some miners. Did one of them give Sadie a map to a treasure of gold?"

"Yeah. We called him Bushy Bill on account ya could hardly make out his face with the beard and them eyebrows. When he knew he was dyin', he drew this map and gave it to Miss Sadie as thanks for tendin' him."

"What did Sadie do with the map?" asked Cort.

Nettie shrugged. "Stuck it away in a drawer somewhere I s'pose. Maybe she threw it away. Bushy Bill was out of his head at times and would go on about findin' this mountain of gold. None of us believed the map was true. Miners was always givin' Sadie things to thank her. Ask Frank. He might know more about it. Can I go now? Chandler and Mrs. Toller are comin' to dinner," she said with a grimace.

"Matt is coming to dinner tonight?"

"Yeah. I have half a mind to lace the gravy with mineral oil. I don't know who is worse—that snake or the missy's mother," grumbled Nettie. "Ain't nothin' ever right for that woman."

"Cort, me and Bridget are plannin' to eat at the hotel tonight," said Brett. "Bein' what we talked about, maybe Bridget and me should stay put at the house."

"No, you and Bridget carry on with your plans. Nettie, can you set two more places at the table?" asked Cort.

"I s'pose so. Somethin' goin' on, Marshal?"

"Just bringin' an old friend to supper," he replied. "You can leave now but keep this talk between us."

When Nettie left, Cort turned to his deputy again. "Brett, ask Frank Stilwell to step over here, then go and keep an eye on Chandler."

"Yes, sir."

A short while later, Stilwell entered the jail office. "Brett said you wanted to see me, Cort." His step faltered when his eyes shifted to the rough looking visitor. "Is something wrong?"

"Just need some information, Frank. You remember David Cook."

Stilwell relaxed and smiled. "Yes, of course, I remember. Didn't recognize you with that lip duster."

Cook stood and they shook hands.

"It has been a while, Frank. Sorry to hear about Sadie."

The attorney's features clouded over. "Yes, her absence has been keenly felt," he replied. "What brings you to Blue Springs?"

"I'm chasing a lead," replied Cook.

"What sort of lead?"

"David is a major general in the Colorado Militia now," said Templeton. "He has Belle in custody up at Fort Collins, and she told him about a map that a miner had given to Sadie to a cache of gold he supposedly found. We wondered what you knew about it."

"None of us had put much stock in the story," said Stilwell. "I told her to get rid of that map and not to speak of it anymore. Just the mention of gold somewhere makes people do crazy things." He looked at Cort, curious. "Why the interest?"

"It's possible that map leads to a treasure worth over half a million dollars," interjected Cook.

Stilwell looked at Cort and General Cook, astonished. "The devil you say."

"David thinks that Bushy Bill stumbled upon a Confederate shipment of gold coins that was buried around here at the end of the war," explained Cort.

"Why is the Colorado Militia involved?" asked Stilwell.

"The treasure belongs to the Knights of the Golden Circle, and they are looking for it," replied Cook.

"The Knights of the Golden Circle…they disbanded years ago at the end of the war."

"They appear to be reorganizing," said Templeton. "According to David, they have caches of silver, gold, and jewelry buried all over the country to finance another war."

Stilwell raised his brow in surprise. "Do you really think the KGC is a threat?"

"As far as the federal government has been able to tell at this point, they number about 50,000," said Cook. "If they get their hands on large amounts of gold, they won't have trouble raising an army. And, with all the scandal and corruption in President Grant's administration, the government is weak. Public confidence is at its lowest ebb. This would be a good time for the KGC to strike."

"My God," murmured Stilwell.

"Frank, do you have any idea where the map might be?" asked Cort.

Stilwell shook his head. "Sorry. I assumed Sadie threw it away. If I think of anything that might be of help, I'll let you know."

He started for the door.

"Hold up," said Cort. "There is something else you should know, Frank."

Stilwell stopped. "What is it?"

Cort told him about Belle's confrontation with Sadie at the time of Sadie's death.

Stilwell stared in disbelief at Templeton. "Belle was responsible?"

"She claims it was an accident, that Sadie lost her balance, and we can't prove otherwise," said Cort. "Belle made it appear that Sadie had been taking opium so there would be no question about it…and possibly as an act of revenge."

The attorney was silent for a long moment. "At least it puts to rest that story. Perhaps now, Sadie can rest in peace. Where is Belle?"

"The military has her in custody for the time being."

Stilwell passed a hand over his face. "Are we done now, Cort? I need a drink."

"Yeah, but keep this conversation to yourself."

The attorney nodded and left.

Cook looked at Templeton "Frank has the right idea. Got any whiskey?" he asked.

Cort pulled out the bottle and a cup and shoved them over to Cook, his mood pensive.

"What are you thinking?" asked Cook, pouring himself a drink.

"Did Belle go back into the house after Sadie died?" inquired Cort.

Cook shook his head. "She said she hadn't. I gather she was too afraid to go near the scene of her crime. Why?"

"Mrs. Wainwright said it looked as though someone had gone through her aunt's belongings searching for something," said Cort.

Cook took a swig of his whiskey. "It was probably Miss Waters."

"Did Belle say how she had gotten into the house the day Sadie died?"

"She said she went in the back door," answered Cook. "Sadie always left a key in a flowerpot. Why?"

"Someone else might have been searching the house between the time that Nettie and the girls departed and Mrs. Wainwright arrived."

"What makes you think that?"

Cort explained about the secret passageway. "Sadie closed it up when she caught clients sneaking out without paying. Sometime after her death, someone reopened it. Hagen was using it for a time to hide after he escaped the federal marshals, but I doubt he was the one who opened it. He probably didn't know about it then."

"You think it was Chandler?"

"Matt said he wasn't aware of the passageway," replied Cort. "But he could have learned of it from Belle. With the passageway opened, he or KGC agents could search for the map unnoticed while the house was empty."

Templeton paused with a new recollection. "Matt tried to buy the house after Sadie had died, but Frank told him that he couldn't sell it to him. When Mrs. Wainwright arrived in town, Matt offered to buy the house from her. When that wasn't possible, he bought all the furnishings she didn't want when she remodeled—"

"Hoping to discover the map among them," finished General Cook. "Obviously, he didn't find anything if he is looking to marry Mrs. Wainwright."

He shoved the bottle back to Templeton.

"What are you going to do about it?"

Cort poured himself a drink and took a swig. "Force Matt's hand."

The classroom was reconverted back to a dining room for the evening. The blackboard was removed, and Nettie managed to find a tablecloth to cover the crude table. Despite the effort and the fine china and crystal settings from the cupboard, Devon's mother was not impressed.

"Honestly, daughter, this is little better than sitting in the kitchen," she complained as she awkwardly seated herself on the long bench.

Out the corner of her eye, Devon could see Nettie bristle and she sighed knowing that she was in for a long evening.

"I told you that I would meet you at the restaurant, Mother. Frankly, I am surprised that you agreed to come here," said Devon.

"Mr. Chandler and I thought it would be a more private place to talk," replied Mrs. Toller.

"About what?" asked Devon, as if she didn't know.

"Why don't we have a glass of wine," suggested Chandler, hearing the contention in Devon's voice. "I brought a fine Bordeaux." He uncorked the bottle and poured a glass of wine for each of them. "Mrs. Toller, I know that you are averse to alcohol, but perhaps you will make an exception tonight."

"I am opposed to spirits, Mr. Chandler. I do not consider a fine wine to be in that category," she replied accepting the glass.

Devon resisted rolling her eyes, and rather than sip the wine as etiquette dictated, she took a gulp of it.

"Bridget and Brett are taking supper at the restaurant, Nettie. You can remove the extra place settings," she said.

"Ain't fer them," responded Nettie.

"Well, I certainly didn't invite anyone," said Mrs. Toller.

Devon looked at Chandler. "Matt?"

He shrugged, just as mystified. "I had hopes for a private evening."

"Well, the least they can do is be on time," complained Mrs. Toller. She looked at Nettie. "Who are these guests?"

Nettie smiled. "You'll see."

A few minutes later, the front door opened, and Templeton strolled into the dining room with Cook. "Sorry, we're late," he said.

Everyone but Nettie regarded the men with surprise.

"I hope you don't mind that I have brought a guest, Mrs. Wainwright. This is Major General David Cook of the Colorado Militia," said Cort.

"No, of course not," replied Devon, grateful for additional company. "You are welcome at our table, sir."

Cook gave her a slight bow. "Thank you, Mrs. Wainwright. You are most kind."

Templeton continued the introductions. "David, this is Mrs. Toller, Mrs. Wainwright's mother and Sadie's sister."

Cook bowed again. "I see there is a strong resemblance to your sister, madam."

Agatha Toller bristled. "I quite assure you, sir, there is not," she responded crisply.

"My apologies. I meant no disrespect," replied Cook. "I greatly admired your sister."

Mrs. Toller bristled again, and Devon quickly invited the men to sit down before her mother erupted into regrettable discourse.

Chandler regarded the newcomers curiously as they took their seats on the other side of the table. "I thought you had the watch tonight, Marshal."

"We do take time to eat, Matt."

"There is a restaurant across the street from the jail," he pointed out.

Templeton smiled. "I thought David would enjoy one of Nettie's home cooked meals after a long trip."

Chandler turned his attention to the major general. "I didn't expect to see you, sir, after so long a time."

"Likewise. I'm surprised you are still in Blue Springs, Mr. Chandler."

"I am a man of opportunity, General." Matt smiled at Devon and reached for her hand. "And I am hopeful that my fortunes are changing in another direction."

Devon pulled her hand free. "I believe we can start dinner now."

Nettie began passing plates and dishes of food, again to Mrs. Toller's disapproval. "Dishes should not be passed around like cards. Guests are to be served," she remarked critically.

"This is not Boston," Devon quietly reminded her mother.

"What brings you to Blue Springs, General?" queried Chandler.

"I brought news to Marshal Templeton that Belle Waters is in the custody of the military at Fort Collins. I regret to say that not all of your aunt's jewelry can be returned to you, Mrs. Wainwright. Many of the pieces were sold."

"What jewelry? Who is Belle Waters?" Agatha Toller demanded to know.

"It's a long story, Mother. I'll tell you later," said Devon.

"And you came all this way to tell Marshal Templeton. Wouldn't a wire have sufficed, General?" questioned Chandler dryly.

"David is here on a higher mission," said Cort.

"What mission is that, sir?" asked Devon.

"I'm tracking a Confederate gold shipment that disappeared just before the end of the war," replied Cook.

"Good heavens. After all these years, how do you know that it wasn't found already?" asked Mrs. Toller.

"It is quite possible that it was," interjected Cort. "Four years ago, a miner came into town claiming that he had found a large cache of gold coins. When he fell ill during the cholera epidemic, he gave Sadie a map just before he died to where he had hidden it."

Templeton looked at Chandler. "Belle must have told you about the map, Matt."

Chandler shrugged. "She might have mentioned it. I discounted it like everyone else familiar with the story."

Mrs. Toller scoffed. "Well, it sounds fanciful to me. Clarissa always could spin a good tale."

"It weren't no story," retorted Nettie. "I seen Bushy Bill give it to her."

Agatha Toller rolled her eyes. "It doesn't mean that this man's claims were true. He was probably delirious with fever."

"Where is the map?" asked Chandler casually.

"That's a good question," replied Cort, eyeing him closer. "But we know people are looking for it."

"Then I was right," said Devon. "Someone had gone through my aunt's drawers. Was it Belle?"

"I don't believe so," responded Cort. "She was after the jewelry."

He proceeded to give Belle's account of her thievery and of Sadie's death.

Nettie snorted. "It weren't no accident."

Devon's mother was appalled. "Prostitution, drugs, murder…I knew my sister's life would have no good ending."

"Sadie never took drugs, and she weren't no prostitute," protested Nettie.

"Hush, the two of you," said Devon. "So, the other person who had searched the house had to be Hagen. He was the only one who knew about the passage."

"There was another," replied Cort.

Devon looked at him in surprise. "How do you know that?"

"Sadie had sealed the passage. That's why Belle had to use Sadie's hidden key to get in," he explained. "By the time Alice Graham and Hagen learned of the passage, someone had already unsealed it to search for the map."

"How could someone else have learned of it?" quizzed Devon.

Templeton shrugged. "Belle or one of the girls who used to work for Sadie could have mentioned it in idle conversation."

Devon shook her head in wonder. "Was Belle a spy for Hagen, too?"

Mrs. Toller's jaw dropped. "Devon, what kind of place is this?!"

"Be quiet, Mother."

"Belle was a pawn," continued Cort.

Devon wrinkled her brow in confusion. "I don't understand."

"Nor do I," declared Mrs. Toller impatiently.

"We're dealing with a conspiracy, madam," broke in General Cook.

"What kind of conspiracy?"

"Did you ever hear of the Knights of the Golden Circle?"

"I remember them from the war," said Mrs. Toller. "Dreadful people. They were always blowing up something. They very nearly succeeded in their plan to burn New York City to the ground."

"They did a lot more than that," responded Cook. "And they are biding their time to start another insurrection. All they need is the money to do it. This missing shipment of gold is key to their goal."

"Good heavens!" exclaimed Mrs. Toller. She looked accusingly at Chandler. "Do you know anything about this?"

Chandler gave her a smile of forbearance. "Believe me, dear lady, I have no inclinations toward an insurrection nor the desire to fight another war."

"But you did fight for the South, Mr. Chandler. You must have some knowledge of how the organization works," commented Cook.

"I was a soldier on the field, General. I had no dealings with the KGC."

"Now that you have exposed their plan, isn't the danger passed?" asked Devon.

"Not until the agent in charge is found," said Cort.

"Mr. Goodnight you mean."

"Yes."

"Well, I don't know why it should be so difficult to find the man. You know his name," remarked Mrs. Toller.

"It's an alias," said Devon.

"Ask that outlaw or that schoolteacher where this Mr. Goodnight is."

"They're both dead, Mother."

There was a clatter when Mrs. Toller dropped her fork. "Dear God!"

Devon looked at the marshal. "What about Belle? You said she was a pawn."

"Alice Graham supported Belle's addiction for opium in exchange for useful information," explained Cort. "At first it was just about the payroll schedules. Then it became clear that Belle knew other things of value to them."

"The secret passageway and the map?"

Templeton nodded. "She had no idea that she was being exploited by the KGC."

"Perhaps Mr. Goodnight has left the area," suggested Chandler.

"I don't think so," interjected Cook. "He still needs the map."

"He will be unmasked," Templeton assured everyone.

"How is that?" asked Chandler.

"Goodnight made a big mistake recruiting Billy Hagen. He hadn't counted on Hagen's war with me being more important to him than his war with the federal government," replied Cort. "That's why Goodnight sent someone to kill him on the ridge—or maybe Goodnight did it himself."

Devon looked at the marshal in surprise. "I thought Hagen was killed by a wild animal."

"There was a second shot that night—a rifle shot. Doc says that's what killed him."

"That's it," declared Mrs. Toller, throwing down her napkin. "Devon, either you marry Mr. Chandler, or you return to Boston with me this week and marry Mr. Birdwell. I'll not allow you to stay in this den of thieves and murderers any longer if I have to pay to have you kidnapped myself. Conspiracies, secret tunnels, agents…you are not safe here. Mr. Chandler, please escort me back to the hotel."

"Mother, we haven't finished eating."

"I have. Who can possibly eat with talk of such things. Mr. Chandler, if you please."

The men rose from their seats and Chandler helped Devon's mother navigate her way off the bench, the awkwardness of which only intensified her disgruntlement.

"Perhaps the marshal will see you to the hotel, madam," he suggested. "With this Mr. Goodnight on the loose, I should stay with Devon to make sure she is safe."

"Thank you, Matt, but that is not necessary," intervened Devon. "Marshal Templeton sealed the tunnel, and he and his deputy are boarders. Besides, I want to be alone for awhile to sort out everything. All of this has given me a headache and much to think about."

At a nod from Cort, General Cook stepped forward. "I'll walk with you and Mrs. Toller, Chandler. I have a room at the hotel as well."

Chandler hung back, hoping to appeal once more to Devon, but Mrs. Toller grabbed his arm and marched him to the door with her. The major general thanked Devon for dinner and followed after them, throwing Cort a meaningful look. As the trio collected their hats and coats in the foyer, Mrs. Toller could be heard complaining all the way out the door.

Finally, there was blissful silence.

Nettie took herself to the kitchen while Devon remained seated at the table. She poured herself another glass of wine.

"Well, dinner certainly went well," she commented satirically as Cort returned to his seat.

"It was a lot to drop on you, but there was a purpose to it," he said.

"I gathered that you think Matt is Mr. Goodnight."

"I don't know, but it is clear that he has an interest in the map," replied Cort. "He is mixed up in this business somehow." Templeton paused. "After tonight, he's going to put more pressure on you to marry him to gain access to the house."

"That's flattering," quipped Devon.

"Sorry. I didn't mean for it to sound that way. I'm sure Matt has feelings for you, Mrs. Wainwright, but you have to be careful until we know what he is up to."

Bridget and Brett came noisily through the front door then and entered the dining room.

"We saw Chandler and General Cook walkin' Mrs. Toller to the hotel," chortled Brett. "She sure wasn't happy. How was dinner?"

"David and I accomplished what we needed to," replied Cort.

Devon stood up. "Excuse me. It has been a long evening."

As she hastily exited the room, Brett and Bridget glanced at each other.

"Is Miss Devon all right?" asked Bridget, her brows knit in concern. "She doesn't seem herself."

"She has a lot to think about," said Cort.

Templeton lay on his bed that night, his hands behind his head, thinking. He tried to keep his mind on the issue of the lost gold and Mr. Goodnight, but thoughts of Devon kept intruding. He could hear her moving restlessly about her suite. He thought about going to her, but decided she needed time to sort things out as she had said—and so did he.

Everything was quiet then. He started to drift off, when there came a light knock on the door. Cort quickly rose to answer it.

"I couldn't sleep," said Devon, walking past him into the room.

Cort closed the door. "I know. I heard you."

Despite the chill in the room, he was shirtless and wore knee length drawers. As her eye took in his virile physique, that strange little flutter went through her right down to her nether region. And she closed her eyes for a moment to regain her composure.

"What happens next—about Matt and this conspiracy?" she asked.

"I'm working on a plan," said Cort.

"This might help." She held out a creased sheet of paper.

"What's this?"

"I think it's the map that everyone seeks, though it hardly resembles one. I can see why it was so easily dismissed."

Cort looked at her in surprise and took the paper from her. He walked across the room and lit the lamp on the table to study the markings. She was right. The map was so crudely drawn it looked like chicken scratches on a piece of paper. The pencil marks were uneven and hard to decipher. It was obvious that whoever had drawn it had not been in good health.

"Where did you find this?" he asked.

"I was going through my aunt's clothes looking for a suitable wedding dress for Bridget, and the paper fell out of the pocket of one of the dresses," recounted Devon. "It's a wonder I didn't throw it away. Do you think General Cook can find the gold shipment with this?"

"I don't know, but the important thing is that the KGC won't find the cache without it if the treasure is the Confederate gold."

Devon nodded. She lingered a few more moments, then moved to leave. At the door, she stopped and turned to him. "I know now that I can't marry Matt. When this is over, I am returning to Boston."

Cort sighed. Though not unexpected, it wasn't what he wanted to hear. "You are going to marry Mr. Birdwell then?"

She grimaced. "I hope to find a way around that."

Cort eyed her closer as she continued to linger. "Is there something more on your mind, Mrs. Wainwright?"

"No," she replied lightly. "This evening was a bit overwhelming is all…. Well, good night, Mr. Templeton."

Devon turned and opened the door. After a moment's consideration, she closed it again and whirled around to him. "I can't leave. I can't leave without knowing what it is that I can't remember."

Cort looked at her perplexed. "About what?"

"About that night...that night that—" She took a deep breath. "I need to know what it is I experienced New Year's Eve that I can't remember."

Cort bit back a laugh and walked over to her. "Shall I refresh your memory?" he asked, his voice low and husky.

A quiver of desire coursed through Devon, and she gazed up at him with wide eyes and nodded. He cupped her face and pressed his lips against hers. Her response was halting, but he knew it was due more from inexperience than reluctance. He dropped his hands and put his arms around her, drawing her closer as his mouth moved across hers in a more sensual manner.

Soon, Devon began to respond with more ardor. Her arms went around his neck, and the floodgates opened. Whatever had happened the night she couldn't remember, he had awakened something in her that had pushed her over the threshold from self-denial to a driving need to know, to feel—at least once—this thing called sexual gratification. And she knew she couldn't entrust herself in such a vulnerable state to any other man but him.

Cort slipped off her robe and moved her onto the bed, and she readily returned the passion of his kisses with an innate instinct that had been too long repressed. She didn't balk when he moved off her to raise her nightgown over her head and remove his drawers.

Driven now by primal instinct, there was no need of preparation as with the first time, and she forgot about her conditions for complete darkness and the cover of blankets. Just the same, he pulled blankets over them when he felt her shiver, then began a seductive assault on her body and senses that took her breath away.

The feelings he invoked in her as his hands and his mouth found every pleasure point were nothing short of wondrous to her. She gasped and moaned, but he gave her no quarter, forcing her to feel with every fiber in her being. It was just as Pearl had said. Every nerve ending, every cell was ignited. Caught in that web of all consuming arousal, Devon didn't care what she was risking.

He pulled the covers down and moved over top of her again, and she curiously ran her hands over his shoulders and his back, feeling muscles cord beneath her fingers, before moving down his sides and over rock hard thighs.

And she felt his response. The flag was raised. She sucked in her breath and gritted her teeth when he separated her legs wider. As he slipped inside her, she was surprised that it didn't hurt. The moment had always amounted to forced entry with her husband for there had been no foreplay, no attempt to raise feelings of desire.

"Relax," Cort murmured in her ear.

As he moved on her, she lay perfectly still as she was taught to do, waiting for "it" to be over, thinking that the golden moments of the engagement were now passed. Not that those moments of foreplay weren't moments to remember, but she deduced that they were just meant to carry a woman through the rest of the not so glorious act.

"Move with me, Devon," he instructed her.

Devon wrinkled her brow in bewilderment. "But I'm not supposed to."

"Forget everything you've been told and listen to me."

Uncertainly, haltingly, she started to move with him. As she fell into sync with him and the rhythm increased, something most amazing occurred. All the wondrous moments that had occurred beforehand were nothing compared to the feeling that was building…building to an intensity that frightened her.

"Keep going," he urged, pushing her to a frenzied point beyond until there came an explosion that showered her with a myriad of sensations that left her gasping for air.

When he moved off her, Devon was speechless.

"Did that answer your question?" he asked.

She nodded vigorously, still trying to catch her breath.

"'Tis little wonder that Bridget and Brett spend so much time in their rooms," she murmured, awed by the scope of what she had been denied all of her married life.

He pulled the covers over them, knowing that as the delirium of lovemaking began to fade, the enormity of what she had done would come crashing down on her.

She continued to stare into space, still enveloped in a sense of wonder. "How could I not remember this?"

"Because it didn't happen then," replied Cort.

Devon turned her head to him. "What do you mean it didn't happen?"

"You had fortified yourself with so much wine you fell asleep before we got to this point."

"What!" She sat upright and looked at him. "All that time you let me think…to wonder—how could you? Why didn't you tell me?"

"If you had known that you had been granted a reprieve, you might have had second thoughts about returning to carry it through," replied Cort, unapologetic.

She flopped back down on the bed. "Why should it matter to you?"

"If you remember, you agreed to the condition that if you started this, you would see it through to the end. Once the flag is raised, it is not so easy to lower, madam. You owed me a second engagement."

"O-o-oh! You are such a man."

"I'll take that as a compliment."

Devon glared at him. "How could you know I would come back again?"

"You are stubborn, and you were a woman on a mission. Those two things insured that you would."

As she started to remonstrate, he leaned over and kissed her, and a shiver went through her when he slipped his hand beneath the covers to find her most sensitive spot.

"The lesson isn't over yet," he murmured against her ear.

And once more, she threw caution to the wind as she succumbed to the low, seductive timbre of his voice and the play of his fingers and lips on her body.

At the conclusion of her lesson, that Devon had gotten more than she had bargained for was an absurd understatement. And she lay still trying to absorb and accept it all. Guilt over the violation of a code that been ingrained in her since childhood versus the pleasures she had just experienced…how was she to reconcile that?

Cort climbed out of bed and pulled on his drawers, then went to retrieve her nightgown for her. He could see that she was struggling.

"Do you want the light off?" he asked.

She nodded.

When the room was dark again, she quickly put on her gown and robe.

"Mr. Templeton, I trust that this will remain between us."

"Of course. But I think we are passed formality now. First names will do."

"I think not, Mr. Templeton," she responded. "People might think that something has occurred between us. As it is, those reporters raised enough of a specter of a romance." She picked up her slippers and moved to the door. With her hand on the knob, she turned to him. "Thank you. It was…most enlightening."

"Happy to oblige. Any time."

"Oh, no. We can never do this again," she was quick to inform him.

As she surreptitiously slipped out the door, the corners of his mouth curled up in a smile. He would take those odds. Regardless of what she said, something very much had occurred between them. He knew that now, and he wondered how long it would take for her to realize and admit it, too. He had no idea what this meant or where it would lead, but he knew it could not be ignored.

C H A P T E R   T H I R T Y - T H R E E

Wrong Idea

Brett shook his head in puzzlement. "I'm tellin' ya, Cort, Mrs. Wainwright is actin' mighty strange again."

Cort looked up from the papers on his desk. "You're probably just imagining it."

"No sir, I ain't, and neither is Bridget and Nettie."

"How is she acting?" asked Cort.

"Well, she jokes and smiles a lot. She sings to herself…and she's nice to me. Don't tell me ya ain't noticed."

Cort smothered a smile. "Can't say. It sounds as though Mrs. Wainwright has made peace with something that has been bothering her."

"That's what Bridget and Nettie said. They think she's made up her mind to marry Chandler."

"Or maybe she has decided to go back to Boston," suggested Cort.

Brett looked at him as though he had grown two heads. "With her mother? I don't think that's likely. Leastwise, she wouldn't be this happy about it."

"Whatever it is, it's her business. Why is it concerning to you that Mrs. Wainwright is in a good mood about something? Just accept it and be grateful."

Brett let out a heavy sigh. "That's what I told Bridget. But she feels a kind of kinship for Mrs. Wainwright, and she's worried that Mrs. Wainwright is about to hitch her wagon to Chandler. When Bridget is worried about somethin', there ain't no sleepin'—or anythin' else—until the worry has passed."

Cort chuckled. "The marriage bed is a little chilly these days?"

"It ain't as accommodatin' as it was," grumbled Brett.

"Why doesn't someone ask Mrs. Wainwright what she's about?"

Brett slapped his knee. "Dang if that ain't just what we said. Bridget and Nettie thought as how you should be the one to ask her," he added.

"Me? What makes you think she will talk to me?"

"You have a way with her, and you don't care if you make her mad."

Cort ran a hand across the back of his neck. How in the hell was he to tell Devon not to be so lighthearted, that her newfound "enlightenment" was sending the wrong message?

"I'll think on it," he said.

"Don't think on it too long."

At the pleading look on Brett's face, Cort reached into his vest pocket and tossed a couple of coins across the desk to him. "Take Bridget and Nettie to supper tonight at the hotel."

Brett's face it up. "Yes, sir."

Devon came down to dinner that night, surprised to find only Cort.

"Where are Bridget and Mr. Sanger?" she asked in a cheery mood.

"They decided to eat at the hotel," said Nettie, bustling in from the kitchen with a tureen of soup and setting it on the table. "I was to go with 'em, but I'm takin' supper with the Walkers, so clean up after yourselves."

Devon stared after Nettie as she rushed out of the dining room. A few minutes later, Devon heard the front door close.

"What was that all about?" she asked in bewilderment as she seated herself on the school bench.

"It's their clumsy attempt to make sure that we are alone," said Cort, sitting down across from her.

"Why?"

"They are afraid that you have decided to marry Matt, and they have charged me with the task of talking you out of it."

"Good heavens. Where did they get that idea?" she asked, ladling out a bowl of the soup and handing it to him.

Cort hesitated. "It seems that you are uncharacteristically in high spirits about something."

Devon was in the process of ladling out a bowl for herself, when she stopped midair and looked at him, realizing the import of what he was saying.

A blush suffused her face, and she set the bowl of soup down and lowered her eyes. "Well, we can't have that now, can we?"

"Nettie and Bridget welcome that you are in high spirits. They just want to know that you are less restrained for the right reason," said Cort.

She looked up at him. "I don't know why it should matter to Bridget and Nettie what decision I make about Matt."

"It matters," replied Cort. "They care about you. But truth to tell, I am here on behalf of Brett."

Devon knit her brows in bewilderment. "Deputy Sanger? How can it possibly concern him?"

"It seems that Bridget is so concerned for you she is too distracted to attend to matters in the marriage bed."

Devon's eyes widened and the blush deepened to a rosier hue. "Oh. Well, Bridget worries too much," she said, uncomfortable with the subject. "You may tell Mr. Sanger that he will have his marriage bed back."

A thought suddenly came to Cort. "Upon further consideration, Mrs. Wainwright, I am inclined to have him wait a little longer."

CHAPTER THIRTY-FOUR

Exposed

"Mr. Chandler, there's someone outside who wants to see ya," said a patron, entering the saloon.

"Who?" asked Chandler distracted by his ledger.

"That real pretty lady…Sadie's niece."

Chandler's head snapped up. Devon had been distant since returning from Aspen Ridge. And after that disastrous dinner, he had decided to give her some space. Now that Templeton knew about the lost gold shipment and the map, he had to watch his step. At least there was one good sign—General Cook had left town.

He quickly made his way outside.

"Devon, what a pleasant surprise. I was getting worried. I haven't seen you about—"

"Matt, I found it," she said, her eyes alight with excitement.

"What, dear heart?"

"The map…I found it. After all that talk at dinner the other night, I started looking for it. It dropped out of the pocket of one of my aunt's dresses."

Chandler was clearly taken aback. "Did you tell anyone about this?"

Devon shook her head. "I didn't know what to do or whom to trust, so I came to you. You are the only one who doesn't seem to have an interest in the treasure. I don't know who Mr. Goodnight is, and I'm afraid of what he will do if he knows that I have the map."

"Apparently, Templeton doesn't share your trust in me," remarked Chandler.

"I know. And while he's watching you, I am fearful that the KGC will strike at me." She shuddered. "After Hagen, I cannot survive another abduction."

"Cort can be pretty single-minded," agreed Chandler. "Where is the map?"

"I gave it to Mr. Stilwell for safekeeping. He put it in his safe for the night," said Devon. "Tomorrow, he's going to place it in the bank vault when it opens. Matt, the map was given to my aunt. That makes the treasure mine if I find it, doesn't it?"

"Only if Cort and General Cook don't learn of it," he replied. "The government may give you a finder's fee, but the bulk of it will be confiscated as contraband. We must keep this between us, Devon."

She reached up and hugged him. "I knew I could count on you. Come to dinner tonight, and we'll celebrate—six o'clock. I have a surprise for you. Marshal Templeton left town for a few days, so he won't be a nuisance."

"Yes, I saw him leave. Where did he go?" asked Chandler, curious.

"I don't know. I suppose to check on the outlying homesteads."

Chandler smiled. "I shall see you at six o'clock then."

"Bring a bottle of one of your best wines," she said with a twinkle in her eye.

At six o'clock, Chandler promptly arrived for dinner with high expectations and was dismayed to find a full table. Pastor Clemmons and Devon's mother were present. When they all sat down, it was clear that Brett, Bridget, and Nettie were joining them too. Neither was the saloon owner thrilled about sharing his prime wine selection with the "help" as Devon filled goblets for everyone.

"Before we enjoy the fruits of Nettie's labor, I would like to make an announcement," said Devon. She looked at Chandler. "Matt, you have been pestering me to marry you for some time, and I have repeatedly said 'no.'"

"And I shall never stop asking," interjected Chandler.

"Well, tonight you can," replied Devon. "I accept your proposal."

Chandler's jaw dropped; Mrs. Toller let out a shriek of delight; and Nettie, Bridget, and Brett exchanged looks of horror. The pastor didn't know what to think.

"You look surprised, Matt. Are you not happy?" asked Devon.

"Yes…yes, off course, dear heart," he replied, struggling to recover his composure. "It's just that you have had such a swift change of mind. Perhaps you should take some more time to be certain."

"Nonsense," broke in Mrs. Toller. "Pastor Clemmons, how soon can you marry my daughter and Mr. Chandler? I would like to return to Boston forthwith."

"Well, I suppose we could arrange for a ceremony tomorrow at the church," replied the pastor, "if you are sure about this, Mrs. Wainwright."

"I am, sir," Devon assured him. She looked at Chandler and smiled lovingly. "I have seen the light."

Chandler reached for his wine and swigged the contents of the glass.

Bridget and Nettie's attention swiveled to Brett.

"You said the marshal would talk to her," whispered Bridget.

"He did," Brett whispered back, just as bewildered.

While Devon and Mrs. Toller excitedly laid out wedding plans over the course of the dinner, the others sat in dismal silence. At the conclusion, Chandler was quick to depart, citing business matters that required his attention. Pastor Clemmons followed soon after, escorting Mrs. Toller to the hotel.

Bridget and Nettie quietly began to clear the table.

Conscious of the cold glares the two women directed his way, Brett rose from his seat. "I—uh—I should go and see if Jasper needs help at the jail…what with the marshal bein' out of town," he stammered.

Devon smiled brightly. "As you will, Mr. Sanger," she replied, helping herself to another glass of wine.

It was nearly 11 o'clock before the town was shrouded in silence for the night. Hidden by the darkness of a starless sky and a new moon, a lone figure quietly jimmied the lock on the door and entered Frank Stilwell's law office.

He made his way to the back room and went straight to the safe. It was an old safe, one he found easy to break into, and he easily gained entry. The intruder lit a match and rifled through the papers until he found the one he was looking for. The map was crudely drawn, and he didn't readily understand the symbols. It would take some studying.

"I didn't expect you to be so late," said Cort.

Chandler whirled about, completely taken by surprise. A smile slowly crossed his features, and he shrugged. "Had to wait until everyone was asleep. I thought you were out of town."

"You shouldn't believe everything you hear, Matt."

Chandler threw back his head and laughed. "I assume that includes the acceptance of my marriage proposal by the fair Miss Devon. I thought I had overplayed my hand when she had that quick change of heart. Well played, Marshal."

"I want the names of the others, Matt."

"The others—oh, you think I'm Mr. Goodnight. Sorry to disappoint you, Cort. I have nothing to do with the KGC. As I told you before, I just take advantage of opportunities when they present themselves."

"Like Mrs. Wainwright?"

"I like Devon. I would never hurt her," replied Chandler soberly.

"No, you just pretended to court her to gain access to her house to find and steal the map."

Chandler had the decency to look contrite. "Tell her I'll send her half of the proceeds when I find the treasure."

"That's magnanimous of you considering the map belongs to her."

"That's more than the government will give her. You know as well as I do Washington will confiscate the whole cache as contraband."

Templeton motioned with his revolver. "Hand over the map, Matt, and start walking to the jail."

"You can't prove I'm guilty of anything."

"Breaking into Stilwell's office is a start. Then, there is the attempt robbery charge."

"C'mon, Cort. No harm has been done. Let me go, and I'll leave town. You'll never see me again."

"I'll take that map, Mr. Chandler, and that gun, Marshal," said a voice from behind.

Templeton and Chandler both turned in surprise to see that an older, slightly built man with spectacles held them at gun point.

Cort peered closer at their captor in the darkness. "Tobias? What the hell are you doing?"

Chandler laughed. "Tobias isn't just Stilwell's secretary, Cort. He's Mr. Goodnight, I'll wager."

"Shut up," said the man, no longer the attorney's mild-mannered employee. "Throw your gun on the floor, Marshal."

When Cort did as he ordered, Tobias snatched the map from Chandler's fingertips and cocked the revolver. "Nothing personal, gentlemen. I can't leave witnesses."

"Does that include Billy Hagen?" asked Cort.

"Hagen was a fool. Nearly ruined everything by kidnapping Mrs. Wainwright."

"Don't be stupid, Tobias. Everyone in town knows you."

"No one notices someone like me, Marshal. Besides, I'll be long gone before your deputies figure anything out. Now, which one of you wants to go first?"

He turned toward Templeton. In that instant, Chandler ejected a small pistol from his sleeve and shot the KGC agent in the arm, sending the man's shot wild. When Tobias grabbed his injured arm, the map fluttered to the floor. As Templeton subdued the secretary and retrieved his gun, Chandler scooped up the map and ran for the door.

"Matt, stop!" commanded Templeton, training his revolver on him.

"Sorry, Cort, I can't." When Templeton hesitated, Chandler smiled. "Tell Devon I'll miss her," he said and dashed out of the building.

As Cort escorted Tobias from the building, he was met with a throng of people who had heard the gunshots. Jasper came running from the jail, and Brett came running from the house half dressed with his revolver in hand. He was followed by Devon, Bridget, and Nettie wearing coats thrown over their nightclothes.

"Marshal, what happened?" asked Jasper. "I thought you was out of town."

"I'll explain everything tomorrow," said Cort. "In the meantime, take this man to a jail cell."

"Yes, sir." Jasper looked at the prisoner as he took the man in hand. "Tobias…that you? What's he done, Cort?"

"He's an agent for the Knights of the Golden Circle, Jasper. Guard him well."

The deputy's mouth dropped open. "Tobias?"

"I need to see a doctor," protested the man. "The marshal shot me when I caught him and Chandler breaking into Mr. Stilwell's office to steal the map."

"Shut up, you weasel," said Jasper, hustling the prisoner off to jail. "You sure had us fooled."

"Do you want me to fetch the doc?" asked Brett.

"Already here," broke in Dr. Morse. "I heard gunshots. Who's hurt?"

"The prisoner needs attention," said Cort.

As the doctor hurried off to the jail, Templeton dispersed the crowd with the promise of an explanation the next day.

He turned to Brett. "Give Jasper a hand tonight in case there are co-conspirators nearby. Stay vigilant. First thing in the morning, send off a wire to General Cook that we have his man."

"Sure thing." Brett shook his head. "Never would have figured Tobias for Mr. Goodnight. How did you?"

"I didn't."

Briefly, Cort explained about setting up Chandler and the surprising turn of events.

"Then Mrs. Wainwright won't be marryin' Matt Chandler," said Brett in relief.

The last of the crowd melted away, and Bridget and Nettie returned to the house.

Devon walked up to Cort. "Where is Matt? Didn't he appear tonight?"

"He did and took off with the map," replied Templeton.

"Are you going after him?"

Cort shook his head. "I owe him one. By the way, he said he would send you half the proceeds from the gold when he discovers it."

Devon laughed. "You didn't tell him the map was a fake?"

"It will keep him busy," replied Cort with a grin. "Knowing Matt, he will probably find something."

As they walked to the house, he told her about Tobias being Mr. Goodnight.

"I heard you tell Deputy Hale," said Devon. "Tobias was there when I gave Mr. Stilwell the map. He was always so quiet I never took much notice of him."

"He was right," remarked Cort.

"About what?"

"Nobody notices people like him…or Miss Primrose."

"What about Matt?" asked Devon. "Is he a member of KGC, too?"

"No, he's an opportunist just like he said."

Devon sighed. "Poor Matt. He'll always be chasing that rainbow and the pot of gold."

"Don't tell me that Miss Boston with her exacting code of conduct holds a soft spot for a scoundrel," quipped Cort.

She glanced sideways at him, a teasing gleam in her eye. "Matt does have some endearing qualities you have to admit. He did win over my mother."

Cort snorted. "A dubious achievement I am happy to allow him."

When they arrived at the house, all was silent, and they assumed that Bridget and Nettie had returned to bed. Cort and Devon removed their coats and quietly climbed the stairs. They came to his room, and he opened the door. When she started past him, he caught her hand.

She looked up at him. "I can't," she whispered.

Her demeanor told him differently and, by the light of the sconce, he could see in her eyes that she was torn. He leaned down and kissed her, taking the calculated risk that she just needed a little gentle persuasion. Her arms went around his neck, and she responded with more passion.

Nettie had been in the kitchen unaware that Cort and Devon had come in and was making her way to bed, when she happened upon the scene. And as Cort maneuvered Devon into his room and shoved the door closed, the older woman's jaw dropped.

"Well, I'll be..." she murmured.

When she passed by the bedroom, a smile broke across her features. From what she could hear, they weren't just talking.

Inside the room, desire had quickly flamed into passion. Cort pulled off his shirt and trousers and they fell upon the bed in something of a frenzy. Without bothering to further disrobe, Cort pulled her on top of him and instructed her to straddle him. In the heat of the moment, she didn't hesitate or question it. She pulled up her nightgown and got on top of him. He freed his member from the drawers, and she caught her breath as she felt him easily enter her.

Instinctively, she moved on him, encountering a different kind of friction but one just as stimulating as in the other position, and she gasped as waves of pulsating sensations began to course through her. It was like that teasing taste of candy that left one greedily wanting more, and she increased her movements without direction from Cort.

He shifted her slightly and slipped his hands beneath her nightgown to cup her buttocks, holding her tighter against him, creating highly charged impulses that seemed to reach every nerve ending in her body.

She had thought the first time with him had been intense, but this was even more so. Maybe it was because their passion was already heightened when they began this time. Maybe it was the different position. She didn't care as she pressed him for the climax. She cried out when he finally brought the release. When their movements slowed to a stop, she collapsed on top of him, gasping to catch her breath.

"You are becoming quite accomplished," he teased.

Devon blushed. The lack of control and abandon when under the influence of unbridled passion was something she was still trying to reconcile with her high society upbringing.

"Do you think anyone heard us?" she asked in consternation.

"No. Everyone is in bed," he assured her.

"Is…is that normal?"

"What?"

"That position?"

"Devon, anything is normal if both parties are in agreement…. Are you in agreement with that?"

Devon readily nodded.

Cort rolled her onto the bed. "And there is more for you to learn," he murmured, trailing light kisses along her neck.

He moved his hand underneath her garment to fan lightly across her sensitive skin. Still highly charged, she felt a shudder of delight roll through her when his fingers dipped lower. Desire began to build once again. Just as she felt herself start to slip into that state of abandon, she summoned the strength to stop him.

"I have to go," she said, breaking away from him.

"We still have time."

He tried to pull her back, but she slipped away and rose from the bed.

"We can never do this again," she insisted, pulling down her nightgown.

Cort chuckled. "I seem to have heard that before."

"I know, but this time I mean it."

"Devon, if you are worried about your reputation—"

"It's not just that. I'm leaving, and it will make the situation all the more difficult."

Cort got off the bed, rearranged his drawers, and walked over to her. "You don't have to leave, Devon. You have income as the teacher of Blue Springs and are already starting to build a life here. You have friends. I know this is a different world out here than you are used to, but I think you could be happy."

She looked up at him. "You have shown me what I needed to know, and I shall always remember this time with you as special. But I cannot continue as we have."

"We will practice discretion. No one will ever know."

"I will know, and it would make me feel like one of those women in my aunt's salon," said Devon. "That may be fine for Pearl or those other ladies, but it isn't for me. I have to return to Boston, Cort. It's better for both of us this way. I'll stay until another teacher can be found. Until then, I think it best if you move out of the house."

She raised herself up on her toes and kissed him lightly on the lips. "I'm sorry," she murmured.

"You are sure about this?" he asked, his voice husky with emotion.

Devon hesitated. "No, but this is the way it has to be."

When she moved to the door, he didn't try to stop her.

Devon lay awake the rest of the night sniffing back tears as she tried to sort out her feelings.

Cort Templeton was unlike any man she was raised to consider worthy of a woman of her class. Though his education was above par, he was plain-spoken and dismissed the concept of polite society as a disconnect from reality and a license to practice hypocrisy. He more often dressed like a cowboy than a gentleman and possessed a different sense of morality. Yet all things considered and given everything she had learned these past months about herself and him, she would have to say that no woman of her class was worthy of Cort Templeton.

From him, she had learned about life—real life. Heat suffused her face as she thought about their intimate times together, and her heart ached at the thought of leaving him. But this was not her world, and she needed to face that realization before she fell more in love with him.

The next morning, the town was abuzz with the happenings of the previous night. As more details came out, everyone was incredulous, but none more so than Frank Stilwell when he learned that his secretary was a high-level agent of the notorious Knights of the Golden Circle.

At the house, a pall settled over the residence as Nettie and Bridget watched Cort move out. Nettie was completely baffled. She knew she hadn't imagined the scene she had witnessed between him and Devon or the telltale sounds coming from his room the previous night.

When the door closed on the marshal, she and Bridget looked up to see Devon watching morosely from the top of the stairs.

"Don't set a place for me at the table," she said.

As Devon retired to her rooms, Bridget looked at Nettie. "What happened? Why did the marshal move out of the house?"

Nettie shook her head. "Can't figure it myself."

"What did he say?"

"He said as how the danger had passed, and Mrs. Wainwright didn't need him no more," replied Nettie.

General Cook and the militia arrived a week later to take custody of the prisoner and the real treasure map, and, though the little town had settled back into a state of normalcy once again, it was clear that something was very wrong with Mrs. Wainwright and the marshal. And it came as a shock to all that she had decided to return to the East.

CHAPTER THIRTY-FIVE

The Truth Prevails

"'Tis a sad day, missy. The town won't be the same without ya," said Nettie as Devon fastened the last of her trunks.

Devon straightened and turned to the feisty little woman, forcing a brave smile. "Thank you, Nettie. I shall miss Blue Springs." She laughed lightly. "I would never have imagined I would have the occasion to say that."

"Then why ain't ya stayin'?" questioned Nettie.

"The town council has found a new teacher," said Devon. "It is time for me to return to my world, but I promise I shall visit."

Nettie wiped away a tear. "Got something in my eye," she mumbled taking out a handkerchief and blowing her nose. "I'll send Orville up to fetch your trunks."

When Nettie left, Devon looked around the room and wiped away a few tears of her own. She walked over to the dresser and saw the rosewood box that had held her aunt's jewelry. It had been her aunt's most prized possession, she recollected Pearl saying. Devon hadn't paid much attention to it before.

She opened it. It was empty now. The cheap jewelry had been discarded, but she was seized with the desire to take the box with her. She started to close the lid, when she noticed a small button in the corner. The color of it matched the inside and was barely noticeable.

Devon pushed it and was surprised when the base of the box moved to reveal a hidden drawer.

Inquisitively, she pulled it open. It housed what appeared to be a diary and two miniature portraits. One was of her aunt at a much younger age, and Devon marveled at how truly beautiful she was. She looked at the other portrait. It was of a handsome, young man, and she surmised that this was Clarissa's lost love.

Beneath the diary, Devon spied a yellowed newspaper clipping. She pulled it out and read about the loss of a Nantucket whaling ship and her crew in a storm in 1843. Looking further, Devon found newspaper clippings of her society debut and of her wedding. She had barely known her aunt and was surprised and mystified that her aunt would have these items about her.

She picked up the diary then and sat down on the bed. It seemed an invasion of privacy, but something compelled her to open the leather-bound journal and read it.

It began with her aunt's musings about a young sailor who had captured her heart, then moved onto an account of her father's disapproval of him and of the couple's plan to elope after the young man's return from his voyage. But he didn't return.

Though Devon knew the story, nothing had prepared her for the anguish that poured out of the journal as she read about her aunt's love for this man and the despair she had felt at his loss. The sailor was Joshua Barrows. Being able to put a name to the man in the photograph personalized the heartbreaking story even more for Devon.

Devon read on about the cruelty of her aunt's family when her aunt discovered she was with child and how she was left to fend for herself in Paris after losing the baby that she never got the chance to see or hold. It was as Pearl had told her but hearing it in Clarissa's words Devon could see just how dark this period of time was for her aunt. Her pain and fear echoed from every word. Still, Devon was shocked to read that her aunt had been contemplating suicide, when she met Madame Marie Le Bonheur, the owner of a well-known Paris salon.

Devon skipped through her aunt's time in the salon but had read enough to see that Pearl may have been telling the truth. Her aunt hadn't been a courtesan.

She flipped through the journal to her aunt's return to the United States. Clarissa had written about meeting a man aboard ship who had befriended her and had become her protector and benefactor. The name stunned Devon…Frank Stilwell. And she read on in wonderment about the special relationship they continued to share.

Devon's amazement turned to bewilderment at the next page. Her aunt had written about seeing a picture of her sister Agatha with her young daughter Devon in the society section of the Boston newspaper. Again, Devon wondered why her aunt would have such an interest in her. She read the next entries and gasped in disbelief.

There came a knock on the door. "Mrs. Wainwright, 'tis Orville Finch come to pick up your trunks."

"Not now," she shouted.

The young man was nearly to the stairs when Devon ran to the door to call him back.

"Did ya change your mind, ma'am?"

"No. Is Deputy Sanger still in the house?"

"Yes, ma'am."

"Tell him to fetch Mr. Stilwell here straightaway. Then tell Nettie that I want to see her as well when Mr. Stilwell arrives," she commanded, her tone sharp."

"Yes, ma'am."

At half past the hour, Nettie and Frank Stilwell stood before Devon, bewildered as to why they had been summoned, but there was no mistaking the tension in the air. As Devon stared at them, energy crackled around her.

"Is somethin' amiss?" ventured Nettie uneasily.

Devon turned an icy glare on her. In that moment, she was as fearsome looking as Agatha Toller, and Nettie swallowed hard.

"Do you know what this is?" quizzed Devon, setting the journal on the table in front of them.

Nettie paled. "It…it's Miss Sadie's journal," she replied hesitantly. "I-I was lookin' fer it. Where did ya find it…"

Her voice trailed off as Devon fixed her with another chilling glare. "Do you know what it says?"

Nettie slowly nodded.

"Why did no one tell me that my aunt was, in fact, my mother?" she demanded to know, her measured tone rising with her anger.

"We wanted to tell ya," Nettie rushed to explain, "but ya was so angry and disrespectin' of Miss Sadie we thought it better to wait until ya was more acceptin' of her. Then there weren't no good time to tell ya when that witch Mrs. Toller come to town," she said with a disdainful snort.

"Is it no wonder that you disliked her so much from the moment she arrived?" retorted Devon facetiously.

"I didn't like what she and her family done to Miss Sadie, but there ain't nothin' 'bout that woman to like otherwise," declared Nettie.

Devon turned a sharp eye on the attorney. "What do you have to say, Mr. Stilwell?"

Stilwell knew that Devon was like a bomb ready to explode, and he chose his words carefully to try to defuse the moment.

"When Sadie saw that picture in the paper of you and Mrs. Toller, it made her wonder," he began. "You were of the age her child would have been, and you bore a marked resemblance to Sadie, so much so that she had me contact a detective in Paris and in Boston to investigate the possibility that you might be her child. When she got the reports that you most likely were, she traveled to Boston to confront her sister."

"Yes, I read all that," responded Devon impatiently. "I remember when she came. There was a terrible argument between them. Why didn't she tell me who she was then?"

"She was protecting you, Mrs. Wainwright."

Devon scoffed. "Protecting me or herself?"

"That ain't fair, missy," said Nettie.

She stopped when Stilwell warned her off with the shake of his head and stepped in again. "Given her profession, Mrs. Wainwright, Sadie knew that she had little chance in court of being awarded custody of you," he explained.

"The Cains and the Tollers were high society families. It would have been a huge public scandal had she tried," he went on. "You would have been forever marked by it."

Stilwell paused. "It nearly broke her to lose you a second time. To hold you close, she retained the Pinkerton Detective Agency to keep her abreast of your life…. It pained her greatly to know how unhappy you were in your marriage."

Devon remained silent, and the attorney continued. "When your husband died and Sadie learned that you were being forced into another unhappy marriage, she saw an opportunity to help."

"I am aware of no help from her," Devon replied crisply.

"Sadie sent you money so that you would be financially independent enough to refuse the marriage," he said.

"I received no money, Mr. Stilwell."

Stilwell wrinkled his brow in puzzlement. "I don't understand. I know that Sadie sent funds several times."

Images of her housekeeper and Agatha Toller suddenly leaped to Devon's mind, and she knew very well why she hadn't received any money.

"Sadie was also laying plans to close her business and build a ranch on one of her properties so she could invite you for a visit," said Stilwell. "It was her hope that you would want to start a new life here, and that, one day, you could get to a place where she could tell you the truth. But to all our great sorrow, Sadie died before she could follow through with her plans.

Devon turned away struggling with emotions that accompanied the exposure of a secret such as this.

"Who else knows the truth?" she asked.

"Just me, Frank, Pearl, and the marshal," replied Nettie.

Devon turned and looked at her sharply. "The marshal knows? You were all going to let me leave without telling me?"

"Cort said as how it would do too much damage in your state of mind to tell ya," said Nettie. "He reckoned the story needed to come out on its own whenever that might be."

Devon had always imagined a conspiracy afoot to reshape her image of Sadie, but now she realized that it had been a campaign to prepare her for when the truth did come out.

"Tell me, Mr. Stilwell, is it your knowledge that Joshua Barrows was a good and honorable man?" she inquired.

"Yes, Mrs. Wainwright, by all my evidence he was. Sadie asked me to conduct an investigation into his death, which I extended to his character. I can tell you that he was a man of his word. I have the report in my files if you wish to take custody of it."

"I do." Devon paused. "You loved Clarissa—Sadie—even knowing that a part of her heart would always belong to Joshua Barrows?"

The attorney smiled. "She had a big heart, Mrs. Wainwright. I am honored to have known her affections as well."

Just then, they heard Agatha Toller's strident voice carry up the stairs.

Devon stiffened and her features hardened. She looked at Nettie and Stilwell. "You may leave now. Send up Mrs. Toller and have someone fetch me a buggy," she instructed with icy reserve.

Nettie and the attorney glanced at each other and quietly left the room.

It wasn't long before Devon heard Agatha coming down the hall, tapping her cane—a sign that she was perturbed about something.

She entered the room and looked around her. "Your trunks haven't been delivered to the stage line office? You must make haste, daughter, or there may not be room enough for them on the coach."

"I am not leaving on the same coach as you," Devon informed her.

Mrs. Toller caught the edge in her tone and eyed Devon closer noticing her stiff bearing and stony expression. "Are you ill? I shall await the next stage with you."

"No, you will go now," stated Devon in no uncertain terms. "The reason for your presence in Blue Springs no longer abides."

"What is that to mean?" huffed Mrs. Toller. "You are acting most peculiar."

"You came here to keep me from learning the secret that you keep," said Devon.

"I don't know what you are talking about."

Devon pointed to the book on the table. "I found Clarissa's journal."

Mrs. Toller paled. "What do you know?"

"That Clarissa was not my aunt and that you are not my mother. How could you and the family do that to her and to me?"

Mrs. Toller sat down heavily on a chair. "You don't know the circumstances. One didn't cross your grandfather, and Clarissa was selfish. She cared not one whit the consequences of her acts."

"She was seeking love and was perhaps the most selfless of all of you. She gave up her child."

Agatha Toller sniffed. "It was the only good thing she ever did." "What could she have given you?"

"Perhaps love not conditioned on duty."

"You were given a life of privilege and entrance into society."

"Yes, in a world where everything is a matter of strategy and love most often a casualty."

Mrs. Toller scoffed. "Love is overrated. Sometimes one must make sacrifices for the greater good."

Devon gave a humorless laugh. "For whose greater good? Do you not see the irony? The elites barter their daughters just as the madams barter their girls."

"Don't be coarse, Devon. It is not the same thing. One is for the purpose of illicit pleasure, the other is for the perpetuation of wealth and position."

"In other words, yours is the higher cause so that makes it all right."

Mrs. Toller huffed impatiently. "You are twisting my words.

"Did your husband know?" asked Devon.

"Father paid him handsomely to accept the situation. And, as Mr. Toller was impotent, the appearance of fatherhood improved his public image. Oh, don't look so disgusted. Clarissa could not care for you on her own and to bring her back into the family with a baby would have created a huge scandal."

"So you took her child and abandoned her in a foreign country with no resources. How charitable," scoffed Devon.

Mrs. Toller stiffened. "She was supposed to join the nunnery but, as usual, had consideration only for herself. You should consider yourself fortunate, Devon. Father wanted to leave you at an orphanage in Paris, but Mother said 'no.' I do believe it was the first and only time she ever stood up to him. So, you see this was the best way for all concerned. Now hurry. There isn't much time."

"I told you. I am not leaving with you," said Devon. "I'm taking the next stage, but I am not returning to Boston or to the family."

"Daughter, do be sensible—"

"I'm not your daughter." Devon gave a derisive laugh. "That's the problem. I've been too sensible, too dutiful all my life. But don't you worry. Your polite society will not learn of this injustice. I shall keep your secret. Now leave before I change my mind."

Mrs. Toller slowly got to her feet. "I do have affection for you, Devon, and I have come to think of you as my daughter. Surely, you must know that I have always done what I thought was best for you."

"No, you have always done what you thought was best for you," retorted Devon.

Mrs. Toller stiffened. "I am still the only mother you have ever known."

Devon regarded her with a solemn expression tinged with sadness. "You were never a mother. You were an overseer."

Cort looked up when the door opened and sighed heavily as Pearl Donovan walked purposefully into the office.

"I wondered how long it would be before Nettie sent for you," he said. "That woman needs to mind her own business."

"Well, someone has to be the adult," retorted Pearl, perching on the edge of his desk. "Nettie said you and Mrs. Wainwright are as miserable as…as a horse in a stall full of flies."

"Is that the best you can do?"

"Sorry. I didn't want to be crude."

Cort returned his attention to the papers on his desk. "Leave it alone, Pearl. You have done enough interfering. Devon is leaving on the stage with her mother."

"Did you ask her to stay?"

"I did, not that it is any of your business."

Pearl snorted. "I can just imagine how you asked her. You should have taken some charm lessons from Matt while he was here." She regarded Cort quizzically. "Why is Mrs. Wainwright leaving Blue Springs? Didn't she take my advice and ask you to—"

"I said to leave it alone, Pearl."

Pearl cocked her head to one side and smiled knowingly. "As I can only imagine that you obliged her and am personally acquainted with your ability to please, what pray tell is the problem?"

Cort rubbed a hand across his face. "If you must know, now that her curiosity has been satisfied, she said that she would feel like one of Sadie's parlor girls were the practice to continue."

"Well, I never heard that one before," quipped Pearl. "Mrs. Wainwright isn't planning on going into a convent, is she?" she asked, half joking.

Cort gave her a wry smile. "I told you she has a different way of seeing things. I wouldn't discount anything."

"Just be friends then."

"I'm afraid that would prove to be too difficult."

Pearl burst into laughter. "So marry her."

"She has made it quite clear that she has no desire to remarry."

"Of course, she doesn't—not to a man like her husband, which is all that is available to her in Boston. I dare say that she doesn't mean she wouldn't marry you. Did you even ask her?"

When he didn't answer, Pearl rolled her eyes in exasperation. "You're an idiot, Templeton, if you allow her to leave."

"I can't force her to stay, Pearl."

"No, but you could give her a good reason not to go…like telling her that you love her."

Nettie burst through the door then, breathless from running. "Cort, ya gotta come quick to the house."

Cort looked at her in consternation. "Why? What's happened?"

"She knows. Oh Lordy, she knows. Pearl, thank heavens you're here," cried Nettie.

Pearl guided the older woman to a chair. "Calm down, Nettie. Who knows what?"

"The missy. She found Miss Sadie's journal. She knows everything. She called me and Frank to her room. She's got Mrs. Toller up there now."

"Christ," murmured Cort. "How is she taking it?"

Nettie shook her head. "Not good…not good at all."

Cort jumped up from his chair, grabbed his hat and coat, and rushed out the door.

When he walked into the foyer of the house, a pale and anxious Bridget met him. "I don't know what's happenin', sir, but somethin' is wrong with Miss Devon."

"Is Mrs. Toller still up there?" asked Cort.

Bridget shook her head. "She come down the stairs white as a sheet and walked out the door without a word."

"Where is Brett?"

"He went to the livery stable. Miss Devon wanted a buggy brought around. She's s'pose to be leavin' on the stage soon, but she ain't had her trunks brought down." Bridget began to weep. "What's amiss, Marshal? Nettie won't say, but I know she's worried."

Cort put a comforting hand on the young woman's shoulder, then bounded up the stairs and strode down to Devon's suite. The door was ajar. He pushed it open and entered the sitting room. Devon turned and looked at him. The strain she was feeling was plain to see on her face.

"Are you alright?" he asked.

"I don't know," she replied coldly. "How should I be upon discovering that people have been lying to me my whole life. And that you, Nettie, Pearl, and Mr. Stilwell are just as complicit."

"I can't speak for Mrs. Toller, but for the rest of us, it was without malice," said Cort. "We were waiting for the right time to show itself."

"And when it didn't, you were going to let me leave without knowing the truth."

"You weren't ready to hear it. Frankly, I didn't expect that you ever would be."

She walked over to him and slapped him across the face. "That was not your decision or anyone else's to make," she said, her voice shaking with anger.

Cort barely flinched, and his eyes locked on hers. "Actually, Devon, it was. Sadie had hoped to tell you herself one day, but in the event that she wasn't around to do so, she had charged Frank with the task when he thought you ready."

"And if that day never came?"

"Then you were never to know. It would have served no good purpose."

Devon walked away from him obviously struggling, and he waited for her to make the next move.

She picked up a miniature from the table. "This was my father," she said, her voice barely above a whisper. She wiped away a tear and straightened her shoulders. "Has a buggy been brought around?"

"I believe so. Where do you want to go?"

"To the cemetery."

"Shall I drive you?"

After a long pause, Devon nodded.

He took her arm, and they descended the stairs to find Pearl, Nettie, Bridget, and Brett gathered anxiously at the bottom.

"Miss Devon, are you alright?" asked Bridget.

Devon gave her a tremulous smile. "I'll be fine. The marshal and I are going for a drive."

Nettie brought Devon's hat and coat. "Here you go, missy."

Devon put on the bonnet and tied the ribbons beneath her chin. Cort helped her with her coat.

Although only Nettie, Pearl, and Cort were aware of the reason behind it, all keenly felt her fragility at this moment. It was one of those times when one wanted to act, but the best response was silence. And the little group continued to stand by quietly and reverently as Cort escorted Devon outside to the buggy.

Devon wasn't inclined to talk as they traveled along the country road, and Cort left her to her thoughts.

At the cemetery, she stood for a long time at her mother's grave, staring, pondering, weeping. Cort remained with the buggy, patiently waiting for her to come to terms with herself, with her life, with the truth.

When she returned to the buggy, Cort took up the reins, and they started off.

"Are you still leaving Blue Springs?" he asked.

Devon nodded. "I have to."

"Nettie, Pearl, and Frank won't say anything. No one will know your story unless you choose to tell it. You don't have to leave, Devon."

"It is not that. I need to do something important, something fulfilling with my life," she said. "I need to forge a new path. Whatever would I do here that could possibly make a difference?"

"You could turn your house into a boarding house and school for young women and teach them trades, so they won't be driven to the streets," he suggested.

"What kind of trades?" asked Devon with mild interest.

"Well, how to run a general store for one," replied Cort. "The Walkers are getting older. Hiram's arthritis is giving him a fit. I'd reckon they would be open to mentoring someone for the extra help."

"Hmm, an apprenticeship," murmured Devon. "What other opportunities would there be for women?"

Cort thought for a minute.

"Ann Gilbert is always complaining that she doesn't have enough fingers to keep up with orders for her hats," he said. "And Sadie was always saying as how the town needs a good dress designer and seamstresses. The ladies in town who are clever with a needle are too busy sewing for their own families…. I'm sure we can come up with more ideas if we put our minds to it."

As Devon appeared to be considering the matter, Cort continued. "You could also build the ranch that Sadie was planning to build. The orphanages in the East are full of boys. Bring them out here to help build it. I can teach them design and engineering skills, and, later, they can learn how to work a farm. For those who don't wish to farm, you will have given them the confidence and capability to do something different with their lives."

"These are good ideas," acknowledged Devon. "But you know that it would be difficult for us to pretend a simple friendship," she said with a wry smile. "And this town is too small for us to avoid each other."

"Then marry me," said Cort.

Devon laughed. "Careful, Marshal, I might take you seriously."

He pulled up on the reins to stop the buggy and looked her in the eye. "I am serious, Devon."

Devon's eyes widened in astonishment.

"I don't have Matt's gift for words," Cort went on, "but I think you know by now that I mean what I say. I don't rightly know what the future holds, but I'd welcome it more with you by my side…to go to sleep with you every night and wake up with you every morning."

He paused. "What I am trying to say is that I love you, Devon, and I want to spend the rest of my life with you."

Devon was stunned and deeply touched. They were the most beautiful words that anyone had ever spoken to her.

"I-I don't know what to say," she said.

"I am hoping you will say that you feel the same way."

"Yes, of course I do. I have for some time, but it is not that easy," she replied.

"Why isn't it if we both share the same feelings for each other?"

"You are a man, Mr. Templeton—"

"Devon, I just asked you to marry me. Call me Cort."

"You have the freedom to do as you please, Cort," she started again. "But I have learned that freedom for a woman comes only with financial independence. Mr. Stilwell claimed the inheritance for me to keep it from going back to the town, and I am going to accept it. I have that freedom now. I cannot give it up."

"I am not asking you to," said Cort.

Devon dashed away a tear. "Darn you, Cort Templeton. I had my mind made up to things. Why do you have to go and mix everything up again?"

He reached over and took her hand. "It is three days until the next stage comes. Promise me that you will think on it until then."

Devon nodded.

Cort clicked the reins, and they moved on. He glanced over at her a few times as they rode.

"Devon, is there some other assurance that you seek?" he asked. "You appear to be still unsettled."

Devon looked at him. "All my life," she said, struggling to explain, "my worth has been determined by my ability to further other people's interests—my family, my husband, this town in their need for a school. I must know that there is value to me...just me," she finished in a soft tone.

Cort knew what she was trying to say, and he took her hand again in silent acknowledgement. He understood that she, herself, had yet to determine her self-worth.

CHAPTER THIRTY-SIX

A Reason to Stay

Since her return from the cemetery, Devon spent the next several hours in solitary confinement coming to terms. She reread Clarissa's diary, recalled her conversations with Pearl, Nettie, Pastor Clemmons and thought about the town that Sadie had built…about the second chance Sadie had given to so many people…about the second chance that she was giving to the daughter she had never been allowed to know.

Devon picked up the picture of a young Clarissa and the miniature of Joshua Barrows and smiled. They were her parents. She was conceived from love—not from a sense of duty.

Devon picked up a photo of "Sadie" then. She had to respect the incredible strength of this woman and her journey in the face of such sorrow and discrimination, and she laid the photo of her on top of the picture of Clarissa, at last able to fuse the two images together in her heart and mind…proud to call this lady her mother.

Devon immediately felt a heaviness being lifted from her. She was no longer sad or angry but was filled with light, hope, and pride. And her thoughts now turned to Cort.

Throughout the night, she struggled to come to a decision, teetering back and forth between her love for him and a need to preserve her sense of self. She couldn't cede her identity again to a man.

When morning came, Devon still had no answer. She decided it was time to end her period of isolation and re-establish some semblance of normalcy in the house, hoping that it might help to bring her to a decision.

When she entered the kitchen, Nettie and Bridget stopped what they were doing and stared at her.

Sensing their uncertainty, Devon smiled. "I'm all right," she assured them. "But I am sorely in need of food."

Nettie and Bridget fell over each other as they hurried to put a breakfast on the table for her. When Devon sat down to eat, she was aware of their eyes on her as they continued to assess her.

"I promise you that I am fine," she said. "Please stop worrying."

Heartened by her lighter mood and appetite, Nettie and Bridget allowed themselves to relax. Still, they were quiet, and as she ate, Devon became aware that they regarded her now with an air of expectancy.

Finally, she laid down her fork and looked at them. "What is it? I told you I am fine. Please believe me."

"Are ya gonna marry Cort or ain't ya?" asked Nettie with characteristic bluntness.

Bridget glared at Nettie. "I thought we had decided to wait until Miss Devon told us the news herself."

"Humph, if we waited for her to say we'd be here 'til spring."

"Stop!" cried Devon. There was immediate silence, and she swept a stern eye over the women. "How do you know about the proposal?"

"Brett told me and said as how you was takin' until the next stage comes to decide," said Bridget.

Nettie snorted. "Don't know what ya need three days fer to decide."

Devon glared at Nettie and turned her attention to Bridget. "Why would the marshal tell Brett?"

"What's so secret about it?" questioned Nettie.

"I was talking to Bridget," Devon responded sharply.

Bridget shifted uncomfortably beneath her mistress' unyielding gaze. "Brett heard him tellin' Miss Donovan."

Devon let out a cry of exasperation. "This goes no further than this house. Is that clear?"

"Yes, miss."

Devon looked at Nettie. "That goes for you, too."

"Don't know what difference it makes," muttered the older woman.

"It doesn't matter if you know or not," snapped Devon. "Now, I have a few errands to attend. No more shenanigans," she warned.

Devon hadn't been gone for an hour before she returned.

Nettie and Bridget were in the kitchen when they heard the front door slam and Devon yell for them.

"Uh-oh. That don't sound good," remarked Nettie.

At a second commanding shout, Nettie and Bridget scrambled to the parlor where they found Devon pacing the floor.

"Is…is something amiss?" asked Bridget timidly.

Devon stopped pacing and turned to them. "Yes, Bridget, there most certainly is," she replied in a clipped tone. "The news is all over town about the marshal's marriage proposal. How did it get about?"

"I can't rightly say, miss. I ain't told no one. Honest, miss."

"Everywhere I went I was besieged by people wanting to know why I haven't made a decision…giving me advice…asking why did I need three days—"

"That's what I said," broke in Nettie.

Devon's eyes swiveled to her. "What do you know of this?" she demanded to know.

Nettie shrugged. "This is a small town, missy. News travels fast."

"Yes, but from which source did it begin its travels?"

Again, Nettie shrugged.

"Strange how that is, isn't it?" remarked Devon, her tone facetious. "No one can ever say how a rumor starts."

"Ain't none of us blind, missy. Everyone knows that you and the marshal got a hankerin' for each other."

Devon blinked in surprise. She had thought that she and Cort had been discreet in their interactions.

"And it don't make no sense why ya might be leavin' instead of marryin' him," continued Nettie. "If you and the marshal have a hankerin'—"

"Would you please stop using that word. The marshal and I have a high regard for each other," corrected Devon.

Nettie snickered. "Then what's the problem if ya have such a 'high regard' for each other?"

"The matter is complicated," said Devon.

"How?"

"There is a question of…of personal liberty to be figured."

Nettie threw up her hands. "Then ya best figure it quick afore it's too late, missy. Cort ain't gonna wait around forever for ya to come to yer senses."

A wave of uncertainty swept over Devon. That was her fear as well. Was she giving up her one chance at happiness?

* * * * *

A veil of expectancy hung over the town as all awaited Devon's answer. She confined herself to her suite, aware that she and Cort were the main topic of conversation and speculation and was dismayed to learn that wagers had even been placed on the outcome.

In the wee hours of the morning on the last day, she finally came to a decision. When she heard Brett and Bridget stirring in their suite, she knocked on their door. Brett opened it, and she handed him an envelope.

"Please take this to the marshal," she said.

"Yes, ma'am."

Cort was pouring himself a cup of coffee, when Brett walked into the office and held out the missive.

"From Mrs. Wainwright," he said.

Templeton slowly set the coffee pot on the stove and took the letter. He sat down at the desk, opened the envelope, and unfolded the paper. He ran a hand across his face as he read the note. When he finished, he sat for a long moment in thought.

Brett watched him closely. "She's leavin', ain't she?"

Cort nodded. He refolded the note and tucked it in his vest pocket. He stood up then, reached for his hat and coat and walked to the door. "I have some business to see to."

Templeton walked down the boardwalk to Frank Stilwell's office. This time there was no Tobias to bar anyone's way, and he walked through the reception room to the private office.

Stilwell looked up when the marshal strode into the room. "Any word?"

"She has made her decision," said Cort.

The attorney didn't have to ask what it was. He could tell by the marshal's solemn demeanor, and he looked away for a moment. "I had hoped she would stay."

"I want you to draw up a document, Frank."

Stilwell took out a sheet of paper. "What do you want it to say?"

Slowly and carefully, Cort dictated two paragraphs.

The attorney wrote it all down. "You'll be upsetting the applecart, you know."

"Is it legal?"

"Probably not in the East, but it is here."

Cort signed the document, and Stilwell added his signature to it as a witness.

"See that Devon gets this," instructed Templeton. "I have some more business to see to."

"What are you going to do?" asked Stilwell.

"Give her another reason to stay."

At the house, Devon supervised the packing of the rest of her belongings.

"Are you sure about this, Miss Devon?" asked Bridget.

"No, Bridget, I am not, but I think it for the best."

"You will be alone, miss."

"Perhaps I need to be to prove to myself that I can be alone."

Bridget knit her brows in bewilderment. She didn't understand that at all. "But where will you go, miss?"

"I don't know," replied Devon. "Perhaps New York. I have a distant cousin there with whom I have kept in touch."

"We will all miss ye," said Bridget, tears welling up in her eyes.

Devon smiled. "I shall miss you, too. But I've decided to implement the marshal's ideas for a school and boarding house...and perhaps for a working farm. I shall return at times to check on matters. I have left a letter of instruction for Mr. Stilwell. I want you and Nettie to manage the house."

"It ain't the same as havin' you here," the young woman replied. She looked at Devon shyly. "Brett and me be expectin' a wee one."

"Bridget, how wonderful!" exclaimed Devon, giving her a hug. "I am so happy for you."

"We was hopin' that you and the marshal would be godparents."

"Oh, Bridget, I would be honored, and I am sure the marshal will be, too." Devon wiped away a tear and gave a light laugh to cover the heavy emotion in the room. "Now, before I change my mind, please have Orville put the trunks in the wagon and take them to the stage line office."

"Yes, ma'am. Aren't you going to say goodbye to the marshal?"

Devon hesitated. "I don't think that is a good idea," she replied. There was an ache inside her that she would always carry with her as it was. To see him would only make it more difficult for her to leave.

"Mrs. Wainwright, may I have a word with you?"

Devon looked across the room to see Frank Stilwell standing in the doorway. "Of course, Mr. Stilwell. Please come in."

"I'll go and fetch Orville," said Bridget. As she moved past the attorney, she threw him a hopeful look that he could do what no one else had been able to do—convince Devon to stay.

"What is it, Mr. Stilwell?" asked Devon. "If you have come to ask me to change my mind—"

"No, Mrs. Wainwright, I came to give you this."

She took the paper he held out to her. "What is it?"

"Read it," he said.

Devon scanned the document and looked up at him in astonishment. "What does this mean?"

"It is as it says," replied the attorney. "Cort is granting you equal rights in a marriage with him. Every right he is legally granted as a husband he promises to extend to you as his wife. All land and monies that you bring into the marriage will remain under your control to do with as you please. You will have complete independence within the full faith and trust of the marriage vows."

Devon was thunderstruck. "Can he really do this?"

"Yes. It is legal in the territory of Colorado," Stilwell assured her.

"I-I can't believe he did this."

The attorney smiled. "It is a testament to the depth of his feelings for you."

"Missy! Missy, come quick!" yelled Nettie from the foyer.

Devon snapped out of her daze and hurried to the top of the stairs. "What is it?"

"You have to come and see this," cried Bridget.

"Good heavens, what could be so important?" muttered Devon as she descended the staircase. She already had one matter before her to consider. She didn't need another.

Nettie and Bridget stood at the open door gesturing for her to hurry.

"What's wrong now?" asked Devon when she reached the foyer.

"See fer yourself," said Nettie.

With a sigh of impatience, Devon started out to the porch and came to an abrupt halt at the crowd of townspeople gathered out front. The students she had taught were present with their families. The Walkers, the women of the Ladies' Auxiliary, the mayor, and the members of the town council were there. The Johnsons and other homesteaders came riding up in a caravan of wagons.

Astonished, Devon slowly moved onto the porch and the crowd began to cheer. Students called out to her: "Don't leave, Mrs. Wainwright." Others cried out: "We want you to stay."

As more and more people clamored for her not to leave, Devon was overcome.

"It seems that you matter to a lot of people, my dear," remarked the attorney, coming to stand beside her.

Devon's eyes glistened with tears. "I-I don't know what to say."

"Say that you will stay. With Sadie gone, Blue Springs needs direction. Who better to oversee the vision that she had for the town than her daughter?"

Devon gazed out over the crowd and found Cort standing off to the side. She caught his eye, and he smiled. There came a tug on her skirt then, and she looked down to see one of her six-year-old students, Lillian.

"My mama says you should marry Marshal Templeton," she said.

Devon looked at the document in her hand. "Your mama is very wise." She bent down and whispered something in the little girl's ear. Lillian giggled and scampered off.

Devon straightened and canvassed the crowd. Spying Pastor Clemmons standing near the front, she motioned him up to her.

"How soon can you perform a marriage ceremony?" she asked.

There was a twinkle in his eye, and he took out his Bible from a satchel. "How about now?" At the look of surprise on her face, he smiled. "A man of the cloth is always prepared to do the Lord's work. What changed your mind, if I may ask?"

"Everything has become clear to me, Pastor Clemmons. It is all right to please others if you please yourself as well. And it pleases me very much to marry the marshal."

The pastor looked across the yard to see Lillian making her way through the people with Cort in tow. "I believe the sentiment to be returned," he said with a laugh.

And so, with Bridget and Brett standing up for them and the townspeople of Blue Springs bearing witness, the pretty society lady from the East gave her hand and her heart to the handsome, plain-spoken marshal from the West on Miss Sadie's porch.

Nettie, Pearl, and Frank Stilwell exchanged smug smiles as they looked on, their mission to reunite Miss Sadie and her daughter accomplished. And, if in the process, there happened an unexpected wedding, they were happy to take credit for that, too.

About the Author

Kathy Keller is the author of several fiction books that encompass the genres of historical fiction, historical romance, and time travel and has recently turned to screenplay writing. She is a graduate of the American University, Washington, D.C., and holds a degree in journalism. A native of north central Pennsylvania, she currently resides in Leesburg, VA with her husband.

Interview with Author

Q: You have written several books. Which one of your books was the most difficult to write?

A: A Little Gentle Persuasion proved challenging. My research turned up the fact that much of what the world knows about the American Wild West was created by Hollywood. Unfortunately, these myths are deeply ingrained, and the facts are not as exciting, so there was a tightrope to walk between crafting a different and exciting story while still observing as much historical accuracy as possible for the history buffs.

Q: Can you give examples of some inaccuracies?

A: Yes. Lawmen in the Old West preferred rifles and double barrel shotguns to revolvers for long-range accuracy. It was mostly self-proclaimed shooters (gunslingers) who strapped on pistols. As far as the showdown at "high noon," it was a rare occurrence, and it was the bystanders who were most at risk as the participants were usually too drunk to shoot straight. Most shooters preferred to ambush their adversaries.

Also, bank robberies—a staple in western movies—were not as prevalent as people think. The Foundation for Economic Education found less than 10 bank robberies (1859-1900) in 15 frontier states. Banks were usually flanked by other buildings in frontier towns, one most often being the sheriff's or marshal's office, and the lawmen were well-armed. Stagecoaches and trains were poorly guarded and much easier to rob.

Q: What surprised you about the Old West that influenced your story?

A: I was intrigued by the madams of high-end parlor houses in places like San Francisco, San Antonio, and Denver. They were smart businesswomen, often millionaires in the day. They had power and political influence, and they were not shy about exercising it. They exploited the system rather than allowing the system to exploit them.

This was a time when young girls and women had little or no options if poor, orphaned or widowed. Thus, the subject of prostitution in this period is such a gray area. Although some madams mistreated and exploited their girls, there were others who did not. Their girls wore expensive clothes, were domiciled in beautiful houses, ate gourmet food, drank champagne, were allowed to keep part of the money they earned and were protected from disease, childbirth and abuse. The girls were free to choose their clients, some regularly entertaining only one or two. A few parlor madams also encouraged romance and some of their girls actually married wealthy clients.

During epidemics, "soiled doves" often stepped forward. One prostitute (Julia Bulette) in the mining town of Virginia City, Nevada, gave money to hard luck miners and nursed them through an influenza epidemic. She was so revered that the mines and saloons closed down and thousands mourned her death when she was murdered by an itinerant.

Also surprising was that redheads were more in demand (they were thought to be more passionate). So many "ladies of the line" dyed their hair. There is an account of a woman who traveled a distance to claim her sister's body. When she saw that her sister had dyed her hair red, she knew what that meant and refused to claim the body.

Q: What other myths of the Old West did you find?

A: John Wayne's ten-gallon hat did not come into being until the 1920s. Most men wore bowler hats. The quintessential cowboy hat was chiefly worn by working cowboys and was fashioned after the Mexican sombrero. Stetson came out with the Boss of the Plains hat in 1865 with a flat brim and higher crown. Settlers adopted the hat and customized it, changing the brim and crown to fit their needs. Additional shaping came about by how the owner treated his hat. If he picked it up by pinching the crown, it would eventually have a crease. If he handled the hat by the brim, the sides would be curved.

Q: How violent was the Old West?

A: The consensus among scholars and historians is that it was not as violent as movies and novels depict. But certainly, there were areas that were dangerous and chaotic, especially in places where there was gold or other valuable minerals present. As states gained statehood and there was a centralized government, the West became tamer.

Q: How much did a town marshal earn?

A: According to historians, town marshals generally received a base annual salary of $200. Some subsidized their salaries by collecting bounties or owning businesses. The annual nominal wage in 1875 was $651.

Q: What were the bounties in the day?

A: Interesting to note is that the term "bounty hunter" is an age-old term referring to money given to recruits by the military, and it was the meaning in the time period of this book as well. The context of the term as used in movies and today as one who tracks down criminals for money was another invention of Hollywood in the 1950s. Bounties for criminals in the Old West were mostly around $100, but the more notorious outlaws could fetch a bounty of $4000 or $5000. The bounty on Jesse James was reportedly $25,000.

Q: What do you do to prepare for writing a book?

A: I spend a great deal of time researching before I start the book, during the writing of the book, and after the writing of the book. I strive to make my stories as historically accurate as possible. My problem comes when I find conflicting facts of which there are many. I go with the one that fits my story best.

Books by Kathy Keller

A Little Gentle Persuasion
The Homeward Heart
A Love Too Proud
Destiny's Shadow
The Paradox
Lady of the Sea

Books by Kathy Keller & A. J. Billman
Millionaires' Row
Millionaires' Row: The Legacy

Connect with the author—*www.KathyKeller.com*

Excerpt from *Lady of the Sea*

Thackeray grabbed the voucher from his first mate to read it for himself. "Who the bloody hell is M. Sutton!" he bellowed, his deep voice carrying the length of the deck.

"The clerk said her to be the new manager," responded Seaton timorously.

The captain's brows shot up. "*Her*? A woman is managing the counting house?"

"Aye. Mrs. Sutton be her name."

"What does a woman know about trade!" thundered Thackeray.

The first mate cringed beneath the captain's glare. "I cannot say, sir."

Thackeray crushed the voucher in his hand. "I shall see to this myself."

As he stormed down the gangplank, the bosun remarked, "I should like to be a spider in that room."

Duncan nodded. "'Twill be a scene to behold."

"I'll wager a Spanish half dollar the captain will have this Mrs. Sutton seein' his side of it in a quarter hour," said White.

"Not if she is comely," countered Duncan. "Mrs. Hepplewaite had him wrapped around her finger and almost afore a preacher 'til he come to his senses. A pretty lady is used to advances and knows how to play a man. But a woman of plain countenance…she'll drop like a feather to flattery. Hey, Alex," he called out. "What say you? Is Mrs. Sutton a woman of pleasing or plain appearance?"

The first mate walked over to them, still feeling a bit shaky. "I-I did not make her acquaintance," he said. "But the clerk did relay to me that once her mind is made up to a matter, it is set hard and fast."

Duncan shook his head. "A woman of singular mind and stubborn disposition running a man's company—she must be plain. I'll wager she gives into the captain's charms *before* the quarter hour."